HUSH HUSH

LINDA KAVANAGH

POOLBEG

Published 2007
by Poolbeg Press Ltd
123 Grange Hill, Baldoyle
Dublin 13, Ireland
E-mail: poolbeg@poolbeg.com

© Linda Kavanagh 2007

The moral right of the author has been asserted.

Typesetting, layout, design © Poolbeg Press Ltd.

1 3 5 7 9 10 8 6 4 2

A catalogue record for this book is available from the British Library.

ISBN 978-1-84223-268-2

Typeset by Type Design in Palatino 9.7/13.6
Printed by
Litografia Rosés, S.A. Spain

www.poolbeg.com

About the Author

Linda Kavanagh has worked as a journalist for several Irish newspapers and magazines, and was a staff writer on the *RTÉ Guide* for fifteen years. She lives with her partner in Dun Laoghaire, Co Dublin.

Her previous novels, *Love Hurts* and *Love Child*, were also published by Poolbeg.

Author email: lindakavanagh@eircom.net

In loving memory of my mother Anne

Acknowledgements

Sincere thanks to Paula Campbell and the Poolbeg team, to editor Gaye Shortland for her amazing attention to detail, to Mike Gold for all his support and practical help, to John Synnott of John Synnott & Co Solicitors for legal information, and to Garda Tara McManus of the Garda Press and Public Relations Office for details of Garda procedure. If any mistakes have occurred in interpreting any of the information generously given, the fault lies entirely with me.
Finally, thanks to all those who have been buying my novels – I hope you'll enjoy this one!

BOOK 1

CHAPTER 1

"You lucky cow!"

"God – some people have all the luck!"

Olivia Doyle grinned, her freckled face wreathed in a big smile. "It's probably a wreck, but I still can't believe it myself. My own house!"

"It's not just a house – it's a country estate, by the sounds of it!" said Maggie, grinning back at Olivia. She was thrilled for her friend, and excited at the prospect of seeing the new house. Correction, she thought, *old* house. It sounded the perfect project for Olivia. Although a chartered accountant by profession, Olivia had a particular flair for renovation and decoration. She'd made a great job of her mother's home, and had helped Barbara with the colour scheme for her apartment.

"Is there a roof on it?" asked Barbara, dark-haired and serious, looking worried in case Olivia was taking on the project-from-hell.

"Yes – and apparently it's okay. But just about everything else needs sorting out."

1

Olivia was the luckiest young woman in the world, and she knew it. While other people of her age were struggling to save for a deposit to buy a house the size of a matchbox, she'd just been given an old country house on three acres of land by her grandmother and great-uncle.

"I wish I had a generous grandmother like yours," said Maggie forlornly. "I'll be saving up for a country estate until I'm a grandmother myself!"

Olivia linked arms with her two friends. "C'mon – I'll buy you each a drink to celebrate."

Not for the first time, she silently marvelled at how different the two girls were from each other. Barbara, the serious one, was now a junior doctor at the new state-of-the-art South City Hospital, where she loved her job, feeling particularly privileged to get a position there, since it offered fantastic training and had a superb Accident & Emergency unit. So different from Maggie, her short blonde hair forever standing on end, who never missed an opportunity to call a spade a shovel. But her direct manner was an invaluable asset in her job as a psychologist with the Health Board.

The three women had been friends since their schooldays, remaining close throughout their university years, even though each of them had chosen different courses. But if anything, they were even closer now, having seen each other grow from childhood to womanhood, sharing their hopes and dreams along the way.

"Maybe there'll be three gorgeous hunks in the pub," Olivia said.

"Huh, chance would be a fine thing!" Maggie raised

her eyes to heaven, and turned to Barbara. "Quickly, check that woman's temperature! She must have a fever! If there are three fantastic guys in the pub, you can be sure there'll be three wives or partners lurking in the background!"

Olivia grinned. "Think positive, my dear friends – there's got to be three half-decent fellows out there somewhere!"

Of course, no one mentioned Richard Devlin, who had been Barbara's first serious boyfriend, and the love of her life. But after years together and plans for a happy-ever-after, he'd unceremoniously dumped her and married someone else. And she was still smarting from the pain.

* * *

As the trio headed towards the pub, Olivia recalled the day her grandmother and Great-uncle Eddie had told her that they were giving her Bay Tree House. Had it really only been a week ago? The day had started out like any other, until her grandmother had phoned and asked her to call around as soon as she could.

Detecting an unusual note in her grandmother's voice, she began to worry about their health, and made a point of getting there as soon as possible. But there had been nothing sinister to worry about – both her beloved grandmother and her brother Eddie were in good spirits when she arrived.

Since the death of Olivia's grandfather several years earlier, her gran and Great-uncle Eddie, who'd never married, had shared her gran's old home, the home where Olivia's mother had grown up. Olivia loved both of them dearly, and she dreaded to think that inevitably, some day, she'd lose them. But for now, they were both in good health – and they had something very unusual, and wonderful, to tell her.

"Eddie and I have been left a house," said her grandmother, "and since neither of us intends moving from here, we thought it might give you a start on the property ladder."

Olivia looked from Great-uncle Eddie to her grandmother, and back again. "I don't understand . . . a house? For me?"

"Well, if I were you, I wouldn't get too excited," said her grandmother briskly. "It's probably in need of quite a lot of updating. We haven't seen it ourselves, but that's how the solicitor describes it. So that probably means it's a total wreck. But you needn't worry about the gift tax and stamp duty – Eddie and I are paying that for you. All you'll need to worry about is getting any repairs done."

Olivia could feel the excitement rising in her chest. They couldn't mean it – she was dreaming, wasn't she? They'd said a house – for her! No, she must have misheard. She looked over at Uncle Eddie, who sat in a rocking chair, puffing his pipe and smiling expectantly at her.

"You can't be serious – a house – for me?"

"Stop repeating yourself, dear," said her grandmother affectionately, "and shut your mouth, Liv, unless you're trying to catch flies."

Uncle Eddie was grinning happily at her as he sucked on his pipe and, as she looked from one of them to the other, Olivia longed to freeze that moment, so that she could remember for the rest of her life that look of love for her that Gran and Uncle Eddie had in their eyes. A lump rose in her throat, and she feared that she was about to cry.

"Who left you the house?" she managed to say at last. "And where is it?"

Like a well-rehearsed duet, her grandmother and Uncle Eddie took turns interjecting into each other's sentences, until the story was complete, and Olivia learned that the house was fifty miles outside Dublin – a mere commuter's distance these days – and had been left to them by a woman they'd never heard of.

"It's odd, isn't it?" said Olivia. "I mean, being left a house by someone you don't know – but who obviously knows you, or at least, must know about you."

There was an awkward silence as brother and sister looked at each other. It looked as though they were making up their minds about something, and looking to each other for confirmation as to how to proceed.

At last, Olivia's grandmother spoke. "When we were told by the solicitor that we'd been left this house . . . well, Eddie and I immediately assumed that it must have something to do with –"

"There's something we've never told you, Liv," interrupted Uncle Eddie. "Even your mother only knows a few sketchy details."

Her grandmother nodded. "It's been too painful a subject, so we've always avoided talking about it."

"Look, you don't have to tell me anything you don't want to –"

"I think it's time we did talk about it – in fact, it may actually help," said her grandmother. "You do agree,

5

Eddie, don't you?"

Uncle Eddie nodded his head.

"There were actually three children in our family," her grandmother said. "Apart from Eddie and me, there was also our older sister Ada."

"My God, where is she? What happened to her?"

"We don't know. She disappeared," said her grandmother. "That's why we wondered if the woman who left us the house in her will – Mrs Laura Morton – might have been Ada under a different name."

Olivia's mouth was open. She had a great-aunt she'd never known about! And why would her grandmother and great-uncle think that their sister would be living under an assumed name? It was all very mysterious!

"But the solicitor says no," added Eddie, chewing on his pipe.

"It seems there's clear proof that this woman has always been who the will says she is," said her grandmother. "Her name was definitely Mrs Laura Morton, and she'd been Miss Laura Donaghy before she married, so it's quite clear from the documentation that she isn't Ada."

Uncle Eddie arose, with difficulty, from the rocking chair. "I think a cup of tea is called for," he said, heading out to the kitchen to put on the kettle. Obviously, he found the subject difficult to deal with. The two women could hear him opening the caddy where the tea bags were kept, and taking down the mugs from the shelf on the dresser.

"So what actually happened to Great-aunt Ada?" asked Olivia. "And how come you don't you know where she is?

6

Her grandmother gestured towards the kitchen. "Let's wait for the full story until Eddie comes back with the tea. I'll need a strong cuppa to get me through it."

"So you're wondering if there could be some connection between Ada and this woman?" said Olivia.

Her grandmother nodded. "I mean, why else would a woman that neither Eddie nor I know leave us a house? It doesn't make sense."

Olivia grinned mischievously. "Could it be some woman from Uncle Eddie's past – maybe a case of unrequited love, someone who never forgot him?"

Her grandmother smiled, then her expression turned to one of sadness. "I wish that was true – that Eddie had had someone special who'd loved him. But the truth is, Liv – Ada's disappearance put his life, and mine, on hold. It was like we became empty inside after Ada left. There were lots of girls who fancied Eddie, but it was as though he couldn't take that next step – and have a family of his own – until Ada's situation had been resolved."

"Well, *you* got married, Gran – and had my mother."

Her grandmother's face took on a soft, distant look as she stared out the window. "I might never have married either," she said softly. "Eddie wasn't the only one who had difficulty moving on until the whole business of Ada's disappearance was resolved. But then, George Doyle came courting me, and he wouldn't take no for an answer."

Suddenly, it was as though the years had suddenly fallen away as her grandmother spoke. The old woman blushed, and for a brief moment Olivia could see the girl her grandmother had once been. Following her grandmother's gaze out the window, Olivia could almost feel that her late grandfather was coming up the driveway in his old black Ford.

Olivia remembered her grandfather as a great big bear of a man, and she'd loved his fuzzy beard, and the way it tickled when he'd swing her up in the air, then catch her, and hug her on the way down. But now, for the very first time, she saw her grandmother as a woman who'd loved her husband dearly, and whose life had been blighted for a second time through his premature death.

Her grandmother turned away from the window, and began to clear a space on the table as she heard Eddie approaching with the tea. "I often think that we might have been different people if Ada hadn't disappeared. Not knowing was the worst part – if we'd been told that our sister had died, we'd eventually have come to terms with it. But always wondering what happened to her, well – " her grandmother wiped away a tear, " – it still hurts."

Eddie put down the tray and handed them each a cup and saucer. "We're sure she's long dead now, Liv," he added, "but we'd still like to know what happened to her. Helen and I often wondered if she'd developed TB, and been sent away to hospital … it was called consumption back then, and it was rampant throughout the country. Maybe she died in a sanatorium long ago."

Her grandmother bit her lip. "It must seem strange now, but back then, people were ashamed to tell others that there was consumption in their families. They knew they'd be ostracised if they did. So maybe that's what happened to poor Ada. I actually remember her coughing and getting sick as we walked along the road to school."

"We also wondered – " Eddie hesitated for a second

" – if she might have had a baby. It was a disgrace in those days, you know, Liv, to have a child without being married."

Olivia nodded. She'd heard that women back then were punished and ostracised for becoming pregnant without a wedding ring, and she'd been astonished that both Church and community had been united in demonising these unfortunate women. Yet the men who got them pregnant didn't suffer at all! Olivia sighed. Not for the first time, she was glad to have been born in more enlightened times.

"Couldn't you have asked your parents about her, later, when you grew up?" asked Olivia, looking from one to the other. "Surely you had a right to know by then? To see her again, if she was still alive?"

Her grandmother answered, shaking her head sadly. "It wasn't that easy, Liv – it's not like today, where people are more frank and open about problems. Back then, secrecy was part and parcel of life. And you'd never challenge your parents, or the clergy, or question their point of view." Her grandmother's voice shook a little. "In later years, both Eddie and I tried to bring the conversation around to Ada, but our parents refused to say anything at all on the subject. There are only so many times you can try to introduce a topic like that." She sighed. "Over the years, Eddie and I checked several times for a death certificate for Ada, but never found one. That gave us hope that she might still be alive somewhere, but as the years went by, we gave up any hope of ever finding her."

"Don't worry, Gran," said Olivia, throwing her arms around her grandmother. "If there's any connection

9

between Ada and this Laura woman, I'll do my best to find out." She then hugged her great-uncle Eddie. "Oh Uncle Eddie, I can't believe that you and Gran have been so good to me! My own house!"

"Look, it could be a pig in a poke," her great-uncle warned her. "Neither Helen nor I have seen it, and I never believe anything that solicitors or estate agents say." He grinned. "It's bound to be falling apart. So don't get your hopes up, Liv. Now, let's all have a cup of tea."

CHAPTER 2

Despite Great-uncle Eddie's warnings about a pig in a poke, Olivia had been delighted when she'd eventually driven down to see the house. Situated on the outskirts of the town of Cloncullen, about fifty miles from Dublin, it was a fine, detached country house surrounded by several fields, and with a barn and an assortment of sheds behind it. It was also right beside the sea, and Olivia had visions of taking long walks along the nearby beach. The grandeur of the house seemed to indicate that it might once have had a lot more land, which presumably had been sold off over the years. But to a city woman, several acres of land offered the closest thing to paradise, and already Olivia was making plans to grow potatoes, strawberries, raspberries and lettuce. Noticing an old greenhouse against one of the courtyard walls, Olivia mentally added herbs, tomatoes and aubergines to her list. Thrilled, she wandered around the neglected garden at the front of the house, found an old trellis covered with wild roses, and in the neglected flower

11

beds, discovered peonies, and several old varieties of flowers and shrubs. Everywhere, nasturtiums had seeded themselves, and Olivia envisioned her home-grown salads sprinkled liberally with nasturtium flower heads, while everyone congratulated her on her beautiful home and the delightful produce from her own country garden. In her own mind, she was graciously accepting the adulation of her friends, when a male head appeared over the wall, stopping her in her tracks.

"They say that talking to yourself is the first sign of madness."

"I wasn't talking to myself – I was talking to the plants," Olivia replied, annoyed that her reverie had been interrupted.

"That's just as bad," said the annoyingly cheerful voice, as its owner hopped over the wall and appeared directly in front of her.

He was easy on the eye, Olivia had to admit. About six feet tall, with dark-brown hair, brown eyes and a wide grin that revealed a mouthful of wonderful teeth.

"How do you know that plants don't enjoy being spoken to?" she retorted. "My gran talks to her flowers all the time. She has the most fabulous lupins you've ever seen. She says they grow taller, produce more fruit as a result – "

He raised his eyebrows. "Your gran has lupins that produce fruit? That's one for the Horticultural Society. Never heard of that happening before!"

Olivia fumed. So he was trying to be funny at her expense. She decided that she didn't like this clever upstart.

"You know what I mean." She was getting flustered.

"Are you sure you don't mean thigmomorphogenesis?"

"Wh – at?" She wasn't sure if he was using a rude word, or if he actually knew what he was talking about.

"It's a theory whereby if you regularly caress a plant, it grows thicker and stronger as a result."

Olivia blushed, and hated herself for it. Because she couldn't stop herself from thinking about what it would be like to caress a certain part of this man's anatomy and watch it grow thicker and stronger too . . .

"By the way, I'm Brendan Warren."

Blushing again, she shook his hand. "I'm Olivia Doyle."

His handshake was strong and warm, and Olivia felt slightly weak at the knees.

"I'll bet you're wondering how I know such a long and complicated word," he said, his eyes twinkling.

"No, I'm not – I bet you just made it up."

"Would you like me to repeat it?"

"Take a hike. You could make up any word, just to impress me."

"So you think I'm trying to impress you?"

Olivia went puce. "If you were, you'd be wasting your time!" she retorted, bending down to examine a wild flower, in an attempt to hide her burning face. God, she was so angry with herself. She'd just fed him that line!

"By the way, I live just down the road," the young man added, "at Blackberry Cottage. Am I right in assuming you've just bought this place?"

"Well, yes, I'm the new owner."

"Welcome to Cloncullen. Even though the city keeps encroaching, it's still a sleepy little town."

"Until city-dwellers like me move in and ruin it all."

It was the young man's turn to look embarrassed. "No, that's not what I meant at all – sorry, it just came out wrong. If it comes to that, I'm a city-dweller myself, a blow-in from Dublin who came down here to set up a dental practice."

"I hate dentists."

The young man didn't seem unduly hurt by her comment. "Most people do. The secret is – look after your teeth properly and you'll rarely need to see one."

"Anyway, I have my own dentist, thank you, so if you're touting for business, you're out of luck."

The young man laughed. "You are a cheeky cow, aren't you? But I really like you!"

"It really doesn't matter to me what you think," said Olivia ungraciously.

Still grinning, the young man stood his ground. "Well, aren't you going to go inside?"

"I'm saving the inside until last."

Olivia wished he'd go away, since she wanted to experience the house alone. She wanted to walk from room to room, absorbing the spirit of the house, to step back in time and envisage how it must have been in its heyday. Since neither she nor her two benefactors knew anything about the house, she didn't even know if it contained furniture, or maybe old documents or photos, and she didn't want to share these precious moments with an annoying, but good-looking stranger.

But there was no sign of him moving. He was still standing there, looking for all the world like an eager dog, waiting for his owner to throw a ball or stick. Then she reasoned that it might be a good idea to have someone accompany her, just in case the stairs were a bit dodgy, or she fell through a floor or ceiling.

Skirting the edge of the garden, Olivia found herself back at the front door, her faithful follower still close behind. Approaching the front door, she took the key the solicitor had given her and deftly turned it in the big old-fashioned lock, and the heavy door front swung open with a groan. Tentatively, she peered inside. There was dust everywhere, but there was something wonderful about walking into your very own first home. She grinned happily to herself, and stepped into the hall.

"Aren't you going to invite me in for coffee?" said Brendan, standing on the doorstep, a cheeky grin on his face.

"I never invite a man in on the first date," Olivia shot back, then gasped at what she had actually said.

"Well, I hadn't realised we were actually on a date," said Brendan, grinning. "Not only are you good-looking, you're a fast mover as well!"

"Jesus, you're incorrigible!"

"And you know my name too! Thirty-three and still at home with the mammy! Or at least I was, until she told me to go and buy a place of my own."

Olivia couldn't help laughing.

"So I'd better ask you out before all the good-looking men in the town find out that you're here. If I stake my claim early, I might be in with a chance."

"A chance of what? Aaaagh!"

As she tripped over a loose floorboard in the hall, she just managed to grab Brendan's arm to stop herself from falling.

"Hmmm," he said, grinning as he steadied her, "I

15

know I'm irresistible, but I didn't expect you to fall for me quite so quickly!"

"Let go of me – I'm perfectly all right!" said Olivia ungraciously, grabbing the banister and escaping from Brendan's grasp. The man was mental!

"Look, I know you'd rather be alone here – "

Olivia looked at him, surprised at this sudden show of sensitivity.

" – but the place could be unsafe. I'll just stay behind you as you go up the stairs, or would you rather I went in front?"

"I'll be fine, thank you," said Olivia abruptly.

As they gingerly climbed the stairs, Olivia was overwhelmed by the beauty of the staircase. On the landing, there was a beautiful big art deco-style stained-glass window. Light poured through it, casting whorls of coloured light onto the opposite walls. It was enchanting!

"Magnificent, isn't it?"

Olivia nodded. Already, she was in love with the house and everything in it. She glanced down at the carpet on the stairs. It was a ghastly old-fashioned pattern of autumn leaves, but it was still in good condition, which augured well for the rest of the house. The old carpet would do fine for the immediate future, until she had enough money to replace it with something more modern. In fact, she might even opt for bare floorboards in some rooms, if the floors were in good enough condition.

On the top landing, Brendan surveyed the ceiling. "There's a little bit of damp in the corner – probably caused by a few loose slates, but there don't seem to be too many problems here." Cocking his head to one side, he looked down at her. "I presume you had a survey done before you bought the place?"

Olivia felt reluctant to tell him how she'd acquired the house. She didn't want to become a source of local gossip. On the other hand, she reasoned, the locals probably knew all about her already.

"My grandmother and great-uncle gave it to me," she said reluctantly.

Brendan looked at her with genuine delight. "Marvellous! That's just terrific!"

And Olivia couldn't help but feel pleased at his reaction.

The large chilly bathroom left a lot to be desired, but Olivia could see its potential.

"Do you prefer a shower or bath?" asked Brendan.

"Shower for speed, bath for relaxation."

Brendan whistled. "My God, we agree on that too!"

"I wasn't aware that we agreed on anything yet – except, maybe, that you're a pest!"

"To know me is to love me."

Olivia ignored him, but as she walked down the stairs ahead of him, she couldn't help smiling to herself, and was glad he couldn't see her grin.

"I think we should move in here – your place is a lot bigger than mine," said Brendan suddenly.

Olivia looked back at him incredulously. "I beg your pardon? Did you just say what I think you said?"

Brendan grinned. "Yes – I think we should live in this house. Mine would be too small – especially when we have a couple of children."

"Of all the – "

He held his hands up in a gesture of supplication, and

Olivia couldn't help noticing how strong and attractive they were. Against her will, she could almost imagine his fingers caressing her bare skin . . .

"Okay, okay," he said, "we'll discuss it first! After all, you haven't seen my place yet."

Olivia stared at him. "Are you on day-release from some mental hospital?"

"That's very unkind! I can't help it if I'm intuitive. I can hardly be blamed for knowing that you're the woman for me."

"Don't I get a say in any of this?"

"Of course. After all, I'm the new-man type – caring and considerate. Otherwise, I'd have clubbed you over the head already, and dragged you back to my lair."

"Charming! I'm hardly five minutes in the town, and already I've been threatened with extreme violence!"

"I'll tell the judge it was provocation. She's so gorgeous, Your Honour, I couldn't help myself!" He wrinkled his nose. "Anyway, didn't I just suggest we live in *your* lair? I seem to be getting confused . . ."

"You're not the only one!" said Olivia, annoyed and excited at the same time.

By now, they had explored the four bedrooms upstairs, and Olivia had been pleased to note that every bedroom was carpeted – although with patterns equally ghastly as the one downstairs – but at least it made the empty house feel more cosy. Each room was also furnished, and some of the furniture was actually to Olivia's own taste. She looked forward to making decisions about what to keep and what to throw out – when she got rid of this extremely annoying man.

Downstairs in the hall again, Olivia turned to him.

"Don't you have any home to go to?" she said nastily, and instantly regretted it.

"But I thought I was moving in with you!" He gave an expression of mock horror, and Olivia couldn't help laughing. "Look," he went on, his expression serious for once, "let's check out the downstairs rooms, then once I'm certain that there's no danger of a wall falling on top of you, I'll leave you alone to browse around." Then he tried to look stern. "But I'll only go under one condition."

"What's that?"

"That when I invite you to Blackberry Cottage, you'll come quietly, and cause no trouble."

Olivia grinned. "Well then, go on and invite me."

Dramatically, he dropped down on one knee. "Olivia – when you come down to Cloncullen next weekend, will you please come to Blackberry Cottage? Say, Sunday, around noon? By the way, do you prefer tea or coffee? There's so much I've yet to learn about you, my love – "

Olivia laughed. This man was incorrigible! But she liked his open face, his sense of humour, his big strong hands – in fact, there wasn't anything to dislike, except the way he managed to make her feel confused, happy and annoyed in equal measure …

"Tea, please. Thanks, Brendan – I'll be there."

CHAPTER 3

Ada Casey was feeling very annoyed. She'd been having great fun playing football in the lower field with some of the lads from the village, and she'd scored several goals for her team. She could outrun most of them, and she enjoyed the feeling of friendly competition between the two teams, and the tremendous sense of achievement she felt when she got the ball into the back of their makeshift net. What a pity women weren't allowed to play football when they grew up – she'd rather do that for a living than work in some boring office! But Ada knew that in Ireland, in 1950, there was little likelihood of a woman having a career in sport.

And now her mother had put paid to her enjoyment by insisting that she visit Father Dineen, the parish priest.

"Father Dineen thinks that you should be behaving in a more ladylike way," she told her daughter acerbically. "After all, you're nearly fourteen now. It's not right that you should be playing with those lads any more."

"Why not, Mam?" asked Ada, puzzled. "We're only having a bit of fun."

21

"It's just not right," said her mother, knitting her lips tightly together. "Now, go and change into a clean dress, and get over to the presbytery. That dress you're wearing is filthy!"

"If only you'd let me wear trousers or shorts, then playing football would be so much easier," said Ada crossly.

"Dear God, no wonder Father Dineen is worried about you!" said her mother, making the Sign of the Cross.

* * *

"You know, you've turned into a fine young woman," said Father Dineen softly, looking Ada over, and making her feel very uncomfortable as his eyes slid up and down her body. "A bit too forward with those boys than you should be. Tell me, child, do they like it when you touch them?"

Ada looked surprised. "I beg your pardon, Father? What do you mean?"

Father Dineen smirked at her. "Oh my dear child, don't look so innocent! I can guess what you've been getting up to, even if your mother can't. Why else would you be hanging around, pretending to play football and chasing games with those lads from the village? I'll bet you just let them chase you for a little while, before they catch you and have their wicked way with you!"

"Father, I just play football and chasing games with the lads – nothing more." Ada wasn't even sure what she meant by "nothing more", but it seemed like the right thing to say. But it did nothing to appease Father Dineen.

"Don't lie to me, you little trollop! Your poor mother is worried sick about your behaviour. Girls like you always end up in trouble! It starts with kissing games in the woods or the hedgerows, then before long you've gone the whole way!"

Father Dineen was working himself up into a rage. Spittle began flying from his mouth, and Ada was both mesmerised and shocked to see the sudden change in his demeanour.

"And you end up pregnant, and your family is disgraced! Do you want to bring shame on your entire family?"

Ada was shocked at the mention of pregnancy. Surely that was something that happened to married women? And what on earth had it got to do with playing football? Nevertheless, she bowed her head contritely, so as not to enrage the priest any further.

"No, Father," she whispered.

"Then why aren't you concentrating on your studies, child? All this physical activity isn't good for girls. The female constitution isn't designed for running around."

"But Father, I'm very good at running – I'd love to become an athlete when I grow up."

If she'd said she wanted to become a prostitute, it couldn't have had a worse effect on Father Dineen. His face turned puce and his arms jerked about, and Ada feared that he might be having a heart attack. But he quickly gained control of himself, and when he spoke at last, his voice was low and ominous.

"How dare you give me such cheek – I've never heard such impudence!" Then he sneered at her, a cruel smile on his lips. "So you want to run around the country, with hardly any clothes on, disporting your female flesh for everyone to see? Have you no shame?"

He took a step towards her, and Ada feared that he was about to strike her.

Instead he grabbed hold of her long golden hair, twisting it around his hand, and pulling her face near to his.

"I can see it in your face, you little hussy – there's a wantonness there that's the mark of an evil woman. I can just

23

imagine how you lift your skirts for the boys, and let them grope around in your knickers – "

"Father! Please – "

Letting go of her hair, Father Dineen grabbed Ada round the waist, kissing her lips roughly. Struggling, she tried to free herself, frightened now by this weird turn of events. But the more she struggled, the angrier Father Dineen became. He dug his nails into her flesh as he tried to maintain his grip on her, and when he spoke, his breath was coming in short gasps. "So you give it freely to the boys from the village, but you play all coy with me? Well, we'll see about that, you young trollop!"

Ada felt frozen and unable to move as Father Dineen ripped open her blouse and began to grope her young breasts. Confused, she wanted to run, but equally strong was an inbuilt respect and fear of the clergy. Maybe this was some specific punishment Father Dineen was meting out, one designed to show her what might happen if she continued playing football with the lads.

But when she felt something hard pressing into her groin, Ada was overcome by panic, and she tried to break away from the priest's grip.

"Please, Father – leave me alone!"

But the priest was now spurred on by her fear. "Aha!" he murmured. "Now that you realise what happens to girls like you, you're frightened, aren't you? You offer it on a plate, but when someone wants to avail of that offer, you turn into a tease, eh?"

"Please, Father, I've got to go home – "

"You're not going home, child – not until you've washed all those filthy stains from your soul! Not until you've been punished for your wantonness!"

With that, the priest, dragged Ada over to the sofa, threw

her on it, pulled her skirt up and her knickers down. In a daze, she watched, frightened and almost in a state of paralysis, as he pulled down his trousers, extracted his penis and rammed it in between her legs. She screamed with pain as it entered her, feeling as though she'd been split in two. She felt that she must be dying – maybe the priest was trying to dispatch her soul to Heaven before she could commit all those sins he'd accused her of?

As she tried to extricate herself from beneath Father Dineen, he continued to thrust into her, bucking back and forth, each of his movements tearing her insides. Tears streamed down her cheeks. Would this suffering ever end? Whatever she had supposedly done, surely it couldn't deserve such painful retribution?

Eventually, she heard the priest gasp, then he rolled off her. Immediately, the intense pain stopped, leaving only a dull ache between her legs. She put her hand down, and feeling her bruised flesh gingerly, discovered blood between her legs and on her clothes.

As the priest lay slumped across the sofa, exhausted from his activities, Ada seized the opportunity to escape. She jumped up and ran towards the front door of the presbytery. Unlocking it, she rushed out the door, constantly looking behind her, still fearful that he might be following her. But there was no sign of him as she rushed across the dimly lit street and climbed the five-bar gate beside the Post Office, then headed off home across the fields.

She was still sobbing as she eventually reached the house, and in the light from the kitchen window, she gazed in dismay at her torn clothes. What would her mother say?

She felt overcome by shame, as though somehow she was responsible for what had happened. She knew that her mother would kill her, and blame her for what had happened anyway. Maybe there was something inherently wrong with her – why did she want to do all the things that girls weren't supposed to do? Why did she love climbing trees, playing football, and running like the wind?

Looking in through the kitchen window, she could see that her mother, Helen and Eddie were on their knees saying the Rosary. Her mother's hands covered her face while she prayed devoutly, and she clutched her rosary beads between her fingers. As usual, her brother and sister were making faces at each other behind her back, trying to make each other laugh, so that the other one would get into trouble.

Relieved that they couldn't see her, Ada crept round the side of the house, and quickly climbed the sycamore tree whose upper branches reached the attic window where the three children slept. All three of them were adept at entering and exiting this way. It was their own closely guarded secret, since they knew that if their parents ever found out, the tree would undoubtedly be cut down. Every so often, their father grumbled about it and threatened to remove it, but on those occasions, they'd distract him by professing interest in whatever project he was currently undertaking on the farm.

Reaching the attic, Ada climbed in through the window that, by agreement, was always left unlocked. Hopefully, she'd have time to change into fresh clothes before climbing down the tree again, and entering through the back door. Luckily, her mother didn't know which dress she had worn to go to the presbytery. She would be cross with her for missing the Rosary, but she'd claim to have said the Rosary at the presbytery with Father Dineen.

Ada wished with all her heart that she could tell her mother what had happened, but she knew she wouldn't believe her. In fact, she could hardly believe it herself. Momentarily, she wondered if it could have been a dream, but the pain between her legs left her in no doubt. And she was still shaking from head to toe.

Hiding her bloodstained knickers beneath her bed, Ada quickly changed, slid down the tree again, and presented herself at the kitchen door.

*   *   *

Late the following evening, when Helen and Eddie had gone upstairs to bed and her father was out checking on the cattle, Ada and her mother sat alone in the kitchen, darning her father's and Eddie's socks. As she stitched, Ada wondered if somehow she might raise the topic of Father Dineen's brutal behaviour towards her, but decided reluctantly that her mother would never believe her, and anyway, she'd be far too embarrassed.

Suddenly, Ada looked up, realising that her mother was speaking to her.

"I see you've started your monthly bleed – I found your soiled knickers underneath your bed." Her mother leaned forward conspiratorially. "Now that you've started, you'll have a bleed every month until you're an old woman." She chuckled malevolently. "It's called the Curse, but believe me, there'll be many times in your life when you'll be very glad to see it arrive!"

As her mother turned back to her darning, Ada felt both relieved and embarrassed. She'd never discussed bodily functions with her mother before, and she was glad that her mother's brief comments appeared to be at an end. Nevertheless, Ada felt a sudden surge of relief bubbling up inside her – maybe what Father Dineen had done to her was somehow necessary to start this monthly process. Maybe girls weren't told about it in advance, since it was so painful when it happened.

Ada continued her darning with renewed gusto. Hopefully, the worst was over, and everything would be all right from now on.

CHAPTER 4

"So when are we going to see the country estate?" said Maggie, chewing on a salad sandwich. It was lunchtime the following Monday, and the two friends had met up for a quick bite to eat. The two women's offices were close to each other, so they met regularly to moan about their workloads, the state of the nation, and their lack of boyfriends in particular.

"Any time you like," answered Olivia. "In fact, I'm going to take Wednesday afternoon off work and go down for a few hours, so come with me if you like. I want to start sorting out the furniture that's there, and arranging to get quotes for the building work."

"Sounds great – you're on. So far, I've no appointments that afternoon. So I'll just tell everyone I'm already booked up for Wednesday afternoon."

"Better ring Barbara and see if she can come too."

"Yeah," said Maggie, grinning, "she'd die if I got to see it first!"

*   *   *

Around lunchtime on Wednesday, Olivia collected both her friends for their first visit to her new house. The roads out of the city were relatively clear, the sun was shining, and all three women were in good spirits.

Barbara had managed to change her shift with her colleague Fergal, and was every bit as excited as Maggie to see Olivia's house. Of course, when she'd mentioned changing shifts with Fergal, she'd had to endure the usual banter and rude innuendos from the duo. Both Olivia and Maggie were convinced that Fergal could be the one to put the sparkle back in Barbara's eyes.

But Barbara knew differently. When she'd first started working at the hospital, Fergal had made it perfectly clear that he was interested in her. But she'd politely let him know that a romance between them wasn't on the cards. In another lifetime, they might have got together, but the spectre of Richard Devlin always came between her and any man she might think of dating. It was ridiculous, she conceded, that he still exerted such power over her. She'd have to get him out of her head, once and for all.

She'd casually dated several men since they'd broken up almost five years earlier, and she'd enjoyed their company. But she'd never felt that special spark for any of them. They'd simply relieved the monotony of nights that would otherwise have been spent alone in her apartment.

Realising that Olivia was looking at her in the rear-view mirror, Barbara replaced her sad expression with a bright smile.

"It's handy to be working in the new hospital," she said, forcing herself to sound cheerful, "because it means I'll be able to drive down to Cloncullen in minutes rather than hours. Although the old county hospital is probably nearer to Cloncullen as the crow flies, the new hospital has the benefit of the motorway."

Maggie pulled a face. "You're lucky you don't have to cross the city – it takes me half an hour to get as far as the M50."

"Yes, but once you get onto the M50, it's only a forty-minute journey," said Olivia. "I'll be able to commute to work when I move in full-time. It's amazing that Cloncullen is so close to the city, yet it still feels like a rural village. You can also get the Dublin-Cork train from nearby Ballyesmond."

"Give it another twenty years, and it will probably be a suburb of Dublin," said Maggie. "At the rate this city is expanding, it may even reach the outskirts of Cork before long."

"I don't think the citizens of Cork would be too happy about that!" said Barbara, smiling.

"Anyone mind if I put on a CD?" asked Olivia. "I've just got the latest Julia Gleeson compilation."

"Sounds great," said Barbara. "I just adore that woman's voice."

"Can't say I've heard of her," said Maggie. "What kind of stuff does she do?"

"Maggie!" said Olivia, in mock horror. "You must be the only person in the country who hasn't heard of her!"

"Julia Gleeson is our most prestigious mezzo-soprano," Barbara told her, "and she's internationally recognised. She's just come back from a world tour, where she sang to packed audiences everywhere she went. "

"Oh, her!" said Maggie, sniffing. "Yeah, I remember her now."

"Well, now you hear her as well!" said Olivia, turning on her CD player, and the car was at once filled with the melodious sounds of Julia Gleeson's incredible voice.

With stunning views to match the beautiful sounds, the trio enjoyed their journey to Cloncullen. The sun was shining, the roads weren't too congested, and they all felt excited. Barbara and Maggie were looking forward to exploring Olivia's new demesne, while Olivia could hardly wait to step through her own front door again.

She was also relieved that her friends were visiting the house midweek, so that she'd be there on her own at the weekend, when she'd arranged to meet Brendan Warren. She still hadn't told Barbara and Maggie about meeting him, although she couldn't understand why, since the trio shared information on everything, especially where men were concerned. Maybe it was because she really liked him a lot – and it would show. Which would mean that her two friends would tease her unmercifully about him! Besides, it was her little secret, and she liked hugging it to herself for just a little while.

After a pleasant drive through open country, Olivia turned off the road and into the gravel driveway of Bay Tree House.

"My God, it's fantastic!" Barbara squealed.

"I can't believe it!" said Maggie enthusiastically. "I thought it was going to be an awful kip – and I'd have to be polite about it!"

"You've never been polite in your life!" laughed Olivia, as she got out of her car and headed towards the front door.

"It's in a wonderful position, too," said Barbara, gazing around her. "You're quite near the town, aren't you? Yet far enough away to have your privacy."

"But not too much privacy, please," said Maggie. "I'm hoping to spot some of the local talent."

Inside the house, the two visitors disappeared up the stairs and, as Olivia headed for the kitchen, she could hear their exclamations of delight as they discovered the stained-glass window. She smiled as she filled the new kettle she'd brought, and turned it on. A house wasn't a home, she'd decided, until the first cup of tea had been made and drunk there. She'd even brought scones, butter and jam, so that they could have proper afternoon tea!

"This place is gorgeous!" said Maggie, as she and Barbara reappeared. "The bedrooms are really big – and some of the furniture isn't bad either. And you can actually see the sea from the back bedrooms."

"The old dear who lived here obviously had good taste," added Barbara. "Although most of the personal stuff seems to have been cleared out, there are quite a few valuable pieces of furniture upstairs."

"Her name was Laura Morton," said Olivia, feeling quite defensive about the woman whose home she had indirectly inherited. She felt a sense of duty to respect the woman's home and possessions, and treat them with the care they'd obviously received during her lifetime. And, as she'd promised her grandmother, she intended to find out as much as she could about the previous owner. She intended to ask around in the immediate neighbourhood, and check the births and deaths for the area. To the best of her ability, she'd try to discover if there was any link between Laura Morton and her grandmother's sister Ada.

"We're off to look at the downstairs rooms now," said Barbara, as she and Maggie hurried out of the kitchen to explore the rest of the house.

Olivia smiled to herself. They were like children! Then again, she had been just as excited on her first visit. By now, her excitement had been muted to a warm glow of happiness and satisfaction. Don't worry, Laura, she said softly under her breath, I promise you I'll take good care of your home.

After a thorough examination of the house, Barbara and Maggie returned to the kitchen, happily accepting the cups of tea and scones that Olivia had laid out on the large pine kitchen table.

"It's fabulous, Liv!" was Maggie's verdict.

"It's – oh God, it's so divine, I'm actually speechless!" said Barbara. "It's a wonderful house. Livvy – I just know you're going to be so happy here!"

CHAPTER 5

The following Saturday morning, Olivia arrived alone at Bay Tree House. She'd no plans to do anything in particular, merely to wander around, and marvel at the fact that she owned it. She was also excited at the prospect of seeing Brendan Warren again. In fact, she'd hardly thought of anything all week except his cheery face, his strong hands . . . She shivered with delight. Only one more day until she saw him again!

She'd been mildly surprised that he hadn't asked to see her on the Saturday. Given his initial enthusiasm, she was more than a little put out that he hadn't demanded to see her the minute she arrived! Oh well, she concluded, maybe he had some important arrangement he couldn't get out of. Maybe he visited his mother every Saturday . . . She was quite prepared to believe the best of Brendan Warren. Come to think of it, wasn't there some big match on that weekend? Maybe he was watching that. She was well aware how sacrosanct a man's viewing of sporting events could be!

*   *   *

Olivia was enjoying exploring the area. Cloncullen was a pretty little town that still retained it olde worlde character. Its layout was well designed, with a square in the centre, and lots of small streets radiating off it. There was also a beautiful sandy beach nearby, where Olivia hoped to walk as often as she could. But before she'd indulge herself in that pleasure, she'd have to work on the gardens at Bay Tree House!

At the other end of the town, there was a very imposing but austere building, which one of the shopkeepers told her had once been an orphanage. There were also lots of small shops, an upmarket restaurant, a Chinese takeaway and a fish and chip shop –and at least six pubs! Her pleasure turned to delight when she found Larkin's, a quaint little emporium that stocked just about everything. In addition to foodstuffs and fresh local produce, it also stocked toys, needles, thread and elastic, bicycle repair kits, Wellington boots, farm implements, tools, greeting cards and stationery.

Olivia always made a point of avoiding the doubtful products offered by many supermarkets. Chlorine in her pre-packed bag of salad? Hidden sugar in her baked beans and tinned fruit? No thanks! So she was pleased to see a large selection of fresh fruit and vegetables on display, and she knew by their knobbly and irregular shapes that these were locally grown produce. It also felt good to support small local businesses.

Filling up her basket with lots of tasty and healthy produce, Olivia made her way to the counter, where a beaming little woman behind the counter began to check off the items on her till, all the while chattering on about the weather. Smiling, Olivia handed over her money, delighted to also discover that shopping local was cheaper than paying city prices.

"Hello, Liv."

Olivia turned in surprise. Then her eyes glazed over, and her mouth tightened.

"Hello, Richard."

"How are you keeping?"

"Fine, thank you," Olivia answered abruptly. What on earth was Richard Devlin doing in a small country store? She would have expected to see him dressed in a designer suit, ostentatiously waving the keys of yet another brand new BMW. Instead he was wearing jeans and an ordinary-looking waterproof jacket.

"How's Barbara?"

Olivia could feel her hackles rising. How dare he inquire so solicitously about the woman he'd dumped!

"She's fine."

Turning on her heel, Olivia walked quickly out of the shop, put her shopping in the boot of her car and drove off without a backward glance. But when she was sufficiently far away not to be seen, she took a quick look in her rear-view mirror. But clearly Richard Devlin hadn't left the shop yet.

As her heartbeat slowed down to normal, Olivia cursed him once again. How many sleepless nights had she herself endured, supporting poor Barbara, who had cried until she had no tears left? Hopefully, Olivia thought, I'll never see him again.

*   *   *

Although she never wanted to see Richard Devlin again, Olivia couldn't wait to see Brendan Warren. So she made a special effort to look nice as she got ready to go to his cottage the following day. She spent hours in the bathroom and in front of the mirror, trying to achieve a casual but sophisticated look. At first, she tied her red-gold hair up in a pony-tail, then she left it hanging loose around her shoulders. Next she piled on the make-up, only to take it all off again, opting for the natural look instead. In place of the floaty chiffon dress she'd brought down from Dublin, she put on a pair of jeans and T-shirt. After all, she was in the country now! Besides, if he really liked her, he might as well get used to the real person from day one!

When she arrived at Blackberry Cottage at noon as arranged, bearing one of her own home-cooked pavlovas, she was surprised, then annoyed, when she discovered that there was no one at home. Puzzled, she checked her watch. No, she'd definitely got the day and the time right. She decided to wait for a while in case he'd been delayed, but after pacing up and down for half an hour, and feeling thoroughly disappointed, she gave up and went back to Bay Tree House.

Alone in the kitchen of Bay Tree House, Olivia felt miserable. And angry. She'd had so many hopes and dreams about Brendan Warren, and now he'd totally let her down.

Eyeing the pavlova, Olivia went to the kitchen drawer

and took out a knife. There was only one thing for it – she'd have to eat it herself. Helping herself to a huge portion, Olivia made a cup of tea and sat down to indulge herself in its glorious and sweet sticky texture.

To hell with Brendan Warren, she thought vehemently, as she shovelled a heaped forkful into her mouth. How dare he suggest a get-together, then not even have the good manners to turn up, or at least to apologise for his absence! Next time she saw him in the village, she certainly intended to snub him. At least that would give her some satisfaction.

Then she wondered if he'd gone off her. Perhaps he'd decided that she wasn't his type. After all, she'd been quite rude to him when he'd first appeared in the garden at Bay Tree House. Olivia recalled her mother's favourite adage: "Never run after a man or a bus – there's always another one coming." Olivia had always followed it faithfully. She certainly wouldn't be running after Brendan Warren! Even if he was the last man on earth, she wouldn't go within a mile of him now . . . besides, a pavlova was a lot more dependable than any man . . .

Olivia helped herself to another slice.

CHAPTER 6

Two months later, Ada began to feel sick in the mornings. She could barely hold down the steaming porridge that her mother ladled out for her and the other two children before they left for school each morning. No sooner did she reach the gate at the end of the driveway than she threw up into the tiny stream that ran along the farm's boundaries.

At first, she managed to disguise what was happening from her brother and sister. On their way to school – she to the Senior School, they to the Junior – she would hang back, sometimes deliberately dropping her books or pretending to tie her shoelace, and urging them to go on without her. Then, as they walked ahead, she would quietly throw up before running to catch up with them.

Eventually, she was caught out when a particularly nasty bout of nausea and vomiting rendered her prostrate in the hedgerow.

"Are you all right?" Helen called out anxiously, running back to help after she'd heard her sister retching.

"I don't know," Ada gasped. "I think I must have caught

some kind of infection."

"I hope it's not consumption," said Eddie, as he ran back to Ada's side, not realising that he was frightening her even more.

Tuberculosis was rampant throughout the country, and people who caught it either spent years in sanatoriums or died from lung failure. It also stigmatised families, and for this reason, everyone avoided people who had a relative with TB, for fear of catching it themselves. There was also a widely held suspicion that TB ran in families, so whole families were socially isolated and stigmatised as a result.

"Look, I'll be okay in a minute," whispered Ada, "but please don't tell Mam or Dad, or any of the teachers. It can't be consumption because I don't have a cough, but you know how people talk."

Thus sworn to secrecy, the children kept their own counsel. So it was the following week before Ada's mother woke up to the fact that her eldest daughter was no longer playing football, her waist was beginning to thicken and she hadn't had a monthly bleed for three months.

"In God's name, Ada – what have you been up to?"

"What do you mean, Mammy?"

"Jesus Christ, Ada," screamed her mother, "all the signs are there! You must be pregnant! You dirty bitch – Father Dineen was right! You're nothing but a liability. Wait till your father hears about this – you've disgraced the family!"

"But Mammy – "

"But nothing! Oh my God, what will the neighbours say?"

When her father returned from milking the cows later that evening, he found a distraught Ada and her tight-lipped mother. His initial look of concern darkened to one of rage as he was told about Ada's situation.

"How could you do this to us, Ada?" he bellowed, pacing

the kitchen floor. "Why couldn't you wait until you were married? Oh God, I suppose it's my own fault, for letting you run wild with those boys. All the time, I thought you were just having fun – but it was a different kind of fun you were after!"

"But Daddy, I've done nothing!"

Her mother's eyes were venomous, her voice low and menacing as she spoke. "You can't fool us, you hussy – you've been letting some boy into your knickers, haven't you?"

Suddenly, Ada crumpled in shock, her spirit broken. Father Dineen had made her pregnant!

"What's the boy's name?" asked her father angrily. "So help me, I'll give him a good hiding when I catch him! He'll pay dearly for what he's done – "

Ada was weeping now. "It wasn't a boy, Daddy – it was Father Dineen!"

There was a shocked silence as parents and child faced each other. Then, with lightning speed, her mother reached out her hand and struck Ada hard across the face.

"You evil bitch – how dare you try to sully the good name of such a wonderful priest! You're just trying to protect the boy that's done this to you. You're evil, Ada Casey – I can't believe you'd stoop so low!"

"But it's true!"

"That's enough, Ada," said her father quietly. "I know you want to protect whoever did this, but in doing so, you've committed another mortal sin by making such wild accusations. I hope you'll go to church tomorrow and make a good confession."

Ada sat crying quietly. What was the use of telling the truth when no one believed her? And what would happen next – could she really have a baby in her tummy? And if so, what would she do with it? She felt too young and inexperienced to

*look after a child. And all her dreams – of becoming an athlete
and representing her country in the next Olympic Games –
were dashed by what was happening.*

"Get out of my sight!" said her mother in disgust.

*"Yes, go to bed, Ada – we'll talk about this tomorrow," said
her father gruffly.*

*Upstairs in the attic, Ada was relieved to find that her
brother and sister were fast asleep. Right now, she felt
emotionally drained, and was glad that she didn't need to
explain to them why their parents were angry with her.
Quickly, she climbed into bed, burying her face in the pillow so
that her sobbing wouldn't wake up Helen and Eddie.*

*Perhaps when she awoke in the morning, she'd discover
that it had all been a bad dream. Maybe she wasn't pregnant –
she'd just put on weight because she hadn't felt like exercising
down at the playing field for a while. Oh how she hated Father
Dineen! Anyway, maybe he'd admit to what he'd done when he
found out that she was pregnant. If she was pregnant.
Eventually, Ada cried herself into a deep and troubled sleep.*

*　　*　　*

"Your father's been to see Father Dineen – "

*For a moment, Ada's eyes filled with hope. Maybe her father
had finally believed her, and had gone to tackle the priest.*

*"And luckily, he knows of somewhere you can go. After all,
we can't keep you here, disgracing the family." Her mother
looked pointedly at Ada's stomach. "You're being sent to a
convent where the nuns take in wayward girls like yourself.
Father Dineen has managed to secure you a place there, where
he says you'll learn humility and go to Mass daily." Her
mother gave a small satisfied smile. "So you'll have a chance to*

ask God's forgiveness for the shame you've brought on this family."

"But, Mammy – "

"And when the bastard you're carrying is born, it's to be hoped that some decent Christian family might be willing to help it purge its sin."

Ada had no idea what her mother was talking about. How could an unborn child have committed a sin?

"When will I be coming home again, Mammy?" she asked tearfully.

"Stop that crying at once," said her mother coldly. "It's a pity you didn't stop to think of the consequences, when you were letting that boy at you!"

Ada tried another tack. "Will I be away long, Mammy?"

"I don't know – we'll have to see what Father Dineen says." Her mother wagged a finger at her. "You're a very lucky girl to have someone like Father Dineen concerned about your welfare. He's such a wonderful example of Christianity – always caring for others. You'd do well to follow his example, Ada."

Ada was completely bewildered. How could Father Dineen be a good example of Christianity, after what he'd done to her? Her own parents seemed to hold him in high esteem, yet he was the most un-Jesus-like person she'd ever met.

Ada had always been impressed by Jesus. He'd loved everyone, and had asked his followers to do the same – and even to love their enemies! It was a bit like a fairy story, except he hadn't been able to live happily ever after himself. Back then, some people hadn't liked the fact that he loved everyone, so they'd crucified him. But he'd started a new religion before he died, so his ideas of loving your neighbour and forgiving your enemies were handed down through the centuries.

Nevertheless, there was one problem that continued to

puzzle Ada. Somehow, all the values she'd learnt in Religious Knowledge classes didn't seem to apply in practice. The nuns in her school slapped the girls' hands and legs with rulers and the dreaded strap, while at Eddie's school, the boys were hit with rulers, chairs, and anything else that came to hand. How did that equate with love and respect for others?

Ada was also puzzled as to how a child born outside marriage could be any different from one born within it. How could an innocent baby be guilty of a sin? Maybe she hadn't understood properly, for she was certain that Jesus wouldn't have made any such distinction.

Ada bit her lip. On the other hand, maybe she'd missed some important point on one of the days when she'd been daydreaming in class. Maybe Jesus didn't extend his love to unmarried girls and their babies. After all, when Jesus was asked who his neighbours were, he'd said: "My neighbour is all mankind." He hadn't said "womankind", or even "humankind". Nevertheless, the idea of loving everyone, even your enemies, appealed greatly to Ada. She would even try to think kindly of Father Dineen.

CHAPTER 7

Olivia and Maggie were having their usual Monday lunch together, at a city centre café near where they both worked.

"You'll never guess who I bumped into at the weekend," said Olivia, as she carried their coffees to the table.

"I presume you mean down in Cloncullen?"

Olivia nodded. "That's where you'll find me every weekend from now on! There's loads of work to be done on the house, the land needs clearing and I intend to restore the gardens to their former glory."

"Go on – tell me who you met. I hope it was some gorgeous farmer or local businessman."

"No, it wasn't – it was Richard Devlin."

Maggie nearly dropped her coffee cup. "My God – what was he doing there?"

"I don't know – I was getting some groceries in one of the local shops, when he said hello. I presume he was buying something himself, but I got such a shock that I never noticed what."

Maggie laughed. "I can hardly believe it! Richard in his designer suit, slumming among the vegetables! That must have been a sight to see!"

"Actually, he wasn't wearing a suit," Olivia recalled. "He was wearing jeans and some kind of waterproof jacket. It was fairly ordinary-looking stuff – not designer wear at all."

"And what about the BMW?"

Olivia gave an apologetic smile. "To be honest, I was so keen to get away from him that I didn't even notice."

"What did he say?"

"Oh, the usual crap. How was I – then he asked how Barbara was."

"The bastard!"

Olivia nodded in agreement. "He looked sort of sad – which gave me a great sense of satisfaction!"

"Was the wife with him?"

"I didn't see anyone else – I think he was on his own."

The two women were silent, both thinking back to the days when Richard and Barbara had been planning their own wedding. Then they'd broken up after a silly row, and Richard began seeing someone else. Within weeks, he had announced that he was marrying this other woman.

Needless to say, Barbara had been devastated. She and Richard had been childhood sweethearts, and everyone had assumed that their bust-up was just a temporary split, probably due to wedding nerves. But Richard took another woman down the aisle a few months later.

Olivia spoke at last. "Do you think I should mention

it to Barbara?"

Maggie pulled a face. "Not much point, is there? It will only remind her of that bastard, and get her all upset again."

Olivia sighed. "I don't think there's a day when she *doesn't* think about him."

Maggie thumped the table. "God, how I hate that man! I'd be delighted if you were able to report back to her that he'd broken his miserable bloody neck!"

"That wouldn't give her any satisfaction – she still loves him, the poor fool."

Maggie looked sourly at her friend. "I think you and I need to focus on helping Barbara to find someone else. Telling her about seeing that bastard will only slow down her recovery." She sighed. "Even if she doesn't fancy her colleague Fergal, surely there are a few other tasty doctors in the hospital?"

"I don't think she even notices the men in the hospital," said Olivia. "She still compares every other man to Richard."

Maggie took a bite of her sandwich. "Anyway, it was probably just a fluke that you bumped into him. You're hardly likely to see him again."

"I hope you're right," said Olivia. "Because if I do, I'll be tempted to strangle him with one of his designer ties!"

Olivia recalled the good old days, when she, Maggie and Barbara had all been part of a large but close-knit group of friends. But when Richard dumped Barbara, it had repercussions for everyone in their circle, leading to the gradual disintegration of the whole group. Like a hive that had lost its queen bee, the people within it began to drift away, to form new groups of friends elsewhere.

Olivia was disgusted and angry with Richard Devlin. Not only had he destroyed Barbara's happiness; his rejection of their friend had also given her own confidence a knock. After all, if this kind of thing could happen to such a devoted couple, couldn't it happen to them too?

"Another coffee, Liv?"

Olivia nodded, and her friend stood up to go to the counter. But Maggie's mind wasn't really on the coffees. Instead, she was thinking about their futures, and wondering if any of them would ever meet a nice guy. The three of them were approaching thirty, and were well established in careers they loved. But none of them had been lucky in love so far. Her own love life had proved uninteresting to say the least. All through her college years, she'd gone steady with another student who, as soon as they graduated, promptly informed her that he was emigrating to Australia. He'd offered her the option of going with him, but she'd suddenly realised that she neither wanted to go to Australia, nor stay with the guy in question. And Olivia, while she'd dated several really nice guys, had never come close to finding one who might be Mr Right.

Returning with the coffees, Maggie placed them on the table, smiling sadly at Olivia as she sat down. "Do you realise it's been almost five years since Barbara and Richard broke up, yet she still gets upset whenever his name is mentioned? I wonder if she'll ever get over him?"

Olivia grimaced. "I don't know, Mags. But I sincerely hope we won't be seeing Richard Devlin in Cloncullen any more."

Unbidden, an image of Brendan Warren crept into

Olivia's mind, but she dismissed it just as quickly. Barbara might be willing to pine over a man, but *she* certainly wasn't going to!

"Liv – what's the matter?" said Maggie, eying her friend. "You're suddenly looking very fierce!"

"Nothing's the matter Mags," said Olivia curtly, "absolutely nothing at all."

* * *

At last, Brendan Warren heard his mobile phone. It seemed to be ringing across a vast expanse of space before finally reaching his brain. Surfacing from sleep, he groggily groped for it on the bedside locker.

"Hello?"

"Brendan – how are you, man?"

Brendan smiled, recognising the voice of his friend, Sergeant Philip Lynch.

"Hi, Philip, I'm not too bad, thanks. Got a nasty headache, though."

"I'm not surprised after your performance yesterday! You had us all worried – especially when you passed out on us."

Brendan winced as he tried to move his head. "My whole body is aching, and I feel like I've drunk an entire vat of Guinness! I wouldn't want to endure anything like that again in a hurry!"

Philip laughed. "I think you'll definitely be off the drink for quite some time!"

Already, even after such a small exertion, Brendan could feel his eyes closing. His headache was still pounding, and it felt like a manic woodpecker was at work on his skull. Then, just as he began to drift off again, he remembered there was something he urgently needed to ask Philip.

He cleared his throat. "I – didn't do – you know – anything that I shouldn't have?"

Momentarily, Philip thought of winding up his friend. But he resisted the urge, deeming it unfair to tease a man in such a delicate condition.

"No, you were fine – honestly. For a moment, I thought you were going to punch the other guy, but you let it pass, thank God."

With relief, Brendan Warren sank back into his pillows. So he hadn't made a total pillock of himself. He couldn't remember much about the day before. There were vague, jumbled-up memories in his head. He remembered the *craic* and the general camaraderie. But after that, everything went black. He couldn't remember how things had ended, or how he'd ended up in a strange bed. Where on earth was he? He wanted to ask Philip, but he was far too embarrassed. Then again, Philip had rung him on his mobile, so *he* mightn't know where he was either . . .

"Well, I suppose if you *had* knocked the other guy's teeth out, you could at least have offered him complimentary treatment!" Philip added cheerily.

"Very funny," said Brendan sourly, suddenly remembering that he was a dentist, and that he was scheduled to do six fillings and a root canal the following morning.

After Philip had rung off, Brendan settled down beneath the bedcovers of the bed once again. But there was something bothering him. Something lurking at the back of his mind – something he hadn't done, but should have done. He groaned. If only his head would stop pounding . . .

Before the phone call had woken him, he'd been dreaming of a woman with long red-gold hair and the face of an angel. Well, a cheeky angel, anyway! Who was she? Why did she keep intruding into his brain? He wondered if she was a figment of his imagination, some kind of composite of his ideal woman? Brendan closed his eyes. Maybe if he dozed off again, she'd come back and fill his dreams once more . . .

CHAPTER 8

The phone rang at Olivia's house in Rathmines, where she still lived with her mother Doreen, pending her permanent move to Bay Tree House.

"Olivia?"

"Oh, hi, Mags."

"Sorry, Liv – but I can't come down to the house next weekend as arranged," Maggie lamented. "My brothers and their friends have finally agreed to paint my apartment, so I can hardly walk out on them when they're willing to do it free of charge. You know I've been asking them to do it for ages, so I'd better hang around and make tea for them! And Barbara said to tell you she can't make it either – she's baby-sitting for her sister. Will you be okay on your own?"

"No problem," said Olivia, smiling to herself. "I'm probably better on my own – you and Barbara would only distract me from all I have to do! First on my list is to find an architect or surveyor, to give the place a good going-over. Something needs to be done with the

55

chimney in the kitchen, since it doesn't look too safe."

"Oh Livvy, please pick a fine thing – it won't hurt to have a good-looking fella around the place!"

"Listen," said Olivia, laughing, "I need an efficient architect – I'm not scouting round for a man for you!"

"Surely it's possible for him to be good-looking *and* efficient?"

"And good in the sack too, I suppose. Well, since he's going to be *my* architect, I'll be the one checking out all his credentials!" Olivia grinned. "Besides, I could end up using a woman architect, you know. I just want to find the best person for the job."

* * *

As it happened, Olivia was given a recommendation for a very efficient local architect. And much to Maggie's annoyance, he was in his fifties, and married with a grown-up family.

The architect, who visited the house during the week, quickly discovered that the brickwork of the chimneybreast in the kitchen was crumbling and would need to be demolished. But he also devised wonderful plans that would replace the demolished fireplace with an identical one made of bricks from a local salvage store, creating a much bigger kitchen, and also providing a sun-room off to the side. This would enable Olivia to take advantage of the southwest-facing courtyard and garden just outside the newly positioned back door. The change in layout would also provide an ideal opportunity to install central heating.

When she arrived at Bay Tree House the following

Saturday morning, Olivia discovered that two of the workmen had arrived just ahead of her, and already they'd started work on the wall to be demolished. An acro-prop held up one end of the wall, while the two men attacked the fireplace with large sledgehammers, one from inside the house, the other from outside. Rivulets of sweat soaked through their T-shirts as they worked.

"You both look in need of a cup of tea," said Olivia firmly. "I'll put the kettle on right away."

To nods and smiles of agreement, Olivia began busying herself at the back of the kitchen. Despite the fact that it now had a large hole in it, the kitchen already had a homely feel to it, and she smiled happily to herself as she got out the tea bags and took down the mugs from the old dresser. She'd already decided that she would keep Laura's old dresser and pine kitchen table. Apart from the fact that they were perfect for the kitchen, Olivia wanted to preserve as much of the house's previous character as possible. And, in a strange way, it helped her to feel closer to its previous owner, for whom she had developed a strange affinity. I must be mad, she thought, smiling to herself. After all, she knew nothing about Laura Morton, nor had she ever seen a photograph of her. All she knew about the dead woman was that she'd left her home to two people she'd never even met.

Olivia was looking forward to bringing her grandmother and uncle down to see the house. And her mother, too – if and when she could spare the time. As a university lecturer, her mother's head was almost permanently stuck in a book, or else she was correcting exam papers or preparing course work for her students. When Olivia told her mother about being given a house, her mother had replied in her usual vague manner, as though she was addressing a distracting schoolchild.

"That's nice, dear. A house, you say? That's very generous of Mother and Eddie. Now where did I leave that pile of papers? Olivia, did you see a pile of corrected exam papers? They're very important – "

Olivia sighed. Sometimes, she wondered if her mother realised that her daughter was a woman approaching thirty. She knew her mother loved her dearly, and although she'd been reared by a single parent, Olivia hadn't suffered any of the deprivations that many single-parent families have to endure. There was always money for clothing, school trips, pocket money, and good food on the table.

Her father was never mentioned. There were no photographs of him, and his name didn't appear on her birth certificate. As a child, she'd occasionally asked about him, but in the face of her mother's evasive answers, she'd gradually stopped asking. As she grew older, Olivia wondered if, perhaps, her mother had been a victim of rape, or if she herself had been the result of a one-night stand. But it was unlikely she'd ever know.

Nevertheless, her mother's vagueness and involvement in her work had proved a useful asset to the young Olivia, and she'd been able to get away with much more than kids whose parents constantly kept an eagle eye on them. It had never been a problem to get permission to stay over at friends' houses. With an absentminded "Of course, dear – do you need some money?" her mother would shell out whatever Olivia asked, or drive her to a friend's house for a sleepover. Olivia often thought that it was just as well she hadn't been the sort to steal or take drugs, because she doubted if her mother would have noticed. Sometimes Olivia felt that *she* was the parent rather than her mother.

Getting out the butter, Olivia ran her hand down her new, environmentally friendly fridge-freezer. It had been the very first thing she'd bought for the house. The old fridge-freezer had only been fit for the scrap heap, and used a ridiculous amount of energy. Now, she'd stocked the new freezer with a supply of her own home-cooked frozen meals, so she'd be ready for any visitors who dropped in. She'd also discovered a gorgeous bakery just outside Cloncullen, where she'd bought a large selection of cakes and scones. Some of these were also in the freezer, the remainder in the bread crock, ready for any unexpected callers. You never knew when some of the locals might drop by!

Olivia busied herself with the mugs and tea bags. Although she wouldn't allow herself consciously think about him, deep in her heart she was hoping that Brendan Warren might be one of those who dropped by. Full of apologies, he'd arrive carrying an enormous bouquet of flowers . . . In your dreams, Olivia told herself. In your dreams, you silly fool.

Carrying a tray with mugs of tea and the freshly buttered scones to the two workmen, Olivia suddenly realised that the sounds of the sledgehammer had stopped, and there were low mumblings from the two men that sounded ominous.

"Is everything okay?"

As Olivia stepped outside the back door into the debris of the demolished fireplace, she realised that one of the men was holding what looked like a small bundle of cloth.

"Missus – this was in the fireplace," said one of the men. "I think you should take a look at it."

Olivia placed the tray on the edge of the courtyard wall. "Please call me Olivia," she said. "What are you guys called?"

"I'm Joe, and this is Johnny."

But the two men didn't smile back in acknowledgement. Instead, they continued to wear grave expressions. "Honestly, Missus – I mean, Olivia – you need to look at this," said Joe, who seemed to be the more talkative of the two.

"What is it?" Olivia peered at the bundle of old rags, but it didn't look like anything special.

"I think – eh, it seems to be a skeleton. A baby's skeleton. I think you need to call the police."

Olivia looked from one to the other in astonishment. The skeleton of a baby? What on earth was it doing in her chimney?

"The police?" she repeated, feeling suddenly dazed and stupid. Beyond a fine for an out-of-date tax disc, Olivia had never had anything to do with the police. Now she had visions of them swarming all over her house, holding up the building work and generally making nuisances of themselves. "Are you sure it's a baby?" she asked at last.

In answer, Joe put the tiny bundle on the courtyard wall and pulled back the outer covering. There was no mistake. Inside was the skeleton of a tiny baby. The bones looked mottled and brittle, and it had obviously been in the chimney for a long time. Looking at it, Olivia felt a shiver run up her spine. The poor little mite! What had happened to it? And what sort of strange things had been happening in this house?

CHAPTER 9

The following night, Ada was deep in sleep when she felt herself being aroused from her bed.

"Shhh!" whispered her mother, as she pulled back the bedclothes and hoisted her eldest daughter into a sitting position. "Father Dineen is downstairs, and he's taking you to the nuns who'll take care of you. Hurry and get dressed – it's a long journey, and you'll need to get there by morning."

"No, Mam, please – don't send me away with him!"

"Hush, child – stop making a fuss! And don't you dare wake your brother and sister! Now get downstairs quickly – Father Dineen is doing us a big favour by saving this family from the shame you've brought on us!"

When Ada came downstairs a few minutes later, still half asleep, her father and the parish priest were standing together in the kitchen. Ada looked at her father in the hopes that he would save her from this dreadful fate. If anyone would help her, it would be him.

But he said nothing. His eyes were filled with tears, and he turned away rather than meet her gaze. In that moment, Ada knew that her fate was sealed. Then her mother silently pushed her towards the door.

"Please, Mam – let me say goodbye to Helen and Joe."

"There isn't time," said her mother brusquely. "Now hurry along – Father Dineen is waiting. It's a long journey, and he'll be exhausted by the time he gets there."

Briefly, Ada wondered why her mother was showing so much concern about the priest's welfare, but none about her own daughter's.

Still disoriented and confused from lack of sleep, Ada was bundled into the back of Father Dineen's car. Momentarily, she was relieved that she hadn't been seated beside him, but her heart was breaking as he started the engine and the car began to glide forward. Her parents hadn't even hugged her, or said goodbye to her! Sitting up, she craned her neck to see out the back window, but all she could see was the darkness engulfing everything behind them. Her parents had disappeared, swallowed up by the night, and now there was only her and Father Dineen. Fortunately, the priest said nothing as he drove along, and at last, an exhausted Ada curled up on the back seat and resumed her interrupted sleep.

As streaks of dawn crisscrossed the horizon, Ada awoke, feeling cramped and cold. Father Dineen was still driving, and as Ada sat up, she noticed him checking in the rear-view mirror to see if she was awake, but he still said nothing.

By the time it was fully daylight, Ada sensed that their journey would soon be coming to an end. Father Dineen turned the car up a side-road, and Ada looked around her in expectation. Then, as big iron gates loomed up ahead, Father Dineen slowed down the car and turned in through the gates, which were bound by a high stone wall. A winding driveway brought them to an imposing redbrick building. Lit by the early *morning sun, it looked inviting, but Ada suspected that it would be anything but.*

"We're here," said Father Dineen, somewhat unnecessarily, as he parked the car on the gravel driveway outside the main front door, and climbed out of the car.

Ada followed him, keeping at a safe distance.

Anxiously, she waited as he pulled the bell chain beside the front door and stood there expectantly. Soon, the door was opened with a flourish, and several twittering and fawning nuns appeared, and after much shaking of hands and enquiries about his health, Father Dineen was whisked off to the parlour at the end of the corridor. As Ada stood alone in the hall, she could smell freshly baked bread, and as her stomach rumbled, she hoped that she, too, would soon be tucking into a breakfast. Hopefully, someone would come to collect her soon, since by now she felt weak with the hunger. Fearing that she might pass out, she sat down in the hallway and leaned against the panelled wall. She could hear the clink of cups in the parlour, and the smell of bacon frying, and her stomach rumbled loudly once again.

At last, one of the nuns stepped out of the parlour, still smiling from her pleasant encounter with Father Dineen. But when she saw Ada, the smile was replaced by a scowl. And instead of greeting the scared young girl, instead she hauled her unceremoniously to her feet.

"Get up at once, girl!" said the nun angrily. "You're a holy disgrace! You needn't think you're going to sit around here doing nothing!"

Taking Ada roughly by the arm, the nun propelled her down a nearby flight of stairs, and Ada found herself in a dank basement that led out into a large concrete yard. At the other end of the yard stood a large building, where the sound of swishing water and noises like a steam engine could be heard. As the nun pushed her inside, Ada realised that she was in some kind of washhouse.

All around her, young women were working, their foreheads covered in sweat. Some were washing sheets and blankets in large steaming vats, their hands raw and red from the hot water. Two others were operating an enormous mangle that stood above a large tub. Ada watched in awe as one of the young women turned the heavy handle, her face red and contorted from the effort of keeping it moving. Her companion fed in the wet items, then proceeded to collect them into a large basket once most of the water had been removed. Then two other girls collected the heavy basket, and carried it outside and across the yard to a drying shed, where several other girls were engaged in hanging up the damp clothing on a series of clotheslines that ran back and forth across the length of the building. Everyone was working as though possessed, and no one looked up or smiled when the nun brought Ada into the drying shed.

The nun handed Ada a well-worn overall. "Here – get out of those fancy clothes of yours and put this on," said the nun brusquely. "You can change over there – " She pointed to a small cubicle. "And hurry up – then you can start by helping Bridie here. She'll show you what to do."

By now, Ada's stomach was churning, both from hunger and from nerves. What was she doing here? How long would she have to stay? Why was she being asked to work here? Surely, she should be getting on with her studies, rather than helping in a laundry?

"Excuse me, sister," she asked politely, "would you mind if I had something to eat first? It's been a long journey, and I haven't eaten anything since teatime yesterday."

Ada wasn't quite sure what happened next, but she suddenly felt a horrendous pain, as a stick hit her across the back of the legs.

"Aren't you a right little Miss?" the nun screamed malevolently. "Tea time, indeed! You'll learn manners here, my girl – you'll be lucky to get one meal a day, and you'll only get that if your work's done properly! You've sinned against God, and you'll pay for it here!"

The girl called Bridie was keeping her head down, no doubt in fear of getting a wallop herself. She looked very pregnant, and Ada felt a stab of pity for her. Then it dawned on her that before long, she herself would be as pregnant as Bridie. And undoubtedly made to work as hard. Tears stung Ada's eyes, but she quickly blinked them away. She wasn't going to let the nun know that she'd upset her.

After Ada had changed into the overall, she joined Bridie, who was folding dry sheets that had been brought back from the drying shed on the other side of the courtyard. The two girls worked quickly in unison together, and the nun gave a grimace of satisfaction as she watched. Then she checked the time on her watch, and headed out of the laundry building, giving a backward glance to make sure that no one was slacking.

"Get on with your work, you sinful hussies!" was her parting shot. "I'll be back to check on you in half an hour. And God help anyone who's fallen behind!"

When the nun was out of earshot, Bridie finally looked up at Ada. "I'll bet you that bitch is going off to stuff her face!" she whispered. "The nuns eat the best of food, while we get only porridge and dry bread."

"How long each day do we spend working?" Ada whispered back. "I'm new here, and nobody's told me anything so far."

"Nor will they," said Bridie sourly, "and you'll work here

like the rest of us until you drop!"

Ada was appalled. She'd assumed that being brought to the nuns by Father Dineen would involve attending some sort of retreat. Did her father know where she was? Surely not. He'd never want her to suffer like this. She knew she'd disappointed him – but even though he'd chosen to believe the priest rather than her, he'd never willingly want her to suffer.

"How long will I really be here?" Ada whispered, as she and Bridie folded and stacked the clean linen.

"For the rest of your life," said Bridie, brutally. "There's no place for us anywhere else – no wants girls who've got themselves pregnant."

"What? But it wasn't my fault – "

"Shhh!" whispered one of the other girls angrily. "If you don't keep your voice down, you'll get us all into trouble!"

"Better be quiet," said Bridie softly. "If not, Sarah will make you pay for it later."

Ada soon discovered that although the young women were all united in their predicament, there was little solidarity between them. A hierarchy existed whereby some women got easier jobs to do than others. This they achieved through currying favour from the nuns' favourites, or by becoming one of the nun's "pets" themselves. But even being a nun's "pet" was a precarious existence, since a nun could suddenly switch her allegiance, and make another young woman her "pet" instead. The women seemed to have formed their own separate cliques, and if a woman became a member of one particular group, God help her if she was then put to work in the company of another group. Knowing this, the nuns, too, played games with their charges, and watched with malevolent glee as the women turned on each other.

Ada felt that she was in a prison camp. Previously, from the comfort of a cinema seat, she'd seen films where inmates fought each other almost to the death for a few crumbs of bread. This place was obviously no different.

For the first few days, Ada lived in a kind of daze. She spoke only when she was spoken to, and worked with a kind of frenzy. Never had she seen people work so hard, yet surely most of these young women must be pregnant like herself? Weren't you meant to take things easy when you were expecting a baby?

She quickly discovered that Sarah, a large young woman with a ruddy complexion, was clearly in charge. If anyone wanted to go to the toilet, Sarah's permission had to be obtained. If one woman wanted to speak to another, Sarah's permission had to be obtained too. And if Sarah took a dislike to anyone, her life would become even more of a hell, if that was possible.

The situation reminded Ada of books she'd read about concentration camp guards who, while being prisoners themselves, nevertheless carried out the brutal wishes of their oppressors, in the hopes of winning a brief reprieve from death themselves. Ada sadly concluded that preying on those below you seemed to be a universal condition.

Ada found herself alternately boiling hot by day while working in the laundry, and freezing cold by night, when all the women were sequestered in a big old dormitory, where there was no heating, the windows rattled, and the bedclothes they were given were sparse and threadbare. At night in her bed, Ada would try to conjure up images of the heat she'd endured earlier in the day, in an attempt to convince her body that she was really warm. And by day, as the sweat ran down her face and body, she tried to recall the Arctic conditions of the dormitory.

So far, Bridie was the only person that Ada had any real

contact with, and occasionally they'd communicate in whispers as they worked.

"Why is Sarah in charge?" she whispered to Bridie one day. "Isn't she pregnant like the rest of us?"

"Oh, Sarah had her baby ages ago, and it's been taken away," Bridie whispered back.

Suddenly, there was a cracking noise, and Bridie gasped in pain as a stick struck her across the legs.

"I said, no talking!" barked Sarah, her face even more red than normal. That brought the conversation to an abrupt end, and Ada had to wait till the following day to probe the subject any further.

The next day, when both young women were put on mangle duty, far away from where Sarah was working, Ada seized the opportunity to quiz Bridie further.

"Since Sarah's not pregnant any more, why hasn't she gone back to her family?" Ada quickly glanced around to ensure that no one could overhear her. "I know you told me on my first day that I'd be stuck here forever, but I thought you were just being nasty, because I was a new arrival."

"I was telling the truth!" Bridie whispered back. "According to the nuns, we've committed a terrible sin that will take a lifetime to work off." Bridie looked around her surreptitiously, ensuring that neither Sarah nor one of her tittle-tattle friends were around. Then she leaned forward conspiratorially. "The only way out of here is in a coffin," she whispered. "Most families don't want their unclean daughters back home again – you see, no man will marry us, and the families are ashamed of us."

Ada was appalled. She immediately thought of her own parents, brother and sister. Surely they'd want to see her again? But the more she thought about it, the more Bridie's *information seemed likely to be correct. After all, why had she been bundled out of her home late at night? Her parents had obviously been ashamed of her. As for Helen and Eddie – Ada's eyes filled up at the thought of not seeing her brother and sister ever again. It was too cruel! How could this happen to a family?*

"Are you absolutely sure?" asked Ada, but she suspected that Bridie was telling the truth.

As Bridie nodded, Sarah suddenly appeared, aiming a blow at Ada this time. "Get on with your work!" she bellowed, Ada and Bridie nodding meekly as she marched off.

Ada tried to imagine the mental pain that Sarah was coping with – undoubtedly she was missing her baby, and taking out her anger on others. Ada tried to think kindly of her, but it was difficult when Sarah continued to make other young women's lives even more miserable than they needed to be.

CHAPTER 10

Barbara sighed. She was exhausted after doing a double shift at the hospital. And now she had to go and mind her sister's kids for the weekend! She'd much rather be going down to Olivia's place, but on the other hand, her poor sister Jane and her partner hadn't had a break in ages, so she mustn't be selfish. Besides, she really liked her niece and nephew – although she'd like them even more if they weren't quite so noisy!

Taking off her white coat, Barbara gratefully signed herself off duty, said goodbye to the rest of the team and headed for the hospital exit. Her neck was aching and she was longing to soak in a hot bath.

They'd had a particularly busy day, because some guy had been seriously injured during a rugby match, and had been airlifted to the hospital, which meant that all the other cases waiting for attention had been delayed. The weekend was also a time that seemed to produce lots of domestic accidents, so there had been a constant stream of people who'd severed fingers while cutting food, burnt or scalded themselves while in the kitchen, and others who'd sprained or broken limbs when carrying out DIY projects. There had even been a child who'd got his head stuck in a saucepan! That looked so comical that the staff felt the urge to laugh, but it was frightening for the child and its parents, so they had to behave in their most professional manner. Barbara smiled to herself. It was certainly true that more accidents happened in the home than anywhere else!

Before she'd left the hospital, the other staff on duty had been teasing her about having a dirty weekend, but regrettably, she thought, as she walked to her car, that was the last thing likely to happen, either now or in the immediate future. Apart from her baby-sitting stint this weekend, it was so long since she'd been out with a man that she'd hardly know how to behave if it happened!

She knew the other staff wondered at her reticence about getting involved in affairs of the heart, but her private life was a closed book as far as anyone else was concerned. She never spoke to any of them about her life with Richard, or the fact that she'd only been weeks away from getting married when they'd split up.

In a bizarre way, she was still grieving. But maybe, she thought, it wasn't simply about Richard any more, but grief for the loss of trust. And it would take a long time for her to regain it, and to trust somebody new.

When she and Richard had broken up, her heart had taken a battering like nothing she'd ever experienced before. Many nights she'd woken up in a sweat, wondering if it was merely a bad dream that Richard was no longer with her. Richard couldn't possibly be gone – for as long as she could remember, they'd been together and planning a future! They'd been together since their schooldays, and Barbara had always been able to bask in the warmth of a secure relationship. She hadn't needed to be out there in the marketplace, like Olivia and Maggie, scouting around for a possible mate.

But when she'd heard of Richard's hasty marriage, she'd felt light-headed and giddy with the shock. She'd wondered if she was having a heart attack since she could hardly breathe, and her heart was racing so fast that she felt she was going to pass out. Perversely, she welcomed the idea of dying, since it would at least take away the unbearable pain . . .

Luckily, Maggie and Olivia had been the ones to break the news to her, so her two dearest friends had been there to support her when her knees had buckled and the tears had flowed freely.

After Richard's betrayal, nothing in her life had ever been the same again. She'd gone from being a lively, out-going and confident woman to a quiet, efficient automaton. Even after she'd finished her final exams and qualified as a doctor, she'd gone about her hospital work with a quiet efficiency bordering on fanaticism. And since she no longer had a private life of her own, she'd been more than willing to do extra shifts for staff who *did* have a life outside the hospital.

She smiled sadly. Despite Fergal's initial interest in her, and encouragement from both Maggie and Olivia, she wasn't yet ready to start dating anyone, least of all a colleague whom she genuinely liked as a friend. She couldn't, in fairness, become involved with another man unless she felt able to offer him total commitment, and right now, she couldn't offer that to anyone. Maybe she never would be able to love anyone again.

Her parents had been wonderfully supportive too, and her sister Jane had rallied round with invites to parties and theatre nights, and tried to involve her as much as possible in her own family's activities. But as the years had gone by and she'd watched her sister's children grow, Barbara wondered if she'd ever have a family of her own. She'd never had any uncertainty about the future when she'd been with Richard, but now, on a personal level, the future looked cold and bleak.

CHAPTER 11

"Oh Liv, it's really exciting, isn't it?"

Olivia looked sourly at her friend. "It's not exactly my idea of excitement, Mags, but thanks for being here – I know I've messed up your weekend."

Maggie pulled a face. "All I was going to do was make tea and hold the ladder while my brothers and their pals painted the apartment. When they realised that your need was greater than theirs, they agreed to make their own tea! And since I'm staying down here tonight, they've agreed to paint my bedroom walls as well. So it's a bonus, really!"

The two women were standing in the kitchen of Bay Tree House, and Maggie was trying her best to calm Olivia's nerves and be as supportive as she could. Maggie was well aware that since Olivia was an only child, the support of her friends was of vital importance to her. From a large boisterous family herself, Maggie was used to being spoilt as the only girl. And since she was aware how much Olivia envied her large unruly family, she tried, as much as possible, to include her friend in family events and celebrations. In fact, Maggie conceded, for both of them, their women friends were the sisters they'd never had.

Olivia looked guilty. "I really shouldn't have rung you – or Barbara either, for that matter – but I panicked when Joe and Johnny found the baby." She found it difficult to refer to it as a skeleton – since it had once been a living being, she felt it deserved the dignity of being referred to as a person.

"Is Barbara coming down?" Maggie asked.

Olivia shook her head. "Afraid not – I told her what had happened, but there's no way she can get out of baby-sitting, since her sister and her partner are going away for the weekend."

Maggie looked out the window. "That sergeant is cute, isn't he?"

Olivia laughed. "Jesus, Maggie, you're incorrigible! He's probably married with half a dozen children!"

Maggie wrinkled her nose. "I don't think so – he hasn't got that harassed look they all get."

"And you'd know, would you?" said Olivia, laughing.

Maggie raised her eyes to heaven.

"But you're right," added Olivia, "he is rather cute."

"Is this house now a crime scene?" asked Maggie, who was an avid watcher of gory detective series on TV.

Olivia raised her eyebrows. "I don't know – I never thought of it like that."

"Well, there's no statute of limitations on murder, so assuming the child was murdered, the Gardai will be looking for its killer."

"God almighty, you love to create drama!" said Olivia, with an exasperated smile. "After all, the child may just have died naturally."

Maggie shook her head vehemently. "If that was the case, Liv, why wasn't it given a normal burial? You wouldn't stuff your beloved baby into a chimneybreast, would you? No – someone was trying to hide what they were doing."

"Well, since it happened a long time ago, whoever did it is probably long dead themselves," said Olivia.

Suddenly, she wondered if the baby had any connection to Laura Morton. As far as she knew, the woman had never had any children. Could it have been in the chimney much longer than that? Presumably the Garda forensics unit would be able to find out the age of the skeleton.

Just then, the sergeant appeared at the kitchen door, stepping over the debris from the demolished chimney breast.

"Eh, excuse me – "

"Please come in, Sergeant – would you like a cup of tea?" Olivia asked.

The young sergeant's face lit up. "That'd be marvellous," he said, smiling.

"I'm sure they didn't need to send someone as senior as you for something like this," said Maggie, "but thank you for being here. We really do appreciate it."

Olivia was amused by the "we". It looked as though Maggie was taking over the situation – at least for as long as the attractive sergeant was involved!

"Well, I just happened to be on duty when your call came in. So as soon as I notified HQ, and got the lads from forensics, ballistics, mapping and photography organised, I came down here to make sure that the crime scene was preserved."

"Crime scene?" Olivia raised her eyebrows. "Seems a lot of heavy guns are being brought out. I mean, the skeleton is so old, whoever put it there is probably long dead themselves."

"Once it's regarded as a suspicious death – which this undoubtedly is," said the sergeant, "then procedure must be adhered to, regardless of how long ago they died."

"So there'll be a post-mortem?" asked Olivia.

"Yes, I've sent for the state pathologist, who'll do a preliminary investigation on the spot. Then the remains will be taken away for a full post-mortem."

"My God, all that for such a little bundle!" said Olivia, looking sad.

"Well, the state accords everyone – even a newborn baby – the right to justice, assuming there's been foul play." The sergeant glanced at his watch. "The state pathologist should be here in the next hour or two." Then the sergeant braced himself for their reaction when he told them what must happen next. "I'm afraid I must also ask you both to vacate the house for the next few days, while the technical people do their stuff."

The two women looked at each other.

"Then we'll miss all the action!" wailed Maggie, looking thoroughly fed up.

"Well, I suppose we could go back to Dublin," said Olivia, also sounding disappointed, "but Mum is like an Antichrist at the moment. She's having new shelves built in her little library at the top of the stairs, and if I go home I'll somehow get roped into searching for the books she's managed to mislay in the process!"

Maggie sighed. "Well, since my apartment is being painted, we can't stay there either." Suddenly, Maggie brightened. "On the other hand – why don't we stay somewhere local? I'm sure there must be a hotel or B&B nearby."

The sergeant nodded. "Good idea. It'll also keep you out of the way of the press – they'll probably descend on the house like a swarm of locusts in the next few days. Now that I think of it, there's a nice little country hotel about fifteen miles from here – the Glen Hotel."

"Sounds great," said Olivia, smiling across at Maggie. She knew her friend would be pleased at this course of action, since it might mean they'd be seeing a lot more of the sergeant.

"About the baby – what exactly will the post-mortem establish?" Olivia asked.

"First of all, cause of death – then the sex of the deceased," the sergeant explained. "These things can be discovered forensically, but we'll also be carrying out investigations locally. There may be people still alive who can fill us in on what happened."

As Olivia and Maggie silently digested all this information, the sergeant glanced around the large kitchen. "This is a great house, isn't it?" he said at last. "It always fascinated me as a kid. I remember hiding in the orchard, and robbing apples on a few occasions."

"Shame on you – a man of the law, guilty of committing a crime himself!" chuckled Maggie coquettishly, giving him the benefit of a big smile.

The sergeant grinned. "I often wondered why I joined the force – now I know why. I obviously did it to expiate my guilt!" He looked down at Maggie, who blushed, unsure of whether he was teasing her or being smart. "Thank you," he added, addressing Maggie, "for helping me to discover why I'm in this job – are you a mind-reader, by any chance?"

"Actually, I'm a psychologist."

"Same thing, isn't it?"

Maggie started to protest, until she realised that the sergeant was only teasing her.

Olivia smiled, then excused herself and returned to the other end of the large kitchen, to make the tea. There was definitely some kind of spark between those two, so she'd leave them alone to see what would happen. Hopefully, the sergeant wasn't married with a string of children and merely amusing himself by engaging in a bit of friendly banter . . .

When the tea was ready, Olivia brought it to the big kitchen table, where the sergeant and Maggie were still engaged in animated conversation. They broke off as she arrived. The sergeant took off his uniform cap and placed it on the table, and Olivia realised that he was really much younger than she'd thought. Obviously, he was a bright lad to have made it so far up the career ladder at his age, which she assumed was very early thirties.

"About the little baby – " he said, looking slightly embarrassed, and Olivia noted with approval that he'd given it the dignity of being a person, "I hope you're not too upset."

"I'm not upset at all," answered Olivia. "Just a little mystified. I don't know if Maggie told you – but my grandmother and her brother were left this house, and they generously passed it on to me. So I know nothing about the people who lived here. But I'm interested to know what you make of it all, Sergeant."

"Please – my name is Philip. Philip Lynch. Let's dispense with the title." He grinned. "Anyway, I'm only getting used to it myself – I was promoted just a few weeks ago."

"Well, congratulations!" said Maggie, beaming at him. "That calls for a celebration, doesn't it, Liv? Got any of those fancy buns?"

"Coming up," replied Olivia, collecting the plateful of cakes and buttered scones from the dresser.

Soon, the three of them were munching happily at the table.

"So you're a local man?" said Olivia. "I guess you must be, if you robbed the orchard here as a kid."

"Actually, I'm not," Philip replied. "I'm a Dubliner too. But I used to visit my grandmother during the summer holidays. You can imagine the lure of an orchard for a city boy!"

Having drunk his tea and eaten two scones, the sergeant rose reluctantly to his feet.

"Duty calls," he said, grinning at Maggie. "I'd better not be seen slacking when the state pathologist arrives!"

"Oh, must you go, Philip?" implored Maggie. "It's so interesting talking to you!"

"Hang on," said Olivia suddenly. "Philip, you said your grandmother lived here – is she, by any chance, still alive?"

"Very much so, although she'd be well into her eighties now. Why do you ask?"

Olivia's face lit up. "Do you think I could visit her? And would she talk to me? I'm really anxious to find out about the woman who lived here before me."

"Mrs Morton? A nice old lady. I vaguely remember her from when I was a kid, but she was ill a lot of the time. TB, I think." He put on his cap. "I'm sure my grandmother would be happy to talk to you. I'll take you there some day, Olivia, if you'd like."

Olivia could see that Maggie wasn't too pleased at this turn of events, since she had plans to cultivate the sergeant for herself.

"Thanks, Philip," Olivia said, "but I needn't trouble you to that extent. Maybe you could just give me her name and address – " Then she realised that Maggie was making frantic gesticulations behind the sergeant's back. What on earth was her friend trying to tell her? Then it dawned on her that perhaps Maggie was afraid the sergeant would escape, and that any kind of contact was better than none. "On the other hand," Olivia added hastily, "maybe it would be better if you introduced Maggie and me to your grandmother."

Olivia was rewarded with a satisfied grin from Maggie.

"Yes, of course," said the sergeant, getting up from the table. "I'll have a word with my grandmother to see if it's okay, then I'll phone you and let you know when would suit. I assume the weekend is best?"

"Yes," said Olivia, smiling, "both Maggie and I have to work during the week."

"Here's my mobile number, Philip," said Maggie quickly, and Olivia had to turn her back in order to hide her grin.

CHAPTER 12

It was late evening when the two women, following Philip Lynch's directions, arrived at the entrance to the small country hotel, which was at the top of a secluded driveway.

"It's lovely here, isn't it?" said Maggie, sighing happily as Olivia drove up the winding driveway. "I'm looking forward to chilling out for a few days – pity Barbara couldn't join us."

Olivia darted a quick look at her friend. "Maybe it's better that she's busy this weekend. Hanging around here might give her too much time to think." And they both knew who Barbara would be thinking about!

As they drove along, they could see stables to the rear of the big house, which came into view as they turned the last bend in the driveway. "Philip says that they organise horse-riding holidays here too," Maggie informed her friend, "and they give riding lessons to children and adults at weekends."

In the beautiful reception hall they were welcomed by

a dark-haired man in his early thirties.

"Hello," he said. "My name is Mark. You're both very welcome. How can I help you?"

Olivia smiled back. "We're hoping that you have some vacancies."

"You're in luck," said Mark. "Although we're fairly full, I think we can fit you in. How many nights will you be staying?"

"Two, I think," said Olivia, returning his smile. "Do you have two single rooms?"

"No problem – as long as you don't mind them not being together. One is in the main corridor, the other in the annexe."

"That's fine," Olivia replied, after receiving a nod from Maggie.

The two friends grinned at each other, relieved to have somewhere comfortable to rest their heads that night. While they'd have settled for a double room if necessary, they were each also relieved to have their own space. They knew from past experience that Olivia liked to read into the early hours of the morning, and Maggie was unable to sleep with the light on.

"Dinner's over for this evening, but I can make you some sandwiches if you'd like."

"Maggie?" Olivia inquired of her friend who shook her head. "No, thanks, Mark, we're fine."

"Will you be having dinner here tomorrow night?"

"Yes, please," the women said in unison.

"Good. I'll get your luggage taken up to your rooms straight away."

"Oh, we don't have any luggage!" said Olivia hastily. "It's a long story – and a very strange one – all we have is the bare essentials."

"Well, if you'd like to tell me all about it, please feel free to join me in the bar for a complimentary drink," said Mark, smiling from one to the other.

"Oh thanks, but – "

"Go on, Liv – it'll help you sleep," said Maggie, nudging her friend. "As for me, I know I'll be fast asleep as soon as my head hits the pillow!"

"Okay – thanks, Mark," said Olivia, "I'll come down for a nightcap once I'm settled in." She smiled to herself as they climbed the stairs to their rooms. She knew that Maggie would soon be dreaming of a certain Garda Sergeant!

In her room, Olivia surveyed herself in the dressing-table mirror. She was a mess, and all she'd brought as a change of clothes were a clean pair of jeans and a T-shirt. But then, she hadn't been planning on having a drink with such an attractive guy!

She wrinkled her nose. What was she thinking of? She was simply having a drink with the proprietor of the hotel – not going on a date! Nevertheless, she wished she'd brought something a little more glamorous to wear. So she brushed her hair carefully, and dabbed on a little eye shadow before she left the room.

As she made her way downstairs, she grinned at her own self-delusion. Mark was just treating her in the same way that he would treat all the hotel guests. Besides, as he'd signed them in on their arrival, she'd seen a mousy little woman scurrying through the hallway – that was probably Mark's wife.

Mark was already in the small bar off the dining room, chatting to another guest, an older man in his sixties, who was sipping a whiskey as Olivia sat up on one of the bar stools alongside him.

"Ah, Olivia," said Mark, "I'm glad you decided to join us. This is Barney McDaid – Barney, this is Olivia Doyle."

Shaking hands, they exchanged pleasantries while Mark poured Olivia a drink. She'd asked for her favourite, a vodka and coke. Handing her the drink, Mark poured a drink for himself, then the three of them chatted about the weather, politics and the state of the world. As a discussion on the forthcoming by-election gathered momentum, Olivia began thinking increasingly of her bed. She sighed. What had she been expecting – to be exclusively chatted up by Mark? As she sighed, Mark turned back to the drinks optics, and poured her another vodka.

"No, honestly, Mark, I couldn't – "

"Go on, it'll do you good. Help you relax."

Olivia nodded. Perhaps he was right. It had been a very strange day – hopefully the few drinks would help her to sleep like a baby.

As if on cue, Barney got down off his stool, said goodnight to Mark and Olivia then headed slowly upstairs.

Mark poured himself another drink. "Now, Olivia," he said softly, "I'm dying to hear what's brought you and Maggie here." He grinned. "You said it was a long story – but I've got all the time in the world to listen."

His words were like a drug to Olivia. She was sitting with an attractive, charming man – and he wanted to know all about her! Aided by a third and fourth vodka, Olivia told Mark all about inheriting the house, finding the skeleton of the baby in the chimney wall, and how the house was now a crime scene, necessitating their stay at the hotel.

"You poor old thing," said Mark, reaching for her hand, and Olivia wondered if all her birthdays had come together at once. He was gorgeous! She gazed into his big blue eyes, and saw only admiration there. Despite the fact that she must look like a dog's dinner, there was no doubt that he was coming on to her!

But even though her brain was becoming increasingly befuddled by drink, Olivia had one last question to ask. "Mark – the woman I saw in the hallway earlier – is she your wife?"

Mark raised his eyebrows. "My wife? God, no – that's my sister Gwen. We own and run the hotel together – it's a family business."

Olivia sighed inwardly with relief. "Oh, I see." A single, gorgeous man was holding her hand, she was pleasantly inebriated, and all was well with the world.

"Well, now that we've got that cleared up, may I kiss you, Olivia?"

Olivia nodded, knowing she'd never be so blatant if she was sober. But that was what drink did to you – delightfully loosened your inhibitions, right?

Stepping out from behind the bar, Mark gently pulled Olivia from the barstool, slid his arms around her waist and kissed her gently. It was a long lingering kiss, and Olivia threw her arms around his neck, returning his kiss with fervour.

"Oh, Olivia – you're gorgeous!" Mark whispered, nibbling her ear gently. Then he looked into her eyes. "Look, I've got an idea – why don't I take a bottle of wine from the bar, then we can take it up to your room?"

"Sounds great!" Olivia whispered back, a silly grin on her face. What a story she'd have to tell Maggie in the morning!

Mark stepped in behind the bar again. "You go on up, Olivia – I'll be with you in a few minutes. I just need to lock up the bar first."

Olivia nodded, then slowly began making her way upstairs to her room. She felt giddy and giggly, and almost slipped as she reached the top step. Gradually, she weaved her way along the corridor to the annexe at the end. Retrieving the key from her jeans, Olivia tried to find the keyhole, eventually locating it, opening the door and staggering in. In preparation for Mark's arrival with the wine and glasses, Olivia cleared the bedside table of the novel she was reading, her credit cards and keys. Maybe after sitting drinking on the bed, they would eventually fall into it together . . . Suddenly, an image of Brendan Warren crept unbidden into her mind. But he hadn't bothered to contact her, had he? Despite all his jokey protests of finding her irresistible. Well, he could go take a hike.

Nevertheless, her mood suddenly altered, and she had a sobering thought. What on earth was she doing? Presumably, she was intending to sleep with Mark – this comparative stranger – when he came to her room? She was sober enough to know that the wine was only a prelude to something else . . .

In a blinding moment of clarity, Olivia realised that things were moving much too fast. She'd tell Mark that she was feeling too queasy for any further nightcaps. Hopefully, she could stall him until she was more in control of the situation. Besides, he'd probably consider her a tart if she slept with him so quickly.

Suddenly, she heard Mark tapping gently on the door. Gingerly she opened it. "Look, Mark – if you don't mind, I'd rather take a rain-check on the wine – I'm feeling rather queasy."

He didn't look convinced. "Just let me come in, Olivia – maybe I can rub your back, make you feel better?"

Olivia knew exactly how he intended to make her feel better! But she knew that if she let him into the room, all would be lost. She'd give in, and probably regret it afterwards. "Look, I think I'm going to be sick, Mark – excuse me, I'll have to go – "

Quickly, she shut the door, leaving Mark standing outside with the tray of wine and glasses. Then she hurried into the ensuite bathroom and closed the door, so that she wouldn't hear any of his entreaties. Because maybe, just maybe, she'd give in and open the door . . .

Finally, she flushed the toilet, in the hopes that if he was still standing outside, he'd think she'd been sick and leave her alone. A puking female was hardly likely to be an attractive option! The next time she saw him, she'd mention how unwell she'd felt, and hopefully, they could arrange another rendezvous. Maybe next time, assuming there was a next time, she'd take things to their logical conclusion . . .

After a half-hearted attempt at brushing her teeth, Olivia stripped off and climbed into bed. Within seconds she was sound asleep.

CHAPTER 13

As the weeks rolled interminably by, Ada became more and more exhausted. Each morning, when she and the other young women were summoned from their beds by the shrill ringing of a bell, she almost collapsed with hunger and morning sickness. But there was no respite – they were all expected to be in the convent chapel for Mass at 7a.m., after which they were given a paltry breakfast, consisting of a bowl of porridge, one slice of bread and a cup of tea. Then they were all packed off to the laundry, where the backbreaking cycle of work began again.

Although Ada began to feel physically weaker, her spirit became stronger, and in desperation she began to formulate a plan. Somehow, she would escape from the laundry. She wasn't prepared to spend her life stuck on this treadmill of suffering. Somehow, she'd get away, then make her way back to her family. It was incomprehensible to Ada that the people who loved her could allow her to suffer like this. They couldn't possibly know how badly she was being treated, and when they saw how weak and exhausted she was, surely they'd accept her again, and take her back into the bosom of the family?

Tears filled her eyes as she thought of the father she loved, who used to carry her home from the fields on his shoulders when she was young. She knew he was disappointed in her, but surely, if she reached home and told him how terrible the convent was, he wouldn't turn her away? Somehow, they'd all get through this. When her parents learnt how much she'd suffered at the laundry, they'd make more humane arrangements for her. She'd give birth in the local hospital, then if necessary she'd agree to have her baby taken away. But maybe – just maybe – her mother would consider keeping her baby in the family? Helen and Eddie would dote on the baby, and they'd all live happily ever after . . .

Ada wiped away a tear. This was all wishful thinking, she suspected, but thoughts of home helped to get her through the awful, monotonous days in the laundry. Besides, if she managed to escape from the laundry, there was nowhere else to go, was there?

Ada felt bad that she couldn't confide in Bridie, but she feared that somehow her plan might be overheard by others, who'd spitefully report her to one of the nuns. She also felt guilty for not inviting Bridie to escape with her, but she realised that there was less likelihood of two of them making a successful escape. She also felt that if Bridie knew nothing about her proposed departure, she couldn't be punished, or inadvertently made to give something away when the nuns inevitably questioned her.

Besides, Bridie was heavily pregnant, and Ada was acutely aware that she wouldn't know what to do if Bridie went into labour while they were on the run.

Ada carefully studied potential means of escape. She concluded that there was absolutely no chance of escaping in any of the vans that came to collect the clean laundry. The women themselves did the loading, and the nuns carefully supervised each transaction. It was the same when the dirty laundry arrived – the women carried it from the vans to the washroom in great big bags, while the nuns stood by, watching the proceedings.

But there was no such supervision of the bread van. Each morning, trays of delicious fresh bread arrived at the back door of the convent. Little of this ever made its way to the women in the laundry – almost all of it went to feed the nuns, who availed of extra daily supplies – just in case the parish priest or bishop might visit – then consumed it themselves when invariably the bishop failed to arrive.

Ada noticed that the doors of the van were left open and unattended for several minutes each morning, while the bakery's driver carried the huge wooden tray of bread down into the nuns' kitchen. The convent was clearly one of the last stops the driver made on his morning rounds – perhaps the second-last – because just one other tray remained laden with bread. The others were always empty.

For a week, Ada watched the arrival and departure of the bread van from the laundry window. The same pattern was observed every morning, and Ada felt confident that this was her best chance of escape.

The window of opportunity for escape would be brief. Since the work in the laundry was constantly supervised, Ada would only have a few minutes in which to accomplish it. She'd ask permission to go to the toilet, then sneak out and hide in the van. She'd lie on one of the empty wooden bread trays, and hope that the driver didn't notice her in the dark interior of the van. Beyond that, she had no plan. She just hoped that there would be some opportunity to slip out of the van unnoticed.

Without any money, Ada knew that it would be difficult to

make her way home. And since she didn't even know where she was incarcerated, she'd need to find a road sign as soon as possible. Now, she regretted not paying attention to the road signs when Father Dineen had driven her here. Nevertheless, Ada refused to be put off. She was leaving this hellhole of the laundry, and that was that. The night before her planned departure, she could hardly sleep, so she was even more exhausted when the bell rang the following morning. Although she felt nauseated rather than hungry at breakfast, she made sure to eat her full ration of food, knowing that it could be days before she was able to eat again.

As the bread van arrived at the convent, Ada found herself breaking out in a sweat. And as the driver carried in the daily tray of bread, she approached Sarah, who was folding clean sheets.

"Excuse me, Sarah," she said politely, her knees knocking, "would you mind if I went to the toilet? I'll be really quick."

Everything hung on Sarah's next words. If she refused, Ada would have to wait until another day to escape.

"Yes, go on – but get back here quickly!" said Sarah sourly. "I'm going to move you back to the washroom – Sister Immaculata needs an extra load of sheets done this morning."

But Ada hardly heard her words. She was already heading towards the toilet block, and from there she would make a quick turn left, slip behind the van, creep along its flank, then hopefully slip inside.

Ada could hardly believe her luck as she slid in behind the empty trays and held her breath. There would be hell to pay if the driver discovered her as he closed the van doors. After what seemed an eternity, she heard the sound of his boots coming up the basement steps from the kitchen, then Ada heard the van doors closing. She let out a sigh of relief. So far so good.

Hopefully, when the driver stopped for his next delivery, she could slip away unnoticed.

In the darkness, Ada had no idea where the van was going next, or whether it would take her nearer to her home and family. She listened to the drone of the engine, and prayed that the driver wouldn't look too closely at the empty trays when he lifted out the last one.

Suddenly, Ada felt the van slow down. Then it appeared to pull in somewhere, and Ada felt the pull of gravity forcing her over to one side. Scrambling to hang on, she held her breath as the van stopped. Then she heard the sound of whistling, and the doors of the van were flung open. Ada blinked, having been in the dark for so long. Crushing herself tightly against the wooden tray, she hoped that she wasn't visible. Next, she heard the sound of a lower bread tray being pulled out, the whistling faded, and suddenly there was silence. This was the moment!

Extricating herself slowly and with difficulty from the van, Ada finally slid to the ground and looked around her. Fortunately, there was no one about. The van seemed to have stopped outside a grocery store in a small village, while the deliveryman made his final delivery there. Quickly, she slipped down the lane between the grocery store and the hairdresser's next door. She would hide there until the van had departed.

When the van finally left, Ada pondered on her situation. She was still dressed in the convent overall, which marked her out clearly as an escapee from one of the laundries. She would have to get rid of it as quickly as possible. She walked down the laneway behind the shops, noting several clotheslines with fresh laundry blowing in the breeze. On one line, she spied a dress that might fit her. And a cardigan too. But first, she needed to make certain that she wasn't being watched. Checking the back windows, she concluded that no one was in *the back of the houses during the day.*

It was all or nothing. Jumping over the wall into one of the gardens, Ada quickly grabbed the dress and cardigan, half-expecting to hear someone roaring at her. But there was only silence. Jumping back over the wall, she ducked in behind a shed and changed from the overall into the dress. It was a little loose, but otherwise it was fine. The cardigan was an added bonus, since the day wasn't exactly warm.

Quickly, Ada slipped the convent overall into a bin, and walked back to the street in her new clothes. She was acutely aware that someone might recognise the dress and cardigan, so she decided to head out of the village as soon as possible. Ada knew that stealing was wrong, and she made a mental note to reimburse the owner of the clothing when she got some money of her own.

By now, her stomach was rumbling, and she longed to hang around the village in the hopes of finding – or stealing – something to eat, but more than anything else, she wanted to get home. So she set out on the road to the north of the village, not knowing whether she was heading towards home, or away from it.

After several miles, she was no wiser about where she was heading. The signposts she'd passed were no help, since they only supplied the mileage to small towns and villages, none of which she'd ever heard of. By nightfall, she was tired and hungry, and the enormity of her plight made her want to cry.

Exhausted, she came upon a farmhouse situated some distance in from the road. In the gloom, she could just make out the shape of a barn, and somewhere in the distance, the sounds of cattle being milked. Lurking in the bushes, she waited until the milking was over and everyone had settled down for the night. Then, she crept into the barn, climbed up into the hayloft and fell fast asleep.

CHAPTER 14

The following morning, Olivia awoke to the sound of her mobile phone ringing. It was Maggie, who was in bright and breezy form, and ready to go down to breakfast in the hotel dining room. Clearly, the result of an alcohol-free evening!

"Have a good time last night?" she asked Olivia, eager for news of what had transpired the night before.

Olivia groaned and turned over in the bed. "I'll tell you all later. I'll just have a quick shower, and see you downstairs in fifteen minutes."

As she joined Maggie in the dining room a little while later, it was Gwen who took their breakfast order. Olivia explained to her friend that Gwen was Mark's sister, and they both speculated on how different from each other they were.

"She's a mousy little thing, isn't she?" said Maggie, when the young woman was out of earshot and heading towards the kitchen.

Olivia nodded. "She's so timid, too – unlike the

gorgeous Mark."

Maggie grinned impishly. "Okay – so tell me what happened."

"Nothing," said Olivia, now thankful that she hadn't succumbed to Mark's charms the night before. He was gorgeous – there was no doubt about that – but she wanted Mark to think well of her and leaping into bed after only just meeting him would have been the wrong decision. She sighed. Why was it considered acceptable for a man to come on strong, yet if a woman did the same thing – or responded to a man's overtures immediately – she was labelled a slag? So much for equality – there was still a long way to go!

"So, did you snog him?" whispered Maggie, keeping her voice low as several other guests were entering the dining room and sitting down at unoccupied tables.

Olivia nodded reluctantly. "I was a bit drunk," she said defensively, "but I turned down his offer of a drinking session in my room."

Maggie's eyes were like saucers. "Jesus – you're a fast worker! While I'm in my virginal bed, you're off tripping the light fantastic with *mein host*!"

"Shh – " Olivia silence her friend just in time, as Gwen arrived with their fried breakfasts. The woman looked tired and flustered, and Olivia wondered why Mark wasn't helping out. On the other hand, he'd been working late, she reasoned – and would have been on the job longer, if she'd let him have his way!

"Why are you grinning?" asked Maggie, as she buttered her toast.

"It's nothing," replied Olivia hastily, "but I wonder where Mark is? His poor sister looks stressed out."

"Maybe he's cooking breakfasts in the kitchen," said Maggie, loading her fork with bacon and sausage. "He'd hardly leave her to do all of it, would he? And they must have other staff as well."

Suddenly, Maggie's mobile phone rang.

"Hi, Philip!" said Maggie, answering it, a delighted grin on her face. "How are you today?"

But Philip Lynch didn't sound too happy. "Maggie, is Olivia there? Could I have a quick word with her?"

Disgruntled, Maggie handed over the phone to her friend.

"Hi, Olivia – look, I've spoken to my grandmother," he hesitated. "I'm afraid she doesn't want to speak to you, or anyone, about Laura Morton."

"Oh." The thought had never crossed Olivia's mind that Philip's grandmother wouldn't want to talk to her. She'd been labouring under the misapprehension that an elderly woman would be glad to have an opportunity to gossip – now she realised how condescending that sounded.

"Oh, that's a pity, Philip. Maybe the news about the dead baby upset her?"

"Yes, I think it did. She said that she felt the dead should be left to rest in peace."

"Well, that baby never even got the chance to live – hopefully it can soon be properly buried?"

"Of course – when all the investigations are over."

"Maybe your grandmother didn't like Laura Morton?"

"I don't think that's true – in fact, if I remember correctly myself, she was quite friendly with Mrs Morton when I was a kid."

"Could they have had a falling-out?"

"I don't think so, but then I don't know for certain."

Olivia sighed. "That's a pity. I really wanted to find out what Cloncullen was like in the past, and discover what land was originally part of the property." She sighed. "I really love the house, and I want to keep it true to Laura Morton's memory. I thought your grandmother might – " Suddenly, she had an idea. "Philip, do you think your grandmother would like to come and see around the house herself? And maybe she'd like to take some memento from it – something to remind her of Laura Morton?"

"It's worth a try, Olivia. I was a bit surprised myself when she said no – but maybe curiosity will make her change her mind."

When Philip Lynch rang off, Olivia handed the mobile back to her friend.

"Thanks very much," said Maggie ungraciously. "Why is it when I fancy a guy, he wants to chat to *you*?"

"Look, Mags – he's only talking to me about his grandmother – we didn't arrange a secret rendezvous behind your back!" said Olivia, grinning. "Besides, you don't know if he's married or has a partner already. If I were you, that's the first thing I'd find out. No point in wasting your sweetness on the desert air, as the saying goes."

"Well, *I* can't exactly ask him, can I?" said Maggie plaintively. "You'll have to do it for me – it'll sound more natural coming from you." She eyed her friend surreptitiously. "Is it safe to assume you're not interested in him yourself?"

Olivia laughed. "He's all yours – while I can see that

he's a very attractive man, I've no designs on him myself." She took a forkful of bacon. "Besides, it's you he seems to fancy – the two of you spent a lot of time chatting yesterday."

Maggie smiled, gratified at her friend's response. "Good – now that we've settled that, you can quiz him on my behalf." She grinned happily. "I quite fancy myself as a sergeant's wife. I can just hear our names being announced at a state function – Dr Margaret and Sergeant Philip Lynch – sounds good, doesn't it? Who knows, he might even make it to Superintendent before long!"

Olivia offered the rack of toast to her friend. "At the rate he's travelling up the career ladder, he'll probably be Commissioner by the time you two get hitched!"

Maggie sighed as she absentmindedly buttered her toast. "Wouldn't it be wonderful? But with my luck, he probably has at least six children already, and a harridan of a wife!"

Olivia laughed. "Yesterday, you were the one who told me he didn't look harassed enough to have a string of kids!"

"Oh, I don't know what I think – I'm all confused! He's gorgeous, isn't he, Liv?"

"If I said yes, you'd hit me over the head!"

"Oh, you know what I mean!"

Olivia smiled at her friend. "This must be a first for me – I'm more interested in a good-looking man's grandmother than I am in the man himself!"

She ducked just in time, as a well-aimed napkin flew over her head.

As Olivia reached for the butter dish, she discovered that Maggie's lavish spreading of butter on her toast meant that there was none left. But when Mark's sister re-appeared from the kitchen, carrying several breakfasts and looking exhausted, Olivia didn't have the heart to ask her for more. So she reached across to an unoccupied table and took some from there.

"Oh dear, I'm terribly sorry – " It was Gwen, her face pink with exertion. "I could see your butter was running low earlier on, and I meant to get you more, but I've been so busy – "

"Don't worry, we're fine," said Olivia firmly. "We can see that you're rushed off your feet."

Gwen flushed, nodding. "Yes, we're almost full at the moment." She looked at them anxiously. "Is there anything else I can get you? Maybe more toast?"

"Well," said Maggie, "when you've got time, another pot of tea would be great. But there's no hurry . . . "

Gwen nodded. "Of course. Is everything else all right? Are your sausages done enough? And what about – "

"We're fine – honestly," said Maggie, cutting across her.

Relief showed on Gwen's anxious face. "Well, if you're really sure – "

"We are," said Olivia firmly. "By the way, where's Mark this morning? Isn't he around to give you a hand?"

"Oh!" Gwen looked shocked. "Mark doesn't do the morning shift. That's my responsibility. He does the evening shift, which keeps him up until quite late, so he takes a lie-in each morning. But I have someone part-time in the kitchen helping with the breakfasts."

"Well, maybe you need to take on more staff?" said Maggie.

Gwen looked alarmed. "Oh please – don't say

anything to Mark about me being under pressure. He'll think I can't cope!"

"Of course we won't," said Olivia, looking puzzled.

"Excuse me, I've got to go – "

Gwen hurried off as someone from another table gestured in her direction. Soon, she was bustling in and out of the kitchen again, serving more breakfasts and extra pots of tea. However, it soon became obvious that she'd forgotten about the pot Maggie had requested.

"Poor woman," said Olivia, as she and Maggie left the dining room. "She's obviously under terrible pressure."

"She doesn't seem cut out for the hotel business, does she?" said Maggie. "I wonder why they don't take on more staff?"

"I suppose it's hard to make a living from a small hotel like this," said Olivia. "Maybe they've got a huge mortgage on the place, who knows?"

Yet again Olivia wondered why Mark, as the more dynamic of the two, wasn't organising the running of the hotel more efficiently. Clearly, Gwen was unable to cope with the pressure, but didn't want Mark to know. Maybe mousy Gwen felt incompetent in comparison to her more talented and out-going brother?

"They're a very odd duo," said Maggie. "Gwen seems like a child who's been browbeaten all her life, whereas Mark was brought up as the boy who could do no wrong. Could their parents have been responsible for the difference in their attitudes? Maybe there's some weird family trauma at the heart of it all . . ."

Olivia laughed. "Always the psychologist, Maggie! Don't you ever give it a rest?"

"Our childhood is where our basic character is

formed," replied her friend seriously. "There's a wonderful quotation that says: 'In the few streets and fields of your childhood, there, no matter how widely you travel, you will live and die.'"

Olivia nodded. "Very profound. Now let's decide what we're going to do for the rest of the day. I don't fancy hanging around here, watching Gwen falling to pieces."

"Let's go for a drive," suggested Maggie. "We can explore the area, and see if there are any interesting places to visit, or good places to shop." She grinned at Olivia. "And maybe, by the time we get back this evening, lover-boy will have re-appeared."

"Stop calling him lover-boy!" said Olivia crossly, "I told you – nothing happened."

Maggie laughed. "Well, maybe it *will* happen tonight!"

CHAPTER 15

Later that evening, when the two women returned from their travels, Mark was again working behind the reception desk. His eyes lit up when he saw them.

"Welcome back!" he said cheerfully. "Did you have a good day?"

"Brilliant, thanks!" Olivia replied. "We found a great shopping centre near Ballyesmond, and as you can see, our credit cards took a walloping!"

Mark appraised their selection of shopping bags and grinned. "I think this calls for a celebration – why don't I meet you both in the bar in five minutes? First drinks are on the house!"

Olivia nodded, delighted, then the two women traipsed upstairs with their purchases.

"How on earth can he offer us free drinks, when he can't afford extra staff to help his sister?" Maggie muttered darkly. Then she grinned. "Nevertheless, I'm not going to turn down a freebie! Anyway, I suppose he's doing it to get into your knickers, Liv. I'll bet he doesn't provide free drinks for all the other guests here!"

"Shh!" urged Olivia, looking down over the banisters. "He'll hear you!"

The two women giggled as they made their way along the corridor towards their rooms. At the door of her room, Maggie paused and looked at her friend.

"So what's it to be, Liv? Do you intend taking him to your boudoir tonight?"

"I don't know," said Olivia, shrugging her shoulders. "I think I'll just wait and just see what happens."

"But you do still fancy him?"

"Who wouldn't – he's gorgeous, isn't he?"

"Not as gorgeous as Philip Lynch."

Olivia chuckled as she gave her friend a quick hug, then headed down the corridor leading to the annexe. "See you downstairs in ten minutes."

In her room, Olivia surveyed the new dress she'd bought that afternoon. She'd bought it with Mark in mind, and now, as she slipped it on, she was glad she'd thrown caution to the wind, even though it had been very pricey. She felt good in it, and it would give her confidence to see the rest of the evening through – wherever it led her.

Intentionally, Olivia reached the bar first, giving her the opportunity to refer to the previous night's unfinished business.

"Look, Mark, about last night – "

"Don't worry, Olivia," said Mark, smiling gently. "I hope you don't think I was too forward."

Olivia sighed with relief. Perhaps she'd played things just right. "No, of course not. It's just that I had far too much to drink, and ended up getting sick," she lied.

"I hope you're feeling better now?" asked Mark, looking concerned. "Maybe you'd prefer a coffee rather than a vodka and coke?"

Olivia was secretly thrilled that he'd remembered her regular tipple. "No – a vodka will be fine," she replied. She would need extra fortification to help her cope with whatever might happen tonight!

Just then, Maggie arrived and soon both women were sitting up at the bar, which gradually filled up with other hotel guests, including Barney McDaid, whom Olivia introduced to Maggie. As Mark chatted with the other guests, he winked at Olivia, and served them both another free drink. As he put the glasses on the bar, he leaned across and addressed Olivia.

"Will I see you back here after dinner?" he whispered.

Olivia nodded, a tingling sensation running up her spine. Maggie noticed what was happening, and kicked Olivia on the shins.

Most of the guests were having an early evening drink before dinner, so gradually the bar began to empty. Olivia and Maggie followed the general exodus from the bar, and settled themselves in a quiet corner of the dining room.

"Surely poor old Gwen won't be serving dinner as well!" whispered Maggie, as they both eyed the door to the kitchen expectantly.

But this time, it was a different woman who served them, a young woman who looked as though she might be a student. She was efficient and pleasant, and before long, everyone in the dining room was munching happily.

While they were being served, Maggie couldn't resist

asking about Mark's sister. "Is Gwen working tonight?" she asked casually.

The young woman looked surprised at the question. "Oh yes – Gwen cooks all the evening meals. Since we only do a set menu, once Gwen's done all the cooking and preparing, it's my job to serve it to the guests, then clean up and leave everything ready for the morning."

"Well, I must say, the food is wonderful," said Olivia as she tucked into her starter of caramelised onion tart. "I've never tasted anything quite so delicious."

Pleased, the young woman nodded. "Yes, Gwen is a wonderful chef. She's won all sorts of awards for her dishes."

"Are you a permanent member of the staff here?" asked Maggie.

The young woman grinned. "God, no – I'm studying at university. I just help out at weekends and during the holidays."

The two women looked at each other. So Gwen not only worked at breakfast time – she also had to do the evening shift as well. And had hardly any staff to help her.

The second and third courses were equally tasty, and as the teas and coffees were served, Maggie and Olivia were happily sated and relaxed.

Maggie yawned. "God, I'm exhausted – I'm looking forward to snuggling down in my bed."

"Oh no, you're not!" said Olivia darkly. "I can't go back into the bar on my own. You'll have to come for one or two drinks, at least."

Maggie darted a mischievous glance across at her friend as she stretched. "Bloody hell, the things I do for you! At this rate, I'll probably fall asleep across the bar, while you and lover-boy flirt across my knackered body! Do me a favour – get your love life sorted out quickly, so that I can go to bed!" Nevertheless, Maggie was delighted that her friend had found someone to take her mind off the problems back at Bay Tree House. It was a long time since she'd seen Olivia look so happy and excited about a man.

Linking arms, the two women crossed the carpeted hall to the bar once again. Barney McDaid was still perched up on the same bar stool as earlier, and looked as though he'd never left. Briefly, Olivia wondered if he'd bothered to have any dinner – she couldn't remember seeing him in the dining room. Drinking without eating wasn't a wise thing to be doing, particularly at his age, she thought.

As they entered the bar, Mark caught Olivia's eye over the heads of several guests, and immediately he began to pour her and Maggie a drink each. By the time they'd reached the counter, two filled glasses had appeared on the counter top. Olivia fished for her purse, but Mark stopped her by placing his hand over hers.

As they seated themselves at a nearby table, Maggie darted an amused glance at Olivia. "I'm impressed! I hope to God you start dating this guy in earnest – because then I'll get free drinks every time I'm with you!"

"Shh!" whispered Olivia. "Nothing has happened yet."

"But I can see by the glint in your eye that it won't be long before it does!" said Maggie, grinning back.

By about eleven o'clock, the crowd in the bar gradually began to dissipate, and soon only Maggie and

Olivia remained.

"I think this is my cue to head for bed," whispered Maggie. "You owe me big-time, Liv!"

Mark appeared at their table as Maggie stood up. "Sure you won't have another?" he asked her, but it was clear to her that he was hoping she would go.

"No thanks – I'm exhausted," said Maggie, excusing herself. "I'll see you for breakfast in the morning, Liv – okay?"

Olivia nodded, hardly able to speak. She was both excited and scared about what would happen next. By staying, she was making it clear to Mark that she wanted to move things on to the next stage. But she was also scared that he might think of her as brazen and forward. But all her worries disintegrated when he slipped his arms around her, and his lips met hers. She could smell his aftershave, and she loved the faint stubble as his cheek touched hers . . .

"Oh God, Olivia," he whispered urgently, "I thought the bar would never empty tonight! As I watched you chatting to your friend, all I wanted to do was hold you, touch you!"

Breaking away from her, he quickly locked up the bar, then taking her hand led her into the now deserted hallway.

"There's just one more thing I've got to do, Olivia," he told her. "I need to check the stables. We've been so busy all day that I'm not sure if the horses have been fed. Will you come with me? I'm afraid that if I let you go, you'll disappear on me!"

Olivia nodded, pleased that he wanted her to go with him, and happy that he was concerned about the welfare of the animals in his care. Respect for animals was high on Olivia's agenda of essential male attributes. She glanced at his profile. God, he was gorgeous!

Gently, Mark slipped his arm around her shoulder as they walked through the back door of the hotel into the darkness beyond. It was a beautiful starry night, and Olivia gazed up in awe. Living in the city meant that she rarely saw such an amazing sky. No doubt Bay Tree House would have a similar night view, she thought happily. One night soon, she'd lie outside in the garden of her beloved house, and stare up at the constellations above her. Who knows, maybe Mark would be lying there with her, too . . .

As her eyes became accustomed to the gloom, Olivia could see the stable ahead, and could hear the gentle whinnying of the horses as they approached.

"Hello, girl," said Mark softly, reaching to stroke a large bay who had been pawing the ground restlessly as he approached. Now the horse was visibly calmer and Mark encouraged Olivia to stroke her nose and breathe gently into her nostrils.

"Isn't she a beauty?" he whispered softly. "We've had her for about three years now, and she's great with nervous riders and beginners – she seems to know instinctively that they need gentle treatment."

His enthusiasm was infectious, and Olivia found herself becoming sexually aroused by watching him stroke the horse. She shivered with excitement. Hopefully, those same hands would soon be stroking her . . .

Mark gave a sigh of relief after he'd gone from stable to stable, checking the rations. "Good news," he said, "the horses were all fed earlier. Gwen must have fed them before she went off duty."

Poor Gwen, Olivia thought briefly, making and serving breakfasts, preparing and cooking dinner, and feeding the horses too. But she was too excited by the touch of Mark's lips on hers to say anything.

"Oh, Olivia!" Mark groaned. "I desperately want to make love to you!"

Quickly, he pulled her into an empty stall, and they began kissing passionately. Olivia felt intoxicated with joy at finally being in Mark's arms. She could smell the delightful blend of his aftershave combined with the warm smell of hay, horses and the darkness that enclosed them in their own special world.

Gently, Mark began caressing her breasts, and Olivia could hardly control the rush of desire that surged through her. She wanted him to take her now, this very instant, standing up against the wall. Eagerly, she helped him pull off her new dress, not caring if it got torn in the process. It had served its purpose – although she knew that it wouldn't have mattered to Mark what she was wearing. Then he opened her bra, and as he kissed her breasts and toyed with her nipples, she began fumbling for the front of his trousers. She no longer felt any inhibitions with this man – soon, she hoped, he would enter her, and they would experience a glorious orgasm together . . .

Abruptly, Mark stopped.

"W-what's wrong?" Olivia whispered anxiously.

"Did you hear that?" Mark whispered, his voice still hoarse with passion. "I think someone's calling for help!"

"What?"

Together, they listened in silence, their hearts still beating frantically. Then the sound came again.

"Mark! Help! Mark, where are you?"

"Damn!" said Mark angrily, breaking away from Olivia. "It's impossible to get a minute's peace in this place!"

Reluctantly, he pulled up his trousers, the magic of the moment ruined. Then he kissed Olivia briskly.

"Look," he said, grimacing, "I'll have to go and find out what the problem is. Wait here for a few minutes. If it's something straightforward, I'll be back. If not, you can let yourself back into the hotel through the door into the kitchen."

Olivia was nodding as the call came again.

"Mark, for God's sake, where are you?"

Quickly, Mark left the stables, heading off in the direction of the disembodied and frightened voice.

"I'm coming!" Mark called out, and despite her annoyance, Olivia had to smile. He certainly hadn't managed to come with her!

In the silence of the night, she could hear the voices quite clearly.

"Where were you? I think he's going to die!"

"I've been checking the horses," she heard Mark lie, then another voice said something about an ambulance being on its way.

Quickly, Olivia dressed herself, hoping that she'd removed all the straw from her hair, and that she could sneak back into the hotel without being seen. She cursed her bad luck at being so close to consummating her relationship with Mark, but nevertheless she was concerned for whoever was in trouble. If an ambulance had been called, then whatever had happened must be serious.

Her heart gave a sudden and painful leap. Could

something have happened to Maggie? No, that fear was illogical. Last time she'd seen Maggie, she'd been heading for bed – where could she be safer?

Nevertheless the fear persisted, and Olivia felt an urgent need to check on her friend. As she crept back through the grounds and into the hotel through the kitchen, she heard the ambulance racing up the hotel driveway, its siren blaring loudly. The noise of the siren and the interest it generated among the other guests – some of whom were now in dressing-gowns and standing out at the front entrance – enabled Olivia to creep upstairs without anyone seeing her. In her room, she quickly checked in the mirror for any stray pieces of straw that might have escaped her earlier scrutiny. Then, she hurried along the corridor to her friend's room.

When Maggie's tousled head appeared at the door, she looked as though she'd just woken from a deep sleep.

"What's happening?" she asked, yawning. "I presume something's up if you're banging on my door in the middle of the night!"

"I'm not sure what's happening myself," said Olivia, "but an ambulance was called for someone. At least I'm relieved that nothing's happened to you."

Maggie looked at her friend and grinned as she climbed back into bed. "Well, by the look on your face, it's safe to assume that nothing's happened to you either – if you know what I mean!"

Olivia grimaced. "You're right – nothing happened. Yet again. Maybe it'll be a case of third time lucky. Maybe next time, Mark and I will manage to – "

She stopped talking, looked over at her friend and sighed. Already, Maggie had gone back to sleep.

CHAPTER 16

The following morning, Ada was woken by the sound of a cock crowing. Disoriented, she looked around her, then realised with relief that she was no longer a prisoner of the nuns. She experienced a moment of joy as she relished her freedom, then she was filled with apprehension as she realised that the nuns would know by now that she was missing. She felt safe in the warmth of the straw, and momentarily longed to curl up and go to sleep again. She was acutely aware that once she left the comfort of the barn, she risked detection at every turn.

Her stomach rumbled, so loudly that she feared someone might hear it. She peered down from her vantage point high up in the barn, but no one on the farm seemed to be up yet. Hearing chickens clucking softly nearby, Ada suddenly realised that chickens meant eggs! And while she preferred hers fried or poached, a raw egg would at least provide some nourishment. With nostalgia, she remembered the hearty breakfasts in her own family kitchen, and the thought gave her a sense of purpose once again.

Quickly, she climbed down the straw bales, and tiptoed

round to the nearby hen run. Sure enough, there were about a dozen eggs inside the hen house, and hungrily she stuffed one into each pocket of her cardigan, quickly leaving before the hens had time to start a commotion.

Ada had just managed to hide behind the barn when the kitchen door of the farmhouse opened, and a man stepped out. He was dressed in scruffy clothes, a cap and Wellington boots, and Ada surmised correctly that he was on his way up to the field above to bring the cows in for milking. As the door opened, the smell of frying bacon wafted towards her, and she felt weak with hunger. The man was chewing what looked like a bacon sandwich as he headed up to the field, and Ada longed for one. She sighed. She'd just have to stay hungry for the present. Once she was out on the road again, she'd chance eating one of the raw eggs.

Sneaking past the farmhouse, Ada reached the road again without being detected. But she still had no idea in which direction she should be heading! She was also worried about the cars driving past, since any of them could be looking for her. Precisely because she'd successfully thwarted the nuns, she knew they'd make every effort to get her back. And if they caught her . . . she shuddered. Better not to think of that.

After walking for several miles, Ada found a field with a stile leading into it, so she climbed over, and settled down on the far side of the hedgerow. She began to eat one of the raw eggs, but gagged as she tried to swallow it. Despite being hungry, her stomach was clearly holding out for a bacon sandwich!

Basking in the warmth of a brief bout of sunshine, Ada relaxed and watched the tiny birds and field mice who had made the hedgerow their home. The birds were twittering, and several little mice were foraging in the grasses for food, their *little noses twitching as they checked the air to detect the proximity of any enemies. How similar we are, Ada thought. I have to keep watching out for my enemies too.*

Eventually, she rose to her feet, deciding that it was time to continue on her journey. But suddenly, as though out of nowhere, a small boy appeared around the hedgerow, and Ada almost collapsed with fright.

"Who are you? This is our farm – you're trespassing!" the little boy shouted, getting ready to run off and tell that she was there.

Ada thought quickly. "I'm a saint," she said, smiling, even though her heart was pounding, "and saints are allowed to go anywhere they like."

The child's mouth fell open. Then it turned and ran away, and Ada cursed herself for her stupidity. The child had probably been too young to understand, and would probably alert some adult as to her whereabouts. Any child of six or seven who understood the word "trespassing" had to come from a family who didn't exactly welcome interlopers on their land.

As Ada prepared to leave, the child suddenly appeared again, this time with a slightly older girl in tow.

"Hello," said Ada, hoping there weren't any others on their way. "I'm Saint Margaret."

The older child, who was about eight, pursed her lips. "You don't look like a saint," she said sceptically. "Shouldn't you be kind of, well, see-through? You look very real to me."

Ada suddenly knew she could pull this off. "But I'll bet you've never been visited by a saint before, have you?"

The children shook their heads reluctantly.

"There – you see!" said Ada triumphantly. "You're very lucky children – the saints only appear to really special people. God told me to visit you, so you must be really good."

The two children looked at each other.

Then the older one spoke. "I'm not very good, really," she said, reluctantly. "I kicked our dog the other day, and Daddy was very cross with me." Then her eyes narrowed. "But then, you must know that already, right?"

Ada nodded sagely. "Of course I do – I know everything about you. But God knows that it was only a little sin – so He said it's okay for me to appear to you."

"Where's your halo?" asked the little child, suddenly brave in the face of his sister's questions.

Ada smiled benignly, but her heart was pounding. This called for some quick improvisation. "Well, saints don't always wear their haloes. If it's a bright day like today, there's no need for them. So we leave them in heaven."

"But you're not dressed like a saint either – they always wear long skirts and have veils on their heads."

"Well, that's because – " Ada racked her brain for a plausible explanation, " – you see, I'm a modern saint. Modern saints dress in modern clothes. The statues in the churches and the pictures in your religion books at school are from the olden days."

Suddenly, Ada's stomach rumbled. "Is there any chance you could get me something to eat?" she asked the children, "But you mustn't tell anyone I'm here – because God's told me only to appear to you two."

"Then what about our older brother – is he bad?" asked the little child, his lip starting to quiver.

"No, of course not!" Ada told him hurriedly. "This is just our secret for the moment. I'll appear to him another day. I know that he's a good boy too."

The older girl stood her ground. "But why do saints need food? I thought that when you got to heaven, God had parties all the time, with lots of cakes and things?"

"Yes, that's true," said Ada, feeling that she might faint from hunger at any moment, "but while we're appearing on earth to good boys and girls, we have to eat just like anyone else."

The two children continued to stare at her, the little boy now picking his nose and examining the contents. Ada felt queasy at the sight, but did her best to keep smiling.

"I know about Saint Teresa, the Little Flower," said the older girl suddenly, "and if you pray to her, you're supposed to smell roses if she's going to answer your request."

Ada nodded. "Yes, Saint Teresa's a lovely person – and a great friend of mine. We have a great time in heaven together – going to all God's parties and eating lots of cakes."

"And Saint Francis of Assisi, who looked after all the animals." She looked pointedly at Ada. "But I've never heard of you. What do you do?"

"I'm Saint Margaret of the Secrets," said Ada, improvising again quickly. "I appear to children to ask them to do special tasks for God. If they do them all successfully – and keep them secret while they're doing them – they'll get a special place in heaven when they die."

The little boy began to cry. "But I don't want to die!" he roared.

Ada quickly tried to divert him from his wailing, in case some adult was in the area and might come to see what the matter was. "Look, would you rather have a prize in this life?" she asked him urgently.

The crying stopped and he nodded expectantly. "Can I have a new bicycle?"

"Of course you can – but not until you've done all the things I ask of you."

The child nodded, content with this arrangement.

"Okay," said Ada. "The first task I'm setting you is to get me some bread and butter – and maybe some cheese – but you mustn't tell anyone why you want it. Pretend it's for yourselves."

"But isn't that a lie?" asked the older girl, sharp as a razor.

"There are two kinds of lies," Ada told them authoritatively. "Yours will only be a white lie, which is a little one, and doesn't really matter."

"Our teacher says that all lies are wrong."

Ada felt increasingly out of her depth. So she used a technique she'd observed her own teachers using, when unable to answer to a student's question but not wanting to show their own ignorance.

"Do you doubt the words of a saint?" she bellowed. "Hurry up and get me some food – or God will be very cross with you!"

Fearfully, the two children rushed off, and Ada hoped that they'd manage to get the food without alerting anyone else. She felt uncomfortable at using the children's gullibility, but felt she had no other option. She was starving, and even a small amount of food would help her to journey onwards.

Then she had another thought: the children must know where they lived, so hopefully they could give her a sense of direction. Once she was heading in the direction of home, it would all be plain sailing . . .

About fifteen minutes later, the two children returned, doorsteps of bread filled with chunks of cheese in their hands. As she accepted them gratefully, Ada tried not to remember where the young child had had his fingers earlier.

"What marvellous children you are!" Ada told them. "God will be really pleased."

She immediately took a bite and chewed ravenously, the two children staring at her in silence.

"Are you able to fly up into heaven?" asked the little boy, his finger now back up his left nostril.

Ada nodded. "Yes, of course – but only when my work on earth is done. I have lots more people to appear to yet. Can you show me the way to the nearest town?"

The girl looked aghast. "Don't you know?"

"Of course I do," said Ada. "This is just another test – to see if you know."

The child pointed down the road. "It's two miles that way."

Ada was relieved – once she reached it she would be able to head in the right direction for home. This information raised her spirits, and she felt positively happy for the first time since she'd been taken from her parents' home.

Suddenly, the older girl spoke, her lower lip quivering. "Do you think God will be angry with me?"

"For what?"

"Well, I know that you said white lies were okay. But in the end, I couldn't tell one. I hope you won't be cross."

Ada suddenly felt very apprehensive.

"I couldn't really tell Mammy a lie – "

"Go on."

"So when she asked us why we wanted all the bread and cheese, I had to tell her it was for Saint Margaret."

"And?"

"And she said she was going to tell Daddy that there was someone trespassing in the lower field. Then he went to get his shotgun."

Ada cast her eyes around the field, and could make out the shape of a very large man in the distance, gun cocked and heading in her direction. Suddenly, she was on her feet.

"But you'll be all right, won't you?" pleaded the little girl.

121

"Since you're a saint, Daddy's bullets can't harm you, right? Anyway, you can fly back up to heaven, can't you?"

Ada looked around her wildly for a way out of the field. At last she spotted the small opening in the hedgerow, which led to the outside world.

Sensing a change in the atmosphere, the little boy suddenly started to cry. "What about my new bicycle?" he called.

But Ada was already running down the road.

CHAPTER 17

The following morning, as Olivia and Maggie arrived downstairs for breakfast, everyone was talking about the previous night's drama. Apparently, Barney McDaid had had a heart attack.

"Poor man," said Olivia, munching some toast that the harassed Gwen had brought to their table. "I hope he'll be all right. He was such a nice man – we had a very interesting chat about education the other evening. Did you know that he was a professor before he retired?"

Maggie grinned. "I'm surprised you had time to be interested in anyone else, while Mark was around!"

Olivia returned her grin. "Hopefully, it'll be third time lucky! Maybe there's a curse on starting anything with Mark in this hotel – if he meets me in Dublin, maybe things will work out better. He says he's up in town quite a lot."

Maggie wrinkled her nose. "While his poor sister is left running the show, no doubt." She felt a particular empathy with Gwen, since the poor woman was clearly stressed out from trying to make a success of the hotel. Maggie often found the stress of her own job as a psychologist overwhelming. While she wasn't supposed to take on board other people's traumas, sometimes it was impossible not to. Often, she'd find herself mulling over someone's marriage breakdown or bereavement, and Liv or Barbara would tease her about taking her work home with her. Maggie sighed. Poor Gwen! Liv was so blinded by her attraction to Mark, that she didn't seem to realise how close to breaking point Gwen clearly was.

In the background, the two women could see Gwen juggling several breakfasts. At one point, she nearly dropped one of the plates, barely catching it in time before it plummeted to the floor.

"God, I can't watch this!" said Maggie, half-laughing and covering her eyes. "It reminds me of going to the circus as a kid – I never enjoyed it because I was always afraid that the jugglers were going to drop something!"

"The animals in those circuses didn't enjoy it much either," said Olivia dryly. "Thankfully, most don't keep wild animals any more. Can you imagine the poor things – cooped up in tiny cages, when they're meant to be roaming free in their native lands?"

"Well, while I can imagine Gwen as a trainee juggler, I can't quite see her as a wild animal," said Maggie. "If she was one, what do you think she'd be?"

"At the moment, a mouse," replied Olivia, "but she might surprise us, you know. She might yet turn out to be the mouse that roared." She took a mouthful of tea. "Assuming things happen between Mark and me, I'll mention Gwen's situation to him – in a roundabout way," she said thoughtfully. "But shh – here's Gwen coming to take our order."

As the harassed young woman approached their table, Olivia and Maggie both spotted a big gash over her right eye.

"You poor thing – what happened?" asked Olivia sympathetically.

"Oh – it's nothing," said Gwen, becoming even more flustered than usual. "A saucepan fell off a shelf in the kitchen. It was my own fault – I hadn't put it back properly."

"Well, we're in no hurry for our breakfast, are we, Liv? So take your time," said Maggie kindly. "Anyway, it looks as though we're the last people needing to be fed – so why don't you come and sit down with us, and give yourself a break for a few minutes? You look worn out!"

"Yes, please do," added Olivia, pulling out one of the other chairs at the table.

Gwen looked alarmed. "Oh no – I couldn't possibly! There are so many things to do, but thanks all the same. Now, if you'll excuse me, I'll go and get your breakfasts."

She bustled off, leaving Olivia and Maggie feeling quite perplexed.

"There's not much anyone can do, if she won't allow herself to be helped," said Olivia, shrugging her shoulders. "Maybe she's one of those people who loves to be a martyr."

"I think you're wrong there," said Maggie "Didn't you notice her eyes filling up with tears when we showed concern for her? She couldn't fake that."

After they'd eaten their breakfasts, the two women collected their few belongings – and their new purchases – from their rooms and headed downstairs to the reception desk to pay their bills.

Olivia was hoping that Mark might be there, so that they could arrange a further meeting. She blushed as she recalled their mutual passion of the night before, and she hoped that he was equally as anxious as she was to consummate their relationship at the earliest possible opportunity. But it was Gwen who handed them their bills, took their credit cards and gave them their receipts. Olivia was deeply disappointed, but since she'd already given Mark her landline number in Dublin, and her mobile phone number as well, she felt reasonably confident that he would ring.

"Isn't Mark around this morning?" she asked Gwen, trying to look casual about it. "Maggie and I just wanted to say goodbye – and thank him for all his help."

At the mention of the word "help" she received a kick from Maggie, who was behind her back.

"Oh, Mark's gone to the hospital – to see how Professor McDaid is getting on," Gwen said. "Since the poor man's survived the night, hopefully he'll make a full recovery."

"That's great news," said Olivia, smiling back at her.

"I hope everything was okay during your stay?" asked Gwen anxiously.

"Oh, yes, it was great – thank you very much. And please thank your brother for us as well."

Gwen looked at Olivia strangely, and seemed about to say something, but then she closed her mouth and merely nodded.

As they left the hotel and drove away in Olivia's car, Maggie turned towards her friend and gave an impish grin.

"Well, I must say, Liv – Bay Tree House has enabled us to meet some gorgeous men, hasn't it? First, we meet the delectable sergeant, and because he needs us to vacate the crime scene, we meet the gorgeous hotelier!"

Olivia nodded. "I just wish we could find someone nice for Barbara."

Maggie turned to Olivia and grinned. "Maybe Bay Tree House can come up trumps again, for her! If it can produce two gorgeous hunks, why not a third? Maybe Laura Morton is secretly looking after us all."

Olivia smiled. She was looking forward to moving back into her house in Cloncullen. And hopefully, meeting Philip's grandmother. Maybe the invitation to Bay Tree House would make her change her mind. Olivia was also anxious to get on with her research into her grandmother's lost sister Ada. Could Bay Tree House or Cloncullen hold the key?

"Would you mind, Liv," said Maggie mischievously as she languished in the passenger seat, "if Philip and I held our wedding reception in the grounds of Bay Tree House? It seems like the ideal place, since we met there . . ."

Olivia giggled. "Okay, if you really want to – but I have an even better idea. Since Mark and I will already be married by then, why don't you hold it at the hotel? My husband and I will give you a very cheap rate . . ."

The two women chuckled, enjoying their wild flights of fancy. But they both knew that beneath the banter there was a serious uncurrent.

CHAPTER 18

Philip Lynch put down a cup of tea on the low table beside his grandmother's chair. "Gran – why don't you want to see these two women? They're very nice, you know. And Olivia, who owns the house, just wants to know what Laura Morton was like." His smile was gentle. "I think that in a strange way she wants to pay her respects to Mrs Morton."

"I have nothing to tell them!" his grandmother protested.

"Honestly, Gran – they just want to know what the village was like when you grew up here. In fact, Olivia's invited you round to Bay Tree House, if you'd like to see the few changes she's making. And she said you could have any memento of Laura's if you wanted it." His eyes twinkled. "I think she'd also like to ask your advice on lots of things – maybe, as neighbours, you could all become friends."

"Which of them do you fancy?" asked his grandmother bluntly, catching him unawares.

Philip Lynch's face suffused with colour, his cover blown. He grinned back at his grandmother, but said nothing.

"Well then, maybe I will see them," snorted his grandmother. "If you won't tell me which of them you're after, I'll just have to see for myself." Shrewdly, she observed the suppressed delight on her grandson's face.

"Thanks, Gran – when will I take you there?"

"Ask them to come here. At eighty-seven, going out tends to be more of a chore than a pleasure."

* * *

"Gran, this is Olivia Doyle – " Philip Lynch smiled, "and Maggie Roberts."

"Hello, Olivia. Hello, Maggie."

Graciously, the old woman shook hands with the two friends, and accepted the large bunch of flowers that Olivia had picked in the garden of Bay Tree House. "Please come in and make yourselves at home – would you like a cup of tea?"

"No, thanks, Mrs Collins, we're fine."

"Please – call me Carmel."

"Okay, eh, Carmel," said Olivia. "It's very good of you to see us."

In the meantime, Philip had excused himself and headed to the kitchen, where he was preparing tea despite the women's refusal. In his opinion, awkward situations were invariably helped along by the addition of good strong cup of tea.

With some difficulty, Carmel Collins eased herself into an armchair, and sat facing the two women.

"Philip tells me you want to know about Laura Morton."

"Yes, please, Carmel," said Olivia. "Since I'm living in her house, I'm keen to know a bit about her."

"What specifically do you want to know?"

"Well," Olivia thought for a second, "what did she look like?"

Carmel Collins seemed to relax at the question she'd been asked, as though she'd anticipated harder ones.

"Laura Morton was a tiny, very pretty woman. Her hair was long and blonde when she was younger, and she wore it in a plait. As she grew older, of course, it turned grey, and then she used to keep it tied up in a sort of chignon."

"What was she like as a person – was she friendly or shy? Was she the life and soul of the village, or did she keep to herself?"

Carmel Collins took a deep breath, as though playing for time. Eventually she spoke. "She was a very nice woman. I don't suppose you know this – but Laura Morton was ill for a great deal of her life. She suffered from TB when she was younger, which left her with a very delicate constitution. She never made a full recovery, so she led a fairly quiet, sheltered life."

Just then, Philip arrived with a tray and began pouring out the tea.

"Laura Morton left Bay Tree House to my grandmother and great-uncle though they didn't even know her – have you any idea why?"

"No, I haven't. Why on earth would I?" said Carmel Collins acerbically. "Laura Morton was a neighbour, but I wasn't privy to her private business."

Olivia bit her lip. She'd obviously upset Mrs Collins – maybe she should have shelved that question until later. But she also wanted to ask Carmel Collins about her long-lost great-aunt. "Carmel – have you ever heard of anyone called Ada Casey? She'd have been my great-aunt. My grandmother and great-uncle thought she might have had some connection to the house."

Suddenly, there was a crash as Carmel Collins dropped her teacup and saucer onto the carpet. "Oh dear!" she exclaimed. "How clumsy of me! It's my arthritis, you see – it makes it hard to grip things. Silly me!"

Quickly, Maggie was on her knees with paper napkins and a cloth, soaking up as much of the tea as she could. Soon, order was restored again, and it appeared that the carpet hadn't been permanently stained. Philip took the wet napkins back to the kitchen.

"Sorry, girls," said Carmel Collins, as she settled back in her chair. "That was stupid of me."

"Not at all!" said Olivia and hurried on, determined to get an answer to the question she had been posing. "I was just asking you – have you ever heard of someone called Ada Casey?"

Carmel Collins looked vague. "I'm sorry dear – I don't think so."

"Oh," said Olivia, feeling deflated.

The silence lengthened, so it didn't seem likely that Carmel Collins was going to elaborate any further.

So Olivia tried what she hoped would be a more acceptable question. "What happened to Mr Morton?"

For a split second, Olivia thought she saw fear in Carmel Collins' eyes. Then the look was gone, and she wondered if she'd imagined it.

"Oh, he died of a heart attack a long time ago. Laura became a widow when she was quite young."

"What was her husband's first name?"

"Henry."

"What did they do for a living?" asked Olivia, now feeling like an inquisitor. "I presume they had money – and the house – it must have had a lot more land attached to it than it does now?"

Carmel Collins nodded. "Henry Morton was a businessman who travelled abroad from time to time. I don't know exactly what he did for a living, but Laura was independently wealthy. Her family were big landowners, and yes – you're right – originally, the house did have about a hundred acres attached to it. Most of it was let out for tillage, but after Henry died, Laura sold it off. Being of a delicate constitution, she didn't want – or need – the responsibility."

"And the baby that's just been found in the house . . ." When she saw the expression on Carmel Collin's face, Olivia was sorry she'd mentioned it at all. But since she'd started the question, she felt obliged to finish it. "It couldn't have been Laura's, could it?"

Carmel Collins pursed her lips together, the fleeting look of horror now gone. "No, it couldn't. The woman was too poorly to bear a child and why on earth would she put it in the chimney? That skeleton has probably been there since long before Laura's time." She grimaced. "The poor little mite! But I can't help feeling – she's been in that chimney for so long now, what's the point of raking up the past?"

Just then, Philip re-entered the room with a plate of

biscuits, placing it on the coffee table between the women. Obviously he'd heard the tail end of his grandmother's comments.

"I'm afraid we have no choice but to rake up the past, Gran," he said, "to try to find out what happened. But hopefully, everything will be back to normal very soon."

"If Laura wasn't able to get out much, how did she cope with things like shopping and cleaning?" Olivia asked, hoping that she wasn't appearing too pushy by asking so many questions. But she was gradually building up a picture of her indirect benefactor, and she was feeling exhilarated by it.

Carmel Collins gave her a frosty stare. "In a small community like this, people help each other. She didn't lack for help and support."

It was as though the arrival of the biscuits had brought the discussion to an end and as they drank their tea Mrs Collins directed the conversation to more general matters about the area.

Having drunk her tea, she rose unsteadily to her feet, and aided by her grandson, excused herself. "Please – stay as long as you like," she informed her two guests, "but at my age, I need to go for my afternoon nap."

Thanking her profusely for her time, the two women prepared to leave as Philip led his grandmother out of the room. Maggie was anxious to see Philip before they left but Olivia felt that they'd undoubtedly overstayed their welcome.

Just as they were about to let themselves out the front door, Philip reappeared. "She's fast asleep already," he said, smiling, and it was evident to both women that he cared deeply for his grandmother. Definitely a plus, thought Olivia. Hopefully, he could care for Maggie too . . .

"Thanks, Philip – that was great," she said aloud. "I feel that I know a bit more about Laura Morton now."

"Thanks, Philip," said Maggie, giving him her best come-hither smile. "Hopefully we'll be seeing you again soon?"

"Of course," he said, smiling back warmly. "I'll be keeping you both up to date on the investigation, won't I?"

As the two women walked back to Bay Tree House, Olivia was deep in thought.

"Anyone in there?" asked Maggie finally. "I thought you'd be pleased with what you found out, but there hasn't been a squeak out of you since we left."

"Hmm, I was just wondering – wasn't it a bit strange that Carmel Collins dropped her cup when I asked her about my long-lost aunt?"

"What are you getting at? She's an old woman – as she told us herself, she has arthritis. I'm sure that would make it difficult to hold a cup."

"I think she dropped it in fright – or else she was playing for time, in order to compose herself."

Maggie looked puzzled. "Why would she do that?"

"I don't know. But I got the impression she *did* know about my aunt, but didn't want to tell me. And did you hear her refer to the baby in the chimneybreast as 'she'?"

"No, I didn't. Are you sure she wasn't referring to Laura?"

Olivia shook her head. "No – she said 'She's been in that chimney for so long now'."

"Well, so what? Does it really matter? Whether she said 'she' or 'he', either way she has a fifty-fifty chance of being right!"

"That's not the point, Mags," said Olivia, exasperated. "No one knows what sex the child was – even Forensics won't know that for several weeks yet!"

Maggie looked at her friend in surprise. "What exactly are you saying?"

Olivia took a deep breath. "Why didn't she refer to the baby as 'it'? I might also have believed that Mrs Collins knew nothing if she'd referred to the baby as 'he'. I'd have put that down to the sexist attitudes of long ago, when 'he' was used as shorthand for both male and female."

"You mean, like people who still say 'mankind' instead of 'humankind'?"

"Exactly. Someone as old as Mrs Collins might have continued to use the sexist terminology she grew up with. But it would have taken a genuine slip of the tongue to refer to the baby as 'she'." Olivia's eyes were as big as saucers. "It sounded to me like she knew exactly who the child was."

CHAPTER 19

Ada sat in the local police station, on the opposite side of the local sergeant's desk. At least she'd be given something to eat there! But Ada wasn't intending to stay there any longer than was necessary. She eyed the door leading out to freedom, but another Garda was working at a desk between the sergeant's office and the main door.

Damn that bloody farmer! As soon as she'd left the children and run out onto the road, the farmer in hot pursuit, she'd almost run into the path of the local sergeant, who was pedalling into the village to buy some sliced ham for his lunch. Seeing the farmer in pursuit, the sergeant had taken up the chase himself on his bike, and between them they'd cornered Ada in a hedge of nettles.

"Now then, what's all this about?" the sergeant had asked, unaccustomed to such activity, and sweat running down his forehead.

"She's been getting my kids to steal food for her," the farmer told the sergeant. "And she's been posing as a saint, too, may God forgive her!"

The sergeant, a kindly man, had looked down at Ada and frowned. "That's not a very nice thing to do, is it?"

"I was hungry," Ada said earnestly, "and it was the only way I could think of to get some food."

"And where are you from, my dear?" the sergeant asked. "It's a bit odd for a young lady of your age to be wandering the roads with nothing to eat."

"I'm on my way home, Sergeant," said Ada. "My parents live in Leafy Vale, and I'm on my way there."

"Well, now – isn't that a coincidence," said the sergeant, a big smile on his face, "I just happen to know the parish priest there, Father Dineen. We were at school together – and that's neither today nor yesterday!" He laughed at his own little joke. "I'll ring him and tell him that you're safe. Then either he or your family can collect you, and take you home. In the meantime, you can stay at the station. I'm sure you'd like a nice cup of tea, eh?"

Ada, numb with shock at hearing Father Dineen's name, could only nod her head in agreement. What utter misfortune that the sergeant should know the very person who had caused all her problems! But she had no intention of staying there until Father Dineen arrived to take her back to the convent. It was pointless to explain to the sergeant what had really happened – that Father Dineen himself had made her pregnant, and she'd been isolated in a convent, where she and countless other unfortunate girls were treated as slaves and worked almost to death. It was so horrific a story that he'd never believe it.

As she drank the cup of tea she'd been given, Ada listened to the sergeant's conversation on the phone.

"She's a bit overwrought, Father – yes, I guessed that couldn't possibly be the truth." He chuckled. "These young lassies – they have notions at that age, God love them!"

When he came off the phone, the sergeant turned sternly to Ada.

Hmm – so you haven't exactly been telling me the truth, young lady. Father Dineen tells me that you're one of those wayward girls – the kind that needs a guiding hand after all the shame you've brought on your family." He stood up. "So it's back to the convent for you, my dear – where the good nuns will help you to discover the error of your ways."

"Please, no, sergeant – they're vicious and cruel, and they work us half to death!" Ada screamed. "Please sergeant, don't send me back there!"

"My dear, I have no choice," said the sergeant sadly. "You've disgraced your family, so there's nowhere else for you to go." He took Ada firmly by the arm. "And just to make sure that you don't take a notion to escape, I'm going to put you in a cell until Father Dineen gets here." Seeing Ada's look of horror, he chuckled. "Don't worry – it's not as bad as it sounds. You'll be quite comfortable, and I'll see that you get more tea – and maybe even a cream bun. You'd like that, wouldn't you?"

Ada nodded, although she didn't even hear what the sergeant was saying. And as he turned the key in the lock, she was numb at the thought of being incarcerated in the convent once again, where she'd be punished by both the nuns and the other girls. The nuns would punish her because she'd dared to flout their authority, and the other girls would punish her because by escaping she'd had the audacity to think she was better than them.

As she sat in her cell, she could hear the sergeant's voice from his office down the hall.

"Yes, Sister, she's safe and well . . ."

Fury built up inside her. Obviously, one of the nuns was pretending to show concern for her welfare, and the sergeant *had fallen for it, hook, line and sinker.*

"Of course, sister — we'll take good care of her until Father Dineen comes to collect her." The sergeant hesitated. "And sister — she won't be punished, will she? I'd hate to think. . . "

Obviously the nun assured him that nothing like that could possibly happen, and he hung up, satisfied that he was doing the best he could for Ada.

Soon, he appeared at the door of the cell, a mug of tea in one hand and a plate in the other.

"Now then, here's a nice cake for you," he said.

Looking up at his kindly face, Ada wanted to cry. If decent men like him could be fooled, what hope was there for anyone else?

Inside, she was silently screaming. She'd no doubt that the sergeant believed he'd done his duty, and would return home to his family to tell them what had transpired, and they would praise him for it. And while he basked in the warmth of his family's affections, she'd once again be incarcerated among the vicious nuns. She doubted that the man had any idea what went on behind convent walls. Like most people, he undoubtedly believed that religious people could do no wrong.

Within the hour, Father Dineen arrived at the station, and Ada could hear him and the sergeant laughing and talking in the sergeant's office.

In the loneliness of her cell, Ada pondered her future and didn't much like what was ahead. Suddenly, she felt a slight flutter in her stomach, and it gradually dawned on her — it was her baby! Alone in the dark with her child, she could almost forget that it was Father Dineen's as well as hers.

Suddenly, a light was turned on, and the sergeant, followed by Father Dineen, appeared outside Ada's cell.

"Oh dear, Ada," said Father Dineen, a smarmy smile on his

face for the benefit of the sergeant, "you're quite a handful, aren't you? What are we going to do with you?"

Ada longed to raise her hand and smash it across his face. But she knew that while her satisfaction would be short-lived, her punishment would be long and arduous. So she said nothing, willing herself to be in some other place, where she could no longer hear his voice or see his leering face.

"Goodbye, young lady," said the sergeant, as he helped Ada into Father Dineen's car. "I hope you appreciate everything that Father Dineen and the nuns are doing for you."

As they drove back towards the convent, Ada hoped that they might have an accident and die, since even death would be preferable to what would happen to her once they got there. Then she felt guilty for wishing such a fate on her own baby, and she cradled her stomach and apologised to it silently in her mind.

Back at the convent, it wasn't long before the punishments began.

"You're the devil incarnate!" hissed one of the nuns. "I can't believe it – pretending to be a saint! Lying to innocent little children! You're an evil hussy, Ada Casey – and you're going to be punished severely for it! You're not fit to be in decent company, so you can sleep outside with the chickens tonight!"

Briefly, Ada thought that this might offer yet another opportunity to escape, but she was pushed roughly into a shed by one of the nuns, then the door was padlocked firmly behind her. Ada found the company of the chickens preferable to that of the nuns or the other women, but it was bitterly cold in there, and there wasn't even enough straw available to cover herself. As she lay shivering, she wondered if the sergeant was sleeping peacefully in his warm bed, confident in the knowledge that

141

he'd done his duty.

The following morning, stiff and cold from a night with little sleep, Ada was told that she wouldn't be getting any breakfast, but she was expected to start work immediately in the laundry. Filled with dread, she faced the other women in the washroom, noting the malicious gleam in the nuns' eyes, since they knew the women would exact their own form of punishment, and they themselves could watch with glee.

Bridie was sullen and uncommunicative, but Ada found this easier to deal with than outright antagonism. On the other hand, Sarah was downright angry, incensed that anyone under her charge would defy her authority by trying to escape. There was also an element of envy among the others, which manifested itself in spite, and Ada found herself "accidentally" pushed or kicked several times each day. No one would speak to her, as though she'd violated some secret code of conduct, yet Ada never witnessed any solidarity between the women. She felt certain that if they all united, together they could ward off the excessive cruelty of the nuns. But even among the disgraced, there was a hierarchy, and each woman clung tenaciously to the rung of the ladder that placed her above someone else.

Despite her rough treatment by both the nuns and the other women, Ada was determined to escape again. But she was being watched all the time, and the only reason a woman was allowed to leave the laundry was when her labour pains started. And even then, the woman was made to work until the pains became so severe that her delivery was imminent. Only then would she be taken off to give birth.

Since the other women were then expected to complete her workload as well as their own, there was little sympathy for a woman when she started her labour pains. Ada observed at first hand how brilliantly and brutally the nuns had stripped their charges of all decency and kindness, effectively making the disgraced women co-conspirators in each other's suffering.

Ada was still in solitary confinement in the shed each night, but she'd taught herself to adjust to the extreme cold of the concrete floor. It was simply a case of mind over matter, she told herself. If the poor hens could survive it, so could she. During the long hours of darkness, she'd try every method she could think of to open the door, but it remained firmly padlocked. In vain she hoped that some night, the nun on duty might forget to lock the door, but it never happened.

So she began prising off one of the sheets of corrugated iron that made up the roof. She'd discovered that one of them was looser than the others, so each night she would prise it up a little further, pulling until her hands were cut and raw from her efforts. She knew they'd hurt unbearably when placed in the hot water of the washroom the following day, but her determination drove her on. If she could manage to peel back a section large enough to climb through, she could jump to the ground and hopefully escape. It would be a long way down to the ground, and she hoped she wouldn't break her ankle in the process, but it was her best chance yet. And since she'd have a whole night's head start, she'd be well on her way home before she was missed.

Unfortunately, a handyman repairing some fences noticed that there was something wrong with the roof of the shed. He duly informed the sisters, to whom it was immediately evident that the roof had been tampered with. At which point, Ada was taken before the head nun and given a lecture on the evils of vandalising others' property. As she was led away from her audience with the reverend mother, the nun escorting her shoved her roughly through the door so that Ada sprawled *down several steps, cutting her leg and bruising her arm.*

As she sat silently crying in the freezing shed that night, Ada prayed for the first time in years, to a God who seemed to have deserted not only her, but all the other unfortunate women whom society had designated evil. Surely, she implored Him, you're a kind and merciful God? If so, how can you let your nuns and priests treat us as viciously as they do? Look, God, I know I'm a sinner, but surely the likes of Father Dineen are far, far worse . . .

Eventually, cold and exhausted, she fell asleep.

CHAPTER 20

"I think I'll go and visit Barney McDaid in hospital. Do you want to come with me?"

Maggie looked at Olivia, surprised. "Okay. But why on earth do you want to do that? It's not as though you know him well . . ."

Olivia nodded. "I know, but I feel sorry for him – he seems very much a loner. I liked him when we chatted at the hotel – and I felt that behind all his geniality, there was a lot of sadness too. Maybe he has no one else to visit, and he might be glad of the company."

"I think you're just trying to ingratiate yourself with Mark," said Maggie teasingly. "You're hoping that he'll be impressed by your generous and thoughtful nature!"

Olivia grinned. "Well, if I'm going to move full-time to the area, I might as well start getting to know the neighbours!"

"But we don't even know if Barney lives in the area," Maggie pointed out. "He'd hardly be staying at the hotel if he lived locally, would he?"

Olivia looked surprised. "You're right – I never thought of that. Maybe he was just taking a break at the hotel. I think he's retired, so he wouldn't have been staying there for business reasons, would he?"

"Well, what do we bring an old man in hospital? Fruit? A cake?"

"Well, since he was brought there as an emergency case, he might need a few toiletries. Maybe I'll get him some soap, and a toothbrush."

"Isn't that a bit personal, Liv? You hardly know the old geezer! I think I'll stick to fruit!"

*　　*　　*

"Well, isn't this a lovely surprise!" Barney McDaid's eyes lit up as the two women approached his hospital bed in the Intensive Care Unit of the local county hospital.

Olivia had settled for some mineral water and a big bunch of flowers from her garden, and Maggie had brought a selection of apples, oranges and pears.

"You certainly gave us all a shock," Maggie told him, as she kissed his ruddy cheek.

He grinned. "Well, I thought things seemed a bit dull and boring at the hotel. It was time someone livened things up!"

"You certainly did that, Barney!" said Olivia, smiling. "You were the sole topic of conversation the night you were rushed to hospital, and at breakfast the following morning!"

"Well, it's great for an oul' fella like me to have the attention of two gorgeous young ladies like yourselves," he said, beaming from one to the other. "It would almost be worth having another heart attack, if it guaranteed me regular visits from you both!"

"I think you've created enough drama, Barney," said Olivia, grinning back. "But we'll visit you again, anyway – that's a promise. But tell us how you're doing – will you be in hospital for long?"

It seemed that Barney was indeed on the mend, but would have to spend several weeks in hospital before he'd be able to return home.

"And where is home, Barney?"

"Home is where the heart is," said Barney, "but in practical terms, I live alone in Dublin – in Terenure. Do you know it?"

"Indeed I do," replied Olivia, smiling. "My mother and I live quite near – we're in Rathmines."

Barney's face lit up. "That's great! So hopefully, we won't lose contact."

Olivia felt sorry for the elderly man. He seemed so lonely. She'd definitely invite him for a meal at her house some evening. Barney was curious to know why the two women had been staying at the hotel. "I'd assumed you were both businesswomen – probably sales executives or something like that," he commented.

"I couldn't sell anything to save my life!" said Maggie, shuddering.

Olivia explained why they'd been staying there, and Barney was very interested to hear all about the baby's body in the chimneybreast.

"My God, how extraordinary!" he said, "And to think it might have stayed there for another generation or more, if you hadn't been having repairs done!" He looked from one woman to the other, a worried look on his face. "Neither of you were upset, I hope?"

Olivia shook her head, warming to the old man for his concern. "No, but we're certainly curious. It's awful to think that maybe someone hurt a tiny baby."

"And you, Barney – why were you staying at the hotel?" Maggie asked.

Barney sighed and looked a little sheepish. "Oh, well – since I'm retired and haven't a lot to do, I sometimes take myself off for a few days. I like the Glen Hotel – it's small and intimate, and the couple who run it always make me feel very welcome."

"Yes, Mark and Gwen are very nice," said Maggie, grinning and giving Olivia a discreet kick.

Barney sighed. "I worry about poor old Gwen, though – I don't think she's very happy, but she'd determined to give the hotel her best shot."

"Yes, we'd noticed how stressed she gets," said Maggie, "but why on earth don't they take on more staff? Then she could ease up on her workload, or maybe even take a break and leave Mark to run the place for a while."

"Well, I suppose that's because the hotel has always been in her family, and she wants to make a go of it." He sighed. "But since she met and married Mark, things haven't been working out. I think he bosses her around too much. In fact – "

"W – what did you just say?" Olivia's voice was hoarse with shock. "Married Mark? I-I thought Mark was Gwen's brother!"

Barney laughed. "Good lord, no! They got married about four years ago, just after Gwen took over the hotel from her parents, who've retired to the South of France.

Personally, I think Mark had his eye on the hotel rather than on poor old Gwen – she's such a mousy little thing, isn't she?" Barney chuckled, unaware that Olivia's brain was reeling in shock.

Maggie, seeing that her friend had been rendered speechless, took over the conversation to allow her time to recover.

"So – you think Mark is a bit of an opportunist, do you?"

Barney nodded. "On the surface he's a very pleasant chap, and he's very good with the guests, but he gives poor Gwen a hard time. She's always got bruises and injuries of one sort or another, and it wouldn't surprise me if Mark was responsible. Then, of course, he also has an eye for the ladies."

"What do you mean?" asked Maggie, glancing at Olivia, who was still silent and white-faced.

Barney looked sad. "When Gwen's not around, he chats up every attractive woman who stays at the hotel." He looked from one to the other. "I'm surprised he hasn't tried it on with either of you lovely ladies!"

Maggie said nothing, and Olivia continued to look frozen.

Barney sighed, unaware of the effect his information was having. "I don't know if it goes any further than flirting – but I wouldn't like to be in poor Gwen's shoes."

"Do you think she knows what's going on?" Maggie asked.

Barney grimaced. "Who knows? I suspect that she's so in awe of him – after all, he *is* a good-looking chap – that she's afraid to rock any boats."

Maggie looked exaggeratedly at her watch. "I think

it's time we headed off, Barney," she said, kicking Olivia, who still seemed to be in a trace.

"Y-yes, of course," said Olivia, trying to give Barney a bright smile. "Goodbye, Barney – we'll drop in and see you next weekend. Is there anything in particular you'd like us to bring you?"

"Well, I wouldn't mind a drop of whiskey – but you'd have to sneak it in. These harridans of nurses won't let me have anything like that."

Maggie looked sternly at him, but his mischievous expression made her laugh. "And rightly so! You need to build up your strength – and I don't think whiskey is going to do that for you!"

Barney grinned. "Haven't you ever heard the expression 'A little of what you fancy does you good?'"

Waving to him, the two women left the ward and headed down the corridor, Olivia marching ahead like an automaton. Maggie was unsure of what to say to her friend, since she knew how much she must be hurting. "How about a cuppa – or maybe a vodka would be better?" Maggie suggested tentatively. "There's a nice pub just down the road – "

"That bastard!" Olivia exploded at last. "The conniving, two-faced bastard!"

Maggie nodded. Anger was certainly healthier than sorrow in a situation like this. "C'mon, Liv," she said, "let's get a few drinks under our belts. Maybe things won't look quite so bad then."

"That poor woman!" Olivia fumed. "Is Gwen so downtrodden that she'll put up with that lily-livered lounge lizard?"

Maggie couldn't help grinning, despite the

seriousness of the situation. Olivia's vocabulary was second to none when she was piqued!

As they reached the main entrance hall, Olivia was still berating the man whom, only a short time ago, she'd been planning to make love to. "I can't believe it!" she ranted. "How could I have fallen for that smarmy git? I've a good mind to – "

Suddenly, all bravado was gone. And as the tears came, Maggie put her arms around her friend.

"Look, Liv – it could have been worse. You mightn't have found out for ages . . ."

"I feel such a fool!" Olivia sobbed. "How could I have fallen for such a line?" She blew her nose into the tissue that Maggie handed her. "What sort of a man deliberately tricks women like that? And hits his poor wife?"

"A man who doesn't like or respect women – and who has no self-respect either," said Maggie soothingly. "You've had a lucky escape."

Olivia sat numbly in the front passenger seat as Maggie drove towards the small town that was nearest to the hospital, and parked outside the nearest pub. Inside, Maggie quickly ordered drinks. It was still early afternoon, but she felt that the shock Olivia was experiencing called for strong measures. And those strong measures meant double vodkas and coke!

In the pub, Maggie went straight to the counter for her order, and carried the tray of drinks back to the table herself.

"I'll leave the car here, and we'll get a taxi back to your place later," said Maggie, countering Olivia's raised eyebrows when she saw the double measures in their glasses.

Before long, both women were more relaxed, and Maggie was glad to see that Olivia was beginning to get her colour back, and could now begin to joke about Mark's behaviour. But her eyes narrowed as she thought of poor Gwen.

"What do you think we should do, Mags?" asked Olivia. "Do you think Gwen knows what her husband is like?"

Maggie shrugged her shoulders.

"Well, it's obvious now that the gash over her eye wasn't due to any pot falling on her," said Olivia, disgusted. "How could any woman stay with a man who hits her?"

"It's not that simple, Liv," said Maggie sadly. "A violent man can gradually drain away a woman's confidence and self-respect. The woman may even end up blaming herself for making him angry." Maggie sighed. "But as to the other women – I doubt it. Don't they say the poor wife is always the last to know?"

"Jesus, I'd hate that – wouldn't you? Everyone else knowing, yet no one having the decency to tell you what he was up to." Olivia looked earnestly at her friend. "You'd tell me, Mags, wouldn't you? If I was ever with a guy who was sleeping around, and you found out – you'd tell me – promise?"

Maggie smiled. "I promise – and you'd better do the same for me! Although I hope Philip Lynch wouldn't be the type . . ." She sighed dramatically. "Who am I kidding? He's too gorgeous to even look my way."

Now it was Olivia's turn to raise her eyes to heaven. "For God's sake, Mags, I hope you're not picking up Gwen's bad habits! Stop putting yourself down – Philip

Lynch would be a lucky man to have you!"

"Thanks for the vote of confidence, Liv," said Maggie, "but just in case we never find any decent men, we can always retire to a nice nursing home together . . ."

"What an exciting prospect," said Olivia dryly. "Nevertheless, it would be better than being shacked up with someone like Mark Cunningham!"

Several hours and many drinks later, the two women left the pub rather unsteadily. It was now night-time, and after buying fish and chips at a local takeaway, they sat on a seat in the main street, eating ravenously.

They were enjoying their food and chatting animatedly when a patrol car with two Gardai drew up beside them. Surprised, they looked up from their chips, only to find that Philip Lynch was the driver.

He grinned at the two of them. "I hope you're not behaving in a drunk and disorderly fashion? Otherwise, my colleague and I might have to arrest you both!"

"Ooh, I'm scared!" said Olivia sarcastically, sticking her tongue out at him with the bravado of a drunk. "Would either of you like a chip?"

"Oh, please arrest me, Sergeant!" said Maggie, grinning. "I'm guilty of finding you dead sexy!"

The two police officers looked at each other in amusement. "Do you have a car?" the other officer asked them.

"Ha!" said Maggie. "So you think you'll catch us out, and be able to arrest us for driving while under the influence?" She grinned cheekily back at him. "Like good citizens, we've left it in the pub car park, and intend taking a taxi back to Olivia's place. So you needn't prepare our cell just yet!"

"C'mon – hop in," said Philip, grinning. "We'll take you home. And I'll look after those cars keys for you, Maggie."

"Actually, we were thinking of heading off to a nightclub," said Maggie, haughtily, nevertheless handing over her keys. "You can come along too, Sergeant, if you promise to dance with me!"

Philip laughed. "You'll be lucky to find a nightclub in this part of the country, Maggie! This isn't Dublin, you know! The most exciting offer you're going to get tonight is a ride in the patrol car!"

"Ooh, a ride!" said Maggie, deliberately choosing to turn his offer into a *double entendre*. "I'd be delighted to accept your offer of a ride, Philip – it's the best offer I've had all evening!" With difficulty, she climbed into the back seat, almost falling on top of Olivia as she did so.

Within minutes, the two inebriated woman had been dropped off at Bay Tree House. There was a lot of cursing and stumbling before they managed to insert the key and open the front door. Then, with a wave from Philip, the squad car drove off and the women went inside.

"You know," said Maggie, clutching Olivia for support, "I don't know why we bothered to open the door – we could just as well have walked in through the opening in the wall at the back!"

Both women found this inordinately funny, and giggled hysterically as they climbed the stairs to their rooms. Within minutes, they were both in their beds and fast asleep.

CHAPTER 21

"Ooh, my head! Have you any Paracetamol, Liv?"

Olivia shook her head, and yelped from the pain of moving it.

It was the following morning, and the two women were in the kitchen, trying in vain to swallow some toast and drink cups of tea to alleviate the ravages of their previous night out.

"C'mon – drink up," Maggie urged her friend. "We're both dehydrated, so the tea should help."

Obligingly, Olivia downed a mouthful of tea. Then she felt a desperate urge to bring it up again. "Oh God, I want to puke," she said, groaning. "I'm going to the bathroom. Or maybe I'll just go back to bed, Mags."

"Oh, please don't leave me, Liv – I think I made a total fool of myself with Philip last night!" groaned Maggie, holding her head. "What am I going to do? I remember saying something to Philip about wanting a ride from him! Oh God – how could I have been so coarse? He'll think I'm awful – if I'd had any chance with him, I've lost it now!"

"Please lower your voice, Mags! I get a pain in my head every time you wail."

"Well, you'd wail too, if you'd just screwed up everything with the man of your dreams!" Then Maggie remembered that the reason they'd been drinking was precisely because Olivia had, in a manner of speaking, lost the man of her dreams. "Oh sorry, Liv – "

Olivia waved her hand in a magnanimous gesture. "It doesn't matter. It's all water under the bridge now."

"Oh God, I was coming on to him last night, and he's probably married! How could I?"

"Look, even if he is, it's not the end of the world," said Olivia. "I'm sure, like any man in uniform, he gets women throwing themselves at him regularly!"

"Oh God, Liv – is that really what I did? Did I really throw myself at him?"

"No, don't be daft – you were just having fun. We were both having fun. It was a great night, wasn't it?"

The two women sat in silence.

"How are you today, Liv?" said Maggie at last. "I mean, about Mark?"

"Who's Mark?" said Olivia, frowning. "Never heard of him!"

Maggie raised her mug of tea in a toast. "Good for you, Liv – down with the bastard! Hopefully, he'll never bother you again."

"Well, if he ever dares to ring me after what I've found out, he'll be sorry!" said Olivia angrily.

Maggie pushed her toast around on the plate. "What you said about Philip – do you think, if I ever did manage to hook him, that I'd have to fight off all these other women?

"Definitely," Olivia said, grinning. "Especially when he's in his Commissioner's uniform."

Getting up to turn the kettle on for more tea, Olivia looked out the front window. "Mags – is that your car in the driveway?"

Maggie stood up unsteadily and looked outside. "Of course it's my car – I've been driving the same bloody car for the last three years, Liv. Are you going senile?"

Olivia grinned. "Don't you remember your 'ride' home in the squad car last night?"

Maggie nodded, cringing as she remembered her behaviour.

"Well, since we left your car outside the pub, someone must have driven it back for us later. And I suspect that someone was Philip Lynch." She grinned at Maggie's startled face. "Why would he do a favour like that for someone he didn't like? I think, Mags, you might still be in there with a chance."

But Maggie was still determined to be negative. "He's married, Liv – I'm sure of it," she groaned. "You're just going to have to find out, and put me out of my misery!"

* * *

As soon as she arrived back in Dublin, Olivia decided that it was time to visit her grandmother and great-uncle Eddie, and bring them up to date on what was happening with the house.

When she opened the door and saw her beloved granddaughter, Helen Casey's face wore a worried expression.

"Oh Liv, Eddie and I read about the baby's skeleton in

the newspapers – you must be very upset."

Great-uncle Eddie puffed on his pipe as though his life depended on it. "Sorry about everything, Liv," he said. "We thought the house would give you a start on the property ladder, not cause you upset."

"But I'm not upset, Uncle Eddie!" said Olivia hastily. "I love the house and the town – and I've had nothing but excitement since you gave it to me. I couldn't be happier!"

And it was actually true. She was enjoying Bay Tree House immensely, and even the finding of the skeleton and the subsequent invasion by the Gardai was interesting and instructive. And through all that had happened, Maggie might have found the man of her dreams . . . The only blot on the horizon had been Mark Cunningham, and already she was getting over him. Of course, she'd also met Brendan Warren . . . but enough said. He'd turned out to be a disaster too.

"Do you think the baby could have had something to do with Ada?" her grandmother asked anxiously.

"I doubt it, Gran – there's certainly no evidence at the moment that Ada had anything to do with the house, or was ever in it. I spoke to an old woman, a Mrs Collins who still lives in the village – " Olivia blushed, suddenly looking at her grandmother. They were about the same age!

"Don't worry, Livvy," said her grandmother, smiling playfully. "The woman was around my age, right? When you reach this stage of life, vanity plays very little part in it."

"You'll never be old to me," said Olivia, hugging her grandmother.

Then her grandmother turned and looked out the window, as though she was afraid to look at Olivia while she asked the next question. "Did you ask this Mrs Collins if she'd ever heard of Ada?"

"Yes, I asked her, Gran – but she denied ever having heard of anyone of that name. But I'll keep digging – maybe as she gets to know me, she'll be more forthright. Of course, she could just be telling the truth."

"And what had she to say about our benefactor, Laura Morton?"

"Mrs Collins knew Laura Morton, but said that she didn't think the child was hers." Olivia hesitated, looking from one to the other. "But I think she was hiding something – although I'm not sure what, or why. She called the baby 'she' – so I'll be interested to discover if that's also the conclusion of the forensic team." She smiled. "Mrs Collins is also the grandmother of the sergeant who came to investigate the crime scene."

Great-uncle Eddie gave her a sly look. "Is he your latest conquest, Livvy?"

"Not at all," said Olivia, laughing. "But my friend Maggie thinks he's cute, so I'm keeping my fingers crossed for her."

As she was leaving, Olivia hugged both of them, begging them to come down and see the house as soon as possible.

"As soon as my arthritis is a bit better, we'll be down to see it," promised her grandmother.

"I just have to have to get a hearing aid fitted," said Great-uncle Eddie. "Then, there'll be no stopping me."

As Olivia left, she realised that their reluctance to visit the house had nothing to do with their health, but to a very real fear of what might be discovered there. Olivia had never known her grandmother to have a problem with arthritis before, and Great-uncle Eddie could hear a pin drop from a mile away! Nevertheless, she knew she mustn't push them. When they felt ready to see the house, they would let her know. Their arrival would be a pleasure she'd just have to defer for the present.

Back at the house that she shared with her mother in Rathmines, Olivia took a quick shower and got changed. She'd arranged to meet Maggie and Barbara at a city centre hotel later, where the trio intended relaxing over a few drinks, while she and Maggie brought Barbara up to date on what had been happening at Bay Tree House in her absence.

Giving her mother a quick kiss, Olivia left the house and headed down the garden path. She grinned to herself. Her mother had been so engrossed in filling her new library shelves with books, that she'd hardly even acknowledged her daughter's arrival or departure!

Taking a bus into the city centre, Olivia arrived at the hotel just as her two friends were settling down in a cosy booth in the bar.

"Seems like you two have been having an exciting time without me," Barbara groaned. "I could kill my bloody sister for asking me to baby-sit last weekend!"

Soon, Barbara had been told about Philip, the gorgeous sergeant whose praises Maggie kept singing, and about Mark, the sleazebag whom Olivia had the misfortune to meet at the hotel.

"Well, I'm definitely coming down next weekend," said Barbara determinedly. "I can't leave you two to have all this excitement on your own! Besides, there might be a man for me down there as well." She grinned. "From listening to you two, it seems as though there's more available men in Cloncullen than in the whole of Dublin!"

Olivia and Maggie exchanged a glance. It was a positive sign to hear Barbara express an interest in any other man besides Richard Devlin.

While they were talking about the men of Cloncullen, Olivia thought briefly about Brendan Warren again, but there was no point in mentioning him to the others. After all, there was nothing to say, was there? She'd only met him briefly and, despite him being full of bravado, he hadn't turned up for their "date". So he was hardly worth mentioning, was he?

Owing to their antics of the previous night, by ten o'clock both Olivia and Maggie were yawning.

"What a pair!" said Barbara in mock disgust. "I don't know why I bothered coming out tonight, since all you pair want to do is go to sleep."

"You liar – you wouldn't have missed it for the world," said Maggie. "You were dying to hear all about our weekend!"

"Well, I'll make absolutely sure to be there myself, next time – I won't be relying on second-hand accounts from you two!"

By the time Olivia reached home, her mother had already gone to bed. Exhausted, no doubt, thought Olivia, from filling her new shelves with the hundreds of books that had previously lined the stairways and landing of the house. Looking around the hall, which now seemed so spacious, Olivia was pleased to discover she could now move about freely, without falling over stacks of her mother's books, student papers and academic publications.

In the drawing room, she poked the dying embers of the fire, adding some coal before she settled down in front of it. Although she'd been tired earlier in the evening, her brain was still fully alert, and she didn't quite feel like going to bed yet. Maybe she'd read for a while, or make herself a mug of tea, before heading upstairs . . .

Suddenly, the landline phone rang. Olivia looked up in surprise – wasn't it rather late to be calling anyone? She didn't like answering the phone so late, in case it was a pervert or some incoherent drunk dialling the wrong number.

Tentatively, she lifted the receiver. "Hello?"

"Olivia – it's great to hear your voice! How are you?"

Olivia froze. It was Mark!

When she didn't reply, Mark began chattering on. "I'm sorry for calling so late, but the last customer didn't leave the bar until just a few minutes ago! I miss you, Olivia – and I'm looking forward to seeing you in Dublin later this week."

Olivia's hands were shaking, and she could hardly speak, never mind hold the telephone.

"Olivia – are you there? Hello?"

At last, she found her voice. "How dare you call me, you – you cheat!"

"Olivia – what's wrong?"

"You know bloody well what's wrong – somehow, you forgot to tell me you were married!"

"Oh." Mark sounded like a naughty boy, who'd been caught out in some silly misdemeanour.

"You lied to me!"

"I know – look, I'm sorry. But that doesn't change how I feel about you, Olivia. Gwen doesn't matter – it's you I'm crazy about!"

Olivia was almost speechless with rage. How could he treat her – and Gwen – so callously?

"You have a nerve! I never want to hear from you again!"

"Please, Olivia – don't hang up. Surely you and I can have a bit of fun? Why should the fact that I'm married make any difference? There's no need to be so strait-laced! I can still see you when I'm up in town –"

"I know that you've hit Gwen, as well," added Olivia, fury in her voice. "What sort of a man would do that? Go to hell, wife-beater!"

Mark laughed harshly. "Gwen is a stupid cow! She needs an occasional clip around the ear to keep her in line! Now listen, Olivia – "

"And does your wife know about your little flings?" added Olivia angrily. "I think it's about time someone told her!"

"Olivia!" This time when he spoke her name, Mark's voice was low and menacing. "If you dare open your mouth to Gwen, you'll be very sorry. I mean it."

"So you think you can threaten me too? Go to hell!" said Olivia hotly, slamming the phone back into its cradle.

Suddenly, she realised that she was shaking from head to toe. As she huddled close to the fire for warmth, she wondered for the umpteenth time what she had ever seen in Mark Cunningham, and once again, she felt grateful to poor old Barney McDaid for having his heart attack when he did! Otherwise, she'd be feeling much worse, because she'd have given herself completely to Mark in the stables of the Glen Hotel.

Suddenly, Olivia's mother appeared at the drawing room door in her dressing-gown. "Are you all right, love? I heard the phone ringing, then I heard you arguing with someone. Is everything Okay?"

Jumping up, Olivia gave her mother a hug. Right now, she needed to feel her mother's comforting arms around her.

"Everything's fine, Mum," she said. "That was just a guy I don't want to see any more. So I told him to take a hike."

Her mother pursed her lips. "Are you Okay, Liv? You sounded rather stressed to me."

Olivia laughed. "He wouldn't take no for an answer, that's all, Mum! So I may have raised my voice to make him understand."

"Who is this man, Liv? I didn't know you'd found a new boyfriend."

"I haven't, Mum – when I met this guy recently, I thought he was nice, but I've since found out that he's not my type."

Her mother looked unhappy with Olivia's explanation, but she nodded, and started heading up the stairs again.

"By the way, Mum – your new shelves are great. And now there's loads of space down here in the hall."

Her mother smiled back, surprised and pleased at her daughter's comments, and Olivia felt a lump in her throat. I really should show more interest in what poor Mum's doing, Olivia thought guiltily. For years, we've skirted round each other, like ships that pass in the night. I don't even know if Mum has dreams any more, or if she worries about old age, or how she'll cope when I move to Bay Tree House.

"I'm glad you like them, Liv," her mother said. "Goodnight, dear – and sleep well."

"Goodnight, Mum – you, too."

But as she placed the fireguard around the fire and put the chain on the front door, Olivia knew that sleep wouldn't come easily that night. Mark Cunningham had seen to that.

CHAPTER 22

"We're going to have to do something about that dreadful creature, Ada Casey," said Sister Immaculata, pursing her lips in barely suppressed anger.

Sister Concepta nodded. "She's nothing but a troublemaker, and she has all the other girls upset. Running off, indeed! After all we've done for her."

Sister Caritas nodded. "These wayward girls are all the same. They don't appreciate anything that's done for them."

A group of nuns were sitting in the parlour the following evening, having supper before a roaring fire. As Sister Benedictus spread jam on her fourth fruit scone, Sister Immaculata placed a piece of turf on the already blazing fire. "It's unseasonably nippy, isn't it?" she asked rhetorically. "I hope it doesn't freeze tonight, and burst the pipes."

"Isn't it a pity that young hussy, Ada Casey, wouldn't freeze to death in the shed," said Sister Concepta. "Then our most pressing problem would be solved."

The other nuns tittered, unsure of whether they should be seen to openly embrace such an un-Christian attitude.

167

Just then, the door to the parlour opened, and Sister Consolata entered, warmed her hands at the fire, and accepted a cup of tea and a small cake from Sister Benedictus.

"Thank you, Sister – what a chilly evening."

The other nuns nodded in acknowledgement, making way for her to pull her chair closer to the fire.

"We were just talking about that troublemaker, Ada Casey," said Sister Immaculata, whose particular joy was discussing topics that allowed her to flaunt her contempt for most other human beings.

"Indeed, she's quite a handful, isn't she?"

Sister Immaculata nodded. "We were just wondering what we can do to restore harmony to the laundry. She's a terribly bad influence on the other girls. Only yesterday, Bridie Hogan challenged my decision to put her on the ironing roster. Can you believe it? That's all due to Ada Casey's influence."

Sister Consolata smiled. "Well, Sisters, I might have just the answer to your prayers."

The nuns all leaned forward eagerly.

"There's a gentleman who lives about fifty miles from here, in Cloncullen, whose wife is stricken with TB."

The nuns adjusted their expressions to ones of concern.

"When I spoke to him yesterday in the town, he told me that he's looking for a maid or assistant – someone to help with his poor wife's care."

She paused. "He's at the end of his tether, poor man – he's been trying to find someone for ages. But as we all know, it's difficult to find anyone to help out with a TB patient – since it's highly contagious, no one wants to take a job like that." She looked around at all the faces. "So I said I'd look out for someone on his behalf."

"Ada Casey!" said Sister Immaculata, her face lighting up

with delight.

Taking their cue from her, all the sisters beamed in agreement.

"Does he know that she's pregnant?" asked Sister Benedictus.

Sister Consolata shook her head. "I didn't think it was necessary to complicate things. She's not showing too much yet, and she's not due for quite some time – besides, poor Mr Morton is desperate for help! We'll worry about any possible repercussions later." Sister Consolata looked sad. "Besides, it's quite possible that she'll get TB from this woman, and die herself anyway."

The nuns all adopted expressions of sorrow at the inevitable vagaries of fate. Then, in order to lighten the mood, Sister Immaculata leaned across to the table, and began re-filling their cups from the enormous teapot. "Well, Sisters, I think that deserves a nice cup of tea, don't you think?"

The nuns all nodded in agreement, grateful to be relieved of the need to maintain sad expressions any longer, and Sister Benedictus volunteered to get another plate of scones from the pantry.

"After all, Sisters – this calls for a little celebration!" she said, smiling. "Finally, God has seen fit to answer our prayers!"

* * *

Ada was trembling with fear as she was escorted by Sarah to Sister Consolata's office the following morning.

"You must be in terrible trouble," said Sarah, with unconcealed glee. "I'll bet you you're going to be put permanently on the washing roster."

The washing roster was what the women all dreaded the most. It meant having your hands permanently in hot, soapy water, leading to blisters, broken and painful skin that refused to heal. Under normal circumstances, the workers were rotated, each spending a week doing washing, then a week on folding, followed by a week in the drying sheds, then a final week on ironing before returning to the dreaded washing schedule. The roster ensured that no one was ever so badly injured that she couldn't be made to work at normal breakneck speed. But the washing roster was also used by the nuns as a punishment, and any show of spirit was quickly suppressed by the threat of an extra week with painful, cut hands. It also gave the rest of the women a sense of relief, because while someone else was being punished, they themselves were temporarily safe.

Alone in Sister Consolata's office, Ada stood stiffly to attention, her hands clasped behind her back, as though she was already protecting them from the watery hell of the washing roster.

"You're an evil girl, Ada Casey," said Sister Consolata, closing her lips in a tight line.

Ada said nothing, since anything she said in her own defence would be interpreted as cheek, and likely to result in further punishment.

"You've caused nothing but trouble since you arrived here. The other sisters and I have been at our wits' end to know how to deal with you."

Ada opened her mouth, thought better of it and closed it again.

"But I think we may have found the solution."

The nun looked closely at Ada, searching her face for fear, unwilling to put her out of her misery until she saw the telltale signs. Then, as Ada's lower lip began to tremble, the nun felt

170

vindicated, and smiled at her malevolently.

"We've decided to send you away, Ada."

Ada looked startled, unsure of whether this was a good thing or not, but suspecting the latter.

"You've heard of TB?"

Ada nodded. Everyone in the country knew about the dreaded consumption.

"There's a gentleman who needs help with nursing his sick wife. She's dying of TB, and someone is needed to look after her. Since you can't behave yourself here, we felt that you might be able to redeem yourself by assisting him. And you might learn a little humility as well."

At first, Ada's heart was filled with joy and relief at the thought of getting away from the sadistic nuns. She mightn't be kept quite so hungry there, and there was always the possibility of escaping from this man's home . . .

Then, the full impact of caring for a dying woman – one suffering from a highly contagious disease – registered with her, and suddenly, her face filled with fear. The nun saw it and revelled in it, well aware that she was handing Ada a possible death sentence, and taking pleasure in the fact that Ada knew it.

"Mr Morton will be here this afternoon to collect you. Please ensure that your overall is washed, ironed and returned to the storeroom before you leave."

Ada wondered vaguely what was supposed to happen about her ongoing pregnancy. Where would she give birth when the time came? Nevertheless, this didn't seem to be the best time to query anything. She was just relieved at the prospect of leaving the convent laundry forever.

As she left Sister Consolata's office, she wondered if she was expected to return to the laundry and work right up until the last second of her incarceration. Yet it didn't seem such a daunting prospect now, and besides, she needed to wash, dry and iron her overall as a matter of urgency. If that wasn't done properly, they might stop her from going with Mr Morton when he arrived.

CHAPTER 23

"My God – the bastard! He has some nerve!" Barbara squeezed Olivia's hand in sympathy, her eyes wide with concern.

Olivia nodded. "I didn't realise how frightened I was until I'd actually put the phone down."

"Well, hopefully, you'll never hear from him again," said Maggie, giving Olivia a bright smile.

The three friends were having lunch together the following day, and Olivia was telling them about Mark's phone call the previous night.

"Let's go out for a meal this evening," Barbara suggested, determined to be supportive, "I think we all need cheering up – especially you, Liv. And after a weekend with only three kids for company, I desperately need some adult conversation myself!"

The other two nodded in agreement.

"What about the new Indian place in Temple Bar?" Maggie suggested. "I'm dying for a decent curry!"

"As long as you don't expect me to share a taxi home

with you afterwards!" said Olivia, laughing. "The last time you had a curry, I needed a peg for my nose!"

"I can't help it if I've got a lively digestive system," Maggie retorted.

"Well," said Barbara, "let me give you a word of advice, Mags – get Philip to put a ring on your finger before you let him take you for a curry!"

The trio laughed, and Olivia was reminded of how much fun they always had together. She'd been shaken by Mark's duplicity, and by his threats to make her sorry if she told Gwen about his behaviour. So she was grateful for her friends' support. A night out was definitely the best way to put the past firmly behind her.

* * *

"I don't believe it!"

"What?"

Maggie was just about to put a forkful of curry into her mouth when Olivia grabbed her arm.

"Over there! Isn't that Mark Cunningham – or am I going mad?"

"Where?" hissed Barbara. "For God's sake, would someone tell me what he looks like!"

"You're right!" Maggie whispered back to Olivia, the forkful of curry suspended midway between the plate and her mouth.

Both women had turned their heads in the direction of the centre table of the restaurant, where Mark and a very attractive young woman were dining together.

Barbara tried in vain to follow the direction of their eyes. "Is that him?" she whispered urgently, not wanting to miss any of the action. "The guy with the curly red hair?"

"No," said Maggie, her eyes still firmly on Mark and his companion. "Mark's the one with the dark hair, sitting opposite the blonde woman in the beige dress."

Having finally spotted him, Barbara also trained her eyes on the duo at the centre table. "Wow! He's loading on the charm, isn't he?" she whispered, as Mark poured more wine into his companion's glass, giving her hand a gentle squeeze as he did so.

"I presume that's not his wife?"

"No, it's definitely not Gwen," said Maggie, unable to tear her eyes away from the restaurant's centre table.

"Do you think the woman knows that he's married?" Barbara asked, turning sympathetically towards Olivia.

"Unlikely," said Olivia, her heart beating uncomfortably fast. "If I hadn't found out from Barney McDaid, I might just as easily be in that woman's place."

"He doesn't waste time, does he?" said Barbara, eyeing Mark as he continued to flirt with his companion. Her lip curled in distain. "Obviously, he chooses the anonymity of the city for conducting his romantic shenanigans. I feel sorry for that poor woman – she looks besotted by him. She probably thinks she's found her dream man."

Olivia nodded. "I wish he'd taken her somewhere else – he's putting me completely off my food."

"Maybe we should say something," said Maggie. "You know, just let her know that he's married. If she knows already and doesn't care, then she's welcome to him. But at least our consciences will be clear."

Olivia laughed harshly. "If I could take a full-page ad

in the daily newspapers, naming and shaming that bastard, I'd do it!"

Olivia found it difficult to eat, and she kept glancing in Mark's direction throughout the meal. Her curry tasted like sawdust in her mouth, and inwardly she cursed their decision to choose this particular restaurant. She drank her wine faster than normal, and although her head felt progressively fuzzier as the night wore on, she felt powerless to slow down.

"Uh oh – they're getting ready to leave!" hissed Barbara. "He'll have to pass by us to get to the door – what's the plan of action when he comes past?"

"We're going to hold our heads up high!" retorted Olivia, with the bravado of several glasses of wine. "He should be hanging *his* head in shame!"

Mark and his companion headed in their direction, and momentarily, surprise registered on his face when he saw them. But he recovered quickly, and the look of surprise was replaced by a scowl.

"Ah – I see the coven is here!" he sneered, walking past their table, his companion following in his wake.

"Aren't you going to introduce us, Mark?" Maggie called after him. "Is this your *real* sister?"

The woman with Mark looked uneasy.

"How's your wife, Mark?" Olivia called after him. "Does she know where you are tonight? I might just give her a call tomorrow!"

"Go to hell, bitch!" he snarled back. "Or you'll get what's coming to you!"

Then he and his companion were gone.

Eventually, the silence at the table was broken by Barbara. "Well, I must say – there's never a dull moment when I'm with you two!" she chuckled. "Thank goodness I didn't decide to stay home and wash my hair tonight!"

The gloomy mood was suddenly dispelled, and they all began talking at once.

"Let's have another bottle of wine," said Olivia, gesturing to a waiter who was passing by. "I'm in the mood to celebrate!"

"What on earth are we celebrating?"

"My lucky escape," said Olivia, as she raised her glass in a toast.

The trio clinked their glasses in unison.

"He certainly is very good-looking," said Barbara. "I can see why you were smitten, Liv."

Olivia nodded. Then she chuckled as she surveyed Maggie's hardly touched curry. "Well, there's one thing I have to thank Mark Cunningham for," she said, grinning.

"At least it'll be safe to share a taxi home with Maggie tonight!"

*　　*　　*

The friends left the restaurant and joined the throng of merry late-night revellers in the streets outside. They linked arms as they walked along Temple Bar's pedestrian concourse. As they headed in the direction of O'Connell Street, in search of a taxi, Olivia was the first to speak.

"I'm glad we had that extra bottle of wine. It'll insulate us from the cold if we have to wait hours for a taxi!"

Maggie yawned. "I hope we won't have aged a decade before we get home – I'm knackered!"

Barbara grinned. "No matter what age you are, Mags, you'll always be an opinionated cow!"

Maggie made a mock swipe at her friend, nearly tripped, and ended up clutching Barbara's arm for support. The two friends laughed, and stumbled ahead of Olivia down the street towards the nearest taxi rank.

"Excuse me – "

Someone plucked at Olivia's sleeve, and she pulled away quickly, fearing it might be a pickpocket. Then she realised it was the young woman who had been dining with Mark Cunningham earlier.

"Oh, hello – "

Maggie and Barbara turned back, nudging each other as they rejoined Olivia.

"Where's Mark?" Olivia asked, looking around her quickly. Was Mark lurking nearby, waiting to cause more trouble?

"No, it's Okay, he's not here – I'm on my own," said the young woman. "I dumped him when I heard you say that he was married."

"Well, good for you!" said Barbara, thumping her on the back. "He's just a sleazebag who preys on women."

"I'd never seen him turn nasty like he did tonight," said the young woman, adding, "He's always been so nice."

"That's the mark of a true sleazebag," said Maggie, "Hey, did you all hear what I just said – the Mark of a true sleazebag! Is that clever, or what?"

The others ignored her.

"So how did you get involved with him?" Olivia asked sympathetically.

The young woman grimaced. "Probably the same as

you – I was staying at the Glen Hotel."

The trio nodded in unison.

"But the reason I'm here isn't just to say thank you for letting me know he was married . . . I felt I should warn you."

"Go on," said Olivia.

"When I told him I wasn't bringing him back to my place tonight, and didn't want to see him any more, he got very angry. Luckily, we were in the street – otherwise, I think he might have hit me."

"He's already done that to his poor wife," said Maggie.

"And he said that it was all your fault – I think he called you Olivia, is that right?"

Olivia nodded.

"Then he said he was going to make you pay for letting me know that he was married. He said you were –" she hesitated, "an interfering cow, and had to be stopped."

The trio were in a state of shock as the young woman said goodnight and began walking away.

"If I were you," she called back to Olivia, "I'd notify the police about him."

CHAPTER 24

When the trio returned to Bay Tree House the following weekend, Olivia roped Maggie into making another visit to Barney McDaid in the county hospital.

They found him in excellent fettle, and delighted to see the two young women. Olivia could have sworn she saw a tear of joy in the corner of his eye as he hugged them both. This time, feeling that they knew him a little better, Olivia brought him some shaving cream, aftershave and a flannel. Maggie took him some magazines and a large bottle of fruit drink.

"Thanks, Maggie," he said, grinning mischievously, "but I don't see any sign of the whiskey . . ."

"That's because we need you to get well, Barney."

"But alcohol is good for you!" Barney protested. "Scientists have been telling us that for ages!"

"I think, Barney, you'll find that they're referring to a single glass of wine a day, Barney, not a whole bottle of whiskey!"

"Well, then – how about a wine glass full of whiskey?"

They all laughed, and Olivia and Maggie were both pleased to see how well he was looking.

As they took their leave of him, Olivia felt a lump in her throat. No doubt the whiskey helped to relieve his loneliness. He probably had no one else to visit him, so before they left she promised him she'd be back to see him again the following week.

As Olivia and Maggie walked down the main corridor towards the hospital exit, Olivia wondered aloud if Mark was likely to visit Barney again, and what she would say to him if she had the misfortune to bump into him.

"Shh!" Maggie grabbed her arm. "Shut up, Liv – there's Gwen!"

Looking in the direction of the Accident & Emergency Department, the two women saw Gwen emerging with her lower arm in plaster.

Almost simultaneously, the three women caught each other's eyes, so there was no way they could avoid greeting each other.

Clearly, Gwen wasn't too keen on making contact either. "Oh, hello," she mumbled, turning her face away from them. "Excuse, me, I've got to go – "

"Gwen!"

Even Maggie was surprised at the authoritative tone of Olivia's voice. Gwen half-turned, looking like a bird poised to take off in flight.

"I think we need to talk."

Gwen blinked. "About what?"

"Now, Liv – " began Maggie, but Olivia shook her off.

"I think you know, Gwen," said Olivia. "Maggie and I are going for lunch, and you're coming with us. I want to know what happened to your arm."

"I-I fell when I was working in the kitchen – "

"No, you didn't," said Olivia. "We know who did that to you."

Taking the bemused Gwen by her good arm, she led her outside, where Gwen's injury was even more obvious in the daylight. Olivia held on to Gwen's arm, almost as though she feared Gwen would bolt if given half a chance. By unspoken assent, they crossed the road and entered a nearby cafe, where Olivia sat close to Gwen while Maggie ordered sandwiches and coffee for all three of them.

"Now, Gwen, tell us what really happened. We know that Mark – your husband – did that to you."

Gwen's bravado began to crumble, and tears began running down her face. "It was all my fault!" she whispered. "I'm not as clever as he is, and sometimes I forget things. I was supposed to order a range of new bed linen and I forgot. So I don't blame him for getting angry with me. He was entirely justified!"

"You must be joking!" said Olivia, a look of disgust on her face. "There's never any justification for a man to hit a woman. And that's not all, is it? That gash you had over your eye when we were staying at the hotel – it wasn't caused by a pot falling off the shelf, was it?"

Gwen shook her head.

Maggie frowned at Olivia, hoping she would soft-pedal a bit. It was obvious that the poor woman was very fragile. Highlighting her stupidity and naivety wasn't exactly helpful.

"Why did you marry Mark?" Olivia asked Gwen, changing tack as she placed her sandwich and coffee in front of her.

For a moment, Gwen's eyes lit up. "He was so good-looking – and he seemed to think that I was wonderful . . ." Her voice trailed off, and Olivia thought cynically that it had been the hotel, rather than the woman, that Mark had regarded as wonderful.

"He was a salesman who came to the hotel selling orthopaedic beds," Gwen added, "and we immediately hit it off. I could hardly believe it when he asked me to marry him . . ."

Olivia and Maggie looked at each other. They could imagine how mousy little Gwen must have felt at receiving such attention. But they doubted Mark would have taken her up the aisle if there hadn't been the prospect of gaining a hotel as well as a bride.

"But that's not a good enough reason to let him walk all over you, is it?" said Maggie, looking sympathetic. "You don't have to shackle yourself to someone who treats you like shit."

"But I promised to love and cherish him always – "

"Well, he's not exactly honouring his own marriage vows, is he?" retorted Olivia angrily.

The three women sat in silence, with Olivia and Maggie both hoping that Gwen was finally accepting, and coming to terms with, her husband's behaviour – in this area, at least. By general assent, neither Olivia nor Maggie mentioned Mark's womanising. Both women felt that getting Gwen to admit to her husband's violence was enough to start with. If they could convince her to leave him, then his womanising mightn't even be an issue.

"So what are you going to do, Gwen?" Olivia asked her pointedly.

"I-I don't know."

"Well, don't wait too long – you can't stay with a man who keeps hitting you. We'll help you, and there are women's organisations that can help too."

"Maybe he'll change – "

Maggie laughed mirthlessly. "That's the oldest story in the book, Gwen – and it's not going to happen. Once a rotter, always a rotter."

* * *

As Gwen drove away – presumably to return to her hotel and errant husband – Olivia and Maggie walked back to Maggie's car.

"God, Mark really is a bastard, isn't he?" said Olivia angrily.

"And a crafty one too," added Maggie. "No doubt he fancied himself as a hotel manager, and found a quick and easy way to get there!"

"Do you think Gwen will have the guts to kick him out?"

Maggie shook her head sadly. "I doubt it. Poor old Gwen has so little self-esteem that's she's grateful to Mark for marrying her. She probably believes that a few thumps round the ear are worth it to have a good-looking and charming husband. I mean, *we* know how easily Mark can fool people."

Olivia coloured, still angry with herself for also being taken in by Mark's charm.

Her faith in her own judgement had been sorely shaken, and she wondered if she'd ever meet a decent guy.

Briefly, she thought of Brendan Warren again. He'd

fooled her too. She'd really believed that there was a spark between them, and she'd genuinely been looking forward to going out with him. So much for her intuition!

She'd also been puzzled that she hadn't bumped into him in Cloncullen, since it was difficult to avoid people in a small town. On the other hand, she conceded, maybe he was purposely avoiding her! She cringed now as she remembered how she'd even made a point of walking past the dental surgery Brendan shared with a colleague. However, it had been business as usual at the surgery, with all the lights on inside, and patients entering and exiting. After that, she'd slunk home, furious with herself for being so pathetic, and worrying in case Brendan had spotted her snooping around. She'd die if he thought she was bothered about him!

"What's the matter, Liv? You've a face on you that would stop a clock!"

Olivia smiled. "Nothing, Mags – I was just thinking how few decent guys there are out there."

"Well, before now, I'd have agreed with you," said Maggie, smiling.

Olivia mimicked the sound of vomiting. "Please, Mags, don't start – I'll get sick if I hear you singing that man's praises any more!"

"Okay, I won't even mention his name. But he *is* gorgeous, isn't he?"

Chapter 25

Philip Lynch whistled as he parked the squad car outside Cormac McCarthy's house, which was situated up a side road a mile outside the village of Cloncullen. Philip remembered the old doctor from his childhood – more than once Dr McCarthy had bandaged up his knee when he fell out of a tree while stealing apples. He doubted if the old man would remember him now, but Philip often saw him collecting his morning newspaper from the local newsagent's. Long retired, he'd been the local GP for many years, so if anyone should know about the Mortons and their household, it was surely him.

"Good morning, Dr McCarthy," said Philip, smiling broadly at the elderly man who opened the door. "I'm Philip Lynch, from the local Garda station – would you mind if I asked you a few questions?"

The old doctor looked annoyed. "I suppose it's about that skeleton you found," he said. "Well, there's nothing I can tell you. So good day to you, young man."

He was about to close the door, but Philip stood firm.

"Please, Dr McCarthy – I need to ask you a few questions. It's just routine and won't take a minute."

The old doctor sighed. "Well, if you want to waste your time, I can't stop you," he said ungraciously, standing back and ushering Philip inside.

In the drawing room of the old Georgian farmhouse, the doctor sat down again, gesturing to Philip to take the chair opposite him.

"Dr McCarthy, did you know Henry and Laura Morton?"

"I did – they were both patients of mine."

"I'm trying to find out who might have given birth to the baby. Do you think it could have been Laura Morton's?"

The old doctor looked annoyed. "How on earth should I know? Since someone stuck it in the chimney, presumably they didn't want anyone else to know about it. But I doubt if it was Laura Morton's – the poor woman had TB for years. She made a reasonable recovery in later life, but she always had a delicate constitution. And why would she do that with the baby anyway?"

"I presume there were other members of the household besides Henry and Laura Morton? Staff, for example? Since Mrs Morton was ill, I presume they'd need staff to run the house?"

"I suppose so. There might have been a maid, or someone who helped out in the garden. But I wouldn't have been familiar with them."

"I'm going to have to track these people down if I can. Are you certain you can't recall any of their names?"

The doctor looked exasperated. "For heaven's sake – you're talking about people who worked there half a century ago! Besides, they're probably long dead by now."

"Those are the exact words my grandmother used too."

"Then maybe you should take heed of what she says," said Cormac McCarthy.

"You know my grandmother, don't you?"

"Well, yes – but not particularly well," the doctor replied.

"I presume she was once a patient of yours?"

The doctor looked wary, as though he hadn't been anticipating such a question. "Eh, yes – I believe so. Why do you ask?"

"But surely if she was your patient, you'd know her quite well?"

"That doesn't necessarily follow," said the doctor angrily. "Before I retired, I had several hundred patients on my books. I couldn't possibly remember each one personally!" He suddenly chuckled, as though to dispel any tension. "Besides, a doctor is a bit like a barman. A good barman remembers you by your tipple rather than your name, and a doctor tends to remember people by their illnesses." He smiled at Philip. "From what little I can recall about your grandmother, she was always a healthy woman – so I saw her very rarely. I hope she's keeping well these days?"

"She's fine," said Philip. "Well, thank you for your time, Dr McCarthy. I'll see myself out."

As Philip walked back to the patrol car, he wondered why the doctor was so anxious to deny anything more than a superficial knowledge of his grandmother. Surely, people who'd lived in the same town for years would know each other well?

He switched on the engine and drove the squad car out through the gates of the doctor's house. There was something very odd going on, he concluded. Especially since he'd seen the doctor and his grandmother talking urgently to each other in the street only a few days before.

CHAPTER 26

Henry Morton was a tall, dapper and handsome man, and the nuns twittered around him as though he was some kind of god. In the nuns' parlour, he charmed them with his wit and repartee, and as Ada waited outside in the hall, she could hear the laughter inside, and began to feel that her salvation might actually be at hand. Henry Morton seemed to be kind and pleasant, and she sighed with relief. Soon, she would be away from here, and a new and hopefully better life would be starting.

But from the moment they left the convent, with the nuns hypocritically waving to Ada and wishing her well, Henry Morton said nothing, and Ada felt that once again she'd been relegated to the position of nonentity. Once or twice, she opened her mouth to make a comment about the weather or the scenery, and then thought better of it.

At last they reached Bay Tree House, and Ada thought it was one of the loveliest houses she'd ever seen. The huge windows glinted in the sunlight, ivy covered the front porch, and two tall bay trees grew in urns on either side of the door.

On either side of the gravel driveway, flowerbeds were packed with a delightful array of plants and shrubs. She felt certain that this was a much loved and well maintained home.

Hardly able to contain her excitement, Ada smiled broadly at her new employer. "Oh Mr Morton – your home is beautiful!"

Henry Morton gave her a sour look. "What my home is like is no concern of yours, young lady. Your job will be to take care of my wife, so see that you do it well. Otherwise . . . "

He left the word hanging, and Ada knew at once that Henry Morton's displeasure would see her being sent back to the convent. Chastened, her initial joy began to dissipate. Obviously Henry Morton's charm was reserved for those whom he felt were worthy of it, and this certainly didn't include her. She sincerely hoped that her new charge wouldn't be as mean-spirited as her husband clearly was.

Bringing Ada round to the side of the house, Henry Morton pushed open a door that led into a huge but cosy kitchen. A woman, possibly in her early thirties, was stirring a large pot on the range, and the delightful smells emanating from it made Ad's empty stomach rumble.

"Mrs Collins, this is the new maid who'll be looking after Mrs Morton. See that she gets an overall, will you? Then take her up to see Mrs Morton. I'm sure my wife will be anxious to meet her new employee."

With that, he was gone, and Ada and Mrs Collins were left looking at each other.

Mrs Collins was the first to offer her hand. "Hello, I'm Carmel Collins," she said, smiling.

"I'm Ada Casey," said Ada, shaking hands.

"You look hungry," said Mrs Collins astutely. "Let me get you a bowl of soup and a sandwich before I take you up to meet

Mrs Morton."

"Thanks — I'm starving," said Ada gratefully.

"I hear that the nuns aren't exactly noted for their kindness to their charges," said Mrs Collins dryly, "but never fear, you'll be well fed in this house, for as long as I'm in charge of the kitchen."

Seeing Ada looking fearfully at the door, Mrs Collins dismissed her fears. "Don't worry — we won't see Henry Morton again this evening. He's gone out to the pub and he'll fall in drunk during the early hours of the morning. Just stay out of his way and you'll be all right, girl."

"But he was so charming to the nuns!"

"That's typical," said Mrs Collins dryly. "You'll see him putting on the same display for the doctor and the priest. But the rest of us have to cope with his surly moods and drunken gibbering. But you'll like Mrs Morton — she's a lovely woman."

After she'd eaten her fill, Mrs Collins gave Ada a clean overall and took her up several flights of stairs, and into a lovely high-ceilinged room. At first, Ada couldn't see anyone in the large bed over near the window, then she realised that there was a tiny, frail form moving within it, and trying desperately to sit up.

"Mrs Morton, this is your new maid, Ada Casey," said Mrs Collins, approaching the bed.

"Ada! How nice to meet you!" said Laura Morton, trying to pull herself up onto her pillows.

Eagerly, Ada hurried forward and helped the bird-like woman into a sitting position.

"Hello, Mrs Morton," she said shyly, "It's nice to meet you too."

"I'll leave you to it, then," said Mrs Collins, as she started to leave the room. "I'll bring your supper up in about half an *hour. Is that all right, Mrs Morton?"*

"That's fine, Mrs Collins," said Laura. "Now, Ada, sit down here and talk to me."

When Mrs Collins footsteps died away, Laura turned to face Ada, an anguished look on her face.

"I'm sorry for you, Ada – it's not right that you should be put in this position. Henry can be very thoughtless. TB is contagious, and I feel that I should offer you the option to leave if you wish."

"Thank you, Mrs Morton – but I've nowhere to go, anyway."

Looking at Ada, Laura suddenly detected the less-than-flat stomach beneath the overalls she was now wearing. Surprised, Laura coloured, embarrassed at what she needed to say. "My God, are you pregnant, Ada?"

"Eh, yes, Mrs Morton, I'm about five months gone. That's why I was sent to the convent."

"You poor thing – I've heard about these places, and the way women are made to suffer in there. How did it happen, Ada – was it with a boy you loved?"

"No, Mrs Morton – it was the parish priest."

"Jesus Christ, what hypocrisy!" whispered Laura Morton. "What sort of a country do we live in, where the clergy can tell us one thing and do the opposite themselves!"

Laura began to cough, and Ada patted her back gently until the spasm ended.

"Let's not say anything to Henry for the present," said Laura, as she lay back on her pillows, exhausted. "I'm sure he assumed you'd already had your baby before you arrived here. He'll be furious if he finds out, and he'll probably want to send you back to the convent straight away."

"Yes, Mrs Morton."

"Please – call me Laura. Except in front of Henry – he's a stickler for protocol." She patted Ada's hand. "Anyway, I think it's best to say nothing about your pregnancy, Ada – until we figure out the best way forward." Lying back on her pillows, she gave a heartfelt sigh. "Dear God, Ada – I wish I could get out of this bed and live a proper life again! Then I could prevent your life and mine from being controlled by my husband! But this TB leaves me feeling so weak. I hear that people all over the country are dying from this illness, and that the state's been building sanatoriums to house all the poor people that have fallen victim to it."

"Well then, you're lucky, aren't you, Miss Laura?" She couldn't bring herself to call the lady just Laura. "Your husband wants to keep to at home, not send you to one of those awful sanatoriums."

Laura laughed bitterly. "You must be joking, Ada – he isn't keeping me at home because he cares about me. If I was in a sanatorium, he wouldn't be able to control me, or my money, in quite the same way. As long as I'm here, I won't get any help – he's hoping I'll eventually die – then he gets all my money and can marry again."

"Surely not, Miss Laura!"

"Believe me, it's true, Ada. My husband is a very callous man." Suddenly, Laura smiled. "We're a right pair, aren't we? You're pregnant and you don't want to be, and I can't get pregnant, although it's what my husband wants most in the world."

"Is it what you want, Miss Laura?"

"Probably not now," said Laura, acknowledging her own feelings for the first time. "I don't love Henry any more, so what would be the point? Besides, I'll never leave this bed, Ada – "

"Don't say that, Miss Laura – of course you will! I'll do

everything I can to help you get well!"

Back in the kitchen, Ada gratefully drank the cup of tea Mrs Collins had poured for her. And she joyfully ate the scone and butter that suddenly appeared on her plate. For the first time in ages, she was being treated like a human being, and it felt good. Despite the presence of Henry Morton, Ada felt that she would enjoy living here. Mrs Collins was a kindly and friendly woman, and Laura Morton was lovely too. Suddenly, she felt as though she had friends for the first time since she'd left home.

CHAPTER 27

The following weekend, Olivia arrived early at Bay Tree House, intending to get some tidying done in the yard before her friends arrived. She was taking an extra day off work and making a long weekend of it. Barbara and Maggie were returning to Dublin early – Barbara for work, Maggie for her parents' wedding anniversary party – so she'd be spending two nights on her own, but in fact, she was looking forward to enjoying the peace and solitude. She'd discovered a lovely old summerhouse in the garden, overgrown with ivy, which she was planning to repaint. She also had plans to clear out the rubbish and rusted implements from the sheds behind the barn.

Olivia grinned to herself as she started to work in the yard. She had no illusions about either of her two friends picking up a hoe or a shovel! They viewed Cloncullen and Bay Tree House simply as a base from which they could explore the area and have fun, and no doubt Maggie would be trying to find an excuse to visit the local police station! Well, thought Olivia, I'll just have to make sure that one of them does the grocery shopping while they're out gallivanting.

On the other hand, she had to admit to herself that she preferred to work alone, because it brought Laura Morton closer to her. She imagined Laura pottering in those same sheds . . . Then she remembered that Laura had suffered from TB, so it was unlikely she'd been able to experience the simple joy of mucking about in her garden. Instead, she'd probably had to watch the world go by from the solitude of her room.

Olivia shivered. How awful it must have been back then, with only the birds outside her window for distraction. TB must have been akin to a prison sentence. She shuddered, knowing that Laura Morton wasn't the only one who'd suffered. Thousands of people in Ireland had spent years in sanatoriums with tuberculosis, and many had never come home again. Perhaps Laura Morton had been lucky not to be sent to a sanatorium. Maybe her husband had loved her so much that he'd wanted to have her cared for at home. Olivia liked to think that Laura had been loved.

When Maggie and Barbara arrived a short time later, they found Olivia standing in the yard, deep in thought.

"Are you okay, Liv?" Maggie asked, giving her a hug.

"Yes, I'm fine," said Olivia, shaking herself out of her reverie. "I hope you two have packed your wellies – there's loads of clearing to do!"

"Do you think we'll see Philip Lynch?" Maggie asked anxiously, ignoring Olivia's teasing remark about working in the yard. Maggie's main reason for being in Cloncullen was to see the handsome sergeant!

"Hopefully," Olivia answered, "because I'd like to meet his grandmother again – maybe I'll invite her round to the house for tea."

"That's a great idea, Liv!" said Maggie enthusiastically, hoping that Philip would be the one to transport his grandmother there.

However, Olivia had another reason for wanting to see Philip Lynch, one that she hadn't told either of her friends. Apart from finding out for Maggie whether he was married or had a partner, she wanted to ask Philip's advice about several calls she'd received during the past week. In fact, they weren't really calls at all. Each time she'd answered the phone, there was nothing but silence from the other end, although she had the distinct impression that someone was there.

The weird calls had occurred on both the landline at her mother's house, and on her mobile phone. She suspected that it was Mark Cunningham, and she hoped he'd get tired of annoying her if she didn't respond. Each time it happened, she'd hung up, but it left her feeling unsettled, and vaguely scared. Presumably, he'd get tired of these childish antics eventually, so maybe there was no need to bother Philip. After all, what could he do about it?

"I'll do the shopping," Barbara volunteered. "It's about time I explored the area, and discovered where all the bargains are. What would anyone like for dinner this evening?"

The trio hadn't brought any supplies from Dublin, since Olivia was adamant that they buy locally. "It's important to support local businesses," she'd told her two friends. "And since I'm now a member of the local community, I ought to give the shops here my support."

She'd glanced over at Maggie, and grinned at her. "Who knows, Mags – you might soon be a member of the local community as well!"

Maggie had rewarded her with a beatific grin. For weeks now, she'd been daydreaming about gorgeous Philip Lynch. If he'd only ask her out, she'd be the happiest woman in the world!

*   *   *

As Barbara loaded the groceries into the boot of her car, she heard a voice calling her.

"Barbara – hello!"

"Oh – hello, Richard." Suddenly, Barbara's heart started pounding. What on earth was Richard Devlin doing in the main street of Cloncullen? Barbara felt as though she'd just walked into a nightmare. Maybe she was dreaming – this couldn't really be happening, could it? After all, she'd only gone to the local stores to get some food!

"How are you?" Richard asked, smiling broadly at her.

"I'm fine thank you." Barbara knew it would be polite to inquire about his welfare in return, but she was determined to be as offhand as possible. Let the bastard think that she didn't care a damn how he was! He could take a hike as far as she was concerned. Nevertheless, her heart was beating painfully, and she hoped that he couldn't see how uptight she really was.

"What brings you to these parts?" he asked, his soft gentle voice still having the power to make her toes curl.

"The same as you, I expect," she said brightly. "I'm visiting friends."

"You mean Liv?"

Barbara was momentarily caught off guard. "Eh – yes."

"I heard that she'd moved down here. In fact, I bumped into her here in Cloncullen recently."

"Is that right?" said Barbara languidly, doing her best to look totally disinterested in who he happened to meet. But inside, she was seething. Liv hadn't told her that she'd met him. When she got back to the house, she was going to kill her!

"Look, Barbs, I'm sorry about – "

As he reached out his hand, she withdrew hers quickly, as though it had been scalded. How dare he try to touch her! And how dare he call her by her pet name – that was reserved for people who cared about her – not for bastards like him!

"Goodbye Richard, I really must fly," she said, mustering up her best smile. "My boyfriend's waiting for me back at Liv's place. We're heading back to Dublin for a dinner party this evening, so I need to get back quickly to shower and change."

With satisfaction, she noted the surprise and dejection on his face. How dare he expect her to be still single, when he'd dumped her for another woman! Quickly, she walked away, pleased with her throwaway line. It was childish, she knew, but there was great satisfaction in scoring a point over him.

Anyway, she'd only told a partial lie. She was returning to Dublin but not until the following evening and then only to do a favour for Fergal by taking over his night shift at the hospital. And Maggie was coming back with her, because she had a family anniversary party to attend.

Resolutely, Barbara kept on walking back to her car, hoping that Richard wouldn't follow her. Thank goodness she'd already done the shopping, because there was no way she was going to remain in the town now! She had to get back to the safety of Liv's place. She had to get away from Richard Devlin. Quickly, Barbara fumbled for her car keys, cursing that she couldn't see the keyhole, because her eyes were filled with tears.

*   *   *

"Liv, I could kill you! Why didn't you tell me you'd seen him?"

"Look, I'm sorry, Barbs," said Olivia apologetically, "I thought it was just a one-off, and that I'd never see him again. There seemed no point in upsetting you."

"Well, now I'm twice as upset! If I'd known he was in the area, I could have prepared myself for bumping into him. Look at me – I'm in a scruffy pair of jeans, and I've no make-up on!"

"You look great – you don't need make-up."

But Barbara would not be mollified. "What on earth is that bastard doing around here?"

Olivia shrugged her shoulders. It *was* peculiar. Was it really just a coincidence that Richard Devlin had been seen in Cloncullen twice?

CHAPTER 28

Slowly, Carmel Collins made her way along Cloncullen's main street. It was a dry, pleasant day, and for once, her arthritis wasn't bothering her too much. The absence of pain made her feel almost young again. She crossed the street and walked slowly towards Larkin's shop, where she intended stocking up on her weekly groceries. She needed tea, bread and butter, cheese, some fruit and vegetables. Mr Larkin himself would deliver the heavier items, like potatoes and turf, later that evening.

She'd just been to visit her old friend Chrissie Delaney, whose cottage was on the outskirts of the village. She and Chrissie had been friends for more than fifty years, ever since Chrissie had first come to the village in her brightly coloured caravan, as a member of the travelling community who regularly camped in Kilcolgan Wood during the summer months.

Now, Chrissie's four children were all adults, some still on the road, others settled in various parts of the country, and Mikey, her husband, long dead from cirrhosis of the liver.

Chrissie had been one of the luckier travellers. Knowing how much Chrissie longed to settle, Laura Morton had eventually bought her the little cottage. Chrissie had turned it into her own little palace, and it was a joy to see her so happy. Yet the pull of the road was still great, and every summer Chrissie would close up her house and take off to visit those of her children who were still on the road.

"There's nothing quite like sleeping under the stars, you know," Chrissie had remarked to Carmel Collins earlier that morning, as they'd both sat drinking tea in Chrissie's kitchen.

"Believe me, I know," Carmel had replied acerbically. "I've been on camping holidays, and all I remember is the rain pouring into the tent, the flies biting, and lying awake freezing with the cold all night."

Chrissie had laughed. "So now you know what the travellers have to put up with! I'm too old now to cope with the road in winter, but in the summer, it's the most wonderful place to be. Even though there are less and less places to camp, and more and more vindictive individuals, and county councils always on your back." Suddenly, Chrissie's face had broken into a smile. "By the way, Carmel, guess who's coming to visit me?"

Carmel had looked at her quizzically.

"Julia."

"Julia who?"

"Julia Gleeson – the singer."

Suddenly remembering, Carmel Collins smiled. "Ah, Julia! Of course. She lived with you for a few years after she ran away from the orphanage, didn't she?"

Chrissie nodded. "She's always been like a daughter to me. And look at her now – an international star! She's also been very good to me, money-wise, you know. She always makes sure I have everything I need. The last time she was here, she bought me all those newfangled kitchen appliances. I never had a dishwasher before."

"You were very good to her, Chrissie." Carmel said, smiling. "Tell her I was asking for her, won't you?"

"You can tell her yourself, when she arrives in a few weeks' time. I'm hoping that you and Dr McCarthy might drop round some evening while she's here."

"Thanks, Chrissie – I'd be delighted," Carmel had replied. "I was always very fond of Julia – and all those poor kids at the orphanage. They had a rough life at the hands of those nuns."

"Except for Sister Angela, God rest her soul. She was always very good to them."

Now, as she was about to cross the road, Carmel Collins was shaken out of her reverie by the approach of two elderly nuns from that very same orphanage. Now that the orphanage no longer existed, and most of the nuns who'd run it were dead, it was rumoured that the orphanage and convent building would soon be sold, probably for conversion into apartments. The two remaining nuns were all that was left of a once flourishing community.

"Hello, Sister Maria, Sister Philomena. How are you both today?"

"We're fine, thank you, Mrs Collins," said Sister Maria. "Lovely day, isn't it? Makes a change to have a bit of sunshine."

"Indeed it does," said Carmel Collins.

"What do you make of the hullabaloo at the Morton house?" asked Sister Philomena eagerly. "Who'd ever have thought that such a thing could have happened in our town?"

Carmel Collins nodded, giving a tight smile.

"I suppose your grandson is involved in the investigations?" asked Sister Maria.

Carmel Collins nodded again. "Yes, it seems to be a nine-day wonder at the moment, but it's hardly worth all the effort, is it? I mean, it all happened so long ago."

"But someone in that house committed murder," said Sister Philomena, shivering exaggeratedly. "I feel sorry for the poor girl who's just moved in – she must be terrified."

"I doubt it – she's a sensible young woman," said Carmel Collins. "Besides, what on earth is there to be terrified of? It's only a poor dead baby. Now, if you'll excuse me – "

"But you've lived in the village a long time, haven't you, Mrs Collins?" said Sister Philomena, gripping Carmel Collins' sleeve, reluctant to let her go. "Maybe you were living here when the awful murder of that baby was committed!"

"Anything is possible, Sister," said Carmel Collins dryly, "but the Gardai haven't yet told us when exactly the murder was committed. So there's no point in speculating, is there?" She looked at her watch. "Now I really must be going, Sisters."

"Goodbye, Mrs Collins," Sister Maria called after her, but Carmel Collins had already hurried off.

CHAPTER 29

As Laura Morton lay in her bed, gazing out at the cloud formations in the sky, she was filled with a terrible sadness. How many more years would she lie here like this? She'd be better off dead.

The emptiness of everything made her want to scream. Was this all that life had to offer her? Her mind was brimming over with ideas, hopes and dreams, whereas her body had placed her in a limbo from which there seemed no escape.

All this talk of a cure was just other people's way of giving her hope. Stupid, blind, unrealistic hope. She didn't believe a word of it herself. Ada and Mrs Collins meant well, and she knew that they genuinely wanted her to get well. In fact, they were the only ones who did. Henry would be glad to see her die. He wanted an heir, and felt cheated by her illness. Nevertheless, their marriage had given him control of all her money, so her death would be a convenient bonus, enabling him to pay off his debts, and find a more fecund wife.

Oh, the dreams she'd started out with! Like every young girl, she'd dreamed of a handsome beau who adored her, a *beautiful white dress and a village church. She'd imagined herself floating down the aisle in a cloud of tulle, to be united forever with the man of her dreams . . .*

She sighed. That's all they'd been – dreams. Henry didn't want her, probably never did. But her wealth had made her attractive to him, and her family had been more than willing to offload her. A single, opinionated female was a liability, and best married off as quickly as possible.

But as soon as the ring was on her finger, Henry had shown his true colours. Contrary to his earlier charming demeanour, he now made it clear that she meant no more to him than a chattel, and that her primary function was to supply him with a son as quickly as possible.

When she became ill, things got even worse. And when TB was diagnosed – which meant years in bed, if not death itself – Henry was furious. His plans for a son and heir had been thwarted! But he consoled himself by spending Laura's money lavishly on his own pursuits, which included, she knew, the company of other women.

Since TB was greatly feared, even Laura's own family now stayed away. Her only visitors were the elderly Dr Walsh – who stayed as briefly as possible and kept his distance from her – and the local parish priest, who urged her, from the safety of the doorway, to spend her time saying the Rosary. Everyone was terrified of being in the company of someone with TB, in case they should catch it.

Laura sighed. Poor Ada had no such choice – she'd been offloaded by the convent, and she had nowhere else to go. Laura fervently hoped that Ada, who'd become her friend and confidante, would stay healthy, since she feared what would happen if she ever succumbed to the dreaded consumption. Henry would certainly evict her at a moment's notice, and the nuns would never take her back. So she'd probably end up alone in some sanatorium, with no one to visit her or care about her . . .

Suddenly, Ada appeared at her bedside, rousing Laura from her reverie. "The parish priest will be up in a minute," she whispered, wishing to prepare her friend, since she knew how much Laura loathed his visits. In fact, Laura's skin crawled every time she heard the sound of his unctuous voice.

Appearing at the door, but being careful not to step across the threshold, the priest smiled condescendingly at her. "How are you today, Mrs Morton? No better? Ah, the Lord works in mysterious ways. My dear child, you must hold a very special place in Our Lady's heart. You've been chosen to bear this special cross, which you must bear with fortitude and courage." He smiled serenely at her. "What are the woes of this life, my child, compared to the Eternal Happiness that awaits you?"

Laura wished she could hit him and she longed to wipe the smarmy smile off his face. If TB was so special, then maybe he'd like to step a little closer so that she could infect him – then he, too, could have a special place in Our Lady's heart!

After the priest had gone, Ada was quickly back at Laura's bedside, plumping up her pillows and trying to cheer her up. She knew how upsetting Laura found the priest's visits, so she was determined to offer her what support she could.

"Is there anything I can get you, Miss Laura?"

"Well, you could bring me my diary – I presume Henry's not about?"

"No, Miss Laura – he's gone out."

"Thank heavens – it's such a relief when he's not here. I can write my daily entry in peace."

Ada helped Laura into a sitting position, then slid her diary out from its hiding place between the mattress and the base, and *handed it to her.*

Laura smiled her thanks, taking the top off her fountain pen. "Thank goodness Henry doesn't know I keep a diary, Ada – and I don't want him to ever find out. Being able to express my true feelings in it is the only thing that keeps me sane right now." Laura turned her head towards Ada. "I used to love Henry once, you know. But that was a long time ago – he was nice back then," Laura's voice soft and dreamy, "and he was kind to me. I knew that he was attracted to my money as well, but I still thought we could have a happy life together." She sighed. "Until I became ill, that is. Then gradually, everything started to change. Gradually he began behaving distantly towards me – " She looked up at Ada, who was still busy straightening the eiderdown, deliberately avoiding looking at her employer. "Oh Ada," she said suddenly, in exasperation, " leave the covers the way they are, and come talk to me!"

"Look, Miss Laura, I don't think you should be talking to me about the Master like this – "

"So you're going to tell him, are you, Ada? Well, you may be more able-bodied than I am, but you're just as much his victim! So please indulge me – who else can I talk to, but you? He doesn't even allow my friends to visit anymore – he tells them all that I'm too 'weak' to receive guests. So I lie here all alone, only able to leave this bed if and when he sees fit." A tear trickled down her cheek. Then she grasped Ada's hand. "Oh my poor Ada! Here I am, thinking only of myself! You must miss your family terribly. I wish I could help you financially – so that you could at least take the bus home to visit them sometimes – but Henry totally controls the purse-strings."

"Don't worry, Miss Laura – my family don't want to see me ever again. Not after having disgraced them."

"But surely you'd like to see your brother and sister again?"

"Of course I would, Miss – I'd give anything to see Helen and Eddie again. But not my parents, even if they wanted to see me." She sighed. "At one stage, I convinced myself that if they knew how badly the nuns were treating me, they would take me back. But I know now I was only fooling myself."

Laura sighed. "Well, then, why don't you go to see your brother and sister – your parents need never know. And Henry needn't know either – you could visit them when he's away. I'm sure we could ask Mrs Collins to discreetly cut back on the weekly grocery bill, so that you'd have enough money for the train fare." Laura's face was aglow with delight at the prospect of being able to help Ada. "If you left early one morning, you could get to Leafy Vale by lunchtime, and see your brother and sister during their school lunch hour. Then, you could catch the late train, and be back here by nightfall. Mrs Collins could make you up a packed lunch."

"Thank you, Miss Laura," Ada said humbly, "but how do I know that Helen and Eddie would want to see me? After all, I don't know what they've been told about me. Maybe they think I'm a disgrace too."

Laura sighed. "I'm sure that's not true, Ada. But in the meantime, why don't you put it to the test by writing to them? Tell them where you are, and that you'd like to see them. If you enclose a stamped addressed envelope, I'm sure they'll write back straightaway." A smile of joy lit up her pâle gaunt face. "We'll ask Mrs Collins to take the money for the stamps from the housekeeping allowance." Then suddenly, Laura looked concerned. "Oh dear, Ada - I suppose your parents might stop them replying to you. I hadn't considered that!"

But Ada wasn't unduly worried. "No, Miss Laura, that won't be a problem. Our postman is so lazy that he refuses to cycle up the mile-long driveway to the house. So he always *leaves the post under a big stone at the gate."* Suddenly, her lower lip quivered and her eyes filled with tears. *"Collecting the post used to be my job, Miss Laura, before they sent me away – I suppose Helen and Eddie collect it now, so there'd be no likelihood of my parents finding any letter from me."*

Laura squeezed Ada's hand supportively. *"That's great news, Ada – in that event, you'll surely have a reply from your brother and sister in no time at all."* Her face was aglow at the prospect of being able to reunite Ada and her siblings.

And Ada smiled back, infected by Laura's enthusiasm. *"Thanks, Miss Laura, that's a great idea. I'll write a letter to them this very afternoon."*

* * *

Henry Morton paced up and down Laura's bedroom, with scant regard for his wife's weakened condition. He was livid to discover that the nuns had tricked him into taking on a pregnant girl as maid to his wife.

"I could kill those fraudulent bitches!" he shouted. *"I assumed they'd given me a girl who'd already had her baby – one who could work hard, not expect to take time off to give birth! I'm going to take her back to the laundry immediately – "*

"Henry – no!" said Laura, her voice as loud as she could make it. *"She's a very good maid, and I won't hear of you sending her away!"* Then she realised that she might be playing into Henry's hands. If he thought she liked Ada, he'd deliberately get rid of the girl to isolate Laura even further. So she quickly added, *"She understands my ways, Henry. I don't want to have to start explaining everything to a new maid."*

Henry Morton continued to pace the floor, as though he hadn't heard. *"I took her on out of the goodness of my heart – "*

she needn't think that I'm going to mollycoddle her, while she wastes my time and money!"

"Henry – you seem to have forgotten something – you don't pay the poor girl anything," said Laura sarcastically.

"Well, she gets bed and board – that's a hell of a lot more than she deserves. Those flighty, troublesome trollops from the laundry are all the same, and I'm not going to have her taking time off to give birth to some man's brat."

"We'll deal with the matter closer to her due date," said Laura, attempting to soothe him. "I'm sure she'll only be away in hospital for a day or two – and Mrs Collins has said she's more than willing to cope on her own."

"Well, she needn't think she's bringing any child back here," said Henry darkly. "I presume it'll be sent to the orphanage?"

"I presume so, Henry," said Laura dryly. "Women like Ada don't have too many choices, do they? In fact, nor do any women in this society."

Just then, the telephone rang in the hall downstairs, and Ada appeared, informing Henry that one of his business associates was on the line. Relieved, Laura sank back into her pillows. Henry would soon forget all about his tirade, now that he was involved in some moneymaking scheme. Hopefully, there would still be time to find a solution to the problem of Ada's pregnancy.

CHAPTER 30

The following morning, after a leisurely breakfast that turned into brunch, Maggie and Barbara set off for Dublin, leaving Olivia alone in Bay Tree House. Before she left, Maggie had repeatedly invited Olivia to join her and the rest of her family for their parents' wedding anniversary celebrations, but Olivia was adamant that she intended using her solo time productively.

Looking from one worried face to another, she'd grinned affectionately at them. "I'll be fine – honestly!" she told them. "I've so much work to do here that I won't even have time to miss you!"

In fact, Olivia was looking forward to spending the rest of her long weekend working hard in the garden. She planned to strip back some of the ivy from the summerhouse to discover exactly what state it was in. The she'd have to see what could be done with the rusty old farm tools that were taking up space in one of the outhouses. Maybe someone would actually want them? If not, she'd have to make arrangements to have them taken away.

The day was fine and there was a fresh breeze blowing in from the sea, and Olivia could smell the salt in the air. She began pulling the ivy off the summerhouse, imagining romantic trysts there in days of old. Did Laura, before her illness, sit inside with her husband on balmy evenings? Or use it to escape from a summer shower? Olivia liked to think that maybe Ada sat here too, enjoying the beauty of the gardens.

Suddenly, as thoughts of Ada came into her mind, Olivia found that she didn't want to work in the garden any more. She'd been mulling over Carmel Collins' comments in her mind, feeling certain that Philip's grandmother knew something about her great-aunt. Now, she realised she had the perfect opportunity to put her ideas to the test. If Ada had ever lived in Cloncullen, she might be buried in the local graveyard!

Taking off her Wellingtons, she changed into trainers and headed for her car. She remembered noticing a small graveyard on a hill just outside the town, and she drove herself there in less than five minutes. The graveyard was deserted but the gate was open, so she stepped inside and gazed around at all the gravestones.

Where would she start? Olivia concluded that it might have been more logical to wait and check parish records, but the idea of finding the actual grave was much more appealing. Since the graveyard was on a rectangular plot, Olivia figured that if she walked through it row by row, she would soon cover every single grave.

Some of the headstones were obviously much older than others, and she found herself lingering over many of them, reading the inscriptions. She noticed recurring names, where whole families had lived and died around the Cloncullen area, and she detected names that tallied with several shops in the town. She found three graves bearing the Larkin name, obviously related to the family who owned the store in the main street of Cloncullen where she'd been doing her regular weekly shopping.

In a corner of the graveyard, Olivia spotted several nuns' graves, and she read off such names a Mother Monica and Sister Angela. No doubt these were the nuns from the old orphanage. Then she came across a grave bearing the name of a Doctor Walsh who had died a few years previously, and she smiled to herself – even doctors, with all their pills and potions, couldn't withstand time itself!

Next, she found the ostentatious grave of Henry Morton. She looked again – surely Laura Morton would have been buried alongside him? But there was no mention of her name on the headstone. Then it dawned on Olivia that since Laura had only died recently, her name might not yet have been etched onto the monument. Yes, that must be it.

Olivia had always found graveyards fascinating, not ghoulish like many people seemed to think. Here was history right in front of her eyes! Some graves were well tended, others had obviously been neglected for years. Slowly, Olivia walked along the paths between them.

She paused at the grave of a little girl named Majella, who had died more then fifty years earlier, at the age of seven. The child's grave was well looked after, so obviously someone still cared about her. Olivia shuddered. She couldn't even begin to imagine the pain of losing your child like that. And even after fifty years, there was someone out there who remembered the child, and was still grieving for her.

After an hour, Olivia felt certain that she'd covered every grave, without finding any marked with Ada Casey's name. In one way, she was relieved, since it meant she could put off the inevitable until another day. On the other hand, it would have been easier for everyone if she'd been able to tell her grandmother and Great-uncle Eddie that she'd discovered where their sister was buried.

Getting into her car, she drove back to Bay Tree House. It was now getting too late to do any further work in the garden, so she opted for a leisurely shower, in preparation for an evening spent reading in the drawing room.

So far, Olivia had resisted installing a television. Apart from the fact that she hadn't had time to watch any programmes, she also wanted to experience life as Laura Morton would have experienced it in the past, before a television set became standard in every living room. Olivia hoped that if she sat in silence, the house might somehow talk back to her, and reveal some of its secrets. For undoubtedly, Bay Tree House held many secrets. If Carmel Collins was hiding something and her great-aunt Ada had really lived there in the past, Olivia hoped that somehow she might be able to find out for herself.

Wandering through the rooms, Olivia felt a thrill yet again at having been given such a wonderful house. Despite the updating that was necessary and the repair needed to the chimneybreast, the house was in remarkably good condition. Many rooms, such as the dining and drawing rooms, needed no changes at all.

Olivia even liked the existing décor – other than the ghastly patterned carpets, which definitely had to go – and she particularly liked the full-length gesso-framed mirrors set into each alcove in the drawing room, which diffused light throughout the room.

Critically, she eyed the mirror over the fireplace. She was decidedly less enamoured of it. While it blended in well with the other two, it was somewhat shabbier, with paint peeling off it at the point where it came in contact with the mantelpiece. Probably due to years of people taking things on and off the mantelpiece, she surmised. Olivia wondered if she could touch it up herself with ordinary gold paint, or was an expert required? It also seemed a little skewed to one side . . .

Leaning forward, she tried to straighten it, then realised that it was screwed to the wall. Of course, it would have to be, given its weight. But the screws weren't quite holding it against the wall . . . she hoped it wasn't going to fall off before she could tighten the screws. Hopefully, she could do it herself, without putting a strain on the gesso frame. Quickly, she got out her toolbox and selected a screwdriver. A few tweaks should be all it required.

Standing on a chair in front of the fireplace, Olivia was about to turn the screwdriver when she noticed the tip of something sticking out from behind the mirror. She sighed. All she needed now was to find that the back of the mirror was coming loose, and she was only going to make things worse by interfering! What was that saying – "If it ain't broke, don't fix it"?

She hovered for a moment in indecision, then decided to push the unsightly bit of whatever-it-was back behind the mirror before tightening the screw. But as she touched the offending material, she realised that it wasn't the backing of the mirror – it felt more like the spine of a small notebook . . .

Using the screwdriver as a lever, Olivia poked and prodded until she could get a grip on the notebook, then realised, as it toppled out, that it wasn't the only one. Fetching a long ruler, she levered several more small books out, then moved her chair over to the other side of the mirror, from where she retrieved several more. Why on earth would anyone go to such lengths to hide a series of notebooks behind the drawing-room mirror?

Stepping down off the chair, Olivia examined the books, realising that they were diaries. Her heart beat faster with excitement . . . there was no name written either on the cover or inside . . . but could these have belonged to Laura Morton . . . or Ada Casey?

*   *   *

"Will you be all right, darling?" Brendan's mother asked solicitously, wiping imaginary dust from the counter top in his kitchen at Blackberry Cottage. Brendan nodded resignedly. His mother was always fussing. Couldn't she see that he was a grown man, who could wipe down his own worktops? Besides, the place was spotless anyway.

His father coughed politely. "The lad is fine, Harriet, leave him alone. He doesn't need you fussing over him."

Brendan shot a grateful glance in his father's direction. His dad seemed to understand how he felt. His mother didn't really mean any harm – she just had a tendency to fuss over him and his brother Andy all the time! "But the two of you are all that I have!" she'd say plaintively any time he objected to her suffocating ministrations.

She'd insisted on him coming to the family home for a big feed earlier, and now he felt uncomfortably stuffed, since he'd had to eat all the meat, potatoes and vegetables she piled on his plate. His mother had declared that she'd spent hours cooking his favourite meal for him, so he'd had little choice but to shovel it down, and hope that it wouldn't all come back up again.

Now, the woman had even more plans for his already queasy stomach!

"Now, listen to me, Brendan – I've put several portions of homemade shepherd's pie in your freezer," she told him, "so you'll have something to keep you going over the next few days."

Conspiratorially, his father winked at him, and Brendan nodded his thanks good-naturedly. Did his mother think there were no shops in the area? Or that he couldn't cook something himself? Even though he had his own home now, his mother continued to fuss over him as though he was still a child. For heaven's sake, he was nearly thirty-five years of age!

Andy had been so envious when he'd managed to buy Blackberry Cottage after he'd qualified and started up in business with Donal. "You lucky old sod,!" his brother had grumbled good-humouredly. "You've escaped! Now I'll be the sole focus of Ma's attention, and I'll end up putting on loads of weight from all the food she'll stuff into me! There are only so many stews and casseroles that I can eat!"

Looking at his parents again, Brendan wished they'd go home. While he loved them dearly, he couldn't take much more of his mother's fussing! Of course, his father always let her away with it, since after all it was only her way of showing how much she loved them all.

Brendan glanced surreptitiously at his watch. It was already late evening, and Evelyn would soon be calling by. He wasn't too keen on his parents knowing about her visit, because no doubt his mother would jump to the wrong conclusions. Neither of his parents were impressed with Evelyn's permanent tan or her over-the-top choice of revealing clothes. But it was his life, and he had to live it in his own way. After that . . . well, he planned to make a very important call.

CHAPTER 31

Sitting in the kitchen of Bay Tree House that evening, Olivia felt very alone and vulnerable. While she'd enjoyed spending the daylight hours alone, she now desperately wished that Maggie and Barbara were there with her.

On the other hand, the solitude would be ideal for studying the diaries she'd found earlier that afternoon. She certainly didn't want to talk to anyone else about them, and since they'd been well hidden behind the mirror, it was obvious that they weren't intended for general reading.

From a cursory glance when she'd first found them, Olivia had concluded that the diaries were written by Laura Morton, and she'd felt a stab of disappointment. There was probably nothing in them that would reveal the whereabouts of her long-lost great-aunt. After all, Laura was unlikely to have had much to say, since she'd spent so many years of her life languishing in bed. How much more exciting it would have been if they'd been written by Ada! Still, it would be interesting to step back into the past, Olivia concluded. And who knows – they might hold some clues about Ada anyway.

Olivia shivered as she now surveyed the empty kitchen. Ever since those silent, menacing phone calls had begun, she'd been jumpy and frightened. She scolded herself. I'm just being ridiculous, she thought. I'm not a little child who's afraid of the dark. But still the fear persisted. What if the caller – presumably Mark – decided to do more than make scary phone calls? What if he decided to visit the house?

Suddenly, the isolation of Bay Tree House – which had previously been its most attractive feature to Olivia – was taking on menacing qualities. The orchard, which she adored by day, was now full of dark menacing shapes by night, and when the wind blew through the trees, she was reminded of the banshee stories of old. The barns and outhouses stood like great hulking giants casting shadows over the courtyard. Olivia shivered again. In fact, since the silent phone calls had started, the house's isolation was becoming downright terrifying.

In view of the gaping hole in the kitchen wall, Olivia wasn't too happy to sit in the room, since her imagination kept running wild, and she imagined a collectivity of axe murderers all peering in together while she sat unaware in the spotlight.

She needed to get an alarm installed as soon as possible. Just as soon as the chimneybreast wall had been replaced. The hold-up, according to the architect, was caused by a query from the planning office. As soon as that was resolved, he'd assured her, it would be plain sailing all the way. Except that now she was terrified out of her wits. While her friends were staying there, the opening in the wall hadn't bothered her. But now, all by herself, she suddenly felt very vulnerable.

Right, Olivia told herself firmly, a mug of tea was called for. Then she would take it and the diaries upstairs to her bedroom, where she would feel less exposed. Then she realised that she'd also forgotten to phone the locksmith about getting the locks on the bedroom doors fixed, but it was pointless to worry about that now. Anyway, from upstairs, she'd be able to hear any sounds coming from below. If anyone tried to enter the house, she could simply barricade herself into her room! Fleetingly, Olivia wished that she'd spoken to Philip about the weird phone calls. But in the daylight, they'd seemed so trivial, especially when the police had so many more urgent demands on their time.

Upstairs in her bedroom, Olivia settled down with the diaries. Her plan was to put them into order based on the year, then she would start reading the oldest one first.

Before long, she had settled down with the first of the diaries, which was dated 1950, and began studying the spidery handwriting that covered each page. It took a while before she managed to decipher the peculiarities of Laura's handwriting but gradually she found she was able to read the contents at a reasonable speed. Disappointingly, the early pages of the first diary seemed to consist mainly of daily weather reports, doctor's visits and the kind of food she was served at mealtimes. Olivia's initial excitement began to wane. On the other hand, what did she expect? Poor Laura's life had been far from interesting. The diaries had probably been a way for Laura to relieve the monotony of her situation. And nowhere was there any mention of her great-aunt Ada.

However, as she continued to turn the pages, Olivia began to notice a subtle change in Laura's perspective. She seemed to become more interested in what was happening around her, and Olivia found herself drawn into the life of 1950s Ireland. Gradually, she began to enjoy Laura's pithy comments and astute observations on the political and social inequities of the time.

Olivia was so engrossed that when she first heard the crunch of gravel outside, it didn't immediately register in her brain. And when she heard the first creaking sound below, she wondered if she'd imagined it. Perhaps, in her excitement to discover any juicy bits in the diaries, her over-active imagination had created its own sound effects inside her head.

Oh God, there it was again! As she put the diary down and listened, the hair stood up on the back of her neck. Someone was definitely moving around downstairs! What was she going to do? The only way out of the house was down the stairs, so she was trapped! The windows were too high off the ground to safely jump out, and there was no way of reaching her car without encountering whoever was lurking downstairs.

Looking around her frantically for a weapon, she spotted the old walking stick she'd found in the bedroom when she'd first arrived at Bay Tree House. That would have to do. If Mark Cunningham was trying to scare her, he was succeeding, but she wasn't going to remain there like a sitting duck! She would defend herself, and show that women could be resourceful, and didn't have to scream or give up without a fight.

Tiptoeing over to the light switch, Olivia turned it off.

That way, the intruder no longer had the advantage. Within seconds, her eyes had become accustomed to the gloom, so she crept out of her room and down the first flight of stairs to the halfway landing. There was a faint light coming from the kitchen and, as she crouched there on the stairs, walking stick in hand, she could see the outline of someone moving down below.

"Olivia!" a muffled and disembodied voice whispered softly up the stairs. "Are you there?"

It was Mark! He had come to finally take his revenge for her imagined crimes! Olivia knew that if she identified herself, he'd quickly climb the stairs and . . . she didn't dare think of what he might have in mind. Hopefully, if he thought she wasn't there, he would go away and leave her alone – at least for tonight. All she had to do was stay perfectly still and he would eventually leave, then she would call the police immediately . . .

Suddenly, to ease a cramp in her leg, Olivia shifted from her crouched position. And the tread of the stairs suddenly creaked. In the total silence, it sounded like a pistol shot. She gasped as she realised she had just given her position away. All Mark had to do now was rush up the stairs and grab her. . .

As the shadowy form began climbing the stairs, she leapt forward and smashed the walking stick down on his head. There was a muffled groan as he slumped in a heap, then rolled back down the stairs and lay inert at the bottom. Too terrified to chance climbing across him, with visions of him grabbing her leg as she passed by, Olivia raced back upstairs again, rushing into her bedroom and barricading herself inside the room by pulling an old chest of drawers across the door. Then with trembling hands, she dialled the emergency number on her mobile phone, telling the person at the other end of the line what had happened.

She remained barricaded in her room until she heard the wail of a police siren, followed by an ambulance. Still shaking, she refused to come out of her room until assured by the police officers that the inert body had been removed from the house and taken away by ambulance. Only then was she willing to open the bedroom door.

"Do you know who he is?" asked one of the officers who were now standing in the hallway as Olivia came downstairs.

Olivia nodded. "His name is Mark Cunningham, he runs the Glen Hotel with his wife, and he's been making weird phone calls for several weeks now."

The police officer wrote down the details in his little notebook. "Well, you don't have to worry about him any longer – he'll be charged with harassment and a number of other charges as soon as he's sufficiently recovered."

"Do you think he might die?" Olivia asked the police officer who'd begun taking her statement. Only now was the impact of what happened beginning to register with her, and she found that she was shaking from head to toe. She'd hit him extremely hard, and she began to feel guilty in case she'd fractured his skull.

"Well, I'm not a paramedic, but I don't think so," the officer assured her. "But one thing is certain – he'll have a very bad headache for quite some time." He grinned. "You gave him quite a clobbering, you know!"

"He deserved it," said Olivia, relieved to know that Mark wasn't actually going to expire. She felt a great sense of satisfaction that she'd had the courage to defend herself. Mark would now know that she wasn't a woman to be trifled with, and she felt confident that he wouldn't be bothering her any more.

CHAPTER 32

"I see your children have got a letter from down the country," said the postman, as he handed Mrs Casey a letter addressed to Helen and Eddie. He was out of breath from having cycled up the mile-long driveway, but he was so curious about its contents that he was prepared to discommode himself in order to find out who had sent it.

"I thought it might be urgent," he said to Mrs Casey, wiping the sweat off his forehead, and hoping that his efforts might be rewarded with a cup of tea at the very least. Normally, he left the Casey's post under a big stone at the gateway, to be collected by one of the children on their way home from school, but today he'd risked giving himself a heart attack in order to gain some valuable snippets of information.

He suspected that the letter might be connected to the topic that was uppermost in his mind, and in the minds of many others in the neighbourhood. There was a rumour going round that the eldest Casey daughter wasn't at home any more, and he hoped that once he was ensconced in the Casey's kitchen, he might be able to raise the matter in a roundabout way.

Mrs Casey took the letter, glanced at it, and stuffed it into her pocket. The postman was deeply disappointed at her reaction. It was clear from her peeved expression that she recognised the handwriting, and he was bursting to know who could have caused her such displeasure. Still, her reaction in itself was enough to supply him with a titbit of juicy gossip to relay at the next house he visited. He'd embellish it just a little by telling the people there that Mrs Casey had received a strange letter from "abroad".

"I didn't know you knew people in that part of the country," added the postman, angling for further information on the letter. But Mrs Casey didn't reply, so he reluctantly accepted that for the immediate future at least, the subject was a lost cause. Maybe he should have just steamed it open while he was making himself a cup of tea in the back room of the Post Office before setting out on his rounds. On the other hand, maybe if he traded a bit of gossip, he might get something in return.

"Did you hear about Mrs O'Brien's gallstones?" he asked.

"No, I didn't," said Mrs Casey, closing the door abruptly in his face. Nosy old so-and-so, she thought, as she took the letter out of her pocket and tore it savagely in two. Then she tore the two halves into quarters, and proceeded to shred the letter until it resembled confetti. Carrying the remains of the letter into the kitchen, she opened the door of the cooking range, and flung the tiny pieces into the flames.

*   *   *

"I'm sure you're wondering how Ada is getting on," said Father Dineen as he sat in the parlour of the Casey's farmhouse. Mrs Casey nodded. She'd never bring up the subject herself,

232

since it was so embarrassing, but she was grateful to the priest for his ongoing concern for her wayward daughter.

"The nuns found her – eh, a little difficult at first. Somewhat on the wild side." He smiled unctuously. "After all, Mrs Casey, you know how headstrong she is."

"You're right there, Father – Ada never went behind the door about stating her opinions," said Mrs Casey ruefully.

The priest nodded. "Yes, she's been finding life at the convent a little dreary." He gave what he hoped was a smile that conveyed affection for Ada. "Not lively enough for her at all!"

He took the cup of tea Mrs Casey offered him, noting with pleasure that she'd served freshly baked scones as well.

"So the nuns thought she'd enjoy a change of scene."

"What do you mean, Father?"

"Well, your daughter's now got a great job with a lovely family, Mrs Casey."

Father Dineen was careful not to mention the dreaded TB and they both studiously avoided any mention of Ada's pregnancy or impending confinement. It was as though they were discussing some delightful holiday that Ada was having. In fact, Father Dineen was hoping that Mrs Casey would be content enough about Ada's care to leave well enough alone.

"That's great, Father," said Mrs Casey, looking pleased. "I really want to thank you for all your help. I don't know what we'd have done without you. Jim is still determined to find the boy who did this to her – and give him a good thrashing."

The priest forced a smile. "Oh dear, Mrs Casey, that's not a very Christian attitude, is it?" he chided gently, "Two wrongs never make a right, you know. Turning the other cheek at times like these is the essence of Christianity." He sipped his tea, and helped himself to a second scone. "Tell Jim it's time he came to confession – he hasn't been for several weeks now. When he does, I'll offer him a few discreet words of advice."

"Oh Father, you're so good! Jim's very angry, you know. A quiet word from you would do him a world of good."

"I'll pray for you all, Mrs Casey," said Father Dineen solemnly, when he eventually stood up from the table. "Now, would you like me to say a decade of the Rosary with you before I leave?"

"Oh, would you, Father?" There were tears of gratitude in Mrs Casey's eyes. "Oh, Father – we're so lucky to have you in our parish!"

Mrs Casey was already on her knees.

CHAPTER 33

After a rewarding day spent working outdoors, Olivia felt a lot more confident about being alone the following night. The night before, when the police had taken Mark away, they'd suggested that she might feel safer back at her mother's home in Dublin. But she'd assured them that she was fine. She hadn't even bothered to contact Maggie or Barbara, knowing that they both had their own work and social commitments. Besides, she needed to stand on her own two feet, and let Mark Cunningham see that she wasn't going to be turned into a gibbering wreck!

Now, as she closed the wooden shutters in the downstairs rooms, Olivia suddenly realised how ridiculous it was to be closing the shutters when there was still a gaping hole in the back wall! But at least she wouldn't be unduly worried about it tonight. The only person she feared was out of action in hospital.

Olivia yawned widely. She was exhausted after the trauma of the previous night. At least tonight she wouldn't worry about the animal noises outside, the bats within the roof, or the wind rustling in the apple trees. Gradually, she was learning to identify and enjoy the sounds of the countryside, while inside she was becoming accustomed to the particular groans and creaking sounds that are unique to every old house.

When she failed to stifle a second yawn, Olivia decided that it was time to make a final cup of tea and head for bed. She'd make some toast as well, then take it upstairs and eat it in bed. There was something infinitely comforting about toast, she thought. Perhaps it reminded her of her childhood, when she and her mother would sit in the kitchen at night in their dressing-gowns, make a big pile of toast, and sit eating it in front of the fire, butter running down their chins, and laughing as they caught the drips before they landed on their pyjamas. Then her mother would brush Olivia's hair until it shone, and now, as she closed her eyes, Olivia could almost feel her mother's touch once again. That had been a rare time of bonding and the thought of it suddenly made Olivia want to cry. After all that had happened, she suddenly longed to run straight home to her mother. But she resisted the urge – after all, she was an adult, wasn't she? And she'd managed perfectly well to look after herself. In fact, she felt proud of the way in which she'd dealt with Mark Cunningham. He certainly wouldn't be bothering her again in a hurry!

Having made tea and two rounds of thickly buttered toast, Olivia loaded a tray and carried it upstairs. She'd prop herself up in bed and start reading the diaries again while she ate her supper, being careful, of course, not to get butter on the diaries, or crumbs all over the sheets!

Leaving the tray on her bedside table, Olivia took off her watch and earrings, before stripping off and slipping into her pyjamas She was excited at the prospect of moving on to the next diary, since they looked like they were getting more interesting. Olivia wondered what changes had taken place in Laura Morton's life to bring about this more positive attitude?

She'd already discovered that Laura Morton hadn't used anyone's full name in her diaries, but identified people by the first letter of their first name. Presumably, this was for their protection as much as hers? Now, as she munched a slice of toast and began working her way through the diary for 1951, Olivia's heart almost stopped. Laura's first entry mentioned someone called "A"! In a state of shock and excitement, she read the entry – "A" appeared to be a maid of some sort, who had arrived at Bay Tree House. As Olivia read on, it became obvious that Laura was becoming very fond of "A", and – shockingly– that she hated "H". Olivia sighed. Who on earth could "H" be? Then she suddenly remembered – hadn't Carmel Collins told her that Laura's husband had been called Henry? As Olivia read on, she realised that Laura's deep affection for "A" was unusual since it became clear that the maid was the object of Henry Morton's lust. Wouldn't Laura have been jealous of the girl?

Suddenly, Olivia stopped what she was doing, her mouth open, her heart pounding. She'd just heard a noise downstairs! Then she gave herself a mental shake – what on earth was she worried about? It was probably a hedgehog shuffling about – or maybe even a fox out scavenging. After all, she'd been leaving her leftovers outside the back door for the local wildlife – so why should she be surprised when they availed of it? She was behaving like a silly town-dweller who couldn't sleep unless there was concrete under her feet! Obviously, she still had a lot to learn about the sounds of night in the country.

Nevertheless, she couldn't stop her heart thumping furiously. Oh God, there was the noise again – and it definitely wasn't the sound of roaming wildlife! It sounded like footsteps, there was no doubt about it. What was she going to do? She looked around wildly for the walking stick, then cursed herself for not putting it back where she'd found it the first time. She was unarmed, and there was definitely someone coming up the stairs!

With a crash, the bedroom door was flung open, and Mark Cunningham stood there, his eyes red and glittering, and looking like a man possessed. Olivia cringed, wondering how on earth he'd made such a recovery. Surely he'd have been detained in hospital for several days, at the very least? She could see no visible signs of injury. Then again, she'd read somewhere that people could become possessed of superhuman strength when the occasion demanded it . . . and Mark would undoubtedly be furious with her for felling him with the walking stick the previous night.

"I've lost everything because of you – you fucking bitch!"

Olivia found her voice. "No, Mark – you lost everything because of *you*! If you hadn't been trying to have your cake and eat it, you'd be fine! *You* chose to play around! "

Mark's face was puce with anger. "You ruined it for

238

me with Tara, that night in Temple Bar," he snarled. "And how dare you advise Gwen to get rid of me, just because I gave the stupid cow a few clips around the ear? Why couldn't you have left well enough alone?"

Olivia felt very frightened, but she wasn't going to let Mark detect her fear. "Gwen deserved to know what a bastard you are," she replied angrily, her fear momentarily on hold. "How could you treat her like that? At least if she knew she had support, she could make her own decision about what to do."

"You were just jealous," sneered Mark. "You wanted me all to yourself – and when you found out I was married, you got spiteful about it!"

"Of all the – " Olivia could hardly believe the man's ego. He obviously thought he was God's gift to women! "Mark, let's be straight about this – I wouldn't touch you with a bargepole now. I don't date married men, and that's all there is to it. And I don't like to see other women being hurt either."

"Aah, the great feminist!" said Mark malevolently. "Willing to wreck other people's marriages in defence of the little woman!"

"Your wife – soon to be your ex-wife, I hope – is no little woman," Olivia retorted. "Hopefully, she's got the guts to give you the heave-ho!"

"You smug, self-satisfied, man-hating bitch!" Mark screamed, spittle running from the corner of his mouth, and Olivia briefly thought of a rabid dog.

Grabbing her arm roughly, he thrust his face into hers, and Olivia saw that the blue eyes she'd once thought so gorgeous were now filled with hatred.

"Not so long ago, you were gagging for it!" Mark

ranted. "That night in the stables, you couldn't get enough of me!"

Olivia felt only relief that they'd been prevented from going the whole way that night, thanks to Barney McDaid's heart attack.

"That was before I knew that you were married, Mark!"

"Aha! So I was quite acceptable when you thought I was someone you could get your claws into?" he sneered. "A single man with a nice little hotel business you could muscle in on!"

"Don't be ridiculous, Mark – I never thought of you that way – that may be the way *your* mind works, but I – "

Suddenly, he grabbed her by the hair, and pressed his face even closer to hers. As he tried clumsily to kiss her, she pulled back from him. His unpleasant breath was making her gag.

"Get away from me, Mark. Don't be stupid!"

"Stupid? I was stupid to have anything to do with you, bitch! Now that my marriage is probably over – destroyed by you, you evil cow – I'll soon be single again, just like you wanted me to be! So now, at last, I'm going to give you what you were begging for in the stables!"

"No, Mark, please!"

Dragging her across the room, he flung her down on the bed, and began tearing off her pyjama top. Olivia kicked him as hard as she could, but she was no match for his strength. As he pinned down her arms, she tried to bite him. But he retaliated by biting her ear, so hard that she thought she might pass out. His anger seemed to have fuelled him with superhuman strength, and she knew without a shadow of a doubt that Mark intended raping her. It would be his revenge for what he perceived she had done to him.

In desperation, Olivia tried to adopt a softly-softly approach, in the hope that it might diffuse the situation, and Mark might yet come to his senses. "Mark!" she managed to gasp. "Please, stop right now! Before you do something you'll regret!"

"You might regret it, bitch," he rejoined, "but I'm going to do what I should have done before now – teach you a much-needed lesson!"

As he began dragging down her pyjama bottoms, Olivia kicked him repeatedly, but he was much too strong for her. As he pushed himself between her legs while undoing his trousers, she let out a blood-curdling scream. It was unlikely that anyone would hear, since the house was off the main road and fairly isolated. But her only hope was that the shock of hearing her scream might momentarily throw Mark off balance, giving her a few seconds to push him off and run for the door…

As Olivia continued screaming, she became aware of the sound of feet pounding up the stairs, then movement on the landing outside, and finally strong hands were pulling Mark off her.

She sobbed with relief as Philip Lynch, in his Garda uniform, grabbed Mark in an arm lock and threw him onto the floor. Mark had been so engrossed in attacking Olivia that he'd been oblivious to anything happening around him. Now, the reality of his situation dawned on him, and a look of horror spread over his face.

"Olivia, tell him that it was all a joke – I didn't mean any harm," he begged, as Philip handcuffed his arms behind his back.

"Shut up!" said Philip contemptuously. "Olivia, are you Okay? I'll send for back-up straight away, and we'll get a female officer to take a statement and look after you. Are either Maggie or Barbara around?"

Olivia shook her head.

Immediately, Philip got on his radio and arranged for a patrol car in the area to be dispatched immediately to Bay Tree House.

Suddenly, Olivia realised that she was shaking from head to toe, and couldn't stop, no matter how she tried. Philip wrapped her duvet around her shoulders, and gave her a sympathetic smile. "As the arresting officer, I have to take this guy to the Garda station. But I'll drop back later, to check that you're Okay." He squeezed her arm gently. "You're in shock, Olivia – which isn't surprising, after what you've been through."

Mark sat whimpering on the floor. "I didn't mean it," he blubbed. "It was all a joke!"

"Save your explanations," said Philip briskly. "I'm arresting you for the attempted rape of Olivia Casey." He pulled Mark to his feet. "As soon as back-up arrives, I'll be taking you to the local station, where you'll spend the night in a cell, before being questioned first thing tomorrow morning."

A few minutes later, the patrol car with two police officers in it arrived, and a female officer took Olivia's statement, while the other one treated her bitten ear and brought her a strong cup of tea, with lots of sugar in it to ward off shock. Then Philip departed, taking Mark off to the police station in his patrol car. To Olivia, everything felt totally unreal. It was like living in a dream, from which she'd eventually awaken, and everything would be back to normal.

Despite assuring the two Gardai that she was feeling all right and could cope on her own, Olivia nevertheless felt very vulnerable, but she didn't want them to think that she was the stereotypical hysterical female! Right now, all she wanted was to curl up in bed and go asleep. She needed time alone to come to terms with what had happened, without her two friends fussing around her. She felt strangely detached from everything, but she realised that this was probably the way her mind was dealing with the shock of what had happened.

Eventually, the two Gardai left, and Olivia made herself another cup of tea. She felt shattered, and aghast that she seemed to be no longer able to judge character accurately. How had she been so taken in by Mark's charm? Why hadn't she seen though his shallow, self-serving nature? Then again, she wasn't the only woman who'd been fooled by him – the woman at the restaurant had been another casualty. Olivia now recalled guiltily that the woman had advised her to contact the police, but she'd felt well able to deal with the matter herself. She shuddered. How wrong could anyone be! Then again, she'd never expected Mark to go so far. Obviously, he'd been determined to have his revenge, since he'd tried to attack her twice!

Olivia jumped when she heard the doorbell ring, but realised with relief that it was probably Philip returning. Then, as a thought occurred to her, she smiled for the first time since Mark had attacked her. Maggie would be furious at having missed the opportunity of chatting up Philip yet again!

"Everything okay?" asked Philip as he stepped into

the hall.

Olivia nodded, still wrapped in her duvet, and Philip followed her through to the kitchen, where he put the kettle on again, and made them both mugs of strong tea.

"Thanks again for saving me, Philip," she said gratefully. "I never thought anyone would hear me scream, but thank goodness you did. But why on earth were you here in the first place?"

"I was driving home, and decided to check on you," he told her. "I was a bit concerned about you being here on your own – especially since the chimneybreast wall hadn't been filled in yet. But when I saw that the lights were off, I assumed the house was either empty or you'd already gone to asleep, so I was about to leave – until I heard you scream."

Olivia shuddered. If she hadn't screamed, Philip would have driven off in his patrol car and she'd have been raped by Mark Cunningham!

He smiled gently. "I guessed you were feeling a bit jittery, especially after the way you whacked poor old Brendan Warren over the head last night."

"Wh-what?"

Philip looked surprised, then a smile spread across his face. "Nobody's told you? The guy you thought was an intruder yesterday – it was only poor old Brendan, calling to see you. I only heard about it when I came on duty this morning. The police car that answered your distress call was from outside the area, so they didn't recognise him," said Philip, grinning. "He had quite a job convincing them that he wasn't Mark Cunningham, and you gave him quite a headache too, by all accounts! Enough to put him in hospital!"

"Oh my God!" Olivia put her head in her hands. "He must absolutely hate me!"

It was all too much for Olivia, and suddenly she was sobbing loudly.

Philip patted her shoulder. "C'mon – it was an accident. I suspect that if you turned up at the hospital to wish Brendan well, he'd be willing to forgive you. He's a very decent fellow, you know." Philip went to the kettle, brought it to the boil once again and poured them both another mug of tea. "But how on earth did that weirdo, Mark Cunningham, end up here this evening?"

Olivia's sobs were now abating. "I met him when we went to stay at that hotel."

Philip looked guilty. "Oh God – I recommended that place, didn't I?"

Olivia dismissed his concern with a wave of her hand. "That's not important – what *is* important is that he tried to rape me, in punishment for advising his wife to leave him because he was hitting her. And it's obviously him who's been making the silent calls to my phone."

Olivia could feel herself blushing, but she wasn't about to tell Philip Lynch how close she'd come to succumbing to Mark's charms herself!

Philip raised an eyebrow. "Why didn't you tell me about these phone calls before now? Nobody needs to put up with that kind of treatment! I could have given him a warning, for starters. That's usually a sufficient deterrent."

"I thought I could handle it," said Olivia humbly. "I never thought he'd actually try to harm me." Gratefully, she took a mouthful of tea. "What happens next, Philip?"

"He'll cool his heels in a cell for tonight, then

tomorrow morning he'll be questioned, and a file prepared for the Director of Public Prosecutions. Then, if we receive directions from the DPP to proceed, we'll bring the case to court."

"How long does all this take? And where will Mark be during this time?"

"I'm afraid that after questioning, Mark will be released while we wait for the DPP's office to give us directions, which could take three to four months. Then we might get into court by early next year."

Olivia looked appalled. "You mean – Mark will be free to continue hassling me?"

"Well, given what's happened, he'd be a stupid man to try," said Philip firmly, "because harassment is also a criminal offence. I'm sure you'll be perfectly safe, Olivia."

Olivia wasn't quite so sure, but she said nothing. Hopefully the threat of an impending court case would keep Mark from doing anything foolish.

"Thanks, Philip – for everything," she said. "I daren't think what might have happened if you hadn't turned up when you did. Will I have to appear in court?"

"I'll be the main witness, but your testimony will also be invaluable," said Philip. "The public need to be protected from people like him."

Olivia nodded, thinking what a kind, decent and likeable man Philip was. Hopefully, he could one day love her dear friend Maggie . . .

"Philip, are you married?" Olivia startled herself by the directness of her question.

"No, I'm not," said Philip, smiling. "Why do you ask?"

Olivia blushed. "Oh, no reason – just curiosity." But

inwardly, she was delighted – now she'd be able to tell Maggie the good news!

"But I'll let you in on a little secret, Olivia," added Philip, smiling. "There's someone that I really like, and I'm hoping to do something about it very soon." He grinned. "So hopefully, I won't be a singleton for too much longer!"

He grinned happily and went off to make another mug of tea, while Olivia's heart plummeted. What on earth did he mean by that? She'd been trying to find out if Maggie had a chance with him, and now she was even more confused! Was he referring to Maggie, or was there some other woman whom he'd set his sights on? Olivia fumed. She was still no closer to an answer . . .

Suddenly, she realised that Philip was speaking to her. "Have you contacted either Maggie nor Barbara to stay with you tonight?"

Olivia shook her head.

"Then why don't you think about going back to your mother in Dublin tonight? Or will I phone her and ask her to come here?"

Olivia shook her head vehemently. She couldn't bear the thought of her mother fussing! She'd end up trying in vain to calm her own mother, which wouldn't do either of them any good. "Look, I'll be fine here, Philip – honestly. Now that Mark's locked up, at least for tonight, I won't be so worried. Besides, the chimneybreast wall should be rebuilt within the next few days. Then, hopefully the house will be intruder-proof."

"But you're still in shock, Olivia. I don't think it's a good idea for you to stay here alone."

"I'm okay, really – "

Philip took out his radio and rang a number. Olivia, deep in thought, wasn't actually listening, until he ended the call by saying "Thanks, Gran".

"Right," he said, smiling as he came off the phone, "you're going to stay with my grandmother tonight."

"But – "

Philip gave an exasperated grin. "Come on, Olivia – what you need right now is to feel safe, and get a good night's sleep! Gran's place is only down the road, and she's looking forward to having you."

Olivia doubted that Mrs Collins would be waiting to welcome her with open arms, but grudgingly she gave in, knowing that Philip was right. She was also grateful to him for realising that she needed support without making an issue of it. Quickly she went upstairs, and as she threw her toothbrush and a change of clothes into a holdall, she considered once again what a nice man Philip Lynch was. He really would be just perfect for Maggie . . .

CHAPTER 34

"You're very welcome," said Carmel Collins, as her grandson deposited Olivia on her doorstep, and wished them both goodnight before heading off. "You've been through a terrible ordeal."

"I'm sorry to trouble you so late at night, Mrs Collins – I mean, Carmel."

"Come in, child, and sit down – here, let me rake up the fire in the grate. Put a piece of turf on, will you, Olivia? While I make us a pot of tea."

Gratefully, Olivia sat down beside the hearth in Carmel Collins' large living room. Selecting a piece of turf from the basket beside the fire, she threw it on and watched gratefully as it connected with the hot smouldering ashes and burst into flame. There was nothing quite as cosy as a real fire when you were chilled to the bone. Right now, Olivia felt tired, cold and strung out. It had been a horrific night, and all she wanted to do now was sleep. Thankfully, Carmel Collins was just as unlikely to want to chat. Judging by her night attire, it

249

was obvious to Olivia she'd either been in bed or heading to bed herself.

Soon, the two women were drinking their cups of tea, Carmel Collins fussing and repeatedly voicing her concern over Olivia's ordeal, and expressing relief that the perpetrator was behind bars – at least for one night. In fact, Olivia sensed that the woman was happy to talk about any topic, as long as it didn't involve Laura Morton, Ada or Bay Tree House.

Eventually, Carmel Collins showed Olivia to her room, and Olivia happily viewed the big double bed with big, plumped-up pillows and freshly laundered sheets. She knew she'd be fast asleep just as soon as her head hit the pillow.

"Thank you, Carmel," she said sincerely. "I'm sure I'll sleep like a log!"

But contrary to what she expected, Olivia found herself unable to sleep right away. Her mind was filled with frightening images, and she tried to blot out the images of Mark screaming at her, holding her down and biting her ear. She shuddered as she allowed herself to think about what might have happened if Philip's intervention hadn't been so timely.

And Brendan Warren. She was overwhelmed with guilt as she remembered the blow she'd struck his skull, thinking he was Mark. He must be furious with her. The thought that he hated her made her feel quite miserable. But why had he been creeping around Bay Tree House so late in the evening? And after such a long time? He hadn't bothered to contact her in weeks, and had stood her up after inviting her to his cottage. It was all very weird.

Olivia felt herself getting angry. Was sort of game was he playing? Suddenly, Olivia jolted upright in the bed. If things had worked out with Brendan, she'd never have got involved with Mark! And she'd have been spared all the trauma and stress as well. So to hell with Brendan Warren, she thought resolutely. He can take a hike as far as I'm concerned. She was sorry about his sore head, but what could he expect if he went creeping around people's houses late at night! But as she drifted off to sleep, she couldn't prevent his endearing and cheeky grin from intruding into her dreams . . .

The following morning, she awoke late, to the sounds of Carmel Collins moving around in the kitchen. Still yawning, she dressed, packed her bag and carried it downstairs, now smelling the distinct aroma of a cooked breakfast wafting up towards her.

"Ah, there you are," said Carmel Collins, as Olivia walked into the kitchen. "Sit yourself down while I make some toast."

"Hmm, smells wonderful," replied Olivia, "but there was no need for you to go to all this trouble!"

"Any friend of Philip's is a friend of mine," said Carmel Collins cheerily. "He'd want me to take good care of you, wouldn't he?"

The two women ate in relative silence, Olivia longing to ask more about Laura Morton, the baby's skeleton and her great-aunt Ada, but she didn't want to alter the pleasant atmosphere. Besides, she reasoned, it would be rude to bring up such topics while she was availing of Carmel's hospitality.

"So you'll be living in Cloncullen permanently, Olivia?"

Olivia nodded. "I hope so. I just love the house, and it's surprisingly easy to get to the city from here. Besides, since my job involves making a lot of phone calls, I can do many of them from Cloncullen just as easily as in the office. "

Carmel Collins nodded slowly, a faint smile on her lips. "So you'll be seeing a lot more of my grandson, will you?"

Olivia nodded enthusiastically. "Oh yes, I hope so. He's been very kind to me."

Carmel Collins nodded. "He thinks a lot of you too, Olivia."

Surprised at the tone of Carmel Collins' voice, Olivia looked up in surprise. And suddenly, she realised in horror that Carmel thought she fancied him!

"I don't think you understand what I – "

Carmel Collins leaned across and patted her hand. "Oh, don't worry, Olivia – I didn't mean to embarrass you. But I think you and Philip will make a lovely couple. I can see that he's very keen on you – I mean, he more or less told me so himself."

Olivia blanched. This was her worst nightmare! Maggie was mad about this guy, so what was she supposed to do? She liked Philip, but certainly didn't fancy him in the way that Maggie did, and would never double-cross a friend anyway.

Her mind went into overdrive. Maybe because she'd asked Philip if he was married, he'd thought she was interested in him! Was that what he'd meant about ending his single status in the near future? Did that mean he was going to make some declaration to *her* soon? Oh God – what was she going to do? She'd have to avoid

Philip in the immediate future, in order to prevent him from making any announcement that might embarrass them both.

Olivia found that she'd suddenly lost her appetite. How on earth was she going to extricate herself from this embarrassing situation? She desperately needed to get out of Carmel Collins' house as fast as she could, before Philip's grandmother made any further awkward pronouncements, or Philip himself turned up and offered to take her home! On the other hand, given Carmel's hospitality, it would be difficult to do that without appearing rude.

"Excuse me, Carmel – I really need to be going," said Olivia, pushing her chair back from the table after what she considered a decent interval, and leaving her breakfast half-eaten. "I've just remembered that I'm supposed to meet someone this morning. Thank you for everything – I hope I'll see you again soon."

Carmel Collins stood up with difficulty, and followed Olivia to the front door where she'd left her overnight bag. "Of course we'll see you again soon," she said cheerfully. "You're almost family now, aren't you?"

Olivia thanked her again, and without looking back headed down the road and away from Carmel Collins' house as fast as she could.

Back within the confines of Bay Tree House, she felt safe. Well, relatively safe, now that Mark had been charged with attempted rape. Nevertheless, she'd need to get the back wall filled in as quickly as possible. Just in case there were any other lunatics marauding around the Cloncullen area. She sighed. And now she had the added problem of dealing with Philip Lynch as well . . .

CHAPTER 35

The last few weeks of Ada's pregnancy were particularly draining. She felt continually tired, yet perversely Henry Morton always needed some job to be done that involved Ada climbing stairs or staying continually on her feet. If it wasn't his trousers needing to be pressed, it was his boots that needed polishing – to his own exacting standards – and she often found herself almost asleep on her feet. So much for being Laura's maid! Henry seemed to delight in ensuring that Ada never had a chance to sit down, although Mrs Collins tried to intervene on several occasions, offering to do the jobs herself. Nevertheless Henry Morton insisted that they all had to be done by Ada.

Luckily, when her labour finally started, Henry Morton was sleeping off a large Sunday lunch, which he'd washed down with several generous glasses of port.

"Oh God, will these pains ever go away?" Ada groaned, clinging to Mrs Collins' arm. Both women were in the scullery off the kitchen, where Ada normally slept, as Ada clutched her stomach in agony. "Is this baby ever going to come?"

"Hush, Ada, for God's sake – don't let Henry Morton hear you!" whispered Mrs Collins, "I really think we should get you to the county hospital. They're better able to deal with situations like this. Besides, it's your first baby, and there could be complications."

"I don't want to go there – they make you suffer if you're not married."

"You're not serious, are you?" said Mrs Collins.

"I am – I heard it from other women at the convent laundry," said Ada defiantly, "and they should know, because their babies were delivered there. So I'm not going to hospital – no matter what you say!"

"All right, as long as you think you can cope with the pain."

"They wouldn't give me anything to relieve the pain in hospital anyway – their aim is to let women suffer, in order to pay for their 'sin'."

"All right, try to relax, Ada – I won't make you go anywhere you don't want to."

"Oooh God!" Ada let out a scream, then stifled it lest Henry Morton should hear. Hopefully, he was still sleeping off his lunch, and wouldn't surface for several hours yet.

"Here – bite on this cloth," said Mrs Collins, handing Ada a clean kitchen towel. "Look, I'm going to have to leave you for a few minutes – I need to let Mrs Morton know what's happening. She'll be worried, since I haven't been upstairs for at least an hour."

"Oh please be quick, Mrs Collins," begged Ada. "I won't know what to do if the baby comes while you're gone!"

Racing quickly but quietly up the several flights of stairs, Mrs Collins hurried into Laura Morton's room.

"Any news yet?" Laura whispered, trying to pull herself up

on her pillows.

"Not yet," said Mrs Collins. "The first is always the longest labour. Poor girl – she's only a child herself."

"Oh God, I feel so useless lying here!" said Laura, her face full of anguish. "You've got to get the baby out of the house before Henry hears about it! You know how livid he was when he discovered that the nuns had given him a girl who was pregnant."

Mrs Collins nodded. "We've agreed that as soon as it's born, I'll take it to the orphanage and say that I found it. It's not an ideal situation, but there's not much else we can do. I can hardly take it home to my own husband and son!"

"Please tell Ada that I'm thinking of her, will you?" said Laura, tearfully, clutching Mrs Collins' hand. "I wish there was something I could do to help!"

"I'll bring your tea up in a few minutes, Mrs Morton, just as soon as I've made sure that Ada is all right."

"Forget about the tea, Mrs Collins!" said Laura, a note of hysteria entering her voice. "Oh God, I wish I could do something useful, instead of lying here like the useless lump that I am!"

"Don't say that, Mrs Morton," said Mrs Collins. "You're already looking a lot healthier since Ada started you on the fruit – it's already bringing a bloom to your cheeks."

"Thanks, Mrs Collins, you and Ada have been a great support to me. But please – go back downstairs and help Ada!"

*   *   *

There were no sounds coming from the kitchen as Carmel Collins hurried downstairs again. Undoubtedly that was a good sign – Ada must have calmed down and her contractions had eased, at least for a little while. Nevertheless it was obvious she was close to giving birth, and Mrs Collins hoped that it would be straightforward, and without any complications when the time came.

Suddenly Mrs Collins jumped with fright as Henry Morton came up the back stairs, but he said nothing, simply grinning malevolently at her as they passed each other. Her heart began thumping uncomfortably. What was Henry Morton doing down there? Normally, a heavy lunch put him into a deep sleep for several hours! She desperately hoped he hadn't been down in the kitchen, for he'd surely have heard Ada's groans if he had.

Down in the darkness of the kitchen, Mrs Collins allowed her eyes a few moments to adjust to the gloom. Then she heard the sound of quiet sobbing coming from the scullery. Inside, Ada lay on her bed, her face white as a sheet.

"What's happened?" Mrs Collins asked urgently, suddenly noticing streaks of blood on the floor and on the bedclothes. "My God, Ada – have you given birth already? Let me see the child!"

"He's taken it, Mrs Collins, he's taken my baby!" Suddenly, Ada was hysterical.

"Who's taken it?"

"Mr Morton's taken it!" Ada screamed hysterically. "He came into the kitchen just as I was giving birth, and he broke my baby's little neck! It only had time to make one little cry, then he twisted its neck, and it was dead!"

A fresh bout of crying assailed Ada and she lay sobbing in Mrs Collins' arms.

"Dear God, what's the world coming to?" said Mrs Collins, rocking Ada back and forth, soothing her as she would a young child. She felt overwhelmed by rage, yet powerless to do anything about it. "Why did he do it? What did he say?"

Ada gulped, another sob catching in her throat. "He laughed and said he wasn't having someone else's bastard in his house. He wrapped it in the tea towel you gave me, and said he was going to dump it!"

For a long time, Ada sobbed hysterically , and Mrs Collins held her tightly in her arms, rocking backwards and forwards, as though this movement could somehow stop all the sadness that had overwhelmed both women.

Tears ran silently down Mrs Collins' cheeks, and she prayed that Ada would somehow be strong enough to survive the appalling treatment she'd received at Henry Morton's hands. And that poor innocent little baby – denied a life simply because it had been to be born on the wrong side of the blanket!

At last, Mrs Collins managed to clear the lump in her throat. "Ada – did you get a chance to see –" She gulped again. "I mean, was it a boy or a girl?"

"It was a little girl."

Mrs Collins let out a groan, which she quickly tried to stifle. "Then maybe it's for the best, my dear," she whispered. "I'm sure you think that's a very harsh thing to say, but what kind of life would she have had – carrying the so-called 'sin' of her birth around with her? Life isn't kind to women, you know."

Ada sat up and made an attempt to dry her red eyes. Her heart was breaking, and she wondered if she'd ever know a moment's happiness again. "Do you think it'll ever be any different for women, Mrs Collins?"

"It has to change, Ada – some day, it has to change."

* * *

"My God, Ada – I wish I could have done something to help. Henry's an absolute brute – even I didn't believe he could stoop to something as evil as this."

Ada straightened the sheets on Laura Morton's bed, her eyes red-rimmed from yet another bout of crying. *"I thought of going to the police, Miss Laura, but Mrs Collins said that since the harm had already been done, I'd only get myself into more trouble. Mr Morton would throw me out and I'd end up back with the nuns in the laundry."*

Laura nodded sadly, her own eyes filling with tears. *"Dear God, what an appalling world we live in, Ada! Mrs Collins is right – the sanctity of life only seems to matter when it provides an opportunity to punish women. Believe me, you'd be the one to suffer, not Henry. Somehow, the facts would be twisted to make you the villain."*

"Please don't distress yourself so much, Miss Laura – you'll make yourself very ill again. Can I get you anything?"

"Dear Ada, you really are so kind! Forget about me – you must take care of yourself – you've only just given birth, and need to take things easy for a while. I think you should see the doctor."

"I don't want any doctor near me," said Ada adamantly.

"Please, Ada – humour me. When he calls to see me tomorrow, can I ask him to check that you're okay?"

"I can't, Miss Laura. That horrible Dr Walsh would be bound to mention it to Mr Morton. Then I'd be in even worse trouble."

Laura groaned and bit her lip. *"You're right – I hadn't thought of that. But Ada, you must at least rest. I don't need anything right now, so why don't you go and put your feet up for a while? Henry is out for the rest of the evening, so there won't be anyone checking up on you."*

"Thanks, Miss Laura, but I prefer to keep working. It means that I don't get a chance to think too much about – " Ada's lower lip quivered, and her eyes filled up with tears again, " – about what happened."

"All the same, I want you to rest – that's an order."

The two women looked sadly at each other, acutely aware of each other's pain and impotence.

"All right, Miss Laura," said Ada, "but you'll have to do something for me in return."

"Of course, Ada – if I can."

"You can – and you will, Miss Laura," said Ada with mock authority, attempting to lift the sombre atmosphere for both their sakes. Otherwise, she felt, they would both start crying again and might never be able to stop. "After I've had my rest, I'm going to peel and bring up a nice big orange. And you're going to eat every bit of it!"

Laura nodded, smiling bravely at her friend, then she turned her face to the wall, overwhelmed by emotion. Dear Ada, she thought, how can she think of others when her own heart is breaking? If only I could live long enough to see Ada safe and out of Henry's clutches. . .

CHAPTER 36

The following morning, Olivia decided that before going home to her mother's house in Rathmines, she'd better visit Brendan Warren in the county hospital, and apologise to him for felling him with a walking stick. Her visit to Brendan would also provide an opportunity to make her regular visit to Barney McDaid, who was in another ward of the same hospital.

Olivia felt more than a little apprehensive about visiting Brendan Warren. Despite what Philip had said about him being really nice, Olivia couldn't see how he wouldn't be annoyed at her. Besides, she wasn't too pleased about his behaviour towards her either!

Well, she might as well get it over with. But she wasn't going to grovel – after all, he hadn't even bothered to turn up when he'd invited her to his house! She'd also decided not to mention Mark's attack on *her*, since she didn't want Brendan Warren thinking she'd been such a gullible fool as to be attracted to a married man. Then she felt doubly annoyed with herself – why should she care what he thought?

Olivia approached Brendan Warren's hospital bed with trepidation, since she'd no idea how he was going to react when he saw her.

"Hello, Brendan."

Brendan Warren's brown eyes lit up when he saw her. "My God, is this an apparition I see before me? Just as I'm dreaming of the gorgeous Olivia, she suddenly appears beside my bed. It must be all these drugs they've been pumping me with – I must be hallucinating!"

Olivia couldn't help laughing. Despite the fact that his head was bandaged, and one of his eyes was partially closed due to bruising and swelling, Brendan Warren was as irrepressible – and gorgeous – as ever!

"I owe you an apology," said Olivia contritely. "I'm sorry for hitting you over the head the other night."

"Don't worry, my precious petal, it only goes to prove that you love me. Why else would you club me over the head and try to drag me into your lair? I love your cavewoman approach!"

"I wasn't sure what to bring you," said Olivia, shyly. "So all I could think of was grapes. Not very original, I know, but then I hardly know you, Brendan, and I certainly don't know your tastes."

"Well, you know all about my taste in women – I'm only attracted to females called Olivia, who have long blonde hair, a lovely smile, and whose taste in men hopefully runs to guys called Brendan. Well, preferably, *one* guy called Brendan."

Olivia laughed. From any other man, comments like that would have sounded downright corny. But coming from Brendan, they were amusing. She experienced a delightful tingling sensation as he gazed adoringly at her, and for a second her spirits lifted. But then she realised that a man like Brendan undoubtedly flirted with every woman he met. He was a just a chancer who made dates with women then didn't turn up, so she should just enjoy the banter and accept there was nothing more to it.

"What on earth were you doing creeping around my house late at night?" she asked, trying to look stern.

"I'm sorry if I frightened you, Olivia," Brendan said, looking contrite and rubbing his injured head gingerly, "but it was the first opportunity I'd got to see you! Even though it was late, I didn't want to waste any more time."

"Well, for someone who was in a hurry to see me, you managed to wait quite a few weeks," said Olivia dryly. "Why on earth would you ignore me for so long, then break into my house late at night?"

Brendan sighed, lying back on his pillows and closing his eyes. "It's a long story, my love –"

"Stop calling me your 'love'!" said Olivia, annoyed. "Nothing you're saying makes any sense!"

"It's hard to think straight when you've been bashed over the head," Brendan replied, rubbing his skull gingerly.

"Sorry – I'm being unfair," said Olivia contritely, "but I still don't understand why –"

Before Olivia could continue, the curtains between his bed and the next one were parted, and a vision in pink appeared, accompanied by an enormous basket of fruit. Olivia was immediately embarrassed by her own small bunch of grapes.

"Darling!" The vision in pink descended on Brendan, and planted a series of kisses on his forehead. "You poor,

poor love! Is there anything I can get my little coochy-coo?"

Looking around, she gazed contemptuously at Olivia, pushing her small bunch of grapes out of the way so that her own large basket of fruit could take pride of place on Brendan's bedside locker.

This vision was wearing a tight-fitting pale pink suit, with a skirt so short that it was barely visible beneath the jacket, and displaying her salon-tanned legs almost up as far as her crotch. Olivia studied the woman's legs for streaks, and was peeved that she couldn't find any. Obviously, Ms Pink Vision went to an expensive beauty parlour, she though sourly. The vision also had masses of curly blonde hair, a heavily made-up face, and was around the same age as Olivia.

Brendan smiled beatifically from one woman to the other, then closed his eyes and drifted off to sleep again, leaving the two women glaring at each other.

"I think you'd better go," said the blonde vision. "He needs to rest now. The doctors say he's not to have too much excitement."

Olivia wanted to punch Ms Pink Vision in the middle of her heavily made-up face. How dare the bitch think she can order me around! she thought angrily.

"Did you bring these?" Ms Pink Vision held up Olivia's grapes contemptuously.

"Eh, yes."

"I'm afraid Brendan doesn't like grapes." She wrinkled up her nose as though they smelled badly. "Maybe you should take them home with you."

"Well, just leave them there," said Olivia, smiling grimly back at her. "Maybe some of his other visitors will eat them."

The pink vision said nothing, but as Olivia turned to leave, she saw her grapes being dropped into the wastepaper basket.

As Olivia left the ward, she was furious. How dare that creature treat her so contemptuously! Now she knew why Brendan Warren hadn't contacted her – he'd been off shagging Ms Pink Vision! Olivia despised the bimbo's over-made-up face, and she wanted to go back and scratch her eyes out. She probably wears fur as well, she thought angrily. There was nothing about the woman that Olivia liked, and Brendan Warren was welcome to her! In fact, Olivia thought to herself, I've just had another lucky escape.

CHAPTER 37

Having decided that she wouldn't stay another night in Bay Tree House until the wall in the kitchen had been closed up and an alarm fitted, Olivia got ready to go back to Rathmines. While it was unlikely that she'd have an intruder three nights in a row, she wasn't prepared to take the chance!

Fortunately, the architect had, by now, sorted out the planning glitch, and was arranging for Joe and John to begin rebuilding the chimneybreast wall and adding the sunroom extension within the next few days. An alarm was being installed by one of the leading security companies in the area, and Olivia had already bought a new landline phone with a caller ID facility on it. When she returned to Bay Tree House next weekend, she'd feel safe at last.

Packing an overnight bag upstairs, aided by Maggie and Barbara, who'd both rushed down to Cloncullen that afternoon when they'd heard what had happened, Olivia tried to be upbeat, and make light of the inconvenience.

"Maybe I'll go and stay at the Glen Hotel again," she said, grinning. "Can you imagine Mark's expression if I arrived at the reception desk with my overnight bag?"

"Why don't you stay with me?" asked Maggie, for the millionth time. "My place is newly painted now, and you can have the sofa-bed in the living room."

"Come and stay with me," urged Barbara. "I have a big spare room, so you'll have your own space."

Olivia shook her head to both offers. "No, I'll go home and stay with Mum," she told them. While she loved her friends dearly, right now she wanted complete privacy to sort out her confused thoughts and emotions. She also needed time away from Maggie and her constant references to Philip. And from Philip himself, if she was to believe what Carmel Collins had told her.

She was also still smarting from her experience at the hands of Brendan Warren's bimbo girlfriend. And since she'd never told either Maggie or Barbara about him, she now had no one to console her. To hell with him! But deep down, she was sorely disappointed. That spark between them had only been in her imagination.

When she arrived back at the house in Rathmines, Olivia knew that coming home had been the right thing to do, and she found herself relaxing back into the peace and tranquillity of the home where she grew up. Although she still stayed at her mum's house on weeknights, since it was more convenient for going to work, it nevertheless felt different this time. During the week, she and her mum were like more like flatmates, each of them getting on with their individual lives. But this time, after the shock of Mark's behaviour, what she really needed was the comfort of her mother's unconditional love.

Doreen was understandably supportive of her daughter – and had immediately guessed that the man on the phone during Olivia's previous visit had been the one who'd attacked her. Though still distracted by the demands of her students' mid-term papers, her mother seemed glad to have her around.

In the drawing room, Olivia sat down and turned on the TV. She needed something to distract herself – maybe a comedy show, or a soap. As she flicked through the stations, a medical drama came on the screen, showing an old man being taken to the Intensive Care Ward, and suddenly, she remembered.

Oh no! She'd forgotten all about her promise to visit Barney McDaid! Because she'd been so upset over the way Brendan Warren's girlfriend had treated her, she'd walked out of the hospital without calling to see him! Olivia was furious with herself, since she prided herself on always keeping her word. The poor lonely man had probably been looking forward to having a visitor, and now she'd let him down. She also felt very grateful to him, since he'd inadvertently saved her from having sex with Mark Cunningham!

She leapt up, went out to the kitchen and turned on the kettle. She'd make a cup of tea for her mum and herself.

Doreen was, as ever, engrossed in reams of student essays when Olivia carried two cups of tea upstairs to her mother's study. Nodding her thanks, Doreen returned her attention to the essay she was marking, sipping her tea absent-mindedly as she ringed one area of it with a flourish of her red pen. As Olivia sat opposite her mother and sipped her own tea, momentarily she felt sorry for the poor student whose work was at the receiving end of her mother's displeasure.

Suddenly, Doreen looked up, noting her daughter's glum expression. "You look sad, love. Look, it's going to take a while to get over what happened to you, Livvy, so don't try to rush it."

"Oh, it's not that, Mum. I'm just annoyed with myself, that's all." Olivia hesitated. "I've let someone down – and I don't know what I can do to remedy the situation."

Her mother looked up. "That's not like you, Liv. What exactly have you done – or not done?"

Olivia grimaced. "I met this old guy when I was staying at the Glen Hotel a few weeks ago, and he had a heart attack while Maggie and I were staying there. We went to see him in the county hospital, and we promised we'd go back – but I've forgotten, and now I'm back in Dublin."

"Well, why don't you send him a card? That should do the trick," said her mother, the matter resolved as far as she was concerned. Her attention was once again focussed on the next essay to be corrected.

Olivia sighed. "I supposed you're right. But I feel so guilty. Poor old Barney McDaid seems to be such a lonely man, and I – "

Her mother's head, which had been buried deep in the next essay, suddenly shot up. "Did you say Barney McDaid? Professor Barney McDaid?"

Olivia nodded, looking surprised.

"Oh dear, the poor man," said her mother, taking her reading glasses off. "What hospital is he in?"

Olivia told her mother, who had suddenly started

fussing around, moving papers about aimlessly.

"Mum, do you know him?"

Her mother's face went a deep shade of pink. "Eh – yes. Many years ago – he was a lecturer in the Department when I was a PhD student."

Olivia smiled mischievously. "How well did you know him, Mum? Was he a boyfriend?"

Olivia was amazed to see her normally distracted mother turning a deep shade of puce.

"Oh dear – yes, I suppose he was." She blew her nose. "What on earth am I saying? Oh Lord, I thought he was living in Australia. It's just so strange, after all these years . . ."

CHAPTER 38

As the months went by, the three women at Bay Tree House continued to support each other silently, all united in spirit against a common enemy who controlled their lives on a daily basis.

As Laura's personal maid, Ada spent a lot of time in the sick room, reading to her mistress and brushing and plaiting her long fair hair. The bond between them had grown stronger with each passing day.

"I don't know what I'd do if I couldn't write down all my anger and frustration in my diary!" said Laura wearily one day. "You're so good to me, Ada – just knowing that someone believes I can get well makes all the difference."

"You will get well, Miss Laura – I'm sure of it," said Ada confidently, as she slid Laura's diary beneath the mattress, to keep it hidden from the prying eyes of her husband. "Already I can see a change in you. You're a lot stronger than when I first arrived here. Now, you can even sit up unaided."

"Henry and Dr Walsh say that I'm putting a strain on my heart and lungs by sitting up," said Laura, "but lying flat on *my back is so utterly boring! Anyway, Henry only pretends to care when the doctor is around – in fact, neither of them give a damn what happens to me."*

"Couldn't you leave him, Miss Laura? Seeing as you're the one from the wealthy background?"

Laura laughed bitterly. "Oh Ada, you kind soul! But by leaving, my 'sin' would be considered as great as yours. Once you're married, no one cares if you're happy or not! In this country, marriage is forever, and you're expected to make the best of it, no matter what happens. Mr DeValera and the Church think that strong family ties make up the backbone of this country."

"But surely there are exceptions to every rule, Miss Laura?"

"Not in their vision," said Laura bitterly. "And as for those strong family ties – well, mine wouldn't last for five minutes if challenged. If I said that I was leaving Henry, I'd be ostracised by all my relatives. Not that they care about me, anyway."

"Well, Mr DeValera's not in power any longer, Miss Laura, and that nice Dr Browne is trying to improve the health service, isn't he? Maybe we'll see some progress over the next few years."

Laura sighed. "I suspect Dr Browne won't get very far. The Church will soon crush him," she said sadly. "It seems to me that we've simply replaced eight hundred years of English oppression with another lot of oppressors." Suddenly, she laughed hysterically. "As if I could leave Henry, anyway! I can't even get out of this bed unaided!"

Ada looked troubled. "I'd help you, Miss Laura."

"Thanks, Ada – I appreciate your support more than you'll ever know. But I don't expect to be around for long, anyway. He's waiting for me to die, you know."

Ada grimaced. "Don't say that, Miss Laura!"

"Oh, it's true, Ada. He wants an heir, you see, but because of my illness, I haven't been able to oblige him. But as soon as I'm gone, he'll take another bride to the altar in double-quick time."

Ada was shocked. While she herself had suffered for not being married, she hadn't realised that women could suffer within marriage as well.

"I'm only telling you what you know already, Ada," Laura replied acerbically, "Henry does exactly what he wants – no doubt he's already out looking for a new wife and spending my money to do it!"

Suddenly noticing that Ada had turned pale, Laura looked at her friend in alarm. "Ada, are you feeling all right? You don't look well. Sit down, for heaven's sake!"

"I'll be fine in a minute, Miss Laura," said Ada quickly. "I just felt a bit light-headed for a momen."

Ada sat down on the edge of the bed, Laura surveying her anxiously. It was a constant worry to her that Ada might develop TB through being constantly in the sick-room with her. However, Laura now noticed that far from becoming emaciated, Ada had actually put on weight . . . Laura's hand flew to her mouth. It couldn't be, dear God, not again!

"Ada" she asked urgently, looking pointedly at Ada's expanding waist, "Ada, please tell me that Henry hasn't . . ."

Her voice trailed off, as Ada hung her head in shame. "I'm sorry, Miss Laura – I wasn't going to say anything to you about it, at least not for the present." Tears filled her eyes. "It happened ages ago, and I kept hoping that if I pretended to myself that it was just a bad dream, I mightn't get pregnant this time – "

"There's nothing to apologise for," said Laura staunchly.

"Oh God, Ada – what are we going to do?" She laughed mirthlessly. "Well, I know what I'm going to do – I'm going to die! But you – "

"No, Miss Laura, you're not going to die – I won't let you! I'll do anything to help you get well!"

"Well, isn't this a cosy scene?" Henry Morton stood in the bedroom doorway. "Ada, please leave me and my wife alone."

"Yes, Mr Morton." Ada hurried out of the room, hoping with all her heart that he hadn't overheard her conversation with Laura. Because if he had, they'd both pay for it.

* * *

"It's preposterous, Henry! I won't hear of it!"

Henry Morton smirked at his wife as she lay in her bed. "Then have the decency to die, my dear. You've been lingering far too long for my liking."

"You're a callous and cruel brute!"

He laughed. "And you, my dear, are just a waste of space lying there!"

Laura closed her eyes tightly to stop the tears escaping. "Any man who could kill an innocent baby is morally corrupt and devoid of all decency. And now, this idea of taking Ada's baby and passing it off as ours –" Laura slumped back into her pillows. "I'll bet you haven't even asked Ada!"

"I don't have to – it's my child anyway," said Henry, now pacing the bedroom floor. "Besides, I only want a son. If it's a girl –" He made a slicing gesture across his throat, and Laura felt sick. "And if you insist on staying alive until Ada's given birth, you'd better be willing to pretend it's yours. After all, you haven't fulfilled your marriage vows and given me a son yourself, have you?"

"For pity's sake, I'm ill, Henry!"

"Well, then, since you're spending all your time lolling around in bed, no one will know that you haven't been pregnant."

As he paced the floor, making plans for his future, Laura studied him coldly.

"When do you intend making Ada aware of your plans?"

Henry Morton gave a nasty smile. *"Since when do I need to consult a servant? That slut will surrender the baby if she knows what's good for her. This is the second time she's been pregnant, and she's barely sixteen. What sort of an example would she be to any child? Besides, she has no means, so she can hardly look after it, never mind look after herself."*

Laura was filled with impotent anger. But she forbore to mention that Ada wouldn't have become pregnant the second time, without his own unwelcome intervention. Oh, how she hated this man! And she suddenly realised, with a growing inner fear, that she had to stay alive until Ada's baby was born. Otherwise, Henry would be free to take a new wife – whom he would expect to quickly provide him with an heir – and Ada and the baby she was expecting would no longer be of any use to him. Either way, it seemed that disaster lay ahead.

Henry stopped pacing and stopped beside the bed. *"She's lucky that we took her in,"* he said, with a self-satisfied grin. *"And when we've got the boy, I intend to get rid of her."*

"What do you mean?"

He gave a horrible laugh. *"Well, old Jasper O'Sullivan is looking for another wife. He needs help with the farm, and those eight children need a mother. If she doesn't agree to that, I'll take her back to the nuns in the laundry."*

Laura shuddered. Jasper O'Sullivan was a revolting old man, and a well-known wife-beater. His first wife had been burdened with endless pregnancies, and died in questionable circumstances. It was rumoured in the village that he'd beaten her to death, although the inquest at the time had claimed that her demise was accidental.

"Why are women always the victims?" Laura asked angrily. "How come you're not penalised for making a woman pregnant, but the woman herself pays the price?"

"That's just the way of the world, my dear. It's a man's world, so just accept it." Just before he left the bedroom, he leaned over the bed and smoothed the top sheet. "Besides, from where you are, my dear, I don't see that you have a lot of choice."

* * *

"This baby of yours – "

"Yes, Miss Laura?"

"Henry admits it's his – in fact, he actually told me so himself, and if it's a boy, he wants to rear it as ours."

Ada looked puzzled.

"Ada – he intends taking your child from you, and pretending that I gave birth to it myself!"

"W-what?"

"He says that if I'm not prepared to die and let him find a wife who'll give him an heir, the least I can do is agree to pass off your baby as ours. Then he'll have the heir he's always wanted. Your child will be as much his as any child I could produce, so it doesn't matter to him who the mother is."

Ada knelt down beside the bed and took Laura's hand in hers. "But, Miss Laura – if that's what you want, I'll do it for you. It would probably be best for the baby anyway. After all, I can't afford to look after it myself, and I'd be able to see it regularly anyway."

"No! Oh Ada – can't you see? Oh God, it's difficult to say this, but – "

"What, Miss Laura?"

"Henry only wants a son! If it's a girl . . ." Laura buried her head in the pillows, unable to say any more.

Ada's heart almost stopped. So if the child had the misfortune to be born female, Henry Morton intended the same fate for her that the previous one had suffered.

"And assuming it's a boy, Henry intends getting rid of you as soon as it's born – he wants to marry you off to Jasper O'Sullivan!"

Ada felt sick. She'd heard terrible stories about Jasper O'Sullivan from Mrs Collins. And most people in the town were terrified of him. There was also a rumour that he sexually abused his own children, although no one in the town was prepared to do anything about it.

"Oh no, Miss Laura – I couldn't – I'd kill myself before I'd marry him!"

"Henry says that if you don't agree to that, he'll take you back to the laundry."

Ada began to cry, and Laura, pulling herself up in the bed, gathered her into her arms. "There, there Ada – I won't let either happen to you – no matter what. Look, I'm getting stronger every day – it's all the fresh fruit you bring me – and soon I'll be on my feet again. I promise you, Ada – I won't let anything happen to you. You have my word."

Ada wiped her tears on the handkerchief Laura had produced from under her pillow. "Thank you, Miss Laura – but you'll get into trouble too, if you help me. Oh God, what am I going to do?"

The two women clung to each other, both of them crying, and neither of them having any idea of how they were going to *deal with the developing situation.*

Laura sighed. "Isn't it unbelievable that both of us should be cowered and controlled by that bastard? By virtue of marrying him, I've effectively given him control of my life – and by extension, yours!"

"Hush, Miss Laura – someone might hear you!"

"Maybe it would be a good thing if he knew how much I hate him!"

"No, Miss Laura – he'd only take out his anger on you. And right now, you need all your strength to get well."

Laura sighed. "You're right, Ada – I should always listen to you – you're a tower of strength. As long as Henry doesn't know how close we are, I can learn more about what he intends to do. Then we must make plans for you to leave – I know we can rely on Mrs Collins to help us."

"Yes, of course – she's been very good to me since I came here. She loathes Mr Morton too. But I don't want to leave you, Miss Laura."

"I'll be fine – don't worry about me. It'll make me happy to know that you're safe." Laura sat up, reaching for her fountain pen. "Has Henry gone out?"

Ada nodded. "He's gone out to the pub, so the coast is clear for the next few hours."

"Then get me my diary again, will you, Ada? I'm in just the mood to fill several extra pages today!"

When Ada had retrieved the diary from underneath the mattress, she handed it to Laura.

Laura smiled. "Thanks Ada – now go and put your feet up, and have a rest, yourself." As Ada prepared to leave the room, Laura suddenly looked at her earnestly. "I was just thinking, Ada – wouldn't it be wonderful if Henry died before I did?"

CHAPTER 39

The following weekend, Olivia arrived back at Bay Tree House early on Saturday morning. Now that the alarm had been installed, the back wall closed up and the extension added, she felt totally secure. And she was looking forward to getting on with some more work in the garden.

Maggie and Barbara were both coming down later – in fact, thought Olivia, grinning to herself, it was proving impossible to keep them away! Barbara had traded shifts with her colleague Fergal, who also worked in the Accident and Emergency Department, enabling her to have several weekends free. And now that Maggie had set her cap at Philip Lynch, she intended to be a regular fixture in the area. But where Maggie was concerned, Olivia was deeply apprehensive about what might, or might not happen, in view of what Carmel Collins had said to her. She'd die if Philip expressed his preference for her over Maggie, and she had every intention of ensuring that she was never again alone with him, nor would she ever give him a second's encouragement.

Olivia smiled to herself as she pulled on her Wellingtons. Barbara was still very pissed off at having missed all the excitement when the baby's skeleton had been found. Olivia didn't see it all in quite the same way, but then maybe she was too sensitive and taking it all too personally. But her friends certainly wouldn't allow her to mope for long!

Olivia was also surprised –and pleased – that Barbara hadn't mentioned Richard Devlin for ages. Hopefully, she was finally getting over him. Maybe the happenings at Bay Tree House had distracted Barbara to such an extent that she was beginning to realise that there really was life after Richard Devlin.

Olivia sighed as she made her way to the back field. Her one regret was that she hadn't yet had time to fully study Laura Morton's diaries. Due to the unfortunate events at Bay Tree House, necessitating her sudden departure to her mother's house, she'd put the reading of the diaries on hold. Now she was hoping – in fact, longing – to decipher them, and learn anything she could about Laura Morton's life. And hopefully, by extension, about her great-aunt Ada.

In fact, she wished she could get going on them straightaway, but the imminent arrival of her friends made it impossible. She didn't want anyone else to know about them yet – it was her little secret, and it made her feel close to Laura Morton. Hopefully, she'd get a chance to go through the diaries later that night in the privacy of her own room. Although she'd only just got started on the second diary before the arrival of her unexpected visitors, the references to someone called "A" had sent a shiver of excitement up her spine. Could this possibly be her long-lost great aunt?

Olivia glanced at her watch. In another hour or so, Maggie and Barbara would be arriving. In the meantime though, she intended getting some work done!

Olivia loved being outdoors and, opening the back door, she eagerly drew the fresh air into her lungs. There was a hint of salt in the air, and Olivia resolved to take a walk along the nearby beach as soon as possible.

Not for the first time, she recalled how lucky she was. Not only had she been given a house, but she couldn't have chosen a more dream location! Bay Tree House was right on the coast, yet within easy reach of the city, situated in a quaint little town, and she had loads of land to develop as she saw fit.

Her first plan was to establish a wild flower meadow alongside the orchard, where insects, birds, butterflies and other wildlife would be welcome. Her land would be a special area where no fertilizer or pesticides would be used, and she'd maintain the old hedgerows around the property so that wildlife could continue to live happily within it.

After a week spent in a busy office, Olivia was craving the chance to work outside in the fresh air. Fortunately the weather was dry and the forecast for the weekend was good, so she was looking forward to turning sods in her own garden, and feeling like a genuine countrywoman! Resolutely grabbing the biggest spade in her arsenal of new garden implements, she headed across the yard. She took a deep breath and filled her lungs with the smell of grass, moss and cow manure. It was wonderful! No doubt, seasoned country folk didn't notice these smells any longer, but to Olivia they were delightful after a week spent choking on city fumes.

It was also a lot more satisfying to work up a sweat doing something useful, as opposed to using machines in a gym. This way, Olivia thought, I'm keeping fit and improving the place at the same time!

She hoped her grandmother and Uncle Eddie would visit the house soon. Neither of them had seen the place yet, but she hoped they'd like the few changes she'd made to update the house and make it more comfortable. She realised that their reluctance was linked to the possibility that Ada had something to do with the house, although Olivia herself had found no direct proof of it. Hopefully, the reference to "A" in the diaries might eventually yield the necessary proof.

The smell of freshly turned earth was deeply satisfying and Olivia smiled to herself as she dug, imagining the comments that Maggie and Barbara would make when they found her knee-deep in soil! She was anxious to get as much soil turned as she could before they arrived, since they both possessed a remarkable ability to distract her from whatever she was doing!

As she worked, Olivia was pleased to discover that the soil beneath all the rubble was actually of very good quality, so her trees would hopefully grow healthy and strong. As well as planting a selection of native trees, Olivia had also decided to plant a few oak trees – which she'd already grown on her office windowsill, from acorns found in her local city park – as a gesture towards the future. Even though she herself would be long dead before these slow-growing trees reached maturity, there was a certain comfort in planning a continuity beyond herself. Maybe my children will see them grow tall and spreading, she thought, and was pleased by such a thought.

The thought of a having a family suddenly brought an image of Brendan Warren into her mind, but she dismissed it just as quickly. She'd been a fool to think that he'd really meant it when he said he'd fancied her. He'd merely been flirting with her, and she'd fallen for it, hook line and sinker. Clearly, he was the kind of guy who flirted with every woman he met, and it was evident that Ms Pink Vision had already staked her claim there. She was welcome to him! Brendan Warren had put up no opposition when the blonde bombshell had pushed Olivia's grapes to the back of the bedside locker, then binned them. To hell with him, she thought, for the millionth time. She'd better things to do with her time than waste it thinking about someone like him!

When Maggie and Barbara arrived together in Maggie's car just after midday, Olivia had finished her digging and had just availed of the new shower she'd recently had installed. When she heard the car, she quickly dressed and hurried downstairs to meet them.

"I'm relieved that you're finished the digging," said Maggie, hugging her friend. "I hope that means we're going to have a nice, leisurely weekend."

"Well, one thing we're not going to do is spend it talking about Philip Lynch," said Barbara. "I'd rather dig up one of Olivia's fields with my nose, than listen to you rabbitting on about him all weekend!"

Olivia smiled. She was glad that she'd never mentioned Brendan Warren to either of them. She'd keep her venomous thoughts about him and his bimbo to herself.

"I've got a very exciting plan for this afternoon," she told them, as they both looked at her expectantly. "We're going shopping for bedroom carpets!"

* * *

As the three women left the carpet store in the business park, where Olivia had selected carpets for all the bedrooms at Bay Tree House, Gwen was coming out of the Cash & Carry pushing a trolley full of produce for the hotel. Initially, when she saw Olivia, Maggie and Barbara, she tried to hide behind the mound of toilet rolls, groceries, kitchen and bathroom cleaning products she was wheeling towards her car. But Olivia called out her name, so she had no option but to acknowledge the greeting.

"Oh, hello," she said, then turned away to begin loading the produce into the boot of her car.

Olivia walked over to her. "How are you, Gwen – how is your arm?"

"It's fine, thank you."

Olivia introduced Barbara to Gwen, and the two women shook hands. As the two women exchanged pleasantries, Olivia and Maggie both noticed that while Gwen's earlier injury had healed, she was now sporting a fresh bruise on her other arm. Realising that they'd seen it, Gwen quickly tried to pull her sleeve down over it.

"Is Mark up to his usual tricks?" asked Olivia angrily.

Gwen opened her mouth, then closed it again, knowing that it was useless to deny it.

Suddenly, Olivia and Maggie locked eyes over the top of Gwen's head. They'd realised simultaneously that

Mark obviously hadn't told Gwen about his impending court case, or that he was likely to be charged with attempted rape.

"Mark hasn't told you, has he?" said Olivia quietly.

"Told me what?"

"That he's been charged with attempted rape."

"W-what?"

"He attacked me in my own house, but luckily the police intervened in time," said Olivia, feeling deeply sorry for Gwen. It was clear that she had no idea what her husband had been up to.

At first, incredulity registered on Gwen's face, then her expression turned to one of anger. "You're making it up, because you want Mark for yourself! He told me that you came on to him, and that you're angry because he rejected you!"

"Look, Gwen – you've got to face facts," Maggie intervened gently. "Since you married him, Mark has been constantly chatting up other women."

Gwen stared defiantly at the three women. "I know that Mark flirts with the woman customers to make them enjoy their stay. He says it's good for business."

"And you're happy about that?"

"Well, no – but we need to build up the hotel clientele."

Olivia sighed. "I'm afraid Mark's antics go much further than mere flirtation. He tried to seduce me in the stables when we stayed at your hotel – and Maggie, Barbara and I met him in a restaurant last week, with another woman."

For a second, Gwen looked angrily at the three women. "Why should I believe you? You're just making that up. Mark would never do that – he goes to visit his mother when he's up in Dublin!"

"Why can't you face the truth, Gwen? Are you going to keep pretending that everything's okay?" asked Maggie gently. "Could you endure a lifetime of him hitting you, and having flings with other women behind your back – in a business like yours, he's got a regular captive audience!"

Gwen said nothing, staring defiantly from one woman to another.

"Surely you must have suspected that something was wrong," said Maggie gently. "Had you really no idea that there were other women in his life?"

Gwen looked at the ground, and suddenly her composure crumpled. As her eyes filled up with tears, she raised her head and looked forlornly at the trio of friends. "Well, just after we were married, I got an STD . . ."

"A sexually transmitted disease?" said Olivia, raising her eyebrows.

Gwen nodded, wiping away a tear. "Mark told me I'd probably got it from a lavatory seat. Until now, I blanked out the possibility that he could have given it to me." She looked across at the others. "We both had to be treated, and he was so kind and nice to me that *I* started feeling guilty, wondering if he was having suspicions about *me!*"

"Well, Gwen, it's time you faced facts and claimed back your life. Your husband is a bully and a sexual predator," said Olivia firmly. "He'll destroy your life, and ruin your hotel business if you don't do something about it. Do you really think guests will want to stay there when details of the attempted rape case come to court?"

"W-when is the court case?"

"It probably won't be for a few months yet. So you've some time to think about it and make decisions. But I wouldn't wait too long, if I were you. I'd see a solicitor as soon as possible."

Gwen nodded slowly. Although she hadn't been able to do it for herself, she would fight tooth and nail for the hotel she loved so dearly.

"If you need any help – " said Barbara,

"Or a shoulder to cry on – " added Maggie,

"We'll be there for you," finished Olivia, handing her a card with her phone numbers on it.

"Thank you," Gwen said, her eyes filling with tears.

CHAPTER 40

Richard Devlin was walking along the main street in Cloncullen, a small child holding his hand. When she saw him, Olivia tried to cross the road to avoid speaking to him. But she had to wait for a tractor to rumble slowly by, which gave Richard time to spot her and call out her name.

"Olivia – can I talk to you for just a minute? Please."

Olivia stood there until they caught up with her.

"Olivia, this is Jack – my son," Richard said, introducing the solemn little boy who was holding his hand tightly, and clutching a toy train engine in the other.

Olivia was stunned to discover that Richard had a child. And horrified as to how she would relay this information to Barbara. Yet in spite of herself, she couldn't resist bending down to say hello to the little boy. After all, it wasn't the child's fault that his father was a low-life.

Straightening up again, she stared frostily at Richard. "Well, what do you want to say to me? You'd better make it quick – I'm in a hurry."

"I-I don't know that I can tell you everything in just a few minutes, but I'm really sorry about what happened between Barbara and me – "

"Save your excuses, Richard. Now, I really must be going – "

"It's a long story, Liv – I just hoped you'd give me a chance to explain a few things. Any time I've tried to talk to Barbara, she just cuts me off."

"Can you blame her?" Olivia retorted. "In her position, I'd do the very same."

"How is she?"

"Barbara's fine. She's going out with a very nice guy at the moment – so I think it's best that you leave well enough alone. She's happy at last – I don't want you spoiling it all for her."

"Liv, honestly, I don't want to intrude into her life – I know that wouldn't be fair. Barbara deserves to be happy, but I just wanted you – her – to know what really happened. I'm not denying that I'm responsible for so much heartache, but – "

"So you want her to give you absolution?" Olivia replied tartly.

He inclined his head sadly, accepting the rebuff. "I just want her to understand exactly what happened. I'm just tired of everyone thinking of me as the bastard. It wasn't like that – although I know I hurt Barbara deeply."

"You did – and none of her friends will ever forgive you either. So what's the point of saying anything? Save your breath, Richard."

"Liv, please – just five minutes."

Olivia looked exaggeratedly at her watch. "Okay –

five minutes."

The local teashop wasn't very crowded, so they found a corner table easily. Richard's little boy sat quietly in his seat as Richard went to the counter to order coffees, and Olivia smiled encouragingly at him, but got no response. He just continued to stare solemnly back at her, while running his toy train engine up and down the table.

"How old is your son?" she asked Richard as he returned to the table with their coffees.

"He's four."

Doing quick mental arithmetic, Olivia's brain registered shock and surprise. It was barely five years since Richard and Barbara had been planning their wedding! Her dislike for him intensified. This meant that he'd barely broken up with Barbara before he'd got another woman pregnant!

Olivia looked at her watch again. "Okay, Richard – what do you want to say? I really do need to go soon."

"This isn't easy, Liv – "

Olivia sat tight-lipped. She certainly wasn't going to make it any easier for him.

"After Barbara and I broke up – "

"Over a silly argument."

"Yes, you're right – it was a silly, stupid, pointless argument. Then I went to a party, and I met Josephine."

"Your wife, I presume?"

"Yes. I went to a party and got pissed. It wasn't meant to be anything more than a one-night stand, and I never expected to see her again. But she contacted me a few weeks later, to tell me that she was pregnant."

"That must have been a surprise," said Olivia dryly.

Richard nodded guiltily. "I was stunned when she

told me. I mean, I was still hoping to get back with Barbara, but when it happened – well, what could I do?"

"Obviously, neither of you took responsibility for contraception, " said Olivia angrily. "Couldn't she have taken the morning-after pill?"

"Well, yes – that's what I thought, too. I mean, I hardly knew her – "

"But you still managed to get her into the sack," said Olivia, knowing it was a cheap shot.

Chastened, Richard nodded.

"So you were the patsy."

Richard darted a glance at his son. "Maybe, in a sense, I was – but how could I not want Jack?" His voice became husky with emotion. "I love him to bits – he means the world to me."

Suddenly, Olivia was seeing another side to the man she'd come to despise. Gone was the image of the high-powered top executive. In his place was a chastened and humbled man, now a father, and one who obviously adored his young son.

"So you married this woman simply because she was pregnant? Pull the other one, Richard."

He sighed. "I did. Josephine had been diagnosed with cancer just before we met. I didn't know any of this at the time, but she was due to start chemotherapy within a few weeks. But when she discovered she was pregnant, she postponed the treatment until after Jack was born. She was thrilled at the chance of having a child." Richard glanced at his son and ruffled the child's hair before continuing. "She phoned me a few weeks after the party to tell me she was pregnant, and that she intended to keep the child. She wasn't asking for anything from me –

she was only contacting me because she felt I had a right to know."

"Then how did she manage to get you down the aisle so quickly?" asked Olivia, still angry on Barbara's behalf.

"Early on in the pregnancy, she collapsed and ended up in hospital. Her family contacted me, so I went to visit her. She looked so brave, so determined to go ahead with the pregnancy regardless of the risks to her own health, that I felt I should give her my full support. After all, this child was mine as much as hers. So I asked her to marry me, and she said yes." Richard looked directly at Olivia. "It wasn't an easy time – I still loved Barbara, would always love Barbara – but I felt I'd no other choice."

Olivia hesitated. It would seem churlish not to enquire about his wife's health, although she didn't want Richard to feel that by doing so she was absolving him of responsibility for his hurtful treatment of her friend. She took a deep breath. "How is your wife's health now? I presume the chemotherapy worked?"

"No, it didn't – she died last year."

"Oh my God – I'm sorry, Richard."

Richard grimaced. "The past few years have been rough – in retrospect, I think Jo had a premonition that she wouldn't come through the cancer, and that she knew Jack was the only child she'd ever have." He looked earnestly at Olivia. "So I don't regret what I did for her – I can at least hold up my head and say that I did the right thing for my son's mother. I gave her the security she needed, supported her through the chemo, and she died knowing that I'd always love and look after our son." He sighed. "That's all I wanted to say, Liv. I just wanted Barbara to know that I didn't abandon her lightly. Even though I married Josephine, Barbara was always the one I loved, but I felt I'd no other choice at the time."

"Why didn't you just tell Barbara that?" asked Olivia.

"I tried, Liv – believe me, I tried. But Barbara would never talk to me. She'd hang up the phone when I rang, and she'd cross the street when I tried to engage her in conversation."

Olivia felt more than a little guilty, since she herself had been one of those who'd urged Barbara to ignore Richard's overtures.

Olivia stood up to leave. Then, just as she was about to go, she had a sudden thought. She quickly turned back to face Richard.

"Did your wife know that you loved another woman?"

Richard nodded guiltily. "She knew I was on the rebound when I met her. But I think she also realised she wouldn't be around for very long, so she accepted she'd just got me on loan for a while." He looked directly at Olivia. "As she was dying, she thanked me for giving her Jack. Her voice was barely audible, but I'll never forget what she said to me. She said: 'I know there was someone special before I barged into your life – maybe it's not too late to find her, and start again.'" He sighed deeply. "It was a traumatic moment, as well as a very emotional one." He looked earnestly at Olivia. "I've always loved Barbara, Liv – you know that. But I wish I'd made a better effort of hiding it from Jo."

"Well, Richard – Barbara's moved on and got over *you*. So I hope you'll respect her enough to leave her alone."

"Of course. I'd never do anything to hurt her – you

know that, Liv. If you truly love someone, you want them to be happy, don't you? And that's all I want for Barbara. I just wanted her to know what really happened."

Olivia nodded, but gave no commitment to pass on Richard's tragic story to Barbara, and wisely, he didn't ask for one.

"Goodbye, Jack," said Olivia, ruffling the little boy's hair, but the child paid no attention to her. "Goodbye, Richard," she said, turning on her heel and leaving the coffee shop.

CHAPTER 41

It was around 3a.m. when the Traveller woman heard it, as she stealthily crossed the courtyard at Bay Tree House. It was a moaning sound, and it was coming from somewhere close at hand. Her first inclination was to ignore it, and run as fast as she could from the place, since she had no right to be there. But suddenly, there came a wail – for all the world like a banshee, she thought – that sent a shiver of fear running through her.

Up to now, it had been a good night for Chrissie. The weather was mild, and someone had carelessly left a window open in the dining room of the big house, so her expedition had netted some silver cutlery. Which meant that Mikey wouldn't hit her, and there would be some money for food when the items were sold. She didn't like stealing – she knew it was wrong – but gradually she'd discovered that there were few other ways to survive.

Now, she risked discovery if she went to investigate. Yet the wail she'd heard was so heartrending that she felt no decent person could ignore it. Perhaps someone else had been doing a bit of housebreaking too, and had stumbled in the dark and injured themselves on a scythe or a pitchfork.

In the darkened silence, her hearing was even more acute than normal, so it proved relatively easy to locate the direction from which the sound had come. It was coming from one of the outhouses in the yard at the back of the house. Wrapping her booty carefully in her shawl, Chrissie laid it to one side of the door and advanced inside. Her heart was beating furiously as she tiptoed through the gloom, and she wondered briefly if perhaps she could be walking into a carefully prepared trap.

Poised for flight in case things suddenly went wrong, Chrissie tiptoed forward. At first, the shed appeared empty, then suddenly she heard what sounded like groaning, followed by a gasp of pain.

"Who's there?" Chrissie called bravely, although she was actually rooted to the ground in terror. The only answer to her words was another groan, so she stepped forward again and peered into the corner where, amid tools and a wheelbarrow, lay a young woman.

Quickly Chrissie assessed the scene, realising that it was one she was all too familiar with. The woman on the floor was about to give birth. Thank God, thought Chrissie, she's had the foresight to bring a few towels into the shed with her. Dropping to her knees, Chrissie surveyed the frail figure in the corner, taking her hand and squeezing it gently. "Don't worry, ma'am, everything's going to be all right. I've got a couple of kids myself and another on the way, so I know what to do. Just relax – for Almighty's sake don't push yet – you'll only tear yourself."

Clasping her hand, Chrissie studied the young woman's face. She now recognised her as the maid from Bay Tree House. Clearly, if she was in labour in an outhouse, no one inside the house was supposed to know. Poor thing, she'd probably spent *the last nine months trying to hide her condition, with no one willing to help her, even though there were probably more than a few who suspected what was going on. Clearly, the man who'd got her into this sorry state was content to ignore his own involvement.*

Not that Chrissie was particularly surprised. She knew a thing or two about the hypocrisy, the prying eyes and the snide remarks that characterised life in many of Ireland's towns and villages. Strange things happened behind closed doors, and even stranger still was people's ability to pretend a situation didn't exist when it wasn't to their liking.

"How long are you in labour, ma'am?"

Ada groaned as another contraction swept over her. "The pains started a few hours ago, just after Mrs Collins went home, and they've been getting more regular since then."

Another contraction took her breath away, and she dug her nails so tightly into Chrissie's hand that she drew blood.

"I'm not due yet – I was planning on running away long before my time came!" She looked imploringly at Chrissie. "Help me, for God's sake – what am I going to do with this baby?"

"Hush now, let's get the child born first," said Chrissie, sounding a lot more confident than she felt. But it was essential to keep the young woman as relaxed as possible – stress would only make the delivery more difficult. Clearly though, this child's future was a problem – Chrissie knew that the world they both inhabited as women was not one that favoured the feminine gender, whether gentry or pauper. It might take two to tango, but only one carried the stigma and the responsibility.

Chrissie stood up but, seeing the terror in Ada's eyes, she reassured her. "It's all right – I'm not leaving you. I'm just going to get the shawl that I left outside. We'll be needing something warm to wrap the wee mite in when it's born."

Quickly, she untied the bundle containing the stolen cutlery, hiding them just inside the shed door. For the time being at least, the shawl would have to serve a more urgent purpose. It wasn't very clean, Chrissie thought ruefully, but for a travelling woman, regular washing was a luxury. Still, it would serve to keep the child warm when it arrived. Her own four children had all been wrapped in it. Perhaps the fifth, which she feared might already be growing inside her, would also feel its warmth.

Anxiously, she looked around, scanning the house and courtyard for any movement. Both women were in a precarious predicament, but for differing reasons. Chrissie found it too frightening to think of the consequences for both of them if they were found there, so she quickly returned to the gloom of the shed. Spreading the towels between Ada's legs, she held her hand once again and squatted down on the floor to wait. It wouldn't be much longer.

Half an hour later, the contractions were coming every few seconds, and Ada's face and hair were soaking with sweat.

"It won't be long now," Chrissie exhorted. "Take short breaths, don't push yet — "

The baby's first cry, when it came, shattered the silence of the night. It was a loud, healthy roar, from a fine healthy baby girl.

"She's a grand child, ma'am," said Chrissie happily, as she wiped off the blood, clamped the cord with a piece of string from her pocket, then cut it with one of the stolen knives, wrapped the child in the shawl and handed her to her exhausted mother.

Ada held her baby in wonderment, looking at the tiny wrinkled face still partly streaked with blood, and the tiny fists that she was attempting to fit into her tiny rosebud mouth. Even though it was still quite dark, every feature, every movement of her child would be etched forever in her mind. How could she part with this flesh of her own flesh? Yet in reality, there was no other choice available.

In her light-headed, slightly hysterical state, Ada now speculated on Henry's reaction if, when she served his breakfast the following morning, she casually announced: "Oh, by the way, Mr Morton, I gave birth to a baby girl last night. She's asleep in the scullery – would you like to see her?"

In reality, she closed her eyes tightly in an impossible bid to stop the tears from escaping. Her body heaved with sobs as the hopelessness of her situation overwhelmed her. In her arms, her tiny daughter slept, oblivious to her mother's tears, and to the fate that lay ahead of her.

* * *

As the thick black of the night sky gave way to the deep purple of early dawn and the first birds began their morning song, Chrissie left the outhouse on the Morton estate carrying a bundle under each arm. In one was the bloodstained towels and placenta that she'd bury in the woods. In the other was a tiny baby, who slept peacefully in the folds of her old woollen shawl, oblivious to its fate and of the hot, bitter tears that her young mother had cried as she held her baby in her arms for the first and last time.

Chrissie held the baby close to her own body for warmth. It was a sturdy little thing, destined for survival. She glanced back over her shoulder as she slipped through the front gates of Bay Tree House.

When safely in the woods, Chrissie sat down at the base of

a large tree and offered the tiny baby her breast – already full of milk for her own youngest child – and it suckled greedily. "God love you, child," she whispered to it, kissing its downy little head, "for I doubt that anyone else in this cruel world will."

Keeping her promise to young Ada, Chrissie – with just one bundle now – emerged at the other side of the woods and made her way along the deserted main street of the town. She held the baby close to her heart, hoping that it wouldn't decide to cry as she walked past a row of houses that faced onto the street. One of them doubled as the police station, and although nothing much ever happened in Cloncullen, old Sergeant Murphy was a light sleeper and saw it as his duty to investigate every incident in the area, no matter how trivial.

Chrissie looked up and saw a light shining upstairs. So the oul' shite was already stirring. Yet in actual fact, Chrissie had to acknowledge that the sergeant was a decent man; he'd once prevented a group of locals from trying to forcibly evict some travelling families from a lay-by out on the Kilcolgan road. It could have become a very violent incident if the sergeant hadn't restored order and threatened to formally charge the perpetrators if they didn't go home immediately.

At the top of the hill, Chrissie finally reached the austere portals of the convent. The big four-storey house where the nuns lived faced out onto the street, while the less imposing and distinctly barn-like orphanage was situated at right angles behind it. What an awful place to live, Chrissie thought. She shuddered, and it wasn't just from the early morning chill.

This was one of those occasions when Chrissie could honestly say that she was glad she hadn't received any formal education. If being in a place like this was the only way to get it, then she'd willingly stay ignorant. At least she could read and write, and she'd taught her own children the basics of reading and writing as well. Her children also had the freedom of the highways and byways, such as they were today. Perhaps this little one in her arms would grow up to be a professor or a prime minister, but would the price of achievement be worth it?

For a moment, Chrissie was possessed of a terrible desire to run as fast as she could away from the convent, taking the child in her arms with her. What sort of life was the wee thing going to have in there? Then she checked herself at her own foolishness; there was nothing she could give this child and besides, hadn't she more than enough of her own already – and possibly another on the way? She could just imagine Mikey's response if she arrived home with no booty, no shawl, but with another baby instead!

Resolutely, she rang the doorbell of the convent, and placed the baby on the steps. Impatiently now, she rang it again, this time keeping her finger on the bell, for she feared that if no one came quickly, she'd snatch up the child and run off with it.

Soon however, she heard the shuffling of slippered feet and the exchange of querying voices from within. Silently, she slipped into the shadows of a nearby building and watched until the door was opened, the baby found and taken inside. It was only when silence reigned again that Chrissie slipped away, and headed back to the camp at Kilcolgan Wood.

*　　*　　*

Back at the Travellers' camp, Mikey was in quarrelsome mood. He was suffering from a hangover from the previous night's drinking, and when Chrissie returned at dawn to the caravan empty-handed, his temper flared.

"Where the hell have you been?" he bellowed, lashing out at

her with his fist, not even waiting for an answer. "That bloody child has been wailing all night!" He gestured towards their youngest child, whose milk she'd shared with the newborn child only an hour before. By now, all the children were awake and screaming, frightened by their father's anger and violence. Silently, Chrissie took the youngest child to her breast.

* * *

Henry Morton was in a rage the following morning.

"We had a break-in last night!" he announced, to anyone who would listen to him. "It looks as though someone got in through the side window of the dining room and took some of the silver cutlery. But luckily, I found it all in one of the sheds later on.

He looked directly at Ada as she placed his boiled egg and toast in front of him.

"It seems that whoever took it was up to something very peculiar," he added. "The ground was trampled in one corner of the shed, and one of the knives I found had blood all over it." He took out his tobacco pouch and began to refill his pipe, his anger visibly rising. "It's probably those bloody tinkers – the ones camping on the far side of the wood. It wouldn't surprise me if they were performing some sort of un-Christian rite in our shed!" His voice quivered with indignation. "I'll have to have a word in the sergeant's ear – to see what we can do about running that thieving scum out of town. The sergeant's inclined to be a bit too lenient. The cheek of those tinkers – interfering with the rights of decent people!"

Ada could barely suppress her anger. Decent people? She certainly didn't think that Henry Morton qualified for that title. But while she longed to defend the kind woman who'd helped her the previous night, she knew her opinion was of no interest to Henry Morton.

She was also relieved that so far Henry Morton hadn't noticed the change in her body shape. The longer she had to recover before a showdown, the stronger and more able to cope she'd be.

A sob rose in her throat and almost threatened to choke her. Fortunately, Henry Morton was now deeply engrossed in his newspaper, so he didn't hear the pitiful groan that escaped her lips, and which she hastily converted into a cough. She was thinking of her little daughter – now an inmate of the town's orphanage – when instead she should have had a loving home with her own mother. How she'd love to nurture the child, and watch her grow day by day . . .

With tears running down her cheeks, Ada quickly fled from the room and headed downstairs towards the kitchen.

CHAPTER 42

It was almost dusk when Barbara arrived in Cloncullen, having finished a late shift at the hospital. She was surprised to find Olivia alone in the house, and expressed her surprise, wondering if Maggie had already gone off to try and snare poor Philip Lynch!

Olivia smiled, pouring her friend a glass of wine. She'd deliberately arranged to get Maggie out of the way, since she needed to talk to Barbara alone. Maggie had been sent off to get a Chinese takeaway for their evening meal, so Olivia knew she had enough time to tell Barbara about her meeting with Richard Devlin. Barbara would undoubtedly tell Maggie about it anyway, but Olivia felt that the choice to tell had to be Barbara's alone.

After she'd told her, Barbara sat staring into space and for a few moments Olivia wondered if her friend had actually heard the information she'd been relaying to her.

"Barbs – are you Okay?"

Barbara turned towards Olivia. "Yeah, I'm okay. A bit shocked, I suppose. So that's why we've been bumping into Richard in Cloncullen – he's obviously living in the area."

Olivia relaxed, glad that her friend seemed to be taking the details of Richard's marriage and child stoically. "To be honest with you," she said, "I was so stunned by what he told me, that I forgot to ask about the practical things, such as where he was living, and whether or not he was still working in IT! Although it doesn't exactly look like it."

Barbara gave a wan smile. "I hope, Liv, you told him that I was having a great time, and living life to the full."

Olivia nodded. "Of course I did," she said loyally. "I told him you'd got on with your life and were doing fine."

"Did he really say he still loved me?"

"He did. That should give you some satisfaction – knowing that he still cares for you, but that you don't feel anything for him any more."

Olivia hoped for a nod of confirmation from her friend, but Barbara seemed to have retreated in to her own world of what might have been.

"Barbs – you don't still love him, do you?" she asked, alarmed.

"I don't know, Liv. He was part of my life for so long that it's hard to think of him not being there. On the other hand, there's been too much water under the bridge – I could never go back to him now."

"Look, it's time you met someone new, and stopped moping over Richard," said Olivia firmly. "He's part of your past, and in years to come, when you've a husband and family of your own, you'll wonder what you ever saw in him."

"I could never love anyone the way I loved Richard," said Barbara stubbornly.

"Okay, I accept that. But you're not getting any younger – none of us are – so you'd want to start thinking positively about your future."

Barbara smiled. "You sound exactly like my mother!"

"Your mother is right – don't waste the best years of your life pining for what might have been. You're an attractive woman – arrange a date with the next man who asks you out!"

"Okay, I promise."

Olivia looked at her friend's sad expression. "But you'd better put a smile on your face first – that miserable puss will put them all off!"

Just then, Maggie arrived back with crispy duck, chow mein, sweet and sour pork, and loads of fried rice. Soon, the trio were tucking into their food with gusto. Maggie was full of glee because she'd bumped into Philip Lynch in the village, and he'd told her she looked great. He'd stopped the patrol car to talk to her, so she felt she was making definite progress there.

Barbara was a little subdued during the meal, but Olivia was hopeful that her friend had taken her advice to heart, and would actively start looking for somebody new.

CHAPTER 43

Early the following morning, Maggie and Barbara had just gone into the town when Philip Lynch arrived at the door of Bay Tree House.

"I've got some news for you," he said, taking off his cap, and settling down into one of Olivia's new sofas.

"Go on," said Olivia, being careful not to sit anywhere near him. While she had to admit that he didn't seem remotely interested in her, she still didn't like being alone with him. Maybe he'd deliberately been waiting until Maggie and Barbara went out? He was in his patrol car and in full uniform, so Olivia assumed that this was an official visit. For that she was much relieved, since he'd hardly make a pass at her in uniform, would he? Then she remembered that women loved men in uniforms, so maybe he'd worn it to impress her, and her relief evaporated.

"Any chance of a cup of tea first?" Philip asked, and Olivia headed off to put the kettle on.

While Olivia got the mugs down from the dresser and

made the tea, Philip chatted about all sorts of inconsequential things. When Olivia served it – being careful to sit on the sofa opposite him – Philip drank his tea with gusto, and devoured two scones from the plate of scones and pastries she'd placed in the centre of the coffee table.

"That was great, Olivia," he said happily, as he popped the last piece of scone into his mouth. "A bachelor like myself doesn't often get a chance to experience good home cooking like that."

Olivia almost choked on her own scone. Was he intimating that she'd make a good wife? Oh God!

Oblivious to her confusion, Philip stretched his legs and proceeded to stand up.

"The news is about the baby's skeleton," he told her at last. "The autopsy's confirmed that the poor baby's neck was broken, and that it was a female baby, no more than a day or two old."

"The poor little thing," said Olivia softly. "Thanks for letting me know, Philip." She was grateful that he was now heading towards the door. "So what happens to the remains?"

"The child will be buried at the Angels' Plot in Glasnevin, next week," he told her.

"Will you and your friends be going? You don't have to, you know."

"I'll be there," said Olivia. "The poor baby deserves a decent send-off."

As he drove away, Olivia looked thoughtful. So Carmel Collins' slip of the tongue had been proven correct. Could this mean she really did know a lot more about the baby than she was prepared to say?

*   *   *

Later that evening, Olivia declined an invitation from Maggie and Barbara to go to one of the local pubs. Instead, she intended finally settling down with Laura Morton's diaries once her friends had gone out. She'd intended getting going on them the night before, but her unexpected meeting with Richard had necessitated telling Barbara all about it, and she'd been emotionally drained herself by the time she'd headed for bed. She smiled to herself. Everything seemed to conspire to prevent her reading them! Anyway, the diaries had remained hidden for many years – another day or two would hardly make much difference. Once she'd become used to Laura's handwriting, Olivia found it surprisingly easy to make progress. It was obvious that "H" was Laura's husband Henry, and "A" was possibly her great-aunt Ada. Mrs C was probably Mrs Collins, Philip's grandmother. There were also several references to another "C", although at this point, Olivia couldn't imagine who that person was. Was it a separate person from Mrs C? Her next task would be to discover who had been the regular people in Laura Morton's life.

One thing Olivia was shocked to discover was that Laura Morton had loathed her own husband. No wonder the diaries had been hidden so carefully! Olivia had always assumed that Laura and Henry Morton had been a devoted couple, and that Bay Tree House had been their own little paradise. Now, she began to wonder what other revelations she was about to uncover! She also wondered if this might account for the fact that Laura's name wasn't on Henry's grave – maybe she'd chosen not to be buried with him at all? Olivia sighed. She felt that there was so much bubbling just below the surface, yet she just couldn't get to the bottom of it. Well, next time she saw Philip Lynch or Carmel Collins, she would ask them where Laura Morton was buried. Olivia smiled to herself. Even today, that sort of thing would surely raise an eyebrow or two.

Olivia felt her heart beating uncomfortably as it gradually became clear that "A" had suffered terribly at "H's" hands, and Olivia felt a frisson of fear run up her spine. Now she began hoping that "A" *wasn't* her great-aunt Ada! How could she tell her grandmother and Uncle Eddie that their sister had been subjected to systematic abuse from Henry Morton in Bay Tree House?

In the earliest diaries, Laura made numerous contemptuous references to "Dr W" and "PP". Gradually, Olivia worked out that PP referred to the parish priest, but as she worked her way through the earlier years, "Dr W" disappeared, and there were initial references to "Dr Mc", then he disappeared abruptly, within a matter of weeks. Olivia puzzled over this. Maybe when she learned more about people living in the town back then, she could understand what was happening. Suddenly, Olivia recalled seeing a tombstone for a Dr Walsh in the graveyard – he'd probably retired or died, and been replaced by Dr Mc. But since she hadn't seen a tombstone for any Dr Mc, hopefully he was still around, and might be able to help her in her quest to find Ada.

Olivia made notes of the pages where particularly interesting or totally confusing references were made, and she was very pleased with her progress. Soon, she hoped, something would fall into place and she'd finally find out what happened to Great-aunt Ada.

*   *   *

Philip sat opposite his grandmother in her sitting room, drinking tea from one of her china cups.

"I learnt something very interesting this afternoon, Gran," he told her. "In trying to find out about the dead baby, I've discovered the names of the people who used to work at Bay Tree House more than fifty years ago. Con Larkin was only too happy to inform me."

His grandmother said nothing. But she recalled the sneaky, snivelling Larkin son, who'd grown into the nosy, mean-spirited adult now running the grocery business started by his parents. If she didn't need to have her groceries delivered, she'd have long ago taken her custom elsewhere.

"And lo and behold, what do I find?" added Philip. "That my own grandmother worked there! I knew you were a friend of Laura Morton's, but not that you were housekeeper there for many years." He smiled gently at her. "Why on earth didn't you say anything to me? It would have saved me a lot of time, and you could have told me the name of the other person working there."

His grandmother sighed. "I'd retired long before you started robbing Laura Morton's orchard," she said dryly, "so it completely slipped my mind."

"The maid's name was Ada Casey – it's odd, isn't it, that Olivia is trying to trace a relative of that very name?" He grinned. "I might have to arrest you, Gran – for perverting the course of justice!"

Carmel Collins said nothing.

"So why didn't you tell me, Gran – have you something to hide?"

His grandmother looked sourly at him. "My dear Philip, my memory isn't what it used to be, I'm afraid, so I don't remember things as clearly as I used to. Wait till you reach your eighties – let's see how smart you'll be!"

"I think, Gran dear, you're a lot smarter than you pretend to be." Philip sighed. "So you're going to make me find out everything for myself? Well, so be it. But I'll get to the bottom of it in the end, Gran, never you fear."

He kissed his grandmother's cheek before he left.

As soon as she heard the front door close behind him, Carmel Collins was out of her chair as quickly as her arthritic joints would allow her.

Quickly, she picked up the phone and dialled.

"Philip knows," she told the person at the other end of the line. "I suppose it was inevitable that he'd stumble on the truth, no matter what we did. He's a clever lad, my grandson." She felt momentary pride in Philip's achievements, but also fear that by unearthing this information, several people could now find themselves in hot water.

"Don't worry," said the voice at the other end of the line. "The truth will have to come out soon, anyway. We just have to make certain we're ready when that time comes."

CHAPTER 44

A week later, Chrissie and her two youngest children were walking by the Post Office when Ada came out, almost colliding with them. Ada had been posting letters for Henry Morton, and she'd welcomed the brief escape from the confines of the house.

Chrissie nodded in recognition, not expecting any acknowledgement in return. However, Ada fell into step with her as she walked down the street, her cheeks now flushed with embarrassment as she recalled their last meeting.

"I-I never thanked you properly for your help," she murmured, glancing around surreptitiously to ensure that no one could overhear them. "I don't know what I'd have done without you. I wish I had something to give you – "

"I don't want your charity," Chrissie said gruffly. "What I did was no more than what any woman would do for another."

Gripping the children by the hand, she continued walking down the street, leaving Ada embarrassed and chastened.

Suddenly, Chrissie stopped, remembering something. She turned towards Ada, then looked around her quickly to ensure that they were still alone. "I hear that they've called her Majella," *she said softly.*

Ada nodded, grateful for the news, yet unable to speak. The pain of loss was already welling up inside her again at the thought of her little daughter in that terrible place. She stopped and groped for a handkerchief as the tears began to fall unchecked. When she looked around, the travelling woman and her children were nowhere in sight.

Majella. What a lovely name. Ada blew her nose and tried to compose herself for the walk back to Bay Tree House. Once again, she thought guiltily of the travelling woman. She'd made a clumsy attempt at conveying her gratitude, which she now realised had been ill-judged and insensitive. She'd hurt the woman's pride, and inadvertently reinforced society's inequality between them. Yet together they'd shared one of the most intimate events in any woman's life.

*   *   *

Hurrying along the main street, Chrissie and her children quickly sought the anonymity of Cloncullen's side streets. When you were a Traveller, it was best to stay out of settled people's way as much as possible. That way, you didn't get so much abuse.

Chrissie liked the maid from Bay Tree House, who'd at least tried, in her own way, to express gratitude for her help. It was a new experience for Chrissie to have anyone acknowledge her value, even though the young woman had been clumsy in the way she went about it. Everyone seemed to think that the Travellers did nothing without being paid for it. Which wasn't true, although there were some Travellers who always kept asking for more, no matter what they were given, and it was

322

them who gave all Travellers a bad name. But the Travellers' way of life was a hard one, Chrissie conceded. So when Travellers found someone who was a soft touch, she could understand why they kept asking, even though she didn't approve of it.

Chrissie had been only sixteen herself when she married big Mikey Delaney. And she was barely seventeen when she gave birth to her eldest child. Now, five years and four children later, she sometimes felt like an old woman, tired in body and in spirit.

At first, Mikey had been good to her. They'd had to share his brother's caravan but then Mikey had won money on the horses and done well over a scrap-metal deal, and they'd been able to buy their own caravan. It was a proud day when they moved in – it wasn't new, but to Chrissie, it was the most wonderful home in the whole world. She'd felt so grown-up to have a place of her own, and when she discovered that she was pregnant, her happiness knew no bounds.

But by the birth of the second child, things had started to change for the worst. Mikey had taken to drinking with a group of travelling men who'd moved into a campsite nearby. So there was less money for the children's food, since most of it now went on beer or cider. By the time the third child arrived, a deal of Mikey's had gone drastically wrong, and in the middle of one night, they were all forcibly evicted from their caravan, by several men who claimed they were taking it in part payment of the debts Mikey owed them.

In summer, it wasn't too difficult to manage – Mikey was able to build them a tent with a frame of large willow branches, sided with pieces of corrugated iron and topped with old coats and curtains. In fact, on fine nights it was lovely to lie out under the stars, and feel at one with the rest of the universe.

But in the winter, it was too cold outside for the children, so they'd had to accept her parents' offer to share their caravan. But in such a confined space, life became a nightmare. Without running water and with only a tiny stove for warmth, the whole family often had to last for weeks without a proper wash or a change of clothing. Yet even in the darkness of the crowded caravan, with children asleep on either side, Mikey always took his drunken pleasure, and once again she was pregnant by springtime.

Sometimes during the day, Chrissie would wrap up the smaller children and take them out begging. She hated having doors shut in her face all the time, but sometimes the effort of it all was worthwhile when she managed to collect enough money to bring back a few bags of chips for the tea, and put a few coppers in the jar she'd hidden from Mikey underneath the bed. She was saving it for a house of her own – it was a pipe dream, of course, but it gave her something to look forward to.

Chrissie knew how a life of squalor by the roadside made the tinkers highly visible to settled folks. It was easy to spot them by their unkempt hair and crumpled clothing that invariably smelled of turf from the campfire or caravan stove. And that made the discrimination all the easier. And where once the Travellers could camp anywhere they liked on Ireland's rolling plains, now almost everywhere they stopped was designated privately owned land.

People said that tinkers were thieves, and you could see settled folks clutching their handbags and checking their back pockets when they realised that there were travelling folk around. Chrissie knew that some travelling people were light-fingered, but when you'd few legitimate ways of earning a living, how else were you supposed to fill the little ones' bellies?

No one wanted pots and pans mended anymore, and the

scrap metal and old batteries that many tinkers collected for resale were considered unsightly and dirty by settled folk. Chrissie found this hard to understand; surely the Travellers were doing more to look after the earth than many settled people, who just dumped their rubbish, whereas the Travellers tried to recycle it. So why were they being punished for it? Yet the travellers were hunted out of towns and villages by these so-called Christian people, condemned for merely trying to earn a living.

Until she was married, Chrissie had never stolen anything. But when it became the only way that she could manage to feed her children, she accepted that she didn't really have a choice. Surely, if God was good, He'd see that she was only doing it out of necessity? While she believed in obeying God's commandments, experience had taught her that most of his earthly ministers were snobs and hypocrites, who looked down on the people of the roads in a way that God himself would never do. She felt certain that God would be more on her side than theirs.

She'd heard that in other countries, people with different-coloured skin or different religions suffered in the same way that the Travellers did. She felt sorry for the people whose skin singled them out and made it easy to persecute them. But what was even more incomprehensible to Chrissie was how people could discriminate against their own kind. For the people of the roads were no different than other Irish people. They had the same surnames – like Walsh, McCarthy and O'Brien. Indeed, weren't the Connors and O'Connors descended from the High Kings of Ireland?

When she'd been a child, sitting round the campfire while her grandfather mended the local farmers' pots and pans, he'd told her that once the Travellers had lived in houses like the *settled people did. But during the Famine of 1845, when the potato crop failed and the English took all the grain out of the country, leaving millions of Irish to die by the roadside or take the notorious coffin-ships to America, today's travellers were the people who'd taken to the roads in search of the means of survival. Others were evicted from their homes on behalf of absentee English landlords, and had no option but to try and earn a living by Travelling from farm to farm mending pots, pans and buckets. They'd been called 'tinkers' then, because of the work they did, and it was a proud name. But today it was a derogatory term, and settled people had contempt in their voices when they used it.*

At other times, her grandfather told her that the tinkers were linked to the Romany gypsies of Europe, and he told her stories of fortune-telling, music, dancing and beautiful costumes. Each time he spoke of the Travellers' origins, he seemed to have forgotten the earlier stories he'd told her, and Chrissie never challenged him about either version. She'd often wondered which, if either, version was true, but she'd never found anyone who could tell her. Most Travellers didn't seem to know much about their origins, and most didn't seem to care. The daily struggle for survival seemed to have stifled all sense of history and hope.

Book 2

Chapter 45

"Majella, have you made your bed?"

"Yes, Mother."

"And have you said your morning prayers?"

"Yes, Mother."

Mother Monica looked at the child closely, eager to find anything wrong so that she could punish the child, and release her own pent-up aggression.

"Well then, since you've got plenty of time before Mass, you can polish the brasses and do the knocker on the front door."

"Yes, Mother."

Feeling vaguely dissatisfied, Mother Monica walked away. She sometimes felt that the children's compliance almost constituted a form of resistance. It was particularly evident in seven-year-old Majella. Although the child had been at St Bernadette's Orphanage since she'd arrived as a newborn foundling, she didn't seem particularly grateful at being given a home. Mother Monica recognised the signs of passive aggression. That child would become increasingly difficult as she got older, and something would have to be done to crush her spirit, before she got totally out of control.

Mother Monica swished her veil and headed towards her office. No doubt these opinionated attitudes were fostered by Sister Angela, who was far too lenient and affectionate with the children. Children were like wild animals, and needed discipline, not cuddles. Mother Monica wished she could transfer the troublesome nun to another convent, but Sister Angela did have her uses. None of the other nuns wished to have any involvement in the children's upbringing, but Sister Angela willingly accepted the extra burden. And since they were designated as an orphanage, and had thirty children in their care, Mother Monica concluded that by getting rid of Sister Angela, she'd be shooting herself and the other sisters in the foot.

When she'd finished polishing the brasses on the convent door, Majella made her way to the basement kitchen, where she knew her friends would be gathered around Sister Angela, who'd be showing them how to make bread or scones. Or, more likely, the nun would be making bread while the girls stood around, idly chatting.

Majella smiled to herself as she hurried down the stairs. Just as well Mother Monica didn't go down to the kitchen very often. She deplored any form of idleness, and believed that if a child wasn't kept busy, the Devil would find work for it to do. On the other hand, Majella often thought that the Devil sounded a lot more fun than God did. And when they were all frozen in the dormitory on winter nights, the idea of experiencing the flames of hell was a very attractive proposition.

Downstairs in the cosy kitchen, with its constant aroma of freshly baked bread, Majella felt happy and content. Soon, they'd all have to attend Mass in the convent chapel, in order to keep Mother Monica from losing her temper. But before then, she'd have a laugh and relax with her best friends Lucy, Julia and Betty – and Sister Angela.

The little nun was the nearest thing any of them had to a mother. Many of the children only knew about mothers from storybooks. Some had hazy recollections of a life before the orphanage, but by virtue of their traumatic arrival there, many had blanked out the pain of what went before.

Majella had no idea who her own mother was, or how she'd arrived at the orphanage. But she had a vivid imagination, and was happy to weave tales of mystery and derring-do when the children got together for storytelling.

"There you are, Majella," said Sister Angela, her face wrinkling into a smile as the seven-year-old entered the kitchen. "Would you like to test my brown bread? You can only have a taste, mind you – but the others think it's quite good."

"It's fantastic!" said Lucy, who'd recently learnt this new word, and now applied it to everything, at every possible opportunity.

Majella chewed a small piece of the loaf Sister Angela gave her, nodding to register her approval.

"I helped Sister mix the dough, didn't I, Sister?" said Julia. "Surely that entitles me to an extra piece?"

Sister Angela laughed. Julia certainly loved her food! "Go on, then, but mind you leave enough for breakfast after Mass!"

"C-can I have a bit too, Sister?" piped up a little voice. Betty was usually so quiet that everyone tended to forget about her.

"Of course, dear," said Sister Angela, looking tenderly at the pale skinny little girl. She liked to see Betty eating, since it might help to put some weight on her. "You're obviously a hungry lot today, so while you're all at Mass I'll bake an extra loaf or two."

The little nun was rewarded with smiles all round, and a chorus of "Thank you, Sister!"

As the children left to attend Mass, their happy expressions quickly replaced by ones of meek gentility lest they bump into one of the other nuns, Sister Angela made herself a cup of tea and sat down. As promised, she intended to bake some extra bread for the poor children, so that they'd all have something nice to look forward to that evening.

Not for the first time, anger boiled up inside her. The thirty children in the orphanage spent most of their lives in a constant state of fear, since the other nuns seemed to relish waging constant war on them. Any show of individuality quickly became stifled through fear. A child's misdemeanour might be nothing more than skipping along a corridor, clumsiness, touching any of the many statues, or speaking any louder than in a whisper. At times – depending on a nun's mood – even whispering was deemed punishable.

God and the Devil also played formidable roles in policing the children. The evil cloven-hoofed satyr and bad-tempered bearded father figure were vigilant even when the nuns were not. The Devil, they were told, tried twenty-four hours a day to lead them into sin, and when God found out about their evildoing – which he always did, since he could see everything – retribution could be swift, perhaps even fatal if he decided to strike them dead.

Sister Angela sighed. It must have fleetingly crossed some of their young minds that the benevolent God they were taught about in religion classes was oddly at variance with this vindictive and violent God of whom the nuns claimed ownership. But even this logical thought would have been quickly stifled. After all, God himself might be listening. The children had learned to trust no one – not even God.

CHAPTER 46

In the doctor's surgery, Sister Angela flopped into the comfortable chair facing Dr Cormac McCarthy's desk. Her arthritis was playing up, and she needed something to keep the pains and aches at bay. She hated the inconvenience of being ill, since she had far too much to do at the orphanage.

"You're obviously working too hard, Sister," said Dr McCarthy kindly. "Why don't you take things a bit easier – maybe delegate a bit more to the other sisters?"

Sister Angela laughed harshly. "Delegate? If I asked any of that lot to give me a hand, I'd still be waiting six months later. They're too busy craw-thumping in the church or sucking up to the priests. As for the bishop – you'd think he was a film star, the way they fawn all over him."

Dr McCarthy smiled. Since he'd set up practice in Cloncullen a few months earlier, he'd had several meetings with the redoubtable Sister Angela. He'd become very fond of this straight-talking nun, who, he suspected, didn't have many opportunities to say how she felt within the confines of the convent. But in his surgery, she could say what she liked – and usually did! In a way, he thought, his surgery was a bit like a confessional. Since his arrival in the area, he'd already heard lots of things about the sober citizens of Cloncullen that they wouldn't want him to know!

"You'll keep an eye on the children, won't you?" Sister Angela suddenly, as he was writing out her prescription.

"My dear Sister, you'll be hale and hearty for many's the year," he replied jovially. "After all, you're only in your middle years."

But Sister Angela wasn't happy to be humoured. "It's not dying I'm worried about – but the possibility that they might move me to another convent, and I'm the only one standing between those children and near starvation," she told him angrily.

"All right, I'll keep an eye on them," he assured her, "but I don't foresee any problems as long as you keep giving them the cod liver oil. Thanks to you, most of those kids are going to grow up strong and healthy."

"Yes – but it's the 'thanks to me' that I'm worried about," she added dryly. Sister Angela knew that she didn't have to spell out everything to Cormac McCarthy. He could see for himself that the children in the orphanage were far from adequately fed, and that if she herself wasn't in charge of the kitchens, their health would be even less of a priority to the other nuns.

Sister Angela knew only too well the discrepancies in the daily diets consumed at the convent, since she herself had to prepare both. To the nuns' dining room each morning went boiled eggs, toast and honey, tea, as well as fresh milk and cream delivered from one of the nearby farms; to the children's table went bread, margarine and black tea. The discrepancy was even more marked in the evenings, when a full dinner was served to the nuns, whereas another round of bread, margarine and black tea was considered good enough for the children.

During the winter months, Sister Angela tried to serve the children with porridge for breakfast as often as she could, surreptitiously making it up the night before in a big pot. As the children all sat shivering in the unheated refectory each morning after Mass, she liked to think that at least they were getting something warm and nourishing inside them. Luckily, Sister Angela could be certain that none of the other nuns were interested in venturing into the cold refectory at that early hour.

Sister Angela liked the new doctor. He was young, had kind eyes, and possessed a compassion and understanding that went far beyond his years. When he'd first arrived in Cloncullen, and she'd consulted him about her worsening arthritis, she'd expressed her concerns about the children's inadequate daily diet.

He'd recommended the daily spoonful of cod liver oil for each child – and had supplied her regularly, free of charge, with enough for all the children. And he'd already used the weight of his position to urge the nuns to supplement the children's diet with cheese, vegetables, and occasionally, even meat. So far, his words had fallen on deaf ears, but Sister Angela was hopeful that he'd eventually succeed.

In the meantime, he tried to ensure that the children didn't want for good food. In the country, many farming folk paid their doctor with a side of beef or a few crates of eggs instead of cash, and when this happened, most of this bounty found its way to Sister Angela, delivered surreptitiously through the back door of the convent kitchen late at night.

Although the children disliked the cod liver oil, and there were always mock groans when Sister Angela administered it after tea each evening, most of the children seemed to have benefited from it. Gradually, they'd lost that pale, sickly look and seemed sturdier, especially the little ones who were growing so rapidly.

"You really should be taking things easy yourself, " Dr McCarthy said. "When I met Mother Superior in the village recently, she said she was worried that your arthritis was getting worse, and – "

"I'm not abandoning those children!" was the outraged reply. "As long as you keep supplying me with pills, I can keep on working. We both know that those children need me." Sister Angela sniffed. "As for Mother Superior's concern over my health – forget it. She only wants me out of the way so that she can cut back even further on the amounts of food the children get."

It was a final statement, to which Cormac McCarthy had no reply.

Sister Angela was, however, determined to keep the conversation on the topic that was foremost in her mind. She continued to look at him stonily. "Your predecessor Dr Walsh was a grumpy old man who never bothered about the children when they were ill – unless a fat fee was involved."

Cormac McCarthy smiled at the implied rebuke. "Don't worry, Sister – I'll call to the orphanage regularly, without charge, for as long as I'm in practice here. Will that satisfy you? I do care about more than money, you know. Anyway – " he grinned across at her, "I'd be afraid that if I didn't, you'd set that God of yours on me!"

"I don't think he's that kind of God," said Sister Angela with a smile. But then her expression saddened. "On the other hand, when I see how some people – not a million miles away from here – treat other human beings, I really begin to wonder . . . "

CHAPTER 47

"The tinkers are coming!"

The news was received in equal measures of joy and anger by different segments of the Cloncullen community. The children at the orphanage looked forward to the arrival of the tinkers in Kilcolgan Wood. They enjoyed watching the arrival of the brightly coloured round-topped wooden caravans, and the idea of living in a wood seemed like a delightful adventure to them.

In contrast, the nuns became apoplectic at the arrival of the Travellers. But from the children's point of view, this meant that for a short time, someone else became the focus of the nuns' wrath instead of them.

When the Travellers came to the area, there was always great discussion about them. They were universally disliked, and everyone began to talk about installing extra locks and maintaining greater vigilance over any valuables they possessed. In the shops, someone always had a juicy story to share with neighbours, about how some tinker had either stolen fruit from their orchard, milk from their churns or plagued them with their begging.

The only person who treated the Travelling people fairly was old Sergeant Murphy, who had the unenviable task of keeping the settled people and Travellers apart – mainly for the Travellers' protection. It was said by many disgruntled locals that he was far too lenient with those thieving tinkers, but the sergeant merely believed that a person was innocent until proven guilty, and that no one – not even the settled residents of Cloncullen – were above the law.

When the Travellers were in town, the Sergeant's popularity tended to hit an all-time low, with some of the town's more prominent citizens suggesting that perhaps he was too old for the job of keeping law and order. Others felt that he was actually responsible for the annual influx of Travellers to the area, since word had spread among the Travellers that Cloncullen was an "easy" town, where they could get away with murder because the sergeant wasn't properly in control.

Prior to the travellers' arrival in the area, Mother Monica would call all the children to the assembly hall. All sorts of lurid tales were used to provide justification for vilifying the poor Travellers. And children were warned to stay well away from the Travellers' camps, because dreadful things might happen to them there.

Of course, as a result of the nuns' instructions, it became an exciting dare to sneak out of the orphanage or dormitory and creep up to the tinkers' camp. Julia had managed it twice without getting caught, and proved it to the others by stealing and bringing back some of the pegs the tinker women sold from door to door. She'd bet them all their jam portions for a week, and for the excitement generated by the escapade, it had been worth eating dry bread at the refectory table while Julia scoffed the whole lot.

It also proved a dare for many of the other children in the village – particularly the boys – who would challenge each other to sneak up to one of the caravans and bang on the door with a big stick to frighten the occupants, or to throw rolls of caps – designed for toy guns – into the campfire, causing a minor explosion and mayhem at the campsite. The children would then laugh loudly and run away, safe in the knowledge that the travelling people's word would never be believed against theirs, should they ever dare to complain.

"Sister, why do the other nuns hate the Travellers so much?" asked Majella one day, her big blue eyes focussed on Sister Angela's face.

Sister Angela shook her head. She found this question impossible to answer, since she couldn't understand why either. On the other hand, it was impossible for her to tell the children that she believed the other nuns were wrong, since surely the message of Jesus was to love everyone?

"I don't know, Majella," said Sister Angela, well aware that such an answer would never satisfy the child.

"I remember you told us about the poor Jews. Hitler hated them so much that he gassed millions of them, as well as gypsies and other people he didn't like."

"Hitler's dead now, and the war's long over, thank goodness, Majella."

The child looked disconcertingly at Sister Angela. "Do you think something like that happened to my parents?"

343

Sister Angela shook her head. "Those awful things happened in Germany and Poland, far away from here."

Majella still looked doubtful. "But Sister, you told us Hitler planned to do exactly the same in Ireland, if he ever got this far. And even though he's dead now, there's a lot of angry people around here too. Do you think that kind of thing could happen to the Travellers?"

"I don't know, Majella, but I hope not."

"But it's the same kind of hate, isn't it, sister? One there's no reason for. What did the Jews ever do to Hitler? Nothing. What have the Travellers ever done to anyone? Nothing."

"Dear God, Majella, let me get on with this baking, or there'll be nothing ready for tea time!" Sister Angela was both exasperated and proud of Majella's burgeoning intellect. In fact, all the children were extremely bright, and she wished they had an equally bright future to look forward to.

And, of course, Sister Angela conceded, Majella's reasoning was perfectly correct. The Travellers had never done anything to the nuns, except dare to inhabit the same planet. It seemed as though the nuns just needed other people to hate.

Sister Angela herself was very fond of Chrissie Delaney, a Traveller whom she looked forward to meeting every summer. Chrissie was a compassionate, caring woman, who spoke a lot of sense, and the two women found that they had much in common.

In the early summer, Chrissie would often venture as far as the convent, knowing it was then the nuns took their annual holidays, leaving Sister Angela to care for the children – and Sister Angela was always happy to see her.

There were a few others in the village of Cloncullen that Chrissie also regarded as friends. Mrs Collins and Ada Casey who both worked at Bay Tree House were always kind to her, and Mrs Collins always gave her any food that was left over at the end of the day.

On a few occasions she'd also met Mrs Laura Morton, who was now recovering well from the TB that had kept her bedridden for years. She'd been gracious to Chrissie, too, and had even invited her to have tea with her in the summerhouse on the lawn.

Of course, Chrissie and Ada Casey shared a secret that Chrissie had sworn never to divulge to anyone. And every time she visited the orphanage, she checked to see how the child was getting on, so that she could tell Ada how strong and healthy her daughter was growing. She sighed. What a pity she couldn't tell her friend Sister Angela that the child was Ada's, but she was sworn to secrecy, and Chrissie's word was her bond.

CHAPTER 48

"Hello, Majella – how are you, today?"

"Hello, Miss Casey," said Majella shyly. "I'm fine, thanks. And you?"

Majella was always pleased to see Miss Casey from the big house. Miss Casey was a very nice person, and was always interested in how Majella was getting on. She often asked Majella about her schoolwork, and inquired as to who her best friends at the orphanage were, and what film stars she liked best. Majella was delighted to be asked, since no one at the orphanage, with the exception of Sister Angela, ever asked her opinion on anything.

As Miss Casey and Majella strolled along together, Majella's friends Julia, Betty and Lucy walked ahead. Majella felt very important that Miss Casey went to the trouble of seeking out her company. It made her feel really grown up.

As always, Miss Casey was concerned about her welfare. "Do they treat you well in the orphanage, Majella? I mean – do they feed you properly and all that?"

Majella nodded. Even though Miss Casey was really nice and she liked her a lot, Majella was afraid to tell her the truth. So many things got the children into trouble; maybe telling Miss Casey the truth would, too. Perhaps if Majella told her about the beatings, the cruel taunts, the children's fear of all the nuns except Sister Angela, it would somehow get back to the nuns and mean more trouble. Maybe well-meaning Miss Casey would say something to the nuns, thinking that she was helping.

Majella shuddered as she imagined the ensuing scene with Mother Monica. "What have you been saying to Miss Casey from Bay Tree House?" the nun would shriek, "She's had the cheek to suggest that you mightn't be getting enough food or attention! I'll show you some attention, you cheeky little notice-box!" And the hands would lash out, momentarily blinding her with their impact round her head. And there would be no supper for several days after.

"You're shivering," said Ada Casey, buttoning up Majella's cardigan solicitously. "Are you sure you've got enough clothes on? I don't want you catching a cold, or something even worse."

Dear God, Ada thought, how I want to take this beloved child of mine into my arms. To take her home with me, to give her all the love I have to give her. Instead, I've consigned her to a life without a name. And all I can give her is a few stolen moments of my time, and the occasional few pennies that Mrs Collins has given me.

"Here – " said Ada, now delving into her pocket and handing Majella a sixpence, "You go and buy yourself an ice cream or some sweets."

Majella took the money and thanked her. It was

double what Miss Casey usually gave her, but she knew that she could never buy any of those treats. The children were supposed to hand over to the nuns any money gifts they received as "payment for their keep". Poor Julia had once been given a few pence for helping to carry a local woman's shopping, and instead of handing up the money she'd bought herself an ice cream. But she'd made the mistake of buying it in Larkin's shop, and young Con Larkin hadn't missed the opportunity of causing trouble. When he'd been helping his father deliver groceries to the orphanage the following day, he'd made sure that the details of Julia's purchase reached Mother Monica's ears. And the wrath of a nun whose rules had been flouted was a spectacle that still aroused fear at the mere thought of it.

Majella had been coming down the corridor as Julia was leaving Mother Monica's office, her face tearstained, rubbing the palms of her hands in her skirt to ease the pain inflicted by lashes of the strap. Ducking out of the way behind one of the large statues in the corridor, Majella had heard Mother Monica calling "Slut!" in Julia's wake. This remark was also heard by Sister Angela, who'd passed the cowering Julia coming in the opposite direction.

"Mother – that's hardly fair!" Sister Angela had said in shocked tones.

"Hrrmph," said Mother Monica, a sneer on her face. "Her and her wanton ways, the little upstart!"

"It wasn't her fault," Sister Angela had replied softly. "How can you blame an innocent child for the sins of an adult? Her father is the one who bears the blame."

Mother Monica had retorted in anger. "She's forever

in trouble, Sister, I think the Devil himself has got to her. Mark my words, Sister, I foresee a life of sin ahead of that young trollop."

Majella now looked intently at Miss Casey and decided to ask her a question that had been bothering her since then. "What is a slut, Miss Casey?" she asked guilelessly, her blue eyes looking intently into Ada's matching ones.

Ada coloured immediately. "Where on earth did you hear that word?" she asked Majella, fearful that someone might have unlocked her own guilty secret, or worse still, levelled the charge against Majella. The child's colouring was becoming so like her own.

"Oh, I just heard it somewhere," Majella replied, deciding that Miss Casey's shocked response must mean that it was a terrible word. "Does it mean the same as trollop?" she added, determined to understand the accusations levelled against poor Julia.

"Y-yes," replied Ada uneasily, "they both mean a woman or girl who is – " She sighed and gave Majella a hug. "They're not nice words – that's all you really need to know at your age. Go on – " she said, giving the child a gentle push, "off you go and buy yourself that ice cream."

Ada watched as Majella walked down the hill and turned back to wave when she reached the point at which she'd soon be lost from sight. And as Ada watched, she pondered on the words "trollop" and "slut", words that reflected the male, religion-dominated world they lived in, in which a woman was either a whore or a virgin.

As Majella turned the corner, she didn't take the turn for Larkin's shop. Although she longed to taste one of those luscious cones with the chocolate flake on top, the fear of retribution was greater than her longing for the short-term pleasure. Instead, she'd hide the money, in case she ever needed it . . .

CHAPTER 49

On cold winter evenings, when the wind howled in from the sea, rattling the shutters and creating draughts everywhere, the children would often huddle together in a corner of the large recreation room and tell stories. This storytelling performed the dual function of providing entertainment, and of distracting the younger ones from the cold, which left their fingers and toes numb and painful, and often made them cry.

"Go on, Julia – tell us the story about your parents again."

The little ones crowded around, eager expressions on their pinched little faces. When the older children told fairytale-like stories about their imaginary families, it was much more exciting than anything that could be found in a storybook. In fact, it wasn't only the younger ones who enjoyed the stories – all the children loved to escape into a world of make-believe. Somehow, fact and fantasy became intertwined.

"Well – my parents were very much in love with each

other – " Julia began, imagining her parents to look like Rock Hudson and Doris Day. "But because they were too young, their own parents wouldn't let them get married. They were – you know – like Romeo and Juliet, only instead of dying, they were sent far away from each other. At least, my mother was sent away to another country when they found out she was having a baby – "

"Well, in that case, wouldn't you've been born in another country?" retorted Lucy.

"Oh. Yes, I suppose you're right," said Julia, chastened and disappointed. It had been such a lovely story. Somehow, she just never seemed to get things right.

But there was another story, one she only vaguely remembered, and which she didn't understand at all. In this particular story, her mother had gone crazy, ending up in a mental home after discovering her husband's sexual abuse of his only daughter. And since there was no one to care for Julia, the orphanage had been the only place she could go . . .

"Where did she get the baby?" intervened six-year-old Mary. "Did God give it to her?"

None of the children were certain where babies came from, although a boy at school had told Majella that a man stuck his thing between a woman's legs and pushed the baby into her belly. Then he'd opened his trousers and taken out a pink wrinkled thing that kept growing as he rubbed it. At first she'd thought it was a ferret, but then he'd tried to get her to hold it, so she'd run away. The implausibility of such a story about babies had caused Majella to keep the information to herself. Clearly, the boy was just trying to frighten her.

"Yes, Mary – God gave it to her. God gives out all

babies," Majella replied. At least, that's what the nuns had told them, and it seemed a far more likely story than the boy's version.

Mary wasn't sure if she was happy with that answer. What on earth would she do if God decided to send her a baby, and she not yet seven years old? This was yet another problem to worry about.

"My parents were very rich," said Betty, taking over the storytelling. "They lived together in a huge house, with servants, gardeners, a swimming pool and a tennis court at the back of the house – "

The other children were silent now, as they pictured this idyllic way of life. "Had they got cars?" asked five-year-old Anna.

"Oh yes," said Betty, warming to her theme, "they had a big shiny black one – that was my father's one – and a lovely red sports car for my mother." Now she lowered her voice to a whisper. "But one day – "

The younger children now looked stricken, since they knew from experience that something awful would soon have to happen in the story, resulting in Betty ending up in the orphanage.

"One day, my parents were out driving in my father's big car, and they were both killed."

"How did it happen?" asked Julia, caught up in the story herself. Last time, it had been a big truck that had ploughed into them, but Betty's recollection of this event could vary. And if she was in good storytelling form, she might even tell them the gory details about the blood and guts that had been spread all over the road.

So stricken with grief was four-year-old Grace, that she began to cry.

"Shut up!" said Lucy fiercely. "How can anyone hear the rest of the story if you keep whinging?"

"Go on," said Majella, as order was restored and Grace silenced – with a dig in the ribs from Lucy on one side, and a hug from Majella on the other.

"Well, they were out for an afternoon drive in the countryside."

"Why didn't they bring you with them?" piped up five-year-old Marian.

"So you want poor Betty to be killed as well?" retorted Julia.

"No, I don't – "

"I was being minded at home by the servants, because I had a cold," Betty explained. "If I'd been well, I would have been with them – then I'd have been killed too," she finished.

"You haven't told us yet how it happened yet – " said Julia, determined to hear the gory details.

"Well, they were driving along when suddenly a big lorry came flying round the corner. It skidded, and went straight into my parents' car – "

The children listened, enraptured. This was a slightly different version than usual, and held the promise of even more gory revelations.

"What happened to the man who was driving it?"

"He was killed too, and there was bits of the car and bits of the people all over the road – so there was no one to look after me any more."

"But if you were rich – "

"Yes, I know – but my wicked cousins came and took over the house and everything, and sent me here to the orphanage. All they wanted was to keep the big house, the tennis court and the swimming pool for themselves."

"And the two big cars!" added little Grace, now smiling at her own cleverness.

"Don't be such an eejit!" retorted Betty. "Didn't I just tell you they were killed in my father's car? It was all smashed up, so there was only one car left." Seeing that she had their full attention, Betty now lowered her voice. "But when I grow up, I'm going back to that house and I'm going to throw those cousins out on the street – "

There were nods of agreement and murmurs of support.

"Then you can all come and live with me, and we'll live happily ever after," she concluded triumphantly.

Lucy now decided that it was her turn. Completing forgetting – or choosing to ignore – the fact that her parents had genuinely been killed in a car accident, she launched into her story.

"My mother is a film star," she said, "But she couldn't make films and look after me at the same time. So she left me here for safekeeping. When she's made lots of money, she's coming back to collect me. Then we're going to live in a lovely big house, and eat cakes and sweets every day!"

"What about your daddy?" said Marian anxiously. "Couldn't he look after you?"

"My daddy was a pirate," Lucy informed the assembly, "but he got killed when he was fighting for treasure with some bad pirates."

"What happened to the treasure?" asked the ever-practical Julia.

Just then, Sister Angela appeared.

"Time for bed, children," she told them, and

obediently they all stood up and began heading upstairs. The older ones would help the younger ones to clean their teeth, undress and put on their night attire.

Sister Angela smiled sadly to herself. She often eavesdropped on the children's stories, and knew how much they all craved a proper home and real parents. Tragedy of one sort or another had brought all the children to St Bernadette's, most of them being the children of women who'd been sent to the cruel convent laundries. But Sister Angela was determined that those tragedies would not be compounded by cruelty and misery at the hands of the other nuns at the orphanage. As long as there was breath in her body, she would love and protect each and every one of them.

CHAPTER 50

As she surveyed herself in the bath, Julia was consumed with self-loathing. Her body was big and awkward, her breasts too large and bouncy, as though they had a life of their own. They also oozed out at the top and bottom of the ridiculously small cast-off bra that the nuns had given her. She longed to be lean – like Majella and Lucy – or even downright skinny, like Betty. Anything would be better than being the way she was. Why had her breasts grown so big and unwieldy? Why couldn't they be non-existent like the other girls? And if only she could get rid of those unsightly wads of fat that straddled each hip . . . She was fed up with being ridiculed by the nuns and called a big fat heap.

In her misery, Julia did the only thing that momentarily eased the hurt and the misery of her size and situation: she ate. She filled her mouth with as much bread and margarine as she could fit. If there was jam too, so much the better. Sometimes, when she'd stuffed as much food as she could into her mouth, and no coherent speech was possible, she'd call the nuns all sorts of awful names, often at the top of her voice, but since no one could decipher the muffled words, they didn't know what she was saying. It gave her a joyful sense of revenge.

Many of the girls, along with Sister Angela, used to tell her she had a lovely singing voice; they'd ask her to sing for them, and the nuns grudgingly got her to sing at Mass on Sundays or when the Bishop was visiting. But to Julia, her voice meant nothing; she didn't even believe that she could sing. She assumed it was just the girls trying to humour her into thinking she had some value. The talent she wanted most was to be thin – something other girls took for granted, but which consumed Julia's life.

Julia loathed her body. There had to be something terribly wrong with it since it made men behave differently towards her than to the other girls. Could she be "an occasion of sin"? She was frightened at the thought. Maybe it was her fault that her father had touched her like that . . . Somewhere, deep in the recesses of her mind, she believed there must be something for which she was terribly to blame . . .

*   *   *

In early summer each year, the nuns took off for what they felt was their well-deserved annual holidays. Sister Angela, who wasn't considered important enough to need or deserve a holiday, was left in charge. As a result, this was the time of year the children loved best, and truth to tell, so did Sister Angela. This time of year also enabled Sister Angela to sort out problems the other nuns had chosen to ignore.

"Julia," said Sister Angela one summer day, "tomorrow, you and I are going up to Dublin."

Julia's mouth dropped open. She'd never been to Dublin in her entire life. Her bottom lip trembled with emotion. Was this a treat, or was there some more sinister reason for going? She knew Sister Angela would never wish her harm, so hopefully there must be a good reason. Or at least, not a bad one.

"Girls," said Sister Angela at breakfast the following morning, "Julia and I have business in Dublin today, and we'll be taking the ten o'clock bus to the city. Can I trust you all to behave yourselves while we're away?"

"Yes, Sister," chorused the entire assembly of girls.

Sister Angela looked stern. "If I come back and find that there's been trouble, we'll all be in hot water. Should anyone call to the convent and ask where I am, tell them I'm off saying my prayers and can't be disturbed." She smiled, looking at the innocent and anxious little faces. "Don't worry. It won't be a lie – I'll be praying all right – on the bus to Dublin. It's in such a bad state of repair that it'll need our prayers to get it there. Just don't tell any callers exactly *where* I'm doing the praying."

Later that morning, leaving the older girls in charge of the young ones, Sister Angela and Julia boarded the bus for Dublin, with Julia in a state of excitement.

"Why are we going, Sister?" she asked, as Sister Angela offered her the window seat.

"We're going to get you some foundation garments," said Sister Angela, her lips pursed. "It should have been done a long time ago."

Julia paled. What on earth were foundation garments?

361

The words sounded ominous. Maybe she was going to be made to suffer after all.

Seeing the child's anxious face, Sister Angela smiled. "Don't worry, Julia, we're only going to get you a few brassieres. We'll go to the foundation department of either Clerys or Arnotts, and get professional advice. There are people who specialise in fitting them, you know. It's important to get the right size for comfort."

Julia looked happier.

"And then, we'll go to Bewley's Café, and have tea."

Julia's eyes lit up. She could hardly believe it – she was being taken to a real cafe! She'd never been in one in her entire life. She was so excited, she could hardly speak.

A few hours later, Julia and Sister Angela were ensconced in Bewley's, with Julia tucking into several of their famous almond buns, while Sister Angela sipped her tea, watching her charge with pleasure.

Their visit to Clerys had proved very successful. Julia was now wearing a properly fitting bra, and experiencing comfort for the first time since her breasts had developed. She had another two equally comfortable bras in a Clerys paper bag beside her chair, and every few seconds, Julia would glance at the bag in wonder, terrified in case she'd forget it when they left. Yet nothing was less likely, given their monumental importance to her.

"Thank you very much, Sister – for everything," said Julia.

Sister Angela smiled. "Just because the other girls don't need brassieres yet, it doesn't mean you're different. You're a few years older than they are, so it's only natural that you've developed before they do. That makes you a leader, Julia – never forget that."

CHAPTER 51

Lucy's eyes were shining. "Guess what – I've got the most wonderful secret in the world!"

"Aw, go on – tell us!"

Lucy was on her way to Mass in the chapel attached to the orphanage, accompanied by Majella, Julia and Betty, her closest friends.

"Okay – but you must promise not to tell anyone."

The trio nodded their heads vigorously.

"I'm going to be adopted!"

The other three children stared at her in amazement. For them, being adopted was the ultimate dream, akin to marrying a prince and becoming a princess, or winning a big prize in the Irish Hospital Sweepstakes. But their initial delight turned to sadness as they realised that this would mean the end of their friendship with Lucy, while emphasising their own continued marginalisation from the real world.

Majella, her best friend, was the first to speak. "Congratulations, Lucy!" she said, hugging her friend.

"That's fantastic!"

"Shhh! Keep your voices down – someone might hear us!" whispered Lucy. Orphans were meant to be ladylike at all times, and showing joy was considered vulgar, and not part of God's scheme of things.

"How did it happen?"

"When did you find out?"

"Where are you going to live?"

The girls all plied her with questions simultaneously, while joyfully Lucy did her best to answer them all.

"I'm going to live with the family of a distant cousin of my mother's – these people were living abroad when my parents were killed. But now they're back, and they're willing to give me a home with them in Dublin. Oh God, I'm so excited!"

*   *   *

Of course, Mother Monica hadn't been pleased at all at Lucy's planned adoption. Apart from losing the subvention paid for the child's care, she disliked anyone else experiencing happiness, especially since it was a commodity so lacking in her own life. Sometimes, in the privacy of her own room, she allowed herself to admit the stark truth – she'd never have become a nun if there had been any other choice. But her brother had been given the farm, she hadn't liked any of the suitors who'd offered to take her off her brother's hands, and all she'd been offered was a dowry for the convent.

Although she and the other nuns had been about to head off for their summer holidays when she'd learnt about the proposed adoption, Mother Monica saw no reason to change her plans. So she'd departed with the rest of the sisters, leaving Sister Angela to hand the child over to her relatives when the appointed day arrived. In fact, she hadn't even said goodbye to the child, or wished her well in her new life.

When Sister Angela had heard Lucy's news, she'd been thrilled and heartbroken in equal measures. "Oh Lucy, I'm going to miss you so much – but I'm delighted for you. A home at last! It's the best news I've heard in ages." As the little nun hugged the young girl, there were tears in her eyes. "Oh dear," she said suddenly, "I won't have my terrible twins any longer!"

Since they'd been babies, Sister Angela had referred to Majella and Lucy as her terrible twins, because they were almost the same age and had exactly the same colouring. And the two girls, in turn, had loved the title, since it made them both feel special.

"But we'll stay in touch, won't we, Sister?" asked Lucy urgently, tears forming in her big blue eyes. "I'll write to you all, and tell you about my new life in Dublin. I'll be going to a new school, I'll have my very own bedroom – oh Sister, I think I'm going to die from excitement!"

CHAPTER 52

The sun was shining and the birds were singing in the trees as Majella and Lucy made their way down the deserted lane to the seashore. The sky was a vivid blue, the warm sand filtered sensuously through their open-toed sandals, and the water looked very inviting. Better still, there was no one else around to have to share it with. It was as though the two girls owned the entire vista themselves.

"I'm so excited!" Lucy said for the hundredth time. "I can hardly believe it – I've got a family after all!"

Majella smiled, willing herself to be happy for her friend. But inside, she felt only a terrible sadness. Now that distant relatives had been found who were willing to give Lucy a home, she was losing her dearest friend. Of course, Lucy had assured her that she would write regularly, but even if she did, things would never ever be the same again. For the thing that bound them together – having no one in the world except each other – was now being altered irrevocably. Majella was aware that she was miserably jealous, but she tried to hide it for Lucy's sake.

The two girls were on their way down to the sea through the dunes to swim, free for a few hours just to be together. It was Lucy's last day at the orphanage, and Sister Angela had urged the two friends to enjoy their last morning together. That evening, Lucy's relatives were due to arrive, and she'd leave the orphanage with them to begin her new life in Dublin. She was clearly excited at the prospect, but a little frightened too.

"Oh, God – I'm so nervous!" she kept repeating excitedly, both to Majella and to no one in particular.

While the other nuns were away, Sister Angela allowed the children more freedom than they had during the rest of the year, and she silently revelled in their joy as they skipped freely and rolled in the grass of the convent garden. She also revelled in the knowledge that if Mother Superior were to witness these events, she might become the victim of a heart attack. This prospect was not an unpleasant one; however Sister Angela's more charitable sentiments quickly reasserted themselves, and she blessed herself fervently.

Sister Angela also ensured that the children got more food than usual at mealtimes, and the atmosphere was much more relaxed and convivial than at any other time of year. In turn, the children did their best to lighten her workload as much as possible, and to ensure that nothing was left undone that might get her into trouble when the other nuns returned. The children stacked wood for the stove, washed the dishes and even washed and rehung all the curtains from the nuns' parlour – nothing was too good for their beloved Sister Angela.

And in the evenings, when the younger children were

asleep in bed, Majella, Lucy, Julia and Betty would sit in the kitchen with Sister Angela. Because of her failing eyesight, they would take turns reading to her as she sat knitting by the range, her experienced fingers rapidly clicking the needles back and forth, her eyes closed in concentration and pleasure. She'd knitted so many of the children's sweaters over the years that she didn't even need to watch what she was doing.

The absence of the other nuns was also a time of general camaraderie in the orphanage, and a time of learning in the kitchen. Without the restraints imposed by the other nuns, the older girls were taught by Sister Angela to bake bread and make apple pies, and then to share with the other children in the wholesome joy of eating them. Those few weeks of the summer were always filled with treasured memories, which many of the children lived on for the rest of their lives.

This year however, the shadow of Lucy's departure hung like the Sword of Damocles over Majella's head. Her anguish also made her feel even further apart from the other children, since they were all excited about Lucy's new family. It was as though one child's dream-come-true might start a chain reaction, resulting in the eventual appearance of everyone else's long-lost relatives. Excitement was running high, and Sister Angela was preparing a little party for the children that evening, to celebrate Lucy's departure. Sister Angela, overcome with excitement herself, felt reckless enough to order several pounds of sausages from the local butcher, which would be served with lashings of fresh bread and butter, then followed by homemade apple-tart and – as a special treat – ice cream.

On the beach, the two girls quickly divested themselves of their clothing. Underneath their frocks and cardigans, both were wearing swimsuits – ancient hand-me-downs that were rarely used in the normal course of events. Since swimming was clearly a pleasure for the children, it was severely frowned upon by the nuns. Besides, in their opinion anything that involved the removal of clothing had to be an occasion of sin, although the meaning of all this was totally beyond the children's understanding. As a result, however, none of the children were ever formally taught to swim; some of the older ones had, by sheer dint of will, taught themselves to float during the weeks of summer when the nuns were away. And they in turn had initiated the smaller ones into the joys of splashing around in the water.

"C'mon – I'll race you in!" cried Lucy, running down to the shore through the soft sand and scattered seaweed, onto the smooth hard sand that was being lapped by the incoming tide. She covered the ground quickly, her red-gold hair fanning out behind her, her pale legs flying across the sand.

We're really so alike, Majella thought, looking down at her own pale legs. Same coloured hair, same skin – no wonder Sister Angela sometimes calls us the terrible twins.

A sob rose in her throat. Why, oh why, she wondered, couldn't she have been the one to have found a new family? However, watching Lucy's exhilaration, she felt a pang of remorse, and the feeling of resentment passed. How could she be so jealous of the friend she loved? Making an effort to smile broadly, Majella followed Lucy into the water, where they splashed each other, laughing and shrieking at the initial coldness of the water.

Quickly, their bodies adjusted to the temperature, and they luxuriated in the tactile pleasure of the water swirling against their skin. They floated among the shimmering waves, gloriously lit by the mid-morning sun, as it gently washed over them. Despite Majella's sadness, the brightness and beauty of the day lifted her spirits. Instinctively, she knew that this day was one that she'd never forget. The memory of Lucy's joy, coupled with the bright, almost fluorescent colours of the water, shore and sky, would be etched forever in her mind.

Treading water happily, Lucy talked endlessly about what her new life would be like; she'd envisioned a home like a veritable palace, and distant cousins who looked, spoke and behaved like movie stars. At last, she'd have a family of her own, like people in the movies did. And in her generosity, she extended their imaginary welcome to Majella as well, inviting her to come for long holidays so that they could both share in the bounty of happy family life. She also had plans to invite the other children along as well – and Sister Angela too. Lucy's enthusiasm was infectious, and Majella couldn't stay out of spirits for long.

"Don't you think it's time we started going back?" said Majella at length, reluctant to spoil Lucy's reverie, but mindful of the help that Sister Angela would need to get things ready for the party.

"Not yet," called Lucy, and she began moving away from Majella, wading out towards the rocks that jutted out from the cliff at the end of the beach.

"Come back!" called Majella. "Lucy, the tide is coming in – you'll be trapped if you go out there!"

But Lucy, insulated by her own happiness, felt no such fear. "C'mon, cowardy custard!" she called good-naturedly. "It's not very far out! I just want to climb up on the nearest rock. I'll bet you there's a great view from there. It'll only take a minute!"

Ignoring Majella's entreaties, Lucy waded onwards through the deep water.

"But we're not allowed go out there!" Majella reminded her urgently.

"Pooh, pooh!" Lucy called back. "We're not allowed to go out there because it's great fun! I want to sit up on the big rock just once before I leave for Dublin. Because I never intend coming back here again!"

Majella was too frightened to follow her, for she could feel the water rising around her, and her own feet being lifted off the ground. "Come back, Lucy! Come back!" she shouted, but by now Lucy was too far away to hear her. Hell-bent on her own sense of achievement, she'd reached the rock, climbed onto it, and was waving from it happily.

But suddenly, as Majella watched, a big wave hit the rock, causing Lucy to lose her balance. Arms flailing, she fell from the rock into the waters below and disappeared from Majella's sight.

Majella watched helplessly, waiting for her friend to reappear. But there was no sight of her.

"Lucy!" Majella screamed. "Lucy, where are you?"

There was no sound except the crashing of the waves. Then briefly, Majella saw her friend again, but she quickly disappeared into the incoming swell. For an eternity, there was no sign of her, and Majella could feel herself becoming hysterical. Then Lucy bobbed up again, further in towards Majella, who now sighed with relief, believing that Lucy was swimming in towards the shore.

But then she realised that Lucy's face was submerged in the water, and her body didn't appear to be moving voluntarily. It was just floating like a rag doll, and being buffeted about by the incoming waves. Screaming now, and clutching at friend as she came within reach, Majella clawed at Lucy's hair, arms and swimsuit straps, as she tried to pull her friend towards the shore. But by now, the lifeless body seemed to weigh a ton. The waves were swirling around her own legs as she neared the shore and were dangerously close to toppling her over. Half-crazy with panic, Majella lost her balance, and the swell of water carried her away from Lucy's body and dumped her, half-choking, onto the beach.

Tears streaming down her face, Majella briefly lay panting on the beach as the incoming tide now threatened to wash over her. Half-staggering, she rose to her feet once again and plunged back into the water. It was easier to pull Lucy now, since the body had become wedged between two smaller rocks where the waves could not drag her outwards. And as she was in shallower water, Majella could at last get a grip on Lucy's hair while still retaining her own balance. Now she cursed the fact that no one was around to help them. Earlier, it had seemed a wonderful bonus not to have to share the beauty of the beach with anyone but each other.

Dragging Lucy's body out of the water, Majella managed to haul it up onto the sand beyond the high-tide mark. All the time she was doing so, she continued talking to Lucy as though she was still alive. In a state of intense shock, Majella couldn't accept that her dearest friend had drowned. Only minutes ago Lucy had been alive and full of excitement and hope for the future. Now she lay cold and unmoving, her wet hair matted with sand, her eyes closed and her face in repose as though she was just sleeping.

Of course that's all it was, Majella told herself, she was just sleeping. Gently, she smoothed the matted hair away from the freckled face of her friend, and wiped the sand from her cheeks, eyes and arms. Then she collected the clothes they'd earlier discarded, and covered Lucy with them.

"You're cold," she told the lifeless body. "I'll try to keep you warm." Gently, she chaffed her friend's ice-cold hands in hers. "Don't die on me, Lucy – please don't die!" she pleaded. "C'mon Lucy, stop pretending, please Lucy, oh please!"

*   *   *

A few minutes later, Dr Cormac McCarthy – out walking his dog before morning surgery – found them. At first, he thought that the two children were sleeping, then he thought that both were dead. Then he realised that the second child was still breathing, but in such a state of trauma that she saw nothing, heard nothing, responded to nothing. It was as though her mind had totally shut down in order to negate all that had happened. Taking the clothing that was covering the dead child, he now wrapped them round the living one, for whom they served a greater need. Reluctantly, having tried and failed to resuscitate her, he left his dog to guard the dead child on the beach, carrying the living one back to his surgery as fast as his legs would carry him. Treatment was urgently needed, or there might yet be a second fatality.

CHAPTER 53

In the children's dining room that evening, there was no longer any party atmosphere. In shocked silence, the children – many of them in tears – ate mechanically, if at all. The many treats – so carefully planned and so much looked forward to – tasted like sawdust in their mouths. The very young ones were incapable of understanding what had happened, but they took their mood from the others. They knew something awful had happened, and the distress of the older children caused them, too, to react with floods of tears. The only one who could eat was Julia, whose misery made her eat more ravenously than ever before.

Several local women had taken charge of the kitchen, the cooking and the care of the children when word of the tragedy became known. This meant that Sister Angela was free to deal with the many responsibilities that had suddenly been thrust upon her shoulders.

"Lucy, Lucy – talk to me," whispered Sister Angela to the small inert figure that lay in the darkened room.

Sitting alone beside the bed, the old nun held the child's cold hand in hers, willing her to respond.

Cormac McCarthy had decided against the county hospital; the journey there would take too long, and anyway, he maintained that the child's chances of recovery lay in being with the people she knew best, rather than with strangers.

At the child's bedside, Sister Angela rambled on, hoping that the sound of a familiar voice might eventually permeate the protective wall that the child had surrounded herself with. "I know it's terrible, losing your best friend like that – but you've got a new home and a new family waiting for you. They'll be arriving soon, and they want to take you away with them. Come on, Lucy – don't just lie there like that – you have so much to live for – "

Suddenly, Majella's eyes opened and she stared up at the nun. "Y-you called me Lucy," she whispered weakly.

"Of course, child – because your name is Lucy," said Sister Angela. "Oh, this is great news – you've no idea how worried we've all been about you. Just wait till I phone Dr McCarthy with the good news!"

Now it all came back to her. She and Lucy on the beach, the sun shining, the two of them running into the sea, Lucy's happiness, then that awful moment when she fell from the rock . . .

It was all too much for Majella to comprehend, but nevertheless she realised that now was decision time. She'd a choice to make that would alter the course of her life forever. She could tell Sister Angela about the mix-up when she came back from the telephone. Her friend was dead, and she was now being given a chance to take her place. In a new family, with a home of her own in Dublin. She would be part of a family at last.

Or she could stay in the orphanage, at the mercy of the nuns, until they finally evicted her, as they did all the children, at the age of sixteen, without any training for life or a career. A sob rose in her throat. How could she think clearly, when she'd just lost her best friend, and her brain was refusing to function?

"Oh, Sister!" she cried to Sister Angela when she returned. "I need to tell you the truth! I'm not Lu – "

"Hush, child – I think that in this instance, you shouldn't say anything," the nun quickly replied. "Don't forget – God helps those who help themselves."

Suddenly, Majella began to cry, and Sister Angela put her arms around her. Now both sobbing, child and nun clung together – in sorrow and in affection, but also in complicity.

Later that evening, a frail figure with a freckled elfin face and long red-gold hair left the orphanage, carrying a battered old suitcase tied up with string, collected by a middle-aged couple driving a maroon Morris Oxford. There were no formal goodbyes, since most of the children had already cried themselves to sleep, and anyway, Sister Angela had advised against it.

"Shouldn't I stay for the funeral?" Majella had asked Sister Angela just before she left.

"No child – go now, while you can," was the reply. "Your friend would have wanted you to." The nun ruffled the child's hair. "You don't have to stand at her graveside, child, for her to know how much you loved her. Let Lu – I mean, let Majella now rest in peace."

*   *   *

On the night of Majella's funeral, as Julia lay in her bed, she could hear sobbing coming from Betty's bed nearby. She longed to be able to comfort her, but there was nothing she could say or do without starting to cry herself.

The enormity of events was only now beginning to fully register as she looked across at the two empty beds on the other side of the small dormitory. Both Majella and Lucy were suddenly gone – one far away to a new home, the other into the cold ground. The monotonous and humdrum regularity that the older girls had so often complained about had certainly been broken – but not in any of the ways that Julia had ever hoped or dreamed of. If only, she thought, life could go back to the way it was a few days ago, she'd never hope, or dream, or ask God for anything again. Maybe if she hadn't prayed to God to send her lots of sweets, He wouldn't have taken Lucy . . .

The funeral, she recalled, had been a sad and dismal affair, with all the children and Sister Angela crying. None of the nuns on holidays had considered it worth their while to return for a mere orphan's funeral, for which the children – and Sister Angela too – were grateful. At least this had meant they'd been free to express their grief and solidarity, without the prying eyes of those who'd never have felt as they did.

Another event had occurred at the funeral that had also upset everyone. Miss Casey, the maid who lived at Bay Tree House had arrived at the graveside, weeping hysterically, so much so that she had to be escorted away by Sergeant Murphy, then taken back to Bay Tree House by Mrs Collins and Mrs Morton.

Julia was frightened and confused. Older people were expected to die – hadn't she often lain awake herself at night, frightened that Sister Angela would suddenly pass away and leave them to the mercy of the other nuns? But Majella had only been a child like herself. To Julia, it seemed as though the whole world had been turned on its head.

She felt as though an enormous cloud of sadness and desolation had descended on Cloncullen. She clenched her lips and teeth tightly together in an effort to stop her jaw from trembling uncontrollably. Because if she let go, even briefly, she was afraid that the moaning sound rising up in her throat would escape into the dormitory, filling everywhere with its sound.

CHAPTER 54

A few weeks later, the nuns finally returned from their holidays. And once again, the punishments, insults and sarcasm became part and parcel of daily life for the children. After she'd been called a tart, slut, fatso, and several names she didn't understand, Julia decided that she'd had enough.

"I'm going, Betty," she told her friend. "I can't take it any more."

"D-don't l-leave me Julia – please!" sobbed Betty, holding out her skinny little arms to her friend. "I'll have nobody to talk to, to be my friend – "

"Then come with me," said Julia, stuffing her extra vest and a towel into her well-worn toiletry holdall.

"I can't – I'm too scared of what they'd do to us when they'd catch us. We'd get at least ten lashes of the strap each!"

"Well, I'm not getting caught," said Julia fiercely, speaking with more confidence than she actually felt. "When I leave here, I don't ever intend setting foot in this place again – now, are you coming or not?"

"I can't," said Betty, with a muffled sob, "I haven't got your guts. Good luck to you – I'm going to miss you so much!" Choking on those last words, she hugged Julia tightly, sobbing into her shoulder.

Julia could feel the hot tears drenching her cardigan, as she comforted this girl who was so special to her. She hardly had the heart to pull herself away.

Quietly, she let herself out through the side door and disappeared into the night.

In the small dormitory – empty now since Majella, Lucy and now Julia had gone – Betty felt frightened and alone. But she had one more task to carry out before she could give in to the luxury of sobbing herself to sleep. Taking the pillows from the other two beds, she slid them under the covers of the one that had been Julia's. Betty, her tears of sadness now turning into a little smile of satisfaction, surveyed her handiwork. If she'd been a sculptor, she couldn't have done better. It really did look big and lumpy like Julia, and the lower pillow looked exactly like Julia's bum.

* * *

"Tell me the truth, Betty," said Mother Superior, looming treacherously over the quaking child. "It's clear that you knew all about this foolhardy escapade."

"I-I don't know anything, Mother," whispered Betty, as clearly as she could. If only her teeth would stop chattering.

Mother Monica paced her office floor, reaching for the much-feared strap as she passed the bookcase on which it normally rested. Menacingly she swished it as she paced back and forth again. That should frighten the little bitch into telling the truth.

"I-I didn't even know that she was going to go, Mother!" Betty ventured bravely. "She – I mean I – " She gulped and closed her mouth once again.

Realising that this tactic wasn't working, Mother Monica opted for a different approach. "Come, come child – you may think that you can get away with lying to me, but surely you're not going to lie before God himself? He knows if you're telling the truth, and if you're not – " she paused for effect, then swished the strap through the air, "you'll have committed a mortal sin that will stain your soul black until you ask God for his forgiveness in confession."

Betty blinked, and tried to envisage God looking into her insides, where her soul – which she imagined must be some kind of white glowing lump – was gradually being darkened by some kind of celestial boot polish.

"And if you die tonight – and God could choose to strike you dead for telling lies – you will go to Hell for all eternity . . . "

Betty gulped, horrified at this last possibility. "I-I think, Mother," she blurted out, "I think she said she was going to cross Kilcolgan Wood – "

"Aha, so you did know!" gloated Mother Monica, now gripping the child's hands and positioning them for the maximum infliction of pain. Then the strap swished through the air once again, this time right on target, and Betty smarted with the pain. But far worse was the bitter sense that she'd betrayed her friend, but was still being punished anyway.

*　*　*

So serious were the events of the night before that Mother Monica decided they warranted a personal visit to the tinkers' camp. In reality, she wasn't concerned about the tiresome child's disappearance – good riddance to the big heap, was her own personal feeling – but it didn't look good for the convent if one of its orphans had run away, especially with the Bishop due to visit the following week. Julia had impressed him with her singing on his previous visit – what would she do if he requested her to sing at Mass this time? With a bit of luck, this matter could be quickly sorted out, and the child reinstated – having been punished severely, of course, as a deterrent to other would-be adventurers – and the whole matter put behind them before the Bishop's arrival. Indeed, it was her very intention to ask for a subvention from His Excellency's diocesan funds under the guise of providing additional advantages for the orphans. It would certainly weaken her case if it became known that one of them had absconded.

If that snivelling little nobody, Betty, was right, then the runaway child would have crossed near the tinkers' camp. She could even be hiding there. Perhaps, Mother Monica thought, she'd be able to intimidate someone there into revealing whether they'd seen her. She sniffed. Respect for the Church was probably the only useful trait that these dreadful tinkers possessed.

*　*　*

"Get away from here, you old witch!" said Chrissie, descending the steps of her caravan, and brandishing a large blackthorn stick. "I got short shrift at your door anytime I called a-begging, so don't you come darkening mine!"

Ignoring Chrissie's insults, Mother Monica stood her ground. "I'm looking for a young girl who is missing from the orphanage. I was hoping that you might have seen her and could tell me which way she went. The poor child has no proper clothes with her, and – "

"How could she have, seeing as you never give any of those children proper clothing?" retorted Chrissie angrily, "And no – I haven't seen any young girl around here, and even if I had, I wouldn't send her back to you lot of craw-thumpin' old biddies!"

"I could ask the sergeant to come and search your caravans," said Mother Monica evenly, "and I'm sure he'd find lots of other things that shouldn't be there."

"Are you accusing the Travellers of stealing?" roared Chrissie. "Get away from here, you black-hearted oul' bitch! And don't forget that I could have you in court for casting aspersions on our good name!"

Realising that she was getting nowhere, Mother Monica turned on her heel and walked out of the camp with as much dignity as she could muster. Everywhere she went, eyes followed her silently, while children and dogs scampered out of the way. Nobody, not even the dogs, had any liking for the nuns at the orphanage.

*   *   *

"Well, now Reverend Mother," said the sergeant,

taking his pipe out of his mouth and examining it
thoroughly, "I don't think that I could do that, you know.
It'd be a terrible imposition on decent folks to go poking
around their caravans – and to be doubting their word."

"You'd take the word of a tinker?" retorted Mother
Monica. "I'm certain that they're hiding the child there.
And a lot of other things that they've probably stolen too.
Sergeant, it's your duty to protect innocent citizens!"

The sergeant looked directly at her, steeliness now in
his eyes. "You're right, Mother – and that's exactly what
I'm doing."

CHAPTER 55

Shortly after Julia's escape from the orphanage, Chrissie called to the back door of the convent kitchen, where she knew she was likely to find Sister Angela.

As usual, at that time of day, Sister Angela was baking.

"Come in, Chrissie, come in," she said, "and close the door after you. There's a terrible gale today!"

Looking carefully around her, Chrissie stepped inside.

"Don't worry," said Sister Angela dryly, "none of the other nuns ever set a foot in here. But they're happy to eat the produce I bake."

"I'm here about Julia, Sister."

"Oh my God – did the poor child have an accident? What – "

"Sister, she's fine! She just wanted me to let you know that she's lodging with us for a while."

Sister Angela blessed herself. "Oh thank God she's all right! I've had sleepless nights worrying about her!" She waved a hand in the direction of the kitchen table.

"Sit down, Chrissie. I'm sure, like me, you could do with a cup of tea!"

Bustling over to the big industrial cooker, she checked the contents of the oven. Satisfied that everything was all right, she came back with a teapot and cups, and lowered herself into a chair opposite Chrissie.

"Of course, if the orphanage was run the way it should be, the poor child wouldn't have needed to run away," said Sister Angela, pouring the tea. "You're very kind, Chrissie – God knows, you've family enough to look after yourself." She hesitated. "But what about Julia's education? She can hardly continue attending the village school! Besides, summer's almost over, so no doubt you'll be moving on soon."

"We will, that's true," said Chrissie, "but I give you my word I'll do all I can to teach Julia myself. It's the only way I can educate my own kids – the travelling way of life means that we're never in one place long enough for the children to go to school. And anyway, there's many settled folk who don't want the children to attend either."

Sister Angela nodded, saddened by the folly and hypocrisy of the human condition. "But I'd hate to see Julia abandon her studies – she's a bright girl, and did you know she has a beautiful voice?"

"No, Sister, I didn't. I'll do what I can to help her. My own mother taught me to read and write – and for that, I'm eternally grateful to her. I'll do my best to keep Julia on her toes!"

The two women smiled at each other. And Sister Angela thought suddenly of another poor child, now dead, and of another one somewhere in Dublin, hopefully happy in her new home.

"Would you be able to use a few apple pies?" said Sister Angela. "I'll be taking them out of the oven in a few minutes. I've baked far too many today, as it happens."

Chrissie smiled. She knew that food was never left over in an orphanage. On the other hand, it would be churlish to refuse Sister Angela's well-meaning hospitality.

"That's very good of you, Sister," she said, smiling. "Thank you, I'd be delighted. My kids will enjoy the treat."

*　　*　　*

As the seasons changed, the Travellers were forced to move camp at regular intervals, invariably moved on, once luminaries from the local community managed to galvanise themselves into a committee of sorts and organise their eviction. At first hand, Julia witnessed these evictions, and wondered at the simple cruelty of ordinary people, and of the unwillingness of seemingly decent people to challenge the accepted way of things. These people reminded her of the nuns, who taught one version of Christianity, but practised another.

But while the winters were the worst time for keeping warm and dry, the Travellers were less likely to be moved at that time, because it meant that settled people would have to leave their own warm firesides and grapple with the elements. Huddled round a central campfire, designed to spread a little heat to all the caravans within its radius, the Travellers would retell stories of their glory days, when they were welcomed by farmers to mend their milk churns, buckets and farm implements.

Often, Julia would sing at the campfire, and her glorious voice seemed to soothe the men's' alcohol-fuelled rages that often led to fights within the camp. As a result, the women would encourage her to sing at every possible opportunity, and she, in turn, developed confidence in the power and effect that her voice had on others. Gradually, she began to accept that perhaps she *did* have a gift, one that might some day help her to earn a living.

Towards the end of her second year on the road with the Travellers, Julia felt that there was a subtle change in Chrissie's attitude towards her. It worried her, since she adored Chrissie, and got along well with Chrissie's own children. Julia helped Chrissie with the four children as much as she could. She felt that it was one small way in which she could repay Chrissie for all she had done for her. She could even tolerate Mikey, although she rarely saw him. Most of the time, he was off drinking, or gathering scrap metal with the other men – except for those nights when he demanded his marital rights with Chrissie, and the caravan heaved until he fell into a drunken stupor.

One evening, as Chrissie shelled peas outside her caravan door, in preparation for the evening meal, Julia could see that something was on her mind.

"Chrissie, what's bothering you?" Julia asked anxiously. "You keep looking at me in a funny way, and I'm wondering if I've done something to upset you."

Having spent her formative years in the orphanage, Julia still sometimes felt that even by breathing she was offending someone.

"Lord, no, child," said Chrissie, smiling. "But you're

right – there is something I've got to say to you. Now please – don't take it the wrong way."

"What have I done?" Julia whispered, fear in her voice. The last person in the world that she'd want to upset would be Chrissie. The Traveller woman had given her a home and, for over two years now, Julia had travelled the roads with Chrissie and her family.

"You've done nothing, dear – except grow up. You've become a woman."

Julia nodded, still mystified and worried.

"And it's time you started planning for your future. And that future isn't here with us, Julia."

"What do you mean, Chrissie?" asked Julia, her voice suddenly hoarse with fear. "You're not throwing me out, are you? You're the only family I have!"

"Of course I'm not throwing you out, but – " Chrissie studiously examined the peas in the bowl rather than look directly at Julia. It was hard for her too, since she was deeply fond of Julia. "I think it's time, for your own sake, that you left us."

"Oh, please Chrissie – don't say that!"

Finally, Chrissie looked up, sadness in her eyes. "If you don't understand what I mean, then I'll just have to spell it out for you." She looked at the peas in the bowl, then back at Julia again. "I've seen the men in the camp looking at you – "

Julia stared at Chrissie uncomprehendingly.

"Looking at you in that special way that a man looks at a woman."

Suddenly, realising what Chrissie meant, Julia blushed.

"You're at the age when what you do – or what's done

to you – will affect you for the rest of your life. So go – before some feckless and handsome young lad steals your heart. Because if that happens, before you know it you'll have several babbies, and your dreams will be over before your life's even started."

Julia's eyes filled with tears at the thought of leaving Chrissie, who'd been like a mother to her.

"If you get trapped here, this will be your life for the rest of your days. And it's a life I wouldn't wish on my worst enemy." Chrissie shuddered. "Vilified by your own kind and living permanently in poverty at the side of some road. Go and make use of that beautiful voice of yours. Make a decent life for yourself, and leave the stigma of the travelling way of life behind you."

"But where will I go, Chrissie?"

Chrissie smiled, relieved that Julia had accepted the inevitability of her departure. Looking around the camp, to ensure that no one else was within earshot, she leaned towards Julia conspiratorially. "I've been putting away a few shillings for this day – so that you'll have enough to live on until you get settled in a job somewhere. And hopefully, there'll be enough left over for singing lessons too."

Chrissie didn't bother to tell Julia that this was the money she'd been saving for a little house of her own. She hadn't managed to put away very much so far, but sometimes, other people's needs were greater than one's own.

Julia gulped. Chrissie's goodness never ceased to amaze her.

That night, as she huddled beneath her blankets on the floor of the caravan, Julia's mind was racing. She was scared, exhilarated and sad all at once. She sensed that she was on the threshold of a new chapter in her life. Where would it lead her? Could she justify Chrissie's faith in her?

The following morning, after a night spent tossing and turning, Julia had decided on a plan. At the earliest opportunity, when Mikey had left to find scrap and the older children had gone begging, she sought a quiet word with Chrissie, who was hanging out the washing on the hedges to dry.

"Remember what we talked about yesterday?"

Chrissie smiled. "As if I could forget, alannah! But take your time about going – don't leave until you feel ready."

"I think I've worked out a plan. But first of all, I need to know when we'll next be camping in Kilcolgan Wood."

Chrissie considered. "Well, the weather's picked up, so I'd imagine we'll leave here and head south within the next few weeks. Then we'll need to stop off to get the horses shod, so it might take us another two or three weeks to get there. But maybe you should leave us before then – I'm sure you haven't forgotten that Cloncullen's where the orphanage is – I don't want that oul' bitch of a Mother Superior catching you."

Julia shook her head. "I've always managed to stay out of the way when we've camped there before. Anyway, this will be my last time to go there. Will you do me a favour when we get there, Chrissie?"

"Of course, child."

"I want you to contact my old friend Betty. This time, I'm not leaving without her."

Chrissie nodded approvingly. "I'll be happier

knowing that you've got company. But Betty's a nervous little thing – are you sure she'll have the courage to go with you?"

"I'll drag her, if I have to," said Julia, smiling.

Chrissie smiled. "I'm looking forward to going back to Cloncullen myself. As you know, I've got some good friends there."

"Mrs Morton and Mrs Collins?"

Chrissie nodded. "And Miss Casey."

"She's the one who got very upset at Majella's funeral, isn't she?"

Chrissie quickly changed the subject. "So how do you plan to convince Betty to leave with you?"

Julia's eyes twinkled. "Since it's the summer term, all the nuns except Sister Angela will be away on holiday. So Betty won't be scared to leave. Besides, you can tell Sister Angela after we've gone. She'll cover for us, and because of that, Betty will be happy to go."

"God bless you both," said Chrissie fervently.

* * *

With the return of the sisters from their holidays at other convents, Sister Angela found herself in hot water. Betty's disappearance was quickly noticed by Mother Monica.

"What? Oh dear, Mother Superior, how could I not have noticed?" said Sister Angela, doing her best to look surprised and flustered. "I could have sworn I saw her here at breakfast this morning. But if you're right, then it must have been some other child. Goodness, it must be these glasses of mine – maybe I need stronger lenses . . ."

"Maybe I should call the police," said Mother Monica, closely watching Sister Angela's reactions. "After all, the child could be in moral danger."

"Oh dear, isn't that a rather drastic action, Mother? I'm sure she'll be back here in no time at all – she's probably gone picking wild raspberries in Kilcolgan Wood."

Mother Superior gave a grim smile of satisfaction. Clearly, Sister Angela knew all about the child's disappearance. Otherwise, she'd be worried in case something genuinely bad might have befallen the child.

Mother Superior flicked her veil, turned on her heel and left the room. Truth to tell, she didn't give a damn about the snivelling Betty. It meant one less mouth to feed, and she'd no intention of notifying the police. The child wouldn't be missed by anyone. But Mother Monica intended storing up the knowledge of Sister Angela's involvement for future reference.

As Mother Monica left the room, Sister Angela did her best to mask the smile that kept breaking out across her face. By now, the two youngsters had several weeks of a head start, so they were unlikely ever to be found. Sister Angela silently wished them luck. As for Majella, who was now Lucy – she hoped the child was now happily settled in her new home. Julia and Betty were intending to contact her, since the real Lucy, poor child, had delightedly told everyone in the orphanage her new address. Sister Angela chuckled. Julia and Betty would get quite a surprise when they discovered that Lucy was actually Majella! She'd thought of warning them in advance, but somehow, it didn't feel right. It wasn't her story to tell.

She sighed, heading towards the refectory. Her arthritic knees were paining her, but there were hungry children waiting to be fed, so she'd no time to put her feet up yet. Now that the other nuns were back from holidays, rations were back at their normal meagre level, and she knew there'd be a gaggle of half-hearted complaints when she gave the children only bread and margarine for tea. But she'd a little treat for them as well – Dr McCarthy had dropped off several dozen eggs, so there'd be a boiled egg for every child as well.

Her heart filled with joy as she headed into the kitchen. This was her domain, and she was never happier than when she was preparing meals for her children. She loved each and every one of them. Nor did she forget the ones who were now far way. Every night, they were all in her prayers.

BOOK 3

CHAPTER 56

At the Angels' Plot in Glasnevin Cemetery in Dublin, the baby's skeleton from the chimneybreast at Bay Tree House was finally laid to rest. Olivia had been adamant that she was attending the burial, since the baby's skeleton had been found in her house. And Barbara and Maggie both volunteered to attend along with her.

"I'm afraid to let either of you out of my sight, anyway," said Barbara, "because when I'm not there, something interesting always happens to you both!"

"Well, I wouldn't describe meeting Mark Cunningham as interesting," said Olivia tersely.

"You know what I mean, Liv. At least you actually met someone – I never meet anyone at all."

"Maybe that's because you spend so much time moping over Richard Devlin," said Maggie blandly, and Olivia shot her an indignant look.

Barbara ignored Maggie's remark, but they both saw her face redden, so they knew she'd heard it.

As they stood a short distance from the tiny grave,

waiting for the priest to arrive, Olivia thought back over all that had happened since she'd been given Bay Tree House. And she thought gratefully of her kind grandmother and Uncle Eddie who had made home ownership possible for her. She had wonderful relations, and she knew how lucky she was. Unlike the poor baby whose remains were about to be interred.

Olivia had considered asking her grandmother and Uncle Eddie if they wanted to attend the burial with her, but decided it might seem a bit odd. After all, they hadn't even visited the house yet!

Olivia saw that Philip's grandmother, Carmel Collins, and the two nuns from the old orphanage had travelled up to Dublin to pay their respects as well. There were also two elderly people, a man and a woman, neither of whom she recognised.

"It's sad, isn't it?" said Barbara. "A poor little baby who never even got a chance to live. I wonder if we'll ever know the full story?"

Olivia looked across to where Carmel Collins was standing, chatting quietly to one of the nuns. "Well, there's someone here who definitely knows what happened. But will we ever get her to tell us about it?"

"Even if anyone knows what happened, they're hardly going to talk," said Maggie quietly. "Murder is a criminal offence, so they won't want to draw the attention of the police. They could be accused of being accessories or of perverting the course of justice."

Just then, Philip Lynch joined the little group, bringing their conversation to an abrupt end.

"Hello, Philip," Maggie gushed.

Barbara nudged her as the officiating priest began to

intone the prayers. And they all fell silent, thinking about the little baby, whose life had been ended before it had even begun.

As they left the cemetery after the burial, Olivia drew Philip aside and pointed discreetly to the woman who was now walking slowly with Carmel Collins. Olivia lived in hope that one day she'd find her missing great-aunt, so every elderly woman she saw increased that hope. But this time she was destined to be disappointed again.

"Philip, who's that elderly woman talking to your grandmother?"

"Her name is Mrs Delaney. She lives just outside Cloncullen and she's a close friend of my grandmother's for many years."

Suddenly, Olivia remembered something she'd heard in the village. "Is she the woman who goes off in a caravan every summer?"

Philip nodded. "Chrissie is a Traveller, and although she settled in Cloncullen many years ago, she still loves to take to the roads during the summer months. She says it's in her blood – she gets itchy feet when the days get longer."

"And who's the man?"

Philip looked down at her, grinning. "Nosy, aren't we? That's Dr McCarthy – he used to be the local GP for the Cloncullen and Ballyesmond area. But he's retired now. I'm surprised to see him here – he usually stays close to home these days. I wonder what's his interest in being here?"

"Probably common courtesy," said Olivia. "You cops always think everyone has an ulterior motive!" She wondered what Philip would say if he knew that his grandmother knew more about the baby than she was letting on. Olivia had also realised that Dr McCarthy was obviously the person Laura referred to as "Dr Mc" in her diaries. And "C" could be Chrissie, couldn't it?

Maggie, who wasn't too happy about Olivia monopolising Philip, joined them and latched onto his arm possessively. He didn't seem to mind, and all three of them left the cemetery together.

As everyone gathered outside the cemetery gates before returning to Cloncullen, Olivia made a spur-of-the-moment decision to invite everyone back for tea – or something stronger – at Bay Tree House. She felt a very real affinity with the baby who'd just been buried, and she somehow felt that a quick burial wasn't enough. Her new carpets had been laid and the place was beginning to look and feel like a real home, so she felt the time was right to invite her neighbours in. Almost everyone accepted her invitation, so she had to stop off on the drive back to get extra supplies of food and drink!

*   *   *

Before long, the small party was in full swing at Bay Tree House, and the kitchen was filled with chatter and the clink of glasses. Olivia had stopped off at Larkin's shop, where she'd stocked up on booze, tea and coffee, ham and chicken, lettuce, tomatoes and cucumber, and in the kitchen, Barbara quickly assembled a decorative and tasty salad, augmented with herbs and nasturtiums from Olivia's garden.

Carmel Collins had come back to the house, as had the

two nuns. Olivia was introduced to both Dr McCarthy and Chrissie Delaney, both of whom she took to at once. Philip Lynch acted as barman, although he wouldn't touch a drop himself, since he was expected back at the Garda station within the hour. He spent most of his time chatting to Maggie, much to Olivia's relief.

Olivia was amused that the nuns each opted for a sherry, and was grateful that she'd brought a bottle back from a holiday in Portugal some years before. It amused her to think that the nuns probably didn't realise that a small glass of sherry actually contained far more alcohol than a normal-sized glass of wine. She grinned as she surmised that both nuns would probably have hangovers later that evening!

When the nuns were leaving, Sister Philomena seemed reluctant to go. "You must come and visit us at the convent," she said, fluttering her hands excitedly. She was clearly delighted to be invited to Bay Tree House, and was determined to maintain the contact now that it had been established.

"I'm sure Olivia would find our convent very dull and basic, after the cosy home she's made here," said Sister Maria, smiling apologetically. "I must say, you've done a lovely job on the house. And you've changed the colour scheme. "

"Oh, so you've been here before, Sister?"

Sister Maria nodded. "When poor Laura Morton was ill, many years ago, some of the sisters, myself included, would sit with her from time to time. Mind you, that's many years ago now. I see you've kept her kitchen dresser and table – they blend in very well with your own style."

"Thank you, Sister, I'm glad you like it. And yes, the dresser and table look great. I love them both – I think they make the place really homely." Olivia hesitated. "Sister, I'm anxious to find out a bit more about Laura Morton – now that I'm living in her house."

"Well, yes, we'd be glad to tell you what we can," said Sister Maria, "but I assumed you knew her? I mean, was she not a relative?"

"It's a long story, Sister," said Olivia. She'd been intending to learn what she could about Laura, then also to casually enquire if anyone named Ada Casey had been in the vicinity, or had been a friend of Laura Morton in the past. Now, she hesitated. Maybe now wasn't the time or place to question the nuns.

"Well, then, you must come to the convent and we can have a good chat," said Sister Philomena. "It used to be an orphanage, many years ago. But it's empty now, and those of us who remain use only a small segment of it." She sighed. "We suspect it'll be sold for development within the next few years. But then, life is all about change, isn't it?"

"I'd love to come, " said Olivia. "And I'm really anxious to learn anything I can about Laura Morton. I really know very little about her."

"I'd be delighted to tell you all about Laura," said Sister Maria. "But what about your own family? Can't they tell you about Laura?"

Olivia shook her head. "They didn't know her at all, Sister," she replied.

"Oh. Was she a distant relative then?" asked Sister Philomena.

"No. Not even related."

"So why did she leave them the house?" asked Sister Maria.

"They don't actually know."

"How odd," said Sister Maria, looking puzzled. "Will your family be visiting the house at some point?"

"I hope so," said Olivia fervently. "There's just my mother, grandmother and Great-uncle Eddie, but I can't convince them to visit yet." She smiled. "I think they want to make sure I've installed all the home comforts first!"

Olivia felt protective of her grandmother and Uncle Eddie, and didn't want to explain the real reason for their reluctance – which was their fear that they'd find some distressing connection to their sister.

* * *

Once the nuns stood up to leave, the exodus towards the door began, and after profuse thanks and promises to meet again, the guests took their departure. Soon there was only Olivia, Barbara, Maggie and Philip remaining.

Philip looked at his watch. "Oh dear, I should be back at the station by now!" He stood up to go. "That was a great little shindig, Olivia," he said, as he prepared to leave. "It was a nice thought to give the poor baby a decent send-off."

"Bye, Philip," said Maggie smiling up at him. "Hopefully we'll see you soon?"

But Philip's parting grin included them all, which left Maggie decidedly peeved.

As Olivia opened the door to let Philip out, she suddenly remembered that she had something to ask him. "Philip – was Laura Morton buried in a different grave to her husband?"

Philip grinned. "There could be a career for you in the Garda detective department, Olivia! Yes, Laura Morton astounded everyone by arranging to be buried in another graveyard. Needless to say, that kind of behaviour was unheard of in these parts."

He hesitated for a second, and she began to worry in case he was going to ask her out. But his next words produced a bombshell she wasn't expecting.

"Olivia, I've been meaning to tell you – I've found out the names of the two people who worked at Bay Tree House as domestic servants during the early 1950s. One was my grandmother – she was the housekeeper – and the other was a young girl called Ada Casey."

Olivia's heart almost stopped beating.

"Isn't that the name of the relative you've been looking for?"

Olivia nodded, unable to speak.

"I'm concerned that my grandmother knew all about this, yet never told me," said Philip. "I get the distinct impression that a number of people around here don't want the police digging into the past."

"You mean your grandmother *knew* Ada?"

"Looks like it. Sorry, Olivia, I have to go now – got to get back to the station. We can talk later."

With that, he was gone, leaving Olivia feeling shocked and disoriented. Quickly, she excused herself and headed for the bathroom, locking herself in to give herself time to think. At last she had news for her grandmother and Great-uncle Eddie!

Now she knew for certain that Ada had actually lived

at Bay Tree House, and was undoubtedly the "A" mentioned in Laura's diaries. This was virtually confirmation that she'd been a victim of Henry Morton's lust while his poor sick wife lay helpless in her bed. But what had happened her? Had she died? Or left and moved elsewhere?

She took a deep breath. She must organise her thoughts and have some questions prepared for when she next saw Philip.

She sighed. Now that she was on the brink of solving the mystery of Ada's disappearance, she was actually reluctant to find out anything more. Because it meant that her grandmother and Uncle Eddie would be shocked and disappointed to learn about their sister's sad life. And she herself would be the bearer of the sad news.

Momentarily, Olivia thought of keeping the truth from them, but realised she'd be dishonouring their right to information on their sister. However unpalatable it was, they still had a right to know.

She'd now have to approach Carmel Collins, and beg her to reveal what she knew. Clearly, Carmel Collins had known about Ada all along, and this time Olivia wasn't going to be fobbed off with vague answers.

CHAPTER 57

The following weekend, as Barbara carried the weekend's shopping along Cloncullen's main street towards her car, she spotted Richard Devlin and his son in the distance. Quickly, she checked her reflection in a nearby shop window, and was annoyed at herself for giving in to feelings of vanity where Richard was concerned. She didn't give a damn about him, so why should she care how she looked? On the other hand, she admitted to herself that she wanted to look good so that he'd realise what he'd missed. And looking good would give her confidence while dealing with him.

"Hello, Richard."

"Hello, Barbara."

Barbara bent down and greeted the small boy holding Richard's hand. "Hello! You must be Jack."

The child, who was clutching a toy train engine in his other hand, held it up for her inspection.

"You like trains, do you, Jack?" Barbara asked, smiling at him.

The little boy nodded.

"Ever since Jack saw his first train, he's been crazy about them. We spend a lot of time in train stations," said Richard, attempting a grin. "We've nearly worn a path to and from the station in Ballyesmond!"

There was a brief, uncomfortable silence, then Richard spoke again.

"How are you, Barbs? I presume Olivia told you . . ." His voice trailed off.

"Yes," said Barbara, giving him the benefit of an appraising smile. "I'm sorry to hear about your wife. It must be difficult rearing a small child on your own."

"We're coping. Obviously, I had to leave the company, but I'm now running a small IT service business from home. I work when Jack goes to nursery school."

"And where is home these days?" As soon as she said it, Barbara could have killed herself for asking. She wanted to appear totally disinterested, but the question had just slipped out.

"After Jo died, I sold the apartment. I thought that it would be better for Jack to grow up in the country, so I bought a house with a few acres of land in Ballyesmond. I even manage to keep a few chickens!"

"So that explains why we've seen you several times in Cloncullen."

"Yes, this is where I do our weekly shop. And Jack goes to nursery school just outside the town." Richard hesitated. "You and Olivia must come and visit us sometime," he said tentatively. "Or maybe I can drop by with some eggs."

"Indeed," said Barbara noncommittally. "Now, if you'll excuse me, I really must dash. I'm on duty at the hospital this evening."

"Can I give you a lift anywhere?" Richard asked eagerly, as they walked along the main street.

"No, thanks," said Barbara. "My car is just across the street."

Once again, she bent down and smiled at the child. "Bye, bye, Jack," she said, and this time was rewarded with a shy smile.

"We're parked just here," said Richard, opening the door of a well-worn Jeep that had clearly seen better days.

"You must miss the BMW," said Barbara coolly.

Richard had the grace to grin. "I certainly do. But it wasn't exactly designed to fit a child car seat, and the weekly shopping! This old Jeep is far better suited to my present lifestyle."

"Bye, Richard," said Barbara, crossing the road to her new Lexus, hoping that he'd keep watching until she reached it and climbed in. It gave her a petty satisfaction to note the present disparity in their vehicles. Previously, it had always been Richard who owned the fabulous car, and she who'd driven a banger, the trademark student's vehicle.

"Bye, Barbara!" Richard called after her. "It was great to see you again."

Barbara didn't reply, but started her engine and reversed quickly out onto the road. She didn't look back as she drove off. She wanted Richard to think that as soon as she'd left his company, she'd forgotten all about him, and that she'd far more important things to think of.

What a pity that wasn't true, she thought angrily. Every time she managed to forget about him and get on with her life, he appeared and played havoc with her heart once more. Well, this time she'd take Liv's advice and accept the next invitation she received from a man. She'd have fun and go to bed with whoever asked her, and she'd allow their unfamiliar caresses to blot out the memories of Richard's passionate lovemaking and his gentle endearments. Go to hell, Richard Devlin, she whispered as she drove along. But her hands were still shaking as she clutched the steering wheel.

* * *

Richard smiled at his son as he placed him in the child car seat and strapped him in. "All right, son?" he asked, giving the child a quick kiss.

The little boy nodded. "Can we get ice creams, Daddy? You promised!"

Richard sighed. Seeing Barbara had completely erased it from his mind. But he'd promised the child, and a promise like that couldn't be broken.

"Of course, Jack. Silly Daddy forgot all about it. Will we get cornets with chocolate flakes in them?"

Jack nodded happily as Richard unstrapped him again. Soon, they were walking back up the main street of Cloncullen to the newsagent's that sold the soft Italian ice cream, Jack still clutching his toy train engine.

Richard swore under his breath. He'd both dreaded and longed for this meeting with Barbara, when she finally met his son. Over and over again, he'd rehearsed in his mind what he intended to say to her. The Barbara in his imaginary scenario had responded to his declaration of love by professing undying love for him in return, and they'd instantly become a couple again. But in reality, of course, nothing had gone according to plan. Barbara had seemed distant and unmoved by their meeting, and he'd felt bereft as a result. Olivia had confirmed that Barbara was seeing someone else, so it shouldn't have surprised him that she'd treated him distantly. He knew he had no right to presume anything where she was concerned, but that hadn't stopped him from hoping.

In the newsagent's, Richard ordered two cornets with chocolate flakes, and was moved by Jack's obvious delight. Leaving the shop, they walked slowly back to the Jeep, the two of them laughing as the ice cream melted faster than the child could eat it, and Richard had to wipe the runny ice cream from his chin.

Briefly, Richard thought of all his colleagues at the IT Company where he'd once worked, and he wondered if any of them would recognise him now. Who'd ever have thought, all those years ago, that he'd eventually trade in his suave man-about-town lifestyle for a country farmhouse and a battered old Jeep? But he could no longer identify with the man he'd been just a few years previously.

Back then, he'd been overly confident about so many things. He'd never questioned his good fortune at finding his niche in the IT business and earning a small fortune. He'd just accepted it as his due, and he'd glibly assumed that his life with Barbara was well mapped out, and that they'd have a long and happy life together. Now he realised – he was ashamed to admit it – he'd been a much shallower man back then. He'd led a charmed life, never experiencing loss or pain, assuming that his future would be as idyllic as his past.

Then, overnight, he'd messed up his life with Barbara, and like a house of cards his comfortable world came tumbling down around him. Now, he had a son whom he loved dearly, but in the process of acquiring him, he'd lost the only woman he'd ever truly loved.

Richard gave a heartfelt sigh. The only thing he now had in common with that man-about-town was his undying love for Barbara. If he could just have his beloved son and Barbara back in his life, he'd never ask for anything else again.

CHAPTER 58

As the weeks went by, Ada gradually recovered from Majella's birth, and so far Henry Morton had detected nothing amiss. She was encouraged to rest by both Mrs Collins and Laura, and Mrs Collins took on extra duties to give Ada time to regain her strength.

Both women had been shocked to learn that poor Ada had given birth in one of the sheds. Mrs Collins had been particularly peeved, since she'd only just left for home when poor Ada had started her labour. But they were both grateful for Chrissie's timely intervention – even though she'd been helping herself to the Morton silver at the time!

Laura Morton was anxious to thank Chrissie in person. "Ada, do you think Chrissie would visit me? I hesitate to ask, in view of my illness, but I really would like to thank her for what she did for you. Obviously, she could only call here when Henry's not around."

"I'll certainly ask her, Miss Laura," said Ada. "In fact, I haven't had a chance to thank her properly myself."

"I look forward to meeting her," said Laura, looking

pleased. "I wish I had something to give her, but as you know, Ada, I can't even get my hands on my own money."

"She'd be insulted if you offered her anything, I can assure you," said Ada.

"Well, at the very least, we could ask Mrs, Collins to bake some treats for her children. How many has she got?"

"Four, I think," Ada replied.

"Well, when Henry goes away next week, maybe you'd ask her to call. And she's welcome to bring her children as well. Even though I can't join them in the garden, I'd love to hear the sound of children's laughter through the window – " Suddenly, Laura looked stricken. "Oh dear, would that upset you, Ada? I wasn't thinking about little Majella when I suggested it – "

"Not at all, Miss Laura," said Ada. "I'd be delighted to hear their laughter too."

*   *   *

Later that week, as Ada took another batch of letters to the Post Office for Henry Morton, she encountered Chrissie coming towards her.

"Hello, Chrissie," said Ada. "Mrs Morton was wondering if you'd call to the house some day next week, while Mr Morton's away. And she said to bring the children if you like." She smiled shyly. "I think she wants to thank you for helping me."

Chrissie raised an eyebrow. "Mrs Morton knows about your child? But I thought her husband was the cause of all your troubles?"

Ada nodded. "Miss Laura hates Mr Morton as much as Mrs Collins and I do. But being ill in bed, she can't do much

416

about it. She also said that if you don't want to come because you're worried about getting TB, she'll understand."

Chrissie gave a harsh laugh. "I've far greater things to fear than a few germs! Tell her I'll be there, as long as I know for certain that her scoundrel of a husband isn't there."

Ada nodded, eyeing the other woman's stomach, which looked remarkably flat. "When is your own baby due, Chrissie?" She lowered her voice. "I remember you telling me, the night you helped me give birth to Majella, that you thought you were pregnant again yourself."

But Chrissie said nothing, looking at the ground instead, and avoiding Ada's gaze.

"Sorry," said Ada, colouring, "I didn't mean to pry. It's none of my business."

"I took something," said Chrissie at last.

Ada looked at Chrissie uncomprehendingly.

"I stopped myself being pregnant."

Ada's jaw dropped. "How did you do that? I didn't think anything like that was possible!"

"Keep your voice down!" Chrissie looked around furtively before she spoke. "Yes, it's possible – if you know what to take. I couldn't face another pregnancy, and another mouth to feed – I've already got four kids under five years of age!"

Ada nodded in solidarity. "So what did you do?"

"I collected special herbs in Kilcolgan Wood, and made up a mixture."

"You can stop it by taking herbs?"

Chrissie lowered her voice almost to a whisper. "As long as you know what you're doing, and only take the exact dose. Too little, and nothing will happen, too much and you could kill yourself. It's also important that you take it as soon as you think you might be in the family way."

Ada was astonished. "How does it work? Does it hurt?"

Chrissie nodded. "It certainly does. You'll wish you could die rather than bear the pain. But assuming you survive it, it's worth it." Her face suddenly darkened. "Now don't you go telling anyone what I've said to you!" She shuddered. "If Mikey found out what I'd done, there'd be hell to pay. But it's easy for him – he doesn't have to do the bearing or the rearing of the children. But he'd still kill me if he found out."

"Of course I won't say anything," said Ada, still amazed that such a possibility, albeit a painful and dangerous one, nevertheless existed for women. And she desperately wished that she'd known about it much earlier.

*   *   *

"You should be due around now," said Henry Morton a week later, eyeing Ada's stomach as she placed his breakfast and the morning newspaper on the dining room table. Suddenly, his eyes narrowed as the realisation dawned on him, and he leaned forward and yanked up her apron and skirt, surveying her already flat belly.

"You bitch! What have you done with it? Where is my child, you ignorant trollop?"

Ada had prepared a story that she hoped would appease him. She didn't dare tell him where the child really was.

"I-it was born dead, Mr Morton," she said meekly. "I went into labour while you were away on business – but it never even cried. So I wrapped it in newspaper and buried it in the woods."

There was silence for a moment, and Ada feared that he was about to explode in anger.

But instead he said quietly: "What was it – a boy or a girl?"

Ada hesitated. "It was a girl, sir."

Henry Morton grunted. "Well, thank heavens for that. I want a son – and the sooner the better." Then he leered up at her. "You'll bear me a son yet, woman – but I want no sissy female babies around here!"

Henry Morton's response confirmed for Ada that she'd done the right thing in getting Chrissie to take Majella to the orphanage. It also brought home to her the shocking realisation that Henry Morton intended making her pregnant again. He was determined to get a son and heir, and since he was no respecter of a woman's willingness to participate, or her state of health, he could rape her again at any time. She had no option but to escape from the house as soon as possible.

But first, she'd have to tell Laura and Mrs Collins. She dreaded leaving them both, since they were the only family she had any more. But she knew they'd understand that she couldn't remain there as a sitting duck, to be raped and made pregnant again at Henry Morton's whim. She was barely sixteen, yet she'd already borne two children! Her body was tired, and she longed for some peace.

A sob rose in her throat. Yet how could she leave, when her beloved daughter was close by? If only she could get a live-in job at some other house in the vicinity. She was more than willing to work hard. Just being safe from Henry Morton was all she wanted.

Later in the kitchen, Ada told Mrs Collins what Henry Morton had said about making her pregnant again.

"How can he do this to me, Mrs Collins?" she asked piteously.

Carmel Collins sighed. "Because he can, Ada – it's a simple as that. He wouldn't dare try it on with me, because I have a husband. But you have no one – beyond me and Mrs Morton –

to defend you, and we're equally at Henry Morton's mercy, albeit in different ways." Her mouth tightened. "But I'm going to have a word with him – I'll threaten to tell my husband if he doesn't stop harassing you, Ada. It's bad enough that you're not being paid, despite working all hours of the day and night looking after Mrs Morton, but this situation can't be allowed to continue."

"But you'll only get into trouble yourself! I don't want you to lose your job on my account."

"Well, if he throws me out, he'll have to find another housekeeper and cook, and I don't think he'd want the inconvenience. Besides, he'd have to explain to Seamus why he sacked me, because I know that my husband would be over here in a flash if I lost my job. We've a son to put through school and university, and we need the extra income I bring home every week."

*   *   *

Mrs Collins looked distraught and guilty as she sat down beside Ada, who was poking the last embers of the fire in the kitchen.

"Can you believe it? Henry Morton laughed in my face, and told me to mind my own business. He said that Seamus was gutless, and that neither he nor any other man in the town would raise a hand to stop him. He said that even if Seamus or I told the sergeant or the priest, neither of them would believe it." Mrs Collins' face was red with anger. "The cheek of him – he said that no one would believe the word of a girl who's come from the laundry, and who'd already been in trouble!"

Ada sagged, feeling utterly defeated. "I've got to leave here, Mrs Collins. You can see that now, can't you?"

Sadly, Mrs Collins nodded her head. "But Ada, where can you possibly go?" she said. "Take my word for it – your family won't take you back, so there's no point in hoping that might happen."

"I realise that – I'd hoped I might have had a reply to all the letters I sent to my brother and sister, but I guess even they don't want to know me any more."

Mrs Collins took off her apron and began folding it. Henry Morton had already retired for the night, and it was time for her to go home. "I know it's terrible to be abandoned by your own flesh and blood – but that's the way people have been made to behave," she said angrily. "In my opinion, it's all the fault of that De Valera fellow – when he was in power, he allowed the Church to gain far too much control. Ordinary people are frightened to disobey that craw-thumping load of old hypocrites!"

"Well, I can't stay here, Mrs Collins. I don't want Mr Morton to get me pregnant again." Ada began to cry softly. "It's not fair, is it? Men seem to be able to do what they want, and women have to suffer the consequences!"

"It's always been that way, girl – I don't know that it'll ever change."

"I hope Miss Laura will be okay. I'm going to miss her, too."

"But, Ada – be realistic! Where can you go? If you're found roaming the streets, you'll end up back at the laundry."

Ada shivered.

"Look," said Mrs Collins, her expression softening, "if you can wait a few weeks, I'll save a bit of money for you from my wages, and I'll cut back on the Mortons' grocery bill, so I can siphon off a few pounds that way too. Then, when you have enough money to go, you can at least take a train or a bus, and get far away from here. Maybe you could get a job in Dublin –

in one of the hotels, where you could live in – and you could make a new life for yourself there."

Ada's eyes lit up with hope. "That would be marvellous – would you really do that for me, Mrs Collins? I'd pay you back every penny – I know you need it for your son's education."

"I don't want to be paid back," said Mrs Collins gruffly. "I just want to know that you're safe and well. But you mustn't mention this to anyone – except Mrs Morton. She deserves to know. She'll be lost without you, but she'll want to put your safety first."

Ada nodded, her eyes filling with tears at the thought of leaving the people she'd grown to love.

"I know she'd help you financially if she could," added Mrs Collins, "but Mr Morton has taken charge of all her finances, and is spending it as though money was going out of fashion. She can't get her hands on any of it."

Ada wiped her eyes. "I know. I hate leaving both of you – you're the only family I have. And Majella – I don't know how I'm going to leave, knowing that she's in the clutches of those nuns."

"Well, you can't stay here, with Mr Morton behaving like a rampant goat. I'll keep an eye on your daughter for you, Ada. We'll keep in touch, and I can let you know how she's getting on. Sister Angela is kind, and she loves all the children, and she told me that she's already spoken to the new doctor, Cormac McCarthy, who's just arrived in Cloncullen. He's promised to shame the nuns into feeding them properly, so Majella will be in safe hands. When you've got a job and saved some money, you'll be in a better position to make decisions."

Ada nodded. What Mrs Collins was saying made good sense. Maybe some day, if the laws were changed and pigs could fly, she'd be reunited with her daughter again . . .

Mrs Collins offered Ada her handkerchief. "Now wipe your face, girl, and go and get a decent night's sleep. You'll need to be fit and well if you're eventually going to get away from here."

*   *   *

"I'm very pleased to meet you, Chrissie," said Laura Morton, extending a tiny pale hand from among the voluminous bedclothes.

"Likewise, ma'am," said Chrissie, taking the little hand in her strong rough one. "Travellers aren't all bad, you know."

Laura smiled. "I know. And settled folk aren't all bad either. Except for people like my husband. Fortunately, he goes away on business from time to time, so we all get brief respites from his temper and cruelty."

Laura tried to pull herself up in the bed and Chrissie quickly helped her to sit up.

"He controls my life, Chrissie, and poor Ada's too. And because I'm ill, that makes it even easier for him. But you're very good to come – I don't get many visitors, and I'm delighted to have the company."

"If you'd like me to call again, ma'am, I'd be only too happy," said Chrissie stiffly, unused to having her company sought by anyone from the settled community.

Laura smiled warmly as the sounds of children's laughter floated up through the air. "I'm so pleased to hear the sound of your children enjoying themselves. Those gardens should be filled with youngsters having fun. Unfortunately, Henry thinks that all possessions should be guarded and preserved. For what, I have no idea. But then, Henry is a very peculiar man."

Chrissie cleared her throat. "I'm sorry about the cutlery, ma'am."

Laura waved her hand dismissively. "I'm not remotely bothered, Chrissie – besides, Henry found it later, anyway." Laura grinned impishly. "I guessed that you had to abandon it when Ada needed your help."

"Yes, ma'am."

"Chrissie, I don't mean to insult you when I say this, but I wish I could help you in some way. A Traveller's life can't be an easy one. But I have nothing of my own. What was mine is now Henry's, and he uses it solely for his own enjoyment."

"Thank you for the thought, ma'am. But we get by."

There was a moment's silence before Laura spoke again. "I can't thank you enough for what you did for Ada," she said softly. "Will you call again please, Chrissie? You've no idea how much joy I get from hearing your children having fun."

Suddenly, the laughter outside ceased and silence filled the air.

Laura smiled. "I think your children have just retired to the kitchen, where Mrs Collins has prepared some treats for them. Go on down and get something to eat yourself, Chrissie – and thanks once again for calling."

"Goodbye ma'am – I'll call to see you again soon." Chrissie grimaced. "As long as I can be sure that your husband isn't around!"

CHAPTER 59

Olivia headed down the corridor of the small county hospital, carrying a large bunch of flowers from her garden, some energy drinks, and a selection of newspapers and magazines. She intended keeping her promise to Barney McDaid while she was down in Cloncullen for the weekend. She'd sent him a card from Dublin, apologising for her oversight, and she now was intent on rectifying the situation. Besides, visiting him was no hardship – she actually liked the old man. Maggie had rolled her eyes to heaven when Olivia had told her where she was going, but to Olivia a promise was a promise. Unlike Brendan Warren – to whom promises obviously meant nothing – Olivia really meant it when she said she'd do something.

As she walked down the corridor towards Barney's ward, Olivia passed the corridor leading to Brendan's ward. She grimaced to herself. She certainly wouldn't be visiting him again! No doubt the bimbo was in there already, crawling all over him, whispering sentimental claptrap in his ear. And he, no doubt, was lapping it all up. Well, she didn't give a damn about either of them. They were well matched.

Unbidden, an image of Ms Pink Vision in bed with Brendan, her salon-tanned legs wrapped around him, forced its way into Olivia's brain. And momentarily, it took her breath away. She sighed. Despite her protestations, his rejection still hurt a lot.

Heading down the ward to Barney McDaid's bed, Olivia halted in surprise. Was that her mother sitting beside him? Her mother had said nothing about leaving the city when Olivia had waved goodbye to her the day before!

Olivia smiled as she approached Barney's bed. She was pleased that her mother was renewing old acquaintances. Maybe she and Barney would get something going between them again. Suddenly, her heart gave a jolt as she realised that her mother and Barney were actually holding hands . . .

"Hello, Barney – hello, Mum."

"Olivia!" Barney exclaimed with delight.

"Hello, love," said her mother, her cheeks blushing a rosy pink. Doreen looked girlishly excited, and younger and prettier than Olivia had seen her look for years.

Barney looked a changed man too. Obviously, his health had improved dramatically, and Olivia couldn't help feeling that her mother's presence might have something to do with it.

"Will we tell her, Barney?"

Barney's eyes twinkled with delight. "Why not? Do you want to be the one to tell her, Doreen?"

"No, you do it, Barney."

"Honestly, Doreen – I think you should be the one to explain it all."

"Which news will we tell her first?" whispered Doreen coquettishly. "Our news, or the other news?"

"I think we should tell her about us, first," advised Barney, raising Doreen's hand to his lips and kissing it tenderly.

Doreen gazed into his eyes, and Olivia felt as though she was seeing her mother in a whole new light.

"Go on, Barney – you tell her."

"I'm far too nervous, Doreen, my love – you do it."

"For goodness sake, will somebody tell me what's going on!" said Olivia, exasperated.

Barney took in a deep breath. "Your mother and I are getting married," he said, grinning at Olivia. "Just as soon as I get out of this hospital bed! I hope you don't mind, Olivia? You see, I've always loved your mother. Never got her out of my system, even after twenty-five years in Australia."

"That's great news!" said Olivia, who couldn't have been happier for them both.

"And we've something else to tell you, Liv, " said her mother softly, glancing quickly at Barney for support. She hesitated. "I don't know how else to say this, Liv – it's probably going to come as a shock to you –"

She hesitated again, and Olivia wanted to shake her.

"But Barney is also your father."

Olivia's jaw dropped open, and her heart almost stopped beating with the shock. She opened her mouth to say something, but no words would come out.

"I hope you're not too upset?" Barney asked her anxiously. "I'm probably a dreadful disappointment to

427

you as a father. You probably hoped for someone more dashing and witty –"

Flinging herself into their arms, Olivia hugged the two of them tightly, laughing and crying at the same time.

"I'm thrilled to have you as my father, Barney!" said Olivia, when she'd finished hugging them both in turn, "but does this mean I'll have to stop calling you Barney and call you 'Dad' instead?"

"Call me whatever you like!" said Barney, tears of happiness streaming down his podgy cheeks.

"Oh Liv, I'm so glad you know about Barney at last!" said her mother shakily. "Over the years, I've often wanted to tell you about your father, but the time just never seemed right. Maybe I hoped you'd ask me yourself as you got older, but you never did. I suppose you were respecting my privacy, and though I really longed to tell you how much I'd loved your father, I just couldn't bring myself to raise the subject. It always upset me to think of what I'd lost, so I kept putting off discussing it with you." Her mother dabbed her eyes, turning to Barney once more. "And if it wasn't for you, Olivia, we might never have found each other again!"

Olivia smiled through her tears. It looked as though her trip to the Glen Hotel might have been worth it after all!

Eventually, after lots of tears, laughter and interruptions, Olivia learned the full story of her parents' romance.

Having worked together at the university for several years, they'd gradually fallen in love. Then Barney had been offered a professorship at a university in Australia, and had asked Doreen to marry him and go with him. They were about to hand in their notice to the university, when they had a stupid row.

"Neither of us can even remember what it was about," said Barney ruefully. "But your mother wouldn't return my phone calls, so I left for Australia without her. I had to accept that she didn't want me any more."

"Yet nothing could have been further from the truth," said Doreen sadly. "But when I discovered shortly afterwards that was I pregnant, my pride wouldn't let me tell him, in case he rejected me, or in case he thought I was trying to trap him."

"Whereas all the time, I was broken-hearted in Australia, hoping each day that your mother would contact me," added Barney. "Because I, in turn, was too proud to let her know how much I still needed her."

"And you never heard from each other again," finished Olivia.

Her parents both nodded, shamefaced.

"We both owe you an apology, Olivia," said Barney. "Because of our stupid pride –" he looked at Doreen for confirmation and she nodded, "we both deprived you of the life you should have had. With two parents to love you."

Doreen nodded, fresh tears running down her cheeks. "My mother and Uncle Eddie were a great support to me during my pregnancy, and after you were born, Olivia," she said. "In fact, they've ensured we wanted for nothing. They'd had a tragedy in their own family, you see. Their sister disappeared, and they've always suspected that she was taken away because she was pregnant. So they didn't want me to suffer as a single parent, and they wanted you to have the best possible life, even without a father."

Olivia nodded as a fresh bout of tears threatened to overwhelm her too. "I know, Mum. Gran and Uncle Eddie told me about Great-aunt Ada."

"I owe them both a huge debt of gratitude," said Barney humbly. "I hope they'll forgive me too, and let me become part of the family again."

As Olivia dried her tears on a tissue from Barney's bedside locker, she thought gratefully of her grandmother and uncle Eddie and their generosity to her and her mother over the years. And she also felt overwhelming sadness for all the years that she and her parents had lost – all because of simple pride. Then she suddenly thought about Barbara – wasn't her friend doing exactly the same thing? Maybe there wasn't a future for Barbara with Richard but they desperately needed to talk through their situation, and resolve it once and for all. Then, if necessary, they could each walk away from each other with a clear conscience, knowing that they'd given it their best shot.

Suddenly, Barney spoke again. "You can imagine my amazement when Doreen turned up at the hospital," he said, smiling at Olivia as he wiped away another tear with an already-sodden tissue. "There I was, lying in my hospital bed, when I saw this woman walking into the ward. Instantly, she reminded me of Doreen, but I was utterly shell-shocked when she stopped at my bed, and said : 'Hello, Barney.' I couldn't believe it!"

He stopped, his voice quivering with emotion, unable to go on until he'd blown his nose. "I'd never expected to see my beloved Doreen again – I always assumed she'd married someone else, so I hadn't even tried to contact her when I retired and came back from Australia. It would have been too painful to have it confirmed that she'd found somebody else." He looked adoringly at Olivia's mother, clutching her hand as though he couldn't bear to ever let it go. "And then to discover that I had a daughter!" He began to weep gently, and Doreen silently slipped her arms around him. "I never, in my wildest dreams, expected to be a father," he finished. "It's the most wonderful and humbling event of my whole life."

Olivia wasn't sure if she wanted to laugh hysterically or cry along with Barney, since her emotions were all jumbled up. She'd come into the hospital having one parent, but now she'd be leaving with two! There were a lot of things that would take time to get used to. But one thing was certain – she and her parents had the whole of the future to look forward to together.

CHAPTER 60

Barbara was pleased to have finished her paperwork at last. Soon, she'd be off duty, and she planned to have a quick shower in the staff quarters of the hospital before heading down to Olivia's place for the weekend. She'd been on Accident & Emergency duty all week, having stood in for a colleague who was on holiday, and she was delighted that her stint was coming to an end. Like most of the junior doctors, she dreaded the Friday night shift, when most of the cases that arrived into the Department were due to a surfeit of alcohol. Luckily, she'd be on the road long before the mayhem began!

Barbara pulled her shoulders back and stretched. She was looking forward to unwinding in the relaxed atmosphere of Cloncullen – the loveliest little town in Ireland, she conceded – only spoiled by occasional sightings of Richard Devlin, which destroyed her peace of mind and made her heart thump uncontrollably. She knew that her two friends were right when they urged her to get on with her life and forget about the man who had caused her so much heartache, but it was difficult.

As her colleague Fergal arrived to relieve her, Barbara began to take her white coat off.

"Hang on, Barbara – give me five minutes, will you?" Fergal pleaded, grinning at her as he slipped on his own white coat and headed for the stairs.

Barbara grinned back, knowing exactly where he was going. Fergal currently fancied one of the new nurses who'd been rostered on the Surgical Ward on the third floor, and he obviously wanted to check if she was on duty. If she was, then he'd try to arrange his coffee break to coincide with hers. Barbara had been helping him to engineer meetings with the young nurse whenever possible, feeling certain that the nurse reciprocated his feelings, but was playing hard-to-get. Silently, Barbara wished him luck – it was good to know that someone else's love life was looking up!

Suddenly, the double doors of the Accident & Emergency Department were flung open, and a man rushed inside, carrying a small crumpled bundle in his arms.

"Excuse me, can you help me, please?" he urgently asked a nurse who was walking down the corridor. "My son's had a bad fall. He keeps losing consciousness, and I don't know what to do!"

Barbara's heart missed a beat. It was Richard Devlin! And the child in his arms was his son Jack. She stepped forward and took his arm.

"Oh God – Barbara," Richard babbled, "I'm so glad you're here! Jack was playing in the barn when I suddenly heard him scream! Luckily, I was repairing the hen house nearby otherwise I mightn't have heard him at

434

all! When I rushed in, he was lying on the ground – he must have climbed up the ladder to the loft and fallen off – at first, I thought he was dead –" He stopped to take a breath. "So I put him in the Jeep and raced here as fast as I could." He gulped. "I brought him here rather than to the county hospital, because you have a special A & E unit here, haven't you?" He was almost in tears. "The roads are better too, so I could get here quicker. I was right to come here, wasn't I? Oh Barbs, can you do something?"

"Calm down, Richard," Barbara said quietly. "Jack is in safe hands now, and we'll do the best we can for him."

The authoritative tone of her voice had an impact on Richard, and he became noticeably calmer.

Making a cursory examination of the child, Barbara concluded that he'd broken his left wrist and had scratches and bruising on both legs, but what concerned her most was his lack of awareness of his surroundings. He'd need an X-ray immediately to detect if there were any fractures to his skull, and if there was bleeding into the brain from a subdural haematoma. Checking his eyes, she was relieved to see a brief flicker as she shone the light directly into each pupil, and he groaned, calling for his father. As Richard clutched his son's hand and whispered endearments, Barbara was relieved to see that the child wasn't actually comatose, but merely in shock.

As one of the nurses on duty filled out a card with the child's personal details, Barbara rang the Radiology Department and arranged for immediate X-rays of his skull and arm. Fleetingly, she wondered where Fergal had got to, and whether or not he'd scored with the nurse on the Surgical Ward. If he'd started his shift at the requisite time, she'd have left for Cloncullen already and been oblivious to what had happened to Richard's son. While on the one hand she wished she hadn't been thrown into this emotional turmoil, on the other she was glad to be of help to a clearly traumatised Richard.

Suddenly Fergal appeared, his cheeky grin denoting a successful dalliance with the new nurse. But it quickly changed to concern as he surveyed little Jack.

"I'll take over now, Barbara – I presume you've ordered X-rays? Good, now you head off for your dirty weekend."

Barbara was gratified to see a momentary flicker of distress flit across Richard's face at the thought that she was about to have a dirty weekend, and she did nothing to deny it. Let him think she was having a great time!

"Thanks, Fergal, but I'll stick around for a while – I know these people and I'd like to be sure that everything's okay before I head off."

An orderly placed Jack on a gurney, and began to wheel him towards the lift that would take him to the Radiology Department.

"Thanks, Barbs – I really do appreciate your help," said Richard, grasping her hand before heading off to accompany his son upstairs.

"No problem," said Barbara in as casual a tone as she could manage.

After Richard had followed the orderly into the lift, Fergal asked her how she knew the man and the child.

"Oh, they're old family friends," she said offhandedly. Then she quickly deflected the conversation away from her own life and onto Fergal's burgeoning love life. "By the way, Fergal, how did you get on in the Surgical Ward?"

Fergal grinned from ear to ear. "I've got a date for next Friday night! Thanks a million for your help, Barbara! I'll gladly return the favour if I can."

Barbara nodded. She was happy to oblige a colleague, especially one she liked as much as Fergal. And she wondered what Fergal would say if she told him that Richard Devlin had once meant the whole world to her.

Fergal and the duty nurses took over the running of the Accident & Emergency Department, so Barbara had little to do as she waited for news of Jack's X-rays. She busied herself with more paperwork, although she hardly saw the forms she was filling in. She was thinking of little Jack's injuries, and hoping that she was right in her judgement that his injuries weren't consistent with a fractured skull. Young heads were remarkably resilient anyway, but she hoped that it was shock rather than actual injury that had caused him to seem confused. Her heart went out to the little boy. He'd be sore from his injuries, and frightened of being in such unfamiliar surroundings. She'd stay until he came back from Radiology, then she'd set his arm with plaster of Paris. One way or another, the child would need to spend several days in hospital, hopefully just for observation.

After what seemed an eternity, Richard returned, wheeling young Jack on a gurney, and bearing a large envelope for Barbara from the Radiology Department. In it were Jack's X-rays. Barbara felt she was about to suffocate and her heart was pounding as she led Richard and Jack into one of the treatment rooms, took the X-rays out of the envelope and hung them up on the light box. Let everything be okay, she pleaded, not sure who she was calling on for help.

Quickly, she scanned the first X-ray, noting the sharp clean break in Jack's wrist. Poor kid – he would certainly need it immobilised with plaster of Paris. As her eyes scanned the second set of X-rays of Jack's skull, her heart was in her mouth. She studied the first one, taken of the front of his head, noting with relief that there was no evidence of any damage. Taking a deep breath, she focussed her attention on the second set of X-rays, which illustrated both sides of the child's skull, and could feel her heartbeat slowing down as she realised that there was no obvious damage here either. Relief suffused throughout her body. Thankfully, she wouldn't be the bearer of bad news. She could happily tell Richard that his son's head looked uninjured.

"Barbs – is it bad news?" Richard's voice was husky with emotion, and he looked as though he was about to cry.

Smiling, Barbara turned towards him. "No, it's good news, Richard. Jack's head seems to be perfectly okay."

"Oh my God!" Croaking his gratitude, Richard flung his arms around her, and she stiffened as she felt the old familiar embrace.

For a split second, she closed her eyes and savoured the feel of his arms around her, then she broke away, trying to appear businesslike and in control of her emotions once again.

"But he'll have to stay in hospital for a few days – just for observation," she cautioned. "I'll make arrangements straight away to have him admitted to the children's ward."

As tears of relief slid down Richard's face, Barbara turned away, unsure of how to cope with the situation, and smiled at the little boy. And as the child smiled back at her, she was overwhelmed with a sudden rush of affection for him. Poor little mite, she thought, he'd been through such a lot in his short little life.

"But first things first," she told Richard brightly. "I'll set Jack's wrist in plaster now."

Speaking directly to the child, Barbara explained what she was going to do, and made it sound so exciting that Jack couldn't wait to have his wrist encased in plaster! She told him how family and friends traditionally wrote or drew pictures on the injured person's plaster, and she made it seem such a wonderful game that her task was quickly accomplished with Jack's full cooperation. The boy wanted his dad to write on his plaster immediately, and laughingly, Barbara had to explain that he needed to allow some time for it to set fully!

"Could you draw a train on it?" he asked her shyly, and she promised him that she'd try, although she'd never been great at art. Barbara was relieved to see that Jack was now alert and happy, and his renewed interest in trains seemed to confirm that he was on the road to recovery.

Already, Barbara had made up her mind that she wouldn't go down to Cloncullen that night. As the doctor admitting Jack to hospital, she wanted to monitor his progress carefully. While there were no obvious signs of trauma, there was always the possibility that something could show up later. Therefore, she'd just go back to her apartment for the night, and then return the following morning to check on the child's progress.

Although the hospital had offered him a bed so that he could stay near Jack, Richard was opting to return to

Ballyesmond. It was only after he learned that Jack was okay, that he'd given any thought to the haste with which he'd left home. He couldn't even remember if he'd closed the front door behind him, or if he'd closed the gate to the hen run. Knowing that Jack was in safe hands, Richard intended to thwart the local foxes from making supper out of his chickens!

Relieved that his son was no longer in danger, Richard asked Barbara if she was going down to Cloncullen that night.

"No, Richard," Barbara said smoothly. "I'm staying in Dublin this weekend. We have tickets for the theatre tomorrow night."

With satisfaction, Barbara noted Richard's sad expression when she'd mentioned "we". She hoped he was assuming that the plural noun meant the man friend she'd invented for his benefit.

"What are you going to see?" he asked, unable to resist any opportunity to find out anything about her life without him.

Barbara smiled with relief. Luckily, she'd read a review about the new play at the Abbey Theatre, so she was able to give him some brief details. It was petty, she knew, but there was great satisfaction in letting Richard Devlin see that she had a happy and interesting life that didn't include him any more.

"Well, I hope you enjoy it," he said, smiling at her, while secretly wishing that he was the one taking her to the theatre. But he'd forfeited that right a long time ago. "Thanks, Barbs, for all you've done for Jack and me tonight". He grasped her hand. "Knowing you personally made it a lot easier to cope with. I needn't tell you, I was petrified that I was going to lose him – " His voice caught, and Barbara felt her own eyes welling up with tears, but she quickly turned away.

"No problem," she said.

Just then, a nurse from the Children's Ward arrived to collect Jack. It was clear that the boy was beginning to revel in his newfound role as the centre of attention, and he happily showed off his newly plastered arm to the nurse, and begged her to write on it, as she wheeled his gurney towards the lift that would take him to the ward.

"Thanks once again, Barbs," said Richard, before following the nurse to the lift.

"Any time," said Barbara flippantly.

After they'd gone up in the lift, Barbara slipped off her white coat, and prepared to leave the hospital for home. Fergal and one of the nurses were attending to a drunk who was loudly objecting to whatever treatment they were proposing, so she checked to see that everything was okay before leaving.

Fergal grinned, well able to handle the complaining drunkard, and he gave Barbara the thumbs-up as she left. "Thanks once again, Barbara," he said, grinning, and she grinned back, knowing exactly what he was referring to. He was so delighted at the prospect of his forthcoming date that he could handle any situation that might occur tonight!

As she climbed into her car, Barbara felt emotionally drained, and relieved that she hadn't encountered Richard again on her way out. No doubt he was still up in the ward, getting his son settled in for the night.

She'd better ring Olivia or Maggie and let them know she wouldn't be coming down to Cloncullen that night.

She sighed. The last time she'd been unable to join them – when she'd had to baby-sit for her sister – they'd had an eventful weekend without her, one that produced a baby's skeleton and two men! Well, one of the men hadn't quite measured up, she conceded – poor Liv had been unlucky with Mark Cunningham. But hopefully Maggie might be in there with a chance where Philip Lynch was concerned . . .

Although she wasn't on duty again until Monday, she would call to the hospital the following morning to see how Jack was getting on. Hopefully, the little boy would soon be well enough to go back home to Ballyesmond.

She sighed as she turned on the ignition. And hopefully Richard Devlin would also be relegated to her past once again. That was where he belonged – wasn't it?

CHAPTER 61

"Now that Dr Walsh has retired, Miss Laura, you must be looking forward to meeting the new doctor," said Ada, as she brushed Laura's hair.

Laura smiled wearily at Ada. "I suppose he can't be any worse than Dr Walsh. On the other hand, maybe he'll recommend that Henry puts me in a sanatorium, or like Dr Walsh he'll lurk outside my room, for fear of catching TB himself."

"Well, we'll soon find out, Miss Laura, because he's sent word that he's coming to visit you tomorrow."

"How exciting!" said Laura dryly. "Still, it is the best offer I've had all week – or all year, for that matter! Get out my best party dress, Ada!"

Ada grinned. "Well, I think it's exciting anyway!"

"What do you know about him, Ada? I'll bet he's old, pompous and opinionated, just like Dr Walsh!"

"No, he's young and very good-looking, according to Mrs Collins, who's seen him in the village. He has a wife too – a very snooty woman, by all accounts, who seems to have delusions of grandeur about herself."

443

"Well, she'll soon lose them in a place like Cloncullen!" Laura said, smiling. "Mind you, she's probably just fed up at having to move to a small town like this, especially if they've come from Dublin. It's not exactly the centre of high society here!"

"I don't know where they're from, but you can quiz the doctor all about it tomorrow! Now, Miss Laura, would you like me to bring you a cup of tea?"

*   *   *

"Hello, Mrs Morton, I'm Cormac McCarthy."

Laura pulled herself up on her pillows, surprised that the new doctor was actually prepared to sit on the edge of her bed.

"You know I've got TB?" she said.

He nodded, but made no attempt to move. "The first thing I'm going to do is open your windows and let in some fresh air," he told her cheerfully. "I want you to leave your windows open on all but the coldest days, and I'd like to see you getting out of that bed, and spending some time outdoors."

Laura looked in astonishment at this good-looking and friendly man as he took out his stethoscope and placed it on her chest. "But Henry thinks the house will be too cold if the windows are open!" she replied. "He insists on every window in the house being shut, day and night."

"Well, that was the old-fashioned way of treating the disease. Originally, it was also believed that people needed to lie quietly in order to immobilise their heart and lungs. Now, fresh air is considered one of the best antidotes to the disease, and since your heart and lungs seem quite strong, I'd like to see you sitting outside in your lovely garden as often as the weather permits." He smiled. "I believe your maid, Ada, has already

444

been encouraging you to eat fruit. So your housekeeper, Mrs Collins, tells me."

Laura nodded.

"And I'd like to see you eating more fresh vegetables too. Healthy eating is also an important way of combating this disease." He smiled at her. "There are also new drugs available for the treatment of TB, so I'd like to try some of those on you as well." He smiled at her. "Don't worry, Mrs Morton, you're going to get well again – I'm sure of it."

As he left, Laura experienced hope for the first time in years.

*   *   *

"He's lovely, isn't he, Miss Laura?" said Ada, as she plumped up Laura's pillows after the new doctor's departure.

"I'm shocked – and amazed," said Laura, her eyes wide with astonishment. "He actually believes I can get better again!"

"Of course you can!"

Laura smiled at Ada. "I know you've been telling me that since you came here, Ada, and I know the fruit has definitely been helping, but I don't think I ever really believed it myself – until today."

"He's very good-looking, isn't he, Miss Laura?"

Laura smiled. "He is, Ada. And I really liked him. But heaven knows what Henry will say when he hears that all the windows in here are to be opened! And I'm to sit out in the garden as well!"

"He can hardly go against the doctor's orders, can he, Miss Laura?"

"Oh, Henry thinks he can do anything he wants." Laura looked pointedly at her friend. "You should know that better than anyone, Ada!"

Ada said nothing.

"How are you feeling, Ada?" said Laura. "I hope Henry hasn't been bothering you again?"

Ada shook her head. "I'm keeping out of his way, Miss Laura," she said noncommittally. "But soon, I'm going to have to leave here." Her lower lip quivered. "I'll really miss you, Miss Laura, but Mr Morton has said to my face that he wants a son – so I have to get away before that happens."

Laura's eyes filled with tears. "Oh Ada – I wish I could protect you! Of course you must go. As soon as possible – you can't afford to delay."

Ada nodded. "But I can't go for a few weeks yet, Miss Laura. Mrs Collins has promised to save a bit of money for me, and cut back on the housekeeping money wherever she can. When I have enough money to get to Dublin, I'll go."

"Oh Ada, if only I had control of my own money!"

"Hush, Miss Laura – don't let Mr Morton hear you say that." Ada smiled brightly. "Now, do you want to hear what Mrs Collins has heard about the new doctor's wife?"

Laura leaned forward eagerly.

"Apparently she's already craw-thumping in church, and sucking up to the priests. I don't think the doctor bothers to go at all. Mrs Collins got the impression that he has a healthy disrespect for what he's been heard to call 'All that mumbo-jumbo'."

"He'd need to be careful about making public statements like that," said Laura, looking worried. "But I don't think they could be a very happy couple, do you?"

"No, she's far too prissy for him."

"She probably only married him because he was a doctor."

Ada nodded. "But why on earth did he marry her?"

"People make mistakes," said Laura abruptly. "My own marriage is living proof of that."

CHAPTER 62

"Barbara's not coming down to Cloncullen tonight," Olivia told Maggie, as she collected her friend for the drive down to Bay Tree House. "She just rang me a few minutes ago, and said that she's been held up at the hospital. She won't be down until tomorrow."

Olivia glanced at Maggie as her friend threw her weekend holdall into the back of the car, and hopped into the passenger seat. "Which is a pity – since I have something amazing to tell you both."

Maggie looked crestfallen as they drove off. "Aw Liv – you're not going to make *me* wait, just because she's not here, are you?"

Olivia grinned. "No, Mags – I don't think I could wait that long myself. I'm dying to tell you!"

"Okay, then – tell me."

Olivia smiled to herself, still savouring the moment. "On the other hand, I think I'll wait until we get to Cloncullen," she said teasingly. "I don't want you grabbing me and hugging me in the car, and causing an accident!"

"Wow! It really must be something really exciting if you're expecting me to react like that!" said Maggie, her blue eyes sparkling. With her unruly hair standing up on end, she looked like an eager poodle about to be taken out for "walkies".

"Have you won the national lottery, Liv?"

Olivia shook her head.

"The Euromillions?"

Olivia grinned. "Nothing like that. Give it a rest, Mags – I promise I'll tell you as soon as we arrive."

Leaning over, Olivia opened the glove compartment. "Now, if it's okay with you –I'm going to stick on a Julia Gleeson CD?"

Maggie waved her hand in agreement, knowing that she wouldn't find out anything further until Olivia was good and ready to tell her. But at least she'd hear about it before Barbara did!

As they drove along, Maggie turned her thoughts to the absent member of the trio. "Poor old Barbs," she said at last. "She works far too hard, doesn't she? All work and no play can't be good for her."

Olivia laughed. "We can't all have cushy state jobs like you have!"

"Being a psychologist isn't exactly easy," said Maggie huffily. "We have to deal with people's traumas and tragedies on a daily basis, and I can assure you, Liv, it's difficult to turn off from people's problems, even when you're off duty."

Olivia reached over and patted her friend's hand sympathetically. Sometimes people thought Maggie was frivolous and flighty, but Olivia knew that the reality was quite different. Maggie took her job and her friendships very seriously, but sometimes Olivia couldn't resist teasing her anyway.

"I never noticed you worrying about other people's problems when Philip Lynch is around," she said grinning, then remembered that she shouldn't be encouraging Maggie to pin her hopes on Philip, in case Carmel Collins' claim was true. Quickly she changed the subject. "Fancy going into Cloncullen for fish and chips as soon as we arrive? I don't know about you, but I'm starving!"

"Yeah, why not?"

Olivia's eyes twinkled. "And then I'll tell you my amazing news."

An hour later, as they ate their fish and chips on a bench in the village square, Olivia told Maggie all about Barney McDaid being her father, and her parents' ill-fated romance. Maggie was astonished and thrilled, and hugged her friend so tightly that she crushed Olivia's bag of chips against her T-shirt, smudging it with grease and vinegar.

Maggie rubbed the stain frantically, making it even worse. "I know you can use vinegar to take out certain stains, but I don't know what you can use to get rid of vinegar!" she said, looking worried.

"Oh, forget about it," said Olivia, grinning. "I may have lost a T-shirt, but I've gained a father!"

They both laughed, and Maggie hugged her again. "It's amazing, isn't it? Who'd ever have believed that your mother and Barney McDaid were once an item? And to think that neither of them ever married anyone else!" She sighed. "It just goes to show you, doesn't it? If someone's meant for you . . ."

Olivia grimaced. "Yeah, but what a pity it took such a long time for it to happen. I'd like to have had a father while I was growing up."

Maggie nodded. "Yes, I know that, Liv. While you had lots more material things than we had growing up, my brothers and I always had each other. Even when they pulled my hair or tied me to the tree in the garden, I never doubted that they loved me." Maggie looked earnestly at her friend. "I often wondered if you missed having brothers and sisters, but I never liked to ask you."

"Of course I did, but you and Barbara became part of my family," said Olivia, "and your parents, and Barbara's parents too, have always made a special effort to include me in whatever family events were going on." She smiled happily. "Now, for the first time – I'll be able to return the favour, by inviting you all to my mother's wedding!"

Later that evening, when they returned to Bay Tree House, the two women acutely felt the absence of their friend.

"It's not the same without Barbs, is it?" said Maggie, throwing down the magazine she'd been reading.

"Thanks very much," said Olivia dryly.

"Aw, Liv, you know what I mean! When the three of us are together, it's like being the Three Musketeers. One for all, and all for one!"

"More like the three witches from Macbeth," said Olivia. "*Hubble, bubble, toil and trouble!*"

"I wish we could make trouble for Philip Lynch – then he'd have to arrest us, and I'd kick up such a racket in my cell that he'd beg me to stay quiet, and I'd inform him that the only way I'd shut my mouth would be if he'd kiss it, over and over again . . ."

"You're mental," said Olivia, looking up from the book she was reading. "To think that you're employed to help people sort out their problems! I think *you're* the one who needs treatment."

"As long as Philip administers it, I'm ready, willing and able!" said Maggie dreamily. "Oh Liv – will he ever ask me out?"

Raising her eyes to heaven, Olivia didn't even bother answering Maggie's rhetorical question. But like Maggie, she desperately wished that he would.

CHAPTER 63

Barbara was surprised to awake and find herself in her Dublin apartment the following morning. Then she remembered Jack's admission to the hospital the night before, and was fully awake instantly. Leaping out of bed and into the shower, she quickly washed herself, dressed, and then prepared herself a quick breakfast of tea and toast. Within twenty minutes of waking, she was in her car and driving towards the hospital.

As she drove along, Barbara wondered how the little boy had coped with a night of separation from his father. Having already lost his mother to cancer, it must have been quite an ordeal for such a young child, even though she knew that the nurses on the Children's Ward would do their best to make him happy during his stay. Assuming he'd developed no complications during the night, he might well be able to go home later that day.

It was a bright, sunny morning, and Barbara wondered enviously if Olivia and Maggie were up yet. Unlikely – most weekends in Cloncullen were lazy and laid-back, with no one climbing out of the pit until nearly lunchtime! Unless, of course, Olivia was having one of her tidying-up days in the garden. If that was the case, she'd already be out there in dungarees and Wellingtons, her nose smudged with clay, and digging frantically like a terrier! Smiling, Barbara planned to drive down to Cloncullen later that afternoon. Assuming Jack was well enough to go home, there was no reason to delay. She didn't need to see Richard again – if fact, she definitely didn't want to see him, since he still had the ability to tug at her heartstrings. She still felt raw and vulnerable when he was around, and right now, she wanted to feel happy and carefree. Yes, she *would* go down to Cloncullen later that afternoon. She always felt safe and relaxed in the company of her two closest friends.

Suddenly, Barbara cursed her bad luck. Dammit. She'd forgotten her mobile phone! She'd left it charging overnight, and had forgotten to put it back in her handbag that morning. Anyway, she'd be going back to her apartment to collect her overnight bag after she'd been to the hospital, so she'd just have to wait until then.

As she pulled into the hospital car park, Barbara was surprised to see several police cars outside the main entrance. Walking past them, she made her way into the hospital lobby, and then took the lift to the Children's Ward. She was looking forward to seeing Jack – almost against her will, she was becoming very fond of the little boy.

As she stepped out of the lift, several uniformed police officers were waiting to step into it, and Barbara looked at them in surprise. Then her heart almost stopped. Surely nothing bad had happened to anyone in the hospital? Maybe the Gardai were investigating a robbery. Drug addicts had probably broken into one of the dispensaries – yes, that was probably it.

But when she stepped into the Children's Ward, she was met with long faces and worried expressions.

"Oh Barbara, you're not going to believe what's happened!" the first duty nurse told her. "That little boy – the one you sent here from A&E last night – he's disappeared!"

"What do you mean by 'disappeared'?" Barbara croaked, her voice suddenly hoarse with fear and emotion.

"He's gone – just disappeared into thin air!" replied the second duty nurse. "One minute he was asleep in his bed, but when the night nurse checked a while later, the bed was empty! I feel desperately sorry for the nurse who was in charge – she's absolutely devastated!"

"Does his father know?" Barbara asked, her heart thumping painfully.

"No, the Gardai have been trying to contact him, but he's not at home," said the first nurse. "He's probably on his way here now – oh God, what are we going to tell him?"

"At what time did Jack disappear?"

"Around 4 a.m. The night nurse said that he'd woken up around 3 a.m., and he was upset because he didn't have his toy train with him. So they drew a picture of a train together, and then he fell asleep. She didn't check on him again until an hour later, and by then he was gone."

The nurse looked near to tears. "The police have been searching all over the hospital for hours, but there's not a sign of the child anywhere on the premises."

"Then I presume they've been checking the grounds as well. And the – " Barbara's heart almost stopped as she thought of the main road that ran adjacent to the hospital. It was horrifying to think of a four-year-old child trying to negotiate that four-lane highway outside.

"Yes, they're checking everywhere. There are patrol cars driving all around the area."

"Did he dress himself before he left?"

"No, his clothes are still here, so he must have worn only his pyjamas. He obviously took his shoes, since they're missing."

Oh God, the poor child would be frozen by now, Barbara thought. Jack wouldn't have realised that the artificially high temperature of a hospital ward bore no relation to the extreme cold of the night outside. A flimsy pair of pyjamas wouldn't be enough to keep him warm! Now, there was also the possibility that he could die of exposure . . .

Just as Barbara was wondering what she could do to help, Richard Devlin stepped out of the lift, and began walking towards the ward. He looked carefree and happy at the prospect of seeing his son, but seeing the worried faces all around him, he turned wordlessly to Barbara. She opened her mouth, but no words would come out. As she frantically tried to think of what to say to him, the hospital's medical director seemed to materialise out of nowhere, and he whisked Richard away, much to her relief.

Nevertheless, Barbara felt that she should stay around to support Richard. She felt utterly helpless, and her heart went out to the little boy, wherever he was. If he was alone, she hoped he was safe from harm. But she couldn't shake off the fear that he might try to cross the four-lane highway at some point along its route, and that the only way he'd turn up would be as another road traffic casualty.

Suddenly, she heard Richard's voice again, and she rushed to his side as he came along the corridor, the medical director at his side. Clearly, the hospital authorities were very worried, since a missing child wasn't good for their reputation. Apparently, the hospital was in the process of checking their CCTV footage for the previous evening, but so far nothing useful had shown up.

The hospital director was relieved to discover that Barbara was still waiting for Richard. He was more than willing to relinquish his charge, commenting that the hospital was doing all it could, and to contact him in his office if he could be of any further assistance.

"The only way he can assist me is by getting my son back," Richard said forlornly, his eyes brimming with tears. "I presume you haven't heard anything further, Barbs?"

Barbara shook her head sadly.

"What do you think happened?" he asked, his face gaunt with fear. "Did Jack leave of his own accord – or did somebody take him? Maybe a paedophile?"

Sheer terror now filled his heart. Instantly he thought of all the children who'd disappeared and never been found. Missing children whose stories had made headlines in the newspapers, and had elicited his sympathy at the time. But that sympathy had been followed by relief that it wasn't his own life that had been thrown into turmoil. Now it was his turn, and he felt paralysed by the enormity of it all.

"I'm going to ring Maggie," said Barbara suddenly. "Since she's a psychologist, maybe she can give us some insight into why he left."

"*If* he left of his own accord," said Richard, his mind in overdrive. "Maybe he was kidnapped by some adoption ring. Maybe they'll take him abroad and sell him to a rich childless couple, and I'll never see him again!"

Richard began to weep, and all Barbara could do was put her arms around him.

"Oh Barbs, I've made such a mess of so many things, haven't I?" he said, holding her close. "First, I lost you. Now, I've lost Jack. I'm not fit for anything – I'm a disaster waiting to happen!"

"C'mon, Richard – calm down. Sitting here weeping won't achieve anything. After I talk to Maggie, I think we should go and look for him ourselves. The police can't possibly cover everywhere."

Cursing the fact that she'd forgotten her own mobile phone, she borrowed Richard's and dialled the phone at Bay Tree House. When Olivia answered, Barbara quickly explained the situation, and asked to have Maggie put on the line.

"Oh Barbs, this is terrible!" Maggie said, as she came on the phone.

"Maggie, I need your advice," Barbara said tersely. "Assuming Jack left the hospital of his own accord, can you tell us what he was thinking about when he left?"

"Hospital would be a frightening place for a four-year-old," Maggie told her. "He probably wanted to be back home with his father, and figured that the only way to find his dad was to set off on his own."

"But he was only going to be in hospital for a day or two!"

"Try telling that to a four-year-old. A day can seem a lifetime at that age. He probably felt abandoned – don't forget that he's lost his mother already. He probably feared that he was about to lose his dad as well."

"The poor little boy!" Barbara's heart was breaking. "He's already been traumatised by his accident, he's got a broken wrist, and he'd have no idea how to get home, anyway!"

Ringing off, Barbara faced Richard once again.

"We can't sit here doing nothing," she said firmly, trying to sound more in control than she actually was. "Let's each take our cars and go search for him. Maggie thinks that he intended heading for home – or at least in whatever direction he thought home was likely to be."

"But he wouldn't have a clue!" said Richard despairingly.

"Don't be so sure of that," said Barbara. "I've read in newspapers about kids of Jack's age who've driven cars and done all sorts of clever things to get to where they wanted to go."

"Oh God – you don't think he's stolen a car as well?" said Richard.

Barbara laughed hysterically, and immediately felt awful for doing so, since poor Richard was clearly distraught. Then suddenly, Richard was laughing too, and he and Barbara reached for each other and clung together tightly, united in their fear for Jack's safety.

CHAPTER 64

"*Come here, bitch – and take that nightdress off!*"

It was midnight, Mrs Collins had gone home several hours earlier and Ada had just drifted off to sleep in her bed in the scullery. She was suddenly woken as Henry Morton climbed into bed beside her, his breath smelling of stale beer, grabbed her roughly and began pulling up her nightdress. Terrified, Ada struggled to get away from him, but he was too strong for her. She sobbed as he forced himself into her, enduring his rhythmic thrusting and grunting, until he eventually fell off her after he'd climaxed. Retrieving his trousers, he left the scullery without a backward glance, leaving Ada weeping and terrified once again.

If anything firmed her resolve to leave Bay Tree House, this was it. But first, she needed help. And there was only one person who could give it to her right now.

*   *   *

The following morning, when Mrs Collins bustled into the

kitchen to prepare the breakfasts, she was confronted by a tearful and subdued Ada.

As Ada faced Mrs Collins, all her grief welled up inside her, and spilled over in a bout of weeping. Mrs Collins comforted her as best she could, in between preparing Henry Morton's breakfast, which had to be served at precisely the same time each morning. Then, while Ada rested, exhausted from crying, Mrs Collins brought Laura's breakfast to her room.

When Mrs Collins informed her mistress that Ada had been raped again, Laura was distraught, and vowed to get better as quickly as she could, so that she could take control of the household again, and protect Ada from her husband's excesses. Mrs Collins had quite a job calming her down too, and it was a while before she returned to the kitchen.

When she finally got there, Ada had stopped crying and was in a surprisingly resolute mood. "I'm going out for a while, Mrs Collins," she said firmly. "There's something I have to do, and I have to do it urgently."

Mrs Collins looked at her, a worried expression on her face. "Are you okay, Ada? You're not going to do anything foolish, are you?"

Ada smiled, reaching out and hugging her friend. "No. I'll be back in an hour. Really. Just make sure Mr Morton doesn't know I've gone out."

Mrs Collins grunted. "Thankfully, he's going away later today, and he'll be abroad for two weeks, so we'll have a bit of peace."

Ada was relieved. This was great news – two whole weeks without living in fear of him. "Why didn't he say anything about it before now?"

"Because he knows the prospect might give us a few extra minutes of enjoyment," said Mrs Collins dryly, "and he can't *stand it. He wouldn't give us the steam off his piss if he could avoid it." Mrs Collins looked closely at Ada. "Where are you going?"*

"To Kilcolgan Wood."

* * *

As they sat in the kitchen of Bay Tree House later that evening, after a day spent washing all the household linen, cleaning the floors and shining all the brasses, Mrs Collins looked at Ada with a quizzical eye. "Are you all right, Ada? You don't look well at all."

Ada sighed. "I don't feel too good, Mrs Collins, but that's only to be expected."

Mrs Collins nodded. "Yes, we've had a very busy day, today. Mr Morton always leaves a long list of thing to be done while he's away." She laughed mirthlessly. "He's determined to make sure we won't have any time to relax while he's gone." She looked closely at Ada. "Anyway, it was probably better for you to be busy today, rather than brooding over what happened to you."

Ada hesitated, unsure of how to tell Mrs Collins what she'd done. "I went to see Chrissie this morning, and got something from her that will stop me getting pregnant," she said at last. "I've already taken it. I know it's not going to be easy – in fact, Chrissie told me it would make me feel terrible." Ada gave a shaky smile. "But it'll be worth it, if it works."

"You poor child!" said Mrs Collins, looking alarmed. "Look, go and lie down, Ada – I wish you'd told me earlier! I can finish off washing the dishes and the pots myself. And I'll tell Miss Laura that you'll be up to see her later, when you're feeling better."

Ada nodded weakly. "Thanks, Mrs Collins – I will lie down, if you don't mind. My stomach is heaving, and I think I might be sick."

"Then take a bucket into the scullery with you," said the ever-practical Mrs Collins. "And assuming you're going to start bleeding at some point, I'll get you some of the old towels from the bottom shelf in the linen cupboard." She patted Ada's shoulder. "And if you've any problems, just call me. I'll check in on you before I go home, after I've served Miss Laura her evening meal. Hopefully, you'll get a few hours of sleep between now and then."

* * *

A while later, Ada was in agony. Sweat had broken out on her forehead, and she'd developed the shivers. Lying in bed, she felt her body convulsing. She'd never known such pain. It was even worse than when she'd given birth in the shed behind the house. Her limbs ached, and she felt that her insides were about to turn out. Waves of burning pain ripped through her body, and as the urge to vomit assailed her, she felt almost too weak to reach the bucket. Luckily, she got to it in time, and as she puked she felt that she was heaving her entire insides into the bucket. At one point, her vision became blurred, and she could hardly breathe. She longed for the oblivion of either sleep or death, but neither would come to ease her suffering. She called out for Mrs Collins, but no actual sounds came from her mouth. Her lips and tongue were dry, and her throat was on fire. As she leaned weakly over the side of the bed to vomit again, she felt contractions in her stomach and had to lean back to ensure there was a towel beneath her, before the bleeding started.

When Mrs Collins finally checked on her just before going home, her expression was grave. "Dear God, Ada – you look terrible." Feeling Ada's forehead, she reeled in shock. "Ada, you're burning up! We'll have to get your temperature down quickly, or else – "

She didn't finish the sentence, because she knew her fears would only frighten Ada further. But it was imperative to get Ada's soaring temperature under control, or there was a very real likelihood that she would die. Frantically, Mrs Collins soaked some towels in cold water, then applied them to Ada's burning body, noticing that she was now bleeding very heavily.

Mrs Collins' own heart was beating frantically. She realised that at this rate, Ada could go into shock, and might not recover. Terrified to leave her, yet knowing she had no other choice, she rushed upstairs to Laura's room.

"What will I do, Miss Laura?" she cried. "Ada's bleeding heavily, and I think she's going to die!"

"You'd better get Dr McCarthy immediately," said Laura, her pale face a picture of concern.

Mrs Collins rushed down the stairs and out of the house as fast as she could. Within minutes, she'd reached the doctor's house on the outskirts of the town and poured out her distressing story to him. Without a second's hesitation, he grabbed his medical bag and headed down the road after Mrs Collins.

*   *   *

The following morning, Ada was still weak, but she'd made a remarkable recovery since being treated with some form of antidote supplied by Cormac McCarthy.

When he'd arrived and looked at Ada the night before, Cormac McCarthy's expression had been grave. "Okay, Mrs

Collins," he said, "you'd better tell me the whole story. Right from the beginning."

When he'd learnt what had happened, and what steps Ada had taken to end a possible pregnancy, he was shocked and deeply angry that a man like Henry Morton could abuse a young girl in such a disgraceful way.

Initially, Mrs Collins had been worried in case Dr McCarthy disapproved of what Ada had done. But she was relieved to discover that his only concern was for his patient, rather than passing moral judgement on her actions.

Dr McCarthy had taken prompt action to bring Ada's temperature down, and had praised Mrs Collins' efforts to help her friend. After an injection, Ada's breathing became more regular, her eyes began to focus once again, and gradually a healthy colour returned to her cheeks. Before long, she had recovered sufficiently to sit up and drink a broth that Mrs Collins had prepared for her on the doctor's instructions.

"How are you feeling now, Ada? You gave us all a terrible fright!" said Mrs Collins. "Miss Laura nearly went out of her mind with worry – I thought I was going to have two casualties on my hands!"

"I'm fine now, thanks to you," Ada said, managing a little smile. "And I'm sorry for causing you all so much trouble. Did I bleed a lot?"

"I thought it was never going to stop!" Mrs Collins confessed. "Thank goodness Mr Morton is away – otherwise, I don't know what would have happened!"

Ada smiled weakly at her. "After all that trouble, I just hope Chrissie's potion worked."

* * *

Laura fluttered her hands in frustration. "I felt so utterly useless, Cormac – poor Ada was lying downstairs in agony, while I was lying upstairs, without the strength to do anything to help her!"

Cormac McCarthy reached out and touched her hand. "Ada knows that you wanted to help her, even though you couldn't," he said gently. "But soon, you'll be back in control of your life again, Laura – honestly. I can see an improvement in your condition already. Soon you'll be strong enough to start walking about on your own, too. Look – I've brought you a surprise!" Smiling broadly, he produced a walking stick. "I want you to start using this every day."

Although she'd only been his patient for a few weeks, Cormac McCarthy had already radically altered Laura's treatment. No longer did she lie in bed all day, studying the clouds through her tightly closed window. Instead, he insisted that Ada help her dress each morning, and support her as she slowly made her way downstairs, and out to the summerhouse in the garden, where Laura would be served her breakfast and read the morning newspapers.

"I want you to start taking an interest in things again," he'd told her. "Henry has turned you into an invalid. You must reclaim your life again, and begin to live it according to your wishes, not his."

He was greatly pleased to hear about the success of Ada's secret fruit and vegetable garden, where she was growing foods to boost Laura's health, in a segment of the garden hidden behind the old stable block, where Henry Morton was unlikely to ever venture. Already, she was successfully growing carrots, cabbages and lettuce there.

But now, as he sat opposite Laura in the summerhouse of Bay Tree House, Cormac's face wore a thunderous expression.

"I only just managed to save her, you know," he said angrily, running his fingers through his hair. "Another hour, and she was a gonner – poor Ada would have died from multiple organ failure, or internal haemorrhaging."

"Thank you for saving her, Cormac," said Laura gratefully. "We really appreciate all that you've done for her."

"I don't want any thanks – I just wish I could change this inhumane society we live in!" he said. Silently, he applauded all those women who took risks to help each other. Sometimes, he had to admit, their methods were crude and could prove almost lethal, but what other choice did they have, when men like Henry Morton could behave with impunity?

Then he looked carefully at Laura. "Mrs Collins told me everything, you know. She had to – otherwise, I wouldn't have known what to treat Ada with." He looked down at the terracotta tiles underfoot, not wanting to look Laura in the eye. "I know all about your husband's behaviour – and I know that you're aware of it too."

Laura coloured. "My husband is a brute, Cormac. If there was divorce in this country, I'd have filed for it long ago. He controls my money, and he's raped Ada several times, because he wants a son. Since I'm too ill to give him one, he says he's prepared to take Ada's child, and pass it off as ours – because it will be his, anyway. How cruel is that, to both Ada and me? But there's nowhere we can turn for help – society seems to condone anything that happens to women."

"Well, you've got me on your side now," said Cormac. "As for your husband – I'll have a word with him. He may have ignored Mrs Collins' entreaties, but I'm damned if he'll ignore mine. I'll threaten to go to the police if he ever goes near poor Ada again."

"Thank you, Cormac," said Laura, smiling gratefully. "You

can't imagine what it means to us to have someone to champion our cause. But I don't want you to end up being victimised yourself. Henry has friends in high places, you know."

Reluctantly Cormac stood up to go. "Your husband may have got away with that kind of carry-on while Dr Walsh was here, but he'll have me to contend with now. If he tries to bully you any more, let me know."

Cormac McCarthy smiled whimsically as he waved goodbye and left the summerhouse. There was nothing he wanted more than to be Laura Morton's own personal champion. But he, too, was trapped in a loveless marriage, from which society offered him no escape.

CHAPTER 65

"Please drive carefully, Richard," Barbara told him as he backed his car out of the hospital car parking space. They had agreed that Richard would drive north along the highway, while Barbara would drive south. Once again, Barbara cursed herself for having forgotten her mobile phone. It would be a lot easier if they were able to keep each other informed of any developments.

Backing her own car out, Barbara followed Richard's car out of the car park, turning in the opposite direction when they reached the main road. Before each of them drove off, they waved to each other, but while Barbara smiled encouragingly at Richard, inside she felt extremely pessimistic.

Since a small boy could hide almost anywhere without detection, finding Jack would be almost impossible, especially if he didn't want to be found. Barbara gave a deep sigh. If he feared being taken back to hospital, as Maggie had suggested, Jack could actively thwart the search himself. Assuming, of course, that he was on his own. Barbara shivered at the thought of someone abducting him for their own nefarious purposes. It wasn't a good idea to think that way, because it would paralyse her from doing anything useful.

The Gardai were checking local outbuilding and industrial premises, and stopping cars on all roads leading to and from the area, so Barbara decided to keep on driving down the motorway for a few extra miles. It was quite possible that given several hours of a head start before he was missed, Jack could have walked quite a distance without detection. She didn't dare think that his little body could be lying somewhere, a victim, this time, of a hit-and-run driver . . .

Racking her brains for any kind of a clue, Barbara tried to put herself in Jack's shoes. Assuming he'd avoided detection and reached the hospital gates, where would he go next? The child was aiming to get home to Ballyesmond, so he might have kept walking along the edge of the motorway in the hopes that somehow it would lead him there. Equally, he could have turned off and taken one of the side roads, if he thought it looked similar to the roads near his home. After all, at four years of age, he'd have little idea of distance. By now, the poor child would be feeling totally alone and frightened. Maybe, in his innocence, he'd approached someone for help, and they'd turned out to be a paedophile . . .

Barbara wiped off the sweat that had gathered on her forehead. Dear God, if she kept thinking like that, she'd become hysterical and be of no use to anyone. Most people were kind and decent and with luck Jack was, at this very minute, sitting in someone's cosy kitchen, eating a hearty breakfast, while that kind person phoned the police . . .

After several hours driving around the area to the south, Barbara reluctantly conceded defeat and turned her car back in the direction of the hospital. Hopefully, when she got there, she'd discover that Jack had already been safely returned to his father. If only she'd had her phone, she could have rung Richard for an update!

However, when she returned to the hospital, she was distressed to discover that there had been no sightings of Jack anywhere. The CCTV had shown no evidence that he'd been abducted from the hospital. In fact, Jack hadn't appeared on any of the CCTV cameras, so a new search of the hospital was also being undertaken. The Gardai were now regarding the child's disappearance as abduction, and were concerned that Jack might have been taken by an opportunist when he left the hospital, and the register of sex offenders was also being consulted, and known paedophiles in the area checked.

Just then, Olivia and Maggie arrived at the hospital, both of them berating Barbara for not answering her phone. "I left it at home," groaned Barbara, "on the one day that it would have been really useful!"

Most of the off-duty hospital staff were joining in the search, and their help was proving invaluable in combing the areas of the hospital that weren't known to outsiders. Already, they'd searched cupboards, storage areas, kitchen presses, broom cupboards and outhouses without success. Finally, a member of the kitchen staff discovered a childish drawing of a train in the back of the food service lift. When confirmed as the drawing the night nurse had made with Jack, his departure route was finally established.

"No wonder nothing showed up on the CCTV – there weren't any cameras tracking the arrival and departure of food trays for the wards!" said Olivia, as she, Maggie and Barbara ate the sandwiches that Olivia had made and brought with her from Cloncullen. Barbara was grateful for her friends' presence, and for the sandwiches that would give her the strength to keep searching for the rest of the afternoon, if necessary. Hopefully, that would be long enough.

The off-duty hospital staff were now organising another search party, so Olivia and Maggie joined them. Each person was given a designated area to search, and in view of the discovery of the drawing, the group were now focussing on the hospital environs, inside and out.

As the group set off, a gaunt Richard returned, and Barbara had the unpleasant task of informing him that no one else had found Jack yet. She also explained about the finding of Jack's drawing of a train, which hopefully meant that Jack had orchestrated his own departure. Handing him one of Olivia's sandwiches, she watched him eat it without tasting it. As far as he was concerned, it was just fuel that would give him the energy to keep on searching.

A phone call on his mobile from the Gardai informed him that they hadn't located Jack either, but he was told that a massive search was underway throughout the county and beyond. What nobody was saying, however, was that every hour spent outside in the cold would lessen Jack's chances of survival.

As Barbara drove off again, this time swapping directions with Richard, she tried to put herself in Jack's place. Think, think, think! She told herself angrily. There must be something that everyone is missing. If I was a little boy trying to get home, what would I do? Maybe I'd try to hitch a lift. But anybody finding a little boy on his own would surely phone the police at once . . . She grimaced. Unless, like me, they'd forgotten their mobile phone. Or were a paedophile. Otherwise, they'd drive him to the nearest police station. No, that wasn't a very likely scenario, because he'd surely have been located by now. No, there had to be something else.

What did he like doing? Presumably, he liked sweets and ice cream. Would he have made his way to a shop? Barbara shook her head. Highly unlikely. If that happened, the shopkeeper would have already reported his presence to the police. And besides, the child had no money . . .

Play school. He went to playschool, didn't he? But Barbara could make no connections here. Playing. What games did Jack like to play? Barbara felt that she was going mad. None of this was helping. She kept watching the road on both sides as she drove along, but there was no sign of Jack anywhere. Nevertheless, the idea of Jack at play was lodged firmly in her mind. It persisted like an itch, and Barbara began to wonder if she had lost the plot altogether.

Poor Jack. Barbara felt overwhelmed with sorrow for the little boy – and for his father. How would Richard survive if anything happened to Jack? She'd seen a very different side to Richard since they'd met again in Cloncullen. Gone was the brash, exuberant and confident man she'd once loved, and in his place was a far less materialistic, deeply caring, and emotional man that she loved even more.

Barbara clutched the steering wheel in shock. Had she just admitted to herself that she still loved Richard Devlin? No, it just wasn't possible! She'd got over him long ago. After all, it was five years since they'd been planning their own wedding. Five years during which she'd qualified as a doctor, and made a new life for herself. Five years during which he'd married someone else, and now had a son. No, she was just imagining it. Feelings were running high at the moment, due to Jack's disappearance. When everything got back to normal, her heart would, too.

To distract herself from analysing her feelings for Richard any further, Barbara resolutely turned her thoughts back to Jack. Maybe by recalling her meeting with Richard and Jack in Cloncullen, she'd remember some obscure fact that might provide a clue to Jack's disappearance.

Richard had told her they were living in Ballyesmond, which was near to Cloncullen. He'd also told her Jack attended nursery school on the outskirts of Cloncullen. What else had he said? Now Barbara was cursing herself for not paying proper attention. But she'd been so stressed at each meeting with Richard that she hadn't been listening properly to anything Richard actually said. She'd been concentrating on her own feelings, and hoping that she looked good, and that he'd be sorry he'd lost her. How pathetic!

Wait – hadn't Jack been carrying a toy train engine, when she'd met him and Richard in Cloncullen? Now she remembered – Richard had told her that Jack loved trains! And he'd dropped the drawing of a train in the kitchen lift as he'd made his escape.

Had anyone checked the nearest train station? There was one several miles from the hospital, heading south. Was it possible that Jack intended taking a train home to Ballyesmond? He knew that trains stopped in Ballyesmond daily, on their journey from Dublin to Cork. And being only four years old, he probably assumed that all trains stopped at his own hometown. No, it wasn't logical. Jack couldn't possibly know that there was a train station nearby!

Nevertheless, Barbara made a quick decision. She took the next exit off the motorway, then came back onto the motorway heading south. It was a slim chance, but everything else had failed so far. Of course, since she'd no phone and couldn't be contacted, it was quite possible that Jack had already been found. But one way or another, it would do no harm to check out her hunch. It was perfectly logical that a small boy who loved trains would head to the nearest train station. She could also phone Richard and the hospital from there.

CHAPTER 66

Two weeks later, Henry Morton returned to Bay Tree House, pleased at the success of his endeavours abroad. But he was surprised – and angry – when he discovered that his wife was not in her room.

"She's out in the garden, Mr Morton," Ada told him, being careful to keep her distance from him. She doubted that the doctor could do anything to help her if Mr Morton took a notion to have his way with her there and then. Despite his good intentions, the doctor was a little too far away for Ada's liking.

Ada was relieved when Henry strode off towards the summerhouse, but felt sorry for Miss Laura, who was likely to be the next recipient of her husband's anger.

"Why on earth are you out here in the cold?" Henry bellowed angrily, as he looked down at his wife, who sat reading on a bench in the summerhouse. She looked healthier than when Henry had left, and this didn't please him one bit. "I'll get Ada to take you back to your bedroom straight away."

"I don't want to go back to bed, Henry," Laura replied

evenly. "This is part of my new treatment – Dr McCarthy wants me to get as much fresh air as possible. He hopes that soon I'll be completely cured. Already, I'm walking well with the aid of a walking stick. Dr McCarthy says I just need to keep exercising to get the strength back in my legs, because the muscles have atrophied due to spending so long lying in bed."

Laura's progress didn't suit Henry Morton's plans at all, so he instantly flew into a rage. "You'll get pneumonia!" he railed. "That bloody quack deserves to be struck off!"

Suddenly, his expression changed, and a demonic grin appeared on his face. "On the other hand, that mightn't be such a bad idea, my dear! Pneumonia might hasten your demise, then I'll get all your lovely lolly to spend on whatever I want!" He leered at her, bringing his face close to hers. "Hmm, let me see – maybe I'll buy a new sports car. It'll help me attract all those lovely titled ladies, who'll have even more lolly for me to spend!"

"Stop it, Henry – you're evil!" said Laura, tears in her eyes.

"Then get back upstairs to bed at once!" he roared, as she struggled to her feet. "Since you claim to be able to walk, you can show me by making your own way back to the house!"

He gave her a shove that toppled her over, but he didn't stay to offer her a helping hand. Instead, he walked off, leaving her crying with frustration, on the ground.

*   *   *

"Henry is a vicious, nasty thug!" said Laura, lying back in the comfort of her bed. Ada had gently washed and treated the cuts on her shins, which had resulted from the shove Henry gave her outside the summerhouse. "He doesn't want me to get better – it's more convenient for him if I'm dependent on him. He can spend all my money, and there's nothing I can do about it."

"I wish your relatives would help you," said Ada. "Neither of us has been very lucky where family is concerned, have we?"

Laura snorted. "As far as I'm concerned, I don't have a family! And if, by some wonderful trick of fate, I should outlive Henry, not one of them will inherit a penny!"

"Don't fuss yourself, Miss Laura," said Ada, fluffing up her pillows. "You are getting better. And that's all that matters. When you're strong enough, you'll be better able to deal with Mr Morton."

Laura smiled affectionately at Ada. "You're so kind-hearted, Ada – and you can always see the good side of a bad situation."

"Dr McCarthy is very nice, isn't he?" said Ada slyly, glancing quickly at Laura. "You like him, don't you?"

"He's a very good doctor," said Laura noncommittally.

Back in the kitchen, Mrs Collins was working herself into a frenzy over Henry Morton's callous treatment of both his wife and Ada.

"He's an evil bastard!" she railed, and Ada was amazed to hear such language coming from the usually sedate Mrs Collins. "It's all very well for Dr McCarthy to say he'll help, but he's not here twenty-four hours a day." She banged the pots into the sink. "And I don't see how a few words from the doctor is going to alter Henry Morton's behaviour. In fact, I'd be worried that the doctor himself could end up being wrong-footed, and sent packing from the village. Apart from Sergeant Murphy, Henry Morton has most of the local squires, politicians and so-called dignitaries in his pocket. They'll all support each other when it comes to the crunch."

Ada said nothing. It was a depressing thought, but she surmised that Mrs Collins was right.

*   *   *

It was late in the evening, the children were asleep, and Chrissie was enjoying a brief respite before Mikey returned from the pub. There was only one pub in Cloncullen that allowed Travellers to drink there, and sometimes Chrissie wished it didn't admit them at all. The owners were happy to take all the Travellers' money, but after closing time, when the men were evicted onto the street, they returned home to their caravans penniless and drunk.

Suddenly, Chrissie was surprised to hear a gentle tap on the caravan door. At first, she experienced a jolt of fear, since the travelling community always had plenty to fear from their settled neighbours, who didn't want to be neighbours at all.

Quickly, she opened the door, and was surprised to see a hooded figure standing outside. But recognising the voice, Chrissie immediately relaxed.

"I need your help," said the hooded figure.

Chrissie nodded. "Of course. Come on inside the caravan." She helped her visitor up the steps.

"Are you on your own?"

Chrissie nodded. "He won't be back till the pubs close, and the kids are all fast asleep."

Inside the small caravan, the two women were silent as Chrissie boiled a kettle of water and made a pot of tea. Then she sat down at the small table opposite her visitor, and poured the tea into delicate china cups. Chrissie didn't own much, but she prided herself on cherishing the few decent things that she had. Sometimes she was amazed that her beloved china tea set had so far escaped Mikey's drunken rages.

If the other woman was surprised at the neatness of the

caravan, or Chrissie's beautiful china, she didn't show it. Her mind was on other things – things that weighed heavily on her mind.

"Now," said Chrissie, "what exactly do you need?"

The woman hesitated, unsure of how to word her request. "I know that you're very knowledgeable about herbs."

Chrissie nodded.

"And I know how dangerous some of them are."

Chrissie nodded again. "You have to know what you're looking for."

"I believe there are mushrooms, too, that can kill."

Chrissie nodded. Most people who lived off the land knew all about mushrooms. She often fed her own kids on wild mushrooms, when Mikey had spent all their money in the pub.

"There are three thousand different types of mushrooms growing in the woods of Ireland," Chrissie explained, "and most varieties are poisonous. Lots of them look alike, so you have to be very careful which ones you pick. Some will make you very, very sick, others will kill you."

"Will you pick some for me?"

"Which kind?"

The woman told her.

CHAPTER 67

Dusk was falling as Barbara reached the train station on the outskirts of the city. Quickly, she parked her car and hurried inside. The small Victorian-style station, with its high arched roofs, was deserted, since the last passenger train had already departed. Barbara's heart sank. The child couldn't be on the train, could he? Or could he have taken an earlier one? Could he, at this very moment, be waiting for Richard back home in Ballyesmond? Barbara took a deep breath. It was a worrying thought, and surely an illogical one. No four-year-old would be capable of getting on a train, and travelling alone, without someone detecting him.

Checking at the ticket office, Barbara was informed, by a very disgruntled employee, that he was closing up the ticket office for the night, and no, there weren't any more passenger trains coming through until the following morning. When she asked him if he'd seen a small boy wandering about on his own, he looked at her as though she had two heads.

"Are you absolutely sure?" she persisted. "This little boy has run away from hospital, and the Gardai are searching for him everywhere!"

"Listen, Missus – I've been so busy all day that I haven't the time to notice any small children wandering about!" was the withering reply, and Barbara had to stop herself from bursting into tears.

As the man closed up the ticket desk and left, Barbara felt utterly alone and miserable. At least I'm an adult, she reminded herself. How on earth must poor Jack feel? By now, as the second night of his disappearance approached, he was bound to be cold and hungry, and very frightened.

She went to the phone, intending to phone Richard, and her heart sank further if that were possible. It had been vandalised, the receiver ripped off.

Sitting on one of the public benches, Barbara surveyed the empty station. She felt self-conscious about shouting out his name, which was ridiculous considering there was no on else around to hear her!

"Jack!" she called, walking the length of the platform, shouting out his name at regular intervals. But there was no reply. In the dimming light, Barbara scanned every nook and cranny of the station eagerly. Soon it would be dark, and any hope of finding the child would be gone.

It was only then that Barbara realised there was a siding off to the left of the main station, where several engines and goods carriages were parked. Walking to the end of the platform, she jumped down onto the tracks, realising that what she was doing was not only foolhardy, but could also be considered illegal. On the other hand, the man in the ticket office had told her there'd be no more passenger trains tonight, so she was unlikely to be in danger. And hopefully there was no one around to see her.

The doors of all the engines and carriages in the siding were firmly closed, so Barbara didn't hold out much hope of finding Jack here. Nevertheless, it was just the sort of place that a child might hide, so she tried all the doors, admitting in the end that it was unlikely Jack could climb up to the doors anyway.

Further along another track, an engine with several attached carriages seemed loaded and ready for departure. In the dim light, Barbara couldn't make out what was in the loaded open carriages, but judging by their uneven shapes, she assumed they were stones from the nearby quarry.

Walking along the central track, she counted the open carriages. There were about a dozen of them, with a full-sized goods carriage on the end. She sighed. This was hopeless. There was no sign of Jack, and she was just wasting her time. She'd walk as far as the last carriage, then she'd turn back.

Looking all around her, Barbara strained to see in the increasing darkness. It was becoming difficult to see anything, so she tried calling Jack's name again. Still there was no answer.

As she approached the last carriage, which was different from the others, she concluded that it was possibly a guard's van, or a storage unit for additional materials. The central door was slightly ajar, so she peeped inside. It was stacked with packages and sacks, possibly of cement or some other industrial materials.

"Jack!" she called loudly, never expecting to get an answer.

Then she heard a scuffling movement, and a small voice piped up.

"Is that you, Barbara?"

He'd never spoken her name before, and the babyish sound of it overwhelmed her with love for him. She'd found him at last!

"Jack! Are you Okay? Everyone's been looking for you! Your dad's worried sick about you!"

Jack said nothing, huddling deeper into the corner of the carriage as Barbara jumped in.

"Jack, you're not hurt, are you?"

Still Jack said nothing.

Climbing into the carriage, and skinning her knees in the process, Barbara longed to groan with the pain. But all her thoughts were of Jack, and she didn't want to do anything to frighten or upset him, in case he bolted off again. So she gritted her teeth instead, crawling on her skinned knees towards the corner of the carriage where she could just make out Jack's profile, as her eyes adjusted to the dark. He was seated on the floor, in a small gap between the piles of sacks.

"Oh Jack, you poor love – you must be frozen!" Taking his tiny hand in hers, Barbara was relieved that he didn't resist. She longed to sweep him into her arms and cuddle him, but she knew it would be better to wait until he was ready to come to her. He might well be traumatised by what had happened to him since he left the hospital, so she would wait for as long as it took. Gingerly, she felt his injured wrist, and was relieved to discover that the plaster cast was still intact.

As she sat down alongside him in the dark, he asked her if she had anything he could eat.

"I'm *very* hungry," he whispered.

Barbara was relieved to discover that she still had one of Olivia's sandwiches in her pocket. Good old Liv had come to the rescue again! Handing it to Jack, she watched happily as he gobbled it down.

"Now, Jack – are you ready to come back to the hospital with me?"

"No!" His cry was emphatic, and Barbara felt him try to rise to his feet. Was he going to bolt?

"Okay, Jack," she said quickly, "we needn't go there if you don't want to. But wouldn't you like to see your daddy? He's really worried about you, and misses you terribly."

Jack said nothing, but Barbara was relieved that at least he'd sat down again. She would stay with him in the corner of the carriage until such time as he was ready to leave it. It would probably take some time before she won his confidence, but she couldn't risk him disappearing again. Clearly, he was in a very fragile emotional state.

In silence, the two of them remained sitting on the carriage floor, Jack now resting his head against Barbara's shoulder. She wondered what she would do if he fell asleep. Could she risk trying to carry him back to her car, or would he wake up and try to get away from her?

Suddenly, with a lurch, the train began to move, taking Barbara completely by surprise. Quickly, she looked through the small opening in the door, wondering if it would be possible to jump off with Jack in her arms. A succession of thoughts ran through her mind: would it be safe to jump, or might they land in the path of another train? Could she take Jack's weight, or would she accidentally let him fall? As the train began to gather speed, the brief opportunity to do anything was lost. Soon, it was hurtling off into the night, with Barbara and Jack its prisoners until it reached its destination. Once again, Barbara cursed her stupidity at forgetting her mobile phone.

In the darkness, she could hear the sound of Jack sucking his thumb.

"Looks like we're stuck here for a while," Barbara said, in as jovial a tone as she could muster. "But you like trains, don't you, Jack? So we'll have a bit of an adventure together."

As the train gradually picked up speed, Barbara silently hoped that it would reach its destination soon. But in all likelihood, considering its cargo, it was going all the way to the site of the big new harbour currently under construction in the south of the country. Details had been in all the newspapers, and every politician in the land was claiming to be the one responsible for getting the funding for it from central government.

Settling herself down with her back against the carriage wall, Barbara risked pulling Jack closer to her. She was relieved when he didn't resist. The child was shivering, and Barbara hoped that she could warm him with the heat from her own body.

"Why did you leave the hospital, Jack?" she ventured at last. "Your dad was coming back to collect you today, anyway, so there was no need for you to run away."

There was no reply at first, and Barbara wondered if he'd fallen asleep. Then she heard rapid sucking of his thumb before he spoke.

"My mummy went into hospital – and I never saw her again. Daddy said she died in there." His lower lip quivered. "I don't like hospitals – people die when they go in there – they're bad places."

"Oh Jack, hospitals aren't bad places – they're where people go when they're sick or injured, " said Barbara gently. "Most of the time, hospitals are able to make people better. But sometimes, people are so sick when they go in there, that the doctors and nurses can't help them."

"Is that what happened to my mummy?"

"Yes, love – your mummy was already very sick when she went into hospital. The doctors and nurses tried to make her better, and she wanted to get better too, because she wanted to be with you and your daddy. But," gently, Barbara put her arms around the little boy, "she was too tired to get well any more."

Jack looked up at her. "Daddy said that you're a doctor. Did you look after my mummy in the hospital?"

"No, Jack – I never met your mummy. I wasn't even qualified when your mummy was there."

"What does 'qualified' mean?"

"It means that I was still learning to be a doctor." This time, she risked tightening her hold on the little boy. "I've only been a doctor for the last two years – but I'm glad that I was there when you came in, and that I was able to fix your arm for you. You were so brave! I know your daddy was very proud of you."

"If you'd been a doctor when my mummy was in hospital, could you have made her better?"

Barbara shook her head. "I'm afraid not, Jack, because I'm still learning, even now. It takes a long time, and lots of practice, to learn how to make people better. But your mummy had the best doctors in the country – if they could have made her better, they would have."

Jack sucked his thumb briefly before removing it from his mouth again. "When Daddy left me in the hospital, I thought I'd die in there, like Mummy did."

"Oh Jack, the only reason you were kept in was to make sure that your head was okay! You'd have been going home today, anyway." Barbara felt her eyes fill with tears at the thought of the poor child's distress. How easily adults forgot to explain things in ways that children could understand!

"Will Daddy be cross with me?"

"Of course not. He'll be so thrilled to have you back that he'll hug you over and over again! He loves you very much, you know."

Jack looked pleased to know that he was loved, and he climbed onto Barbara's lap. "Will you tell me a story?" he asked.

"Of course. Do you have a favourite one?"

"I like the one about *Jack and the Beanstalk*. Do you know it? The boy in the story has the same name as me."

Barbara smiled. "And you're every bit as brave as he is!" As the little boy closed his eyes, Barbara began. "Once upon a time, there was a boy named Jack, who took his mother's cow to market. And she was very cross when all he brought home were a few beans . . ."

Barbara didn't need to continue. Unlike the Jack in the story, this little Jack was already fast asleep.

CHAPTER 68

"Where on earth can Barbara have got to?" asked Olivia, worriedly. "She's been gone for hours – I hope she hasn't had an accident."

"Now there are two people missing," said Maggie. "Maybe there's an Irish Bermuda Triangle out there, and they've both been sucked into it!"

"Not very funny," said Olivia. "I'm going to try Barbara's mobile again, just in case she went home to collect it." But her continuous ringing of Barbara's number produced no response.

It was now midnight, and the small groups of hospital employees who'd been helping with the search for Jack were gradually beginning to disband and go home.

Soon, there were only a few stragglers left, including Olivia and Maggie.

Just then, a gaunt-faced Richard reappeared from the car park, having been driving around fruitlessly, searching the same area over and over again, and phoning his nearest neighbour in Ballyesmond, who was regularly checking the Devlin house, just in case Jack had somehow made it home.

"Richard, I think you should go home and get a few hours' kip," said Olivia firmly. "You look totally knackered. Maggie and I will stay here, and let you know if anything happens." As she spoke, Olivia caught Maggie's eye. They were both aware that if "anything happened", it was now as likely to be bad news as good. This likelihood, coupled with Barbara's disappearance, the two friends were not feeling optimistic.

"Thanks, Liv, but I couldn't sleep a wink," Richard replied. "And thanks to both of you for all your help – you've been wonderful. No matter what happens – "

As Richard's lower lip began to tremble, Maggie stepped forward and put her arms around him.

"We've all got to stay positive, Richard," she said, hugging him. "The police are still looking for Jack, so maybe you should leave it to the experts. For a few hours at least."

"I couldn't, Mags – I want to be here for Jack, if – "

"Okay, in that event, let's all go to the hospital canteen, " said Maggie firmly. "The staff have kindly been keeping it open all night, so that anyone helping in the search can get a cuppa when they need it. And right now, you definitely need something to keep you going."

"Good idea," nodded Olivia. "I'll inform the porter's desk where we'll be, so that if there's any news, they can let us know immediately."

The tragedy of Jack's disappearance seemed to have created a truce between them all, temporarily ending hostilities and restoring their relationship to the former close bond that had existed before Richard and Barbara broke up.

"Where's Barbara?" Richard asked, as they walked towards the canteen. "Is she going to join us?"

Olivia and Maggie looked at each other, unsure of what to say. Right now, Richard didn't need to hear any more bad news.

"I think she's still out searching for Jack," said Olivia carefully. "We haven't heard from her in a while."

"Oh God, I love that woman so much!" said Richard, all attempt at subterfuge gone, his feelings raw and at the surface. "Barbara's been so kind to me – I wish I could wipe away the past, and begin again!" Then he gave a tired smile. "Obviously, I don't mean Jack, of course. If I could just have Barbara – and Jack – I'd be the happiest man in the world."

"Do you really mean that?" said Olivia, seriously.

Richard looked surprised. "Of course I do. You know I love her, Liv – always have."

"Then why don't you tell her?" replied Olivia. "I think it's time that the two of you had a real heart-to-heart."

But even as she spoke, Olivia hoped she wasn't offering her advice too late. There was still no sign of Barbara, and both Olivia and Maggie were now seriously worried. Their friend had vanished into thin air! And there was still no sign of Jack.

*   *   *

Early the following morning, as the goods train pulled into a siding at a small station close to the site of the new harbour, onlookers were astonished to see a dishevelled woman and a small boy in pyjamas alight from the last goods carriage.

At first, the lorry drivers from the site of the harbour, who were waiting to load the granite blocks, stared at them in amusement. Then someone made the connection between the missing child who'd been mentioned on radio and television news bulletins over the last two days. All of a sudden, people were running forward to welcome them, to offer them cups of tea – an offer that was gratefully accepted by Barbara – and finally, to phone the police, to let them know that Jack was alive and well.

In the small kitchen behind the station's ticket office, Barbara and Jack were the centre of attention. Smiling although exhausted, Barbara answered questions in between sips of tea, and sandwiches from the ticket clerk's own lunch, which he'd generously donated to the two hungry waifs. Soon, members of the local Gardai appeared on the scene, and arrangements were being made to bring Jack and Barbara back to Dublin by patrol car. Jack was thrilled, and Barbara suspected that police cars might soon supplant trains as his favourite toys and mode of transport!

Having spoken to both Jack and Barbara by telephone, Richard was beside himself with delight. As she listened to the happiness in his voice, Barbara felt that old familiar rush of love for him. It was just like old times, when there'd been only laughter and joy in their relationship. Long before that silly quarrel, about nothing in particular . . .

As she waited with Jack for the patrol car to collect them, Barbara longed for the oblivion of sleep. She was utterly exhausted, and her emotions were all jumbled up.

While she was thrilled that Jack would soon be reunited with his father, she knew that she was going to miss him desperately. She'd grown unbelievably fond of him during their short, but highly charged, time together. She'd been telling the truth when she'd told him she loved him.

In the dark of the railway carriage, they'd established a deep bond. And she'd been deeply humbled by Jack's trust in her, and his belief that she could make everything right.

When Jack had eventually woken up from his sleep, he'd wanted Barbara to retell the *Jack and the Beanstalk* story.

"I went asleep, so I missed the ending," he'd told her solemnly, and Barbara was amused at his innocent assumption that she'd continued telling the story, even after he'd gone to sleep!

After the Jack in the story had successfully escaped from the giant, brought back the golden egg to his mother, and they'd lived happily ever after, Barbara and Jack sat in companionable silence as the train clattered on through the night. Gradually, Barbara noticed that it was getting brighter outside, so hopefully they'd reach the train's destination soon.

Lost in her own thoughts, Barbara was startled when Jack suddenly spoke. She'd assumed he'd fallen asleep again.

"What does 'marry' mean?"

Barbara racked her brains for a simple explanation. "It means that two people love each other, and want to live together always."

Jack digested this information. "Daddy likes you."

"Does he?"

"Yes. He told me that he was going to marry you before he married my mummy, and got me."

Barbara was silent.

"But my mummy's gone, so I don't have a mummy any more." Jack sucked his thumb for a few minutes before he spoke again. "If you married my daddy, you could come and live with us, and be my mummy." He looked up at Barbara. "Would you like to live with us?"

Barbara hesitated, unsure of what to say. If she followed her heart and said yes, she'd lose any advantage with Richard, since Jack would surely report back what she'd said. On the other hand, if she said no, Jack might become upset. Barbara knew how important it was for kids to know that they were loved and wanted. She was glad it was dark, and that Jack couldn't see her burning face.

Deftly, she turned the question around. "Would *you* like me to live with you, Jack?"

The child nodded vigorously, then looked earnestly up at her. "Do you love me, Barbara?"

Surprised, Barbara hugged him. "Of course I do."

"And I love you, too." Contentedly, Jack snuggled close to Barbara, and she slipped her arm around him.

As the train clattered on into the night, the two of them sat huddled together, in their own little world.

As Jack slept, Barbara lay awake, analysing her conversation with Jack. She'd astonished herself at her own admission to Jack that she loved him. But it was true – how could she not love such a wonderful little boy? She longed to ease the hurt he'd suffered when his mother died. It was a huge burden for a small child to carry. And she vowed there and then that she'd try to keep in contact with him, even though she wanted nothing to do with his father. Hopefully, Richard might let her take Jack out for a treat occasionally. The child needed continuity in his life, and if she could help him in any way, she'd gladly do so.

She sighed, alone in the darkness. How simplistic a child's world was! As far as Jack was concerned, love could sort out everything. In his world, there were no such things as pride, jealousy or a broken heart. If you wanted to do something, you simply did it. Barbara wished that the adult world could offer such simple certainties.

CHAPTER 69

It was early evening, and Ada and Mrs Collins were having a cup of tea in the kitchen, prior to Mrs Collins' departure for home.

"I envy you having a home to escape to," said Ada, watching Mrs Collins drink the last dregs from her cup, then put on her coat.

Mrs Collins smiled sadly at her. "I wish you had a home, too. Would you not try to contact your brother and sister again?"

Ada shook her head vehemently.

"All right then, I'll see you tomorrow, Ada. You won't forget to wash up, will you?"

Henry Morton had already been served his dinner in the dining room. He'd been out of sorts all day, complaining alternately of a stomach ache, dizziness and a headache, and Ada had heard him retching in the bathroom earlier. When she'd accidentally encountered him on the top landing that afternoon, he had looked a frightening sight, his forehead all glistening with sweat. Ada and Mrs Collins had both made a

501

point of staying out of his way, since they were well aware that he'd take out his anger on whoever was around.

"No doubt he'll be asleep by now," said Mrs Collins contemptuously, "having consumed a bottle or two of wine with his meal, and several ports afterwards."

Bustling out the door, she waved goodbye to Ada, who now sat alone in the kitchen. This might be the best time of evening for Mrs Collins, but it was the most worrying time for Ada. Without Mrs Collins to act as a bulwark, Ada felt vulnerable when there was only herself and the helpless Laura pitted against Henry Morton.

Laura had already retired for the night, having exhausted herself by repeatedly walking round the garden. Since she'd got back on her feet again, she couldn't get enough of it, even though Henry clearly disapproved. She was filled with a determination to get better as soon as possible, and when Henry was absent from the house, she constantly begged Ada to accompany her on her walks, in case she needed help. Ada, thrilled to see Laura's enthusiasm, was glad to help her whenever she could.

Alone in the kitchen, Ada now wished that she'd asked Mrs Collins to collect Henry Morton's dishes from the dining room. She was filled with a terrible sense of foreboding. Leaving the kitchen, she headed upstairs to the dining room, where she was confronted with the usual sight of Henry Morton asleep across the table.

But this time, he wasn't snoring as he usually did. In fact, he wasn't breathing at all. Just to be sure, Ada held her hand in front of his gaping mouth, but there was no breath coming out. Then she tentatively prodded him, half expecting that he'd sit up and roar at her. But there was no movement of any kind. For several minutes, she stood there transfixed, gazing at the dead

Henry Morton, and wondering what she should do next.

Stepping close to him, she looked with distaste at his bloated features. They still had the power to frighten her, and for one brief second, she thought she'd seen him move, but thankfully, she realised, it was just the gradual and totally natural expulsion of air that occurred in a recently deceased body.

What should she do now? There was no point in telling Miss Laura yet. Ada supposed that contacting Cormac McCarthy was the logical thing to do. And on the way back from the doctor's house, she would call to Mrs Collins' house and give her the good news. Then, while Dr McCarthy was examining the body, she'd tell Miss Laura and help her to get dressed. No doubt Miss Laura would want to be present when Dr McCarthy issued her husband's death certificate.

* * *

As soon as Cormac McCarthy entered the dining room at Bay Tree House, he knew that he wasn't dealing with a straightforward heart attack. When Ada had informed him of Henry's sudden death, he'd immediately assumed that the years of self-indulgence had finally caught up with the master of Bay Tree House. But now, as he looked at the dead Henry Morton with distaste, he realised that the man had probably been poisoned. Initially, he wasn't certain what kind of poison had been used, but it had to be something that was readily available. Which left hundreds of possibilities. But a successful poisoner also had to make sure the victim ingested something that they wouldn't vomit up again. And there weren't quite so many of those.

He smiled grimly. On the other hand, the time of year was a real giveaway. Aided by the recent heavy rain, lots of wild mushrooms were at the height of their fruiting stage. Although he wasn't a mycologist, he knew that some deadly species were currently sprouting at the roots of the oak and poplar trees in Kilcolgan Wood. He'd noticed them as he'd walked his dog through the woods only a few days earlier– in fact, his dog had been attracted to their sickly sweet, almost foetid smell, and he'd had to pull him away to safety.

He'd only come across a single case of mushroom poisoning in his entire life, and that had been in a textbook at the university library. Which was surprising, considering how many poisonous mushroom varieties were available and growing locally.

With distaste, Cormac looked at the dead Henry Morton, observing the telltale jaundice, which told him the man had died of liver and kidney failure. An autopsy would undoubtedly show necrosis of the liver and kidneys, probably due to ingesting something like death cap mushrooms, but it really didn't matter, since he'd no intention of ordering an autopsy anyway.

It would have taken Henry Morton some time to die, he realised, so the mushrooms must have been given to him a day or so earlier. After his initial sickness, shivering and vomiting, there would have been a period of respite before death, and Henry Morton would have felt much better, but all the while, the toxins were still doing their work, ensuring that recovery was ultimately impossible.

Cormac looked down at the body of Henry Morton without pity or remorse. He didn't blame them, whichever one it was. In fact, he didn't even want to know. They deserved some peace, and he wasn't going to make a song and dance about the demise of a man who destroyed everyone he came in contact with.

And he was glad he hadn't been called until it was too late

to do anything. Although there was no antidote to many wild mushroom toxins, he'd nevertheless have been bound by his Hippocratic Oath to make some attempt at saving Henry Morton's worthless life.

As he prepared to leave the room, to face the three women waiting outside, he considered his options. Was there any point in letting them know that he knew? Probably not. Assuming only one of them did it, that person mightn't even have told the others, so there was no point in exposing that person to even greater risk. On the other hand, maybe they were all in it together.

"It looks as though Henry died of a heart attack," he told them gravely, and all three of them had the grace to look sorry. He wondered if it was his imagination, or had he detected an almost inaudible sigh of relief when he'd told them his verdict? As he followed the women into the drawing room, Laura leaning on the walking stick he'd given her, he composed his face into an expression of grave decorum. Now he would formally sign the death certificate and call the undertakers. He knew that the women's sorrowful expressions were only there for his benefit. None of them would regret Henry Morton's passing. And truth to tell, neither would he.

* * *

It was the morning of Henry Morton's funeral, and hundreds of mourners had already gathered outside the church several hours before the funeral Mass was due to begin. Most of the mourners were motivated by curiosity and excitement rather than grief. It wasn't often that someone as important as Henry Morton died, and everyone within a hundred miles of Cloncullen wanted to be seen paying their respects. People also wanted to keep an eye on who else was attending, and curry favour where they could. Funerals were great places to do business, after all. And if it helped to imply that they'd been closer to Henry Morton than they were, well, so be it. In fact, many of those attending had hardly known Henry Morton at all, and they certainly didn't care much about his passing.

At Bay Tree House, Mrs Collins had been baking for days, and a vast array of pies, savouries, cakes and pastries had been prepared for the reception after the funeral. Already, all three women were experiencing a freedom they hadn't known before, and there was a heady atmosphere in the house that was quite unsuited to a funeral!

Ada had already been to one of the local pubs, to arrange delivery of crates of beer and assorted spirits. On the way, she'd met Chrissie, who'd smiled at her and given a discreet thumbs-up signal.

"Please come to the reception, Chrissie," Ada had said, "Things are different now – you won't be turned away."

But Chrissie had shaken her head. "I know that you, Miss Laura and Mrs Collins would welcome me, but I won't be caught dead around that other load of hypocrites who'll all be pretending to mourn Henry Morton!"

And there was nothing Ada could do to dissuade her.

Back in the drawing room, Laura was surveying her figured black suit in one of the long gesso mirrors in the alcoves. The suit was a little old-fashioned perhaps, but having been confined to her bed with TB for so long, shopping hadn't been high on her agenda. Her basic supply of clothing – up to now, mainly nightdresses and dressing-gowns – had been bought for her in the nearby town by Mrs Collins. She'd thought briefly of splashing out on a new outfit for the occasion – then again, did she really want to waste her money on something for Henry's funeral? Laura felt a heady sense of joy at the thought of being back in control of her life. She was even managing to walk about quite easily, with the aid of the stick that Cormac had given her.

"Miss Laura, are you sure it's advisable for you to go?" said Ada, looking at her dubiously. "I know you're feeling a lot better, but the strain might still be too much for you."

Laura laughed. "Ada, the first thing you're going to do is stop calling me 'Miss' Laura. That was only for Henry's benefit. And thankfully, he won't be bothering us ever again."

Looking in the mirror once again, Laura surveyed herself critically. Ada had painstakingly set her hair in curlers the night before, and the result, today, was a halo of delightful blond curls. Laura felt inordinately pleased. In a perverse way, she wanted to look well today. She wanted people to know that she was a person once again, not just a pale shadow of Henry Morton. Laura smiled. She was no longer a wife, but a widow. And she intended to be a merry one.

"And I'm definitely going to the funeral," Laura said, a look of determination on her face. "Even if I have to be carried there! More than anything, I want to make sure that bastard is safely lodged in the ground."

CHAPTER 70

As the crowds of well-wishers dispersed, and newspaper reporters rushed off to file their stories on Jack's safe return, the trio of friends stood alone outside the hospital's main entrance.

"Thank goodness you're both safe," said Olivia, hugging Barbara tightly. "How on earth did you end up on a goods train to Cork?"

"It's a long story," said Barbara, smiling tiredly. "I remembered that Jack loved trains, so I thought the nearest train station was a possibility. The rest I'll explain once I get a few hours' sleep."

"Don't even think of driving!" said Maggie. "I'll drop you off at your apartment as soon as you're ready."

"But you must be as tired as I am!" said Barbara indignantly. "You've been up all night too, haven't you?"

Maggie nodded. "And we're not the only ones. Half the hospital has been helping in the search, and the Gardai and people everywhere have been unbelievably kind."

"Well, I hope Richard appreciates it," said Barbara tartly.

In the hospital, Jack was being checked out before being released to his father, who intended taking him straight home to Ballyesmond. Jack and Barbara had been brought back to the hospital grounds by patrol car, where a grateful Richard hugged then both tightly, before he and Jack were whisked off by the hospital's medical director. It was rumoured that a press conference had been arranged for later. Evidently, the hospital authorities had been hoping that good news would divert attention from questions about the hospital's security system, for the moment at least.

The trio of tired and bedraggled friends headed towards the hospital canteen, which was operating normal hours again. They decided to see if there was any possibility of getting a fry-up there before heading home, since they all knew that once their heads hit their pillows, they'd be out for the count for quite some time.

They were in luck, and before long, each of them was seated before a large plate of bacon, sausages, eggs and toast. As she poured their tea, Barbara explained in detail her hunch about the train station, and the others marvelled at her ability to think laterally under such pressure. And none of them could help wondering what might have happened if Jack hadn't been found until much later . . .

"He's a wonderful little boy," said Barbara, smiling nostalgically. "And so intelligent for a four-year-old! I really loved being with him."

"And what about his father?"

Barbara's face went a dark shade of puce. "I'm glad Richard's got his son back, but there's nothing more to it than that."

"The two of you seemed very close during the search," said Maggie mischievously.

"It's only natural that I'd want to help," said Barbara stiffly. "Now please shut up, the pair of you. I'm tired, and all I want to do is get some kip."

"During the search, Richard told us that he still loves you, and always will love you," said Olivia.

"He did?" There was pain in Barbara's eyes.

"Yes, he did," Maggie confirmed, nodding.

"Look, Barbs – I was wrong," said Olivia humbly. "I told you to ignore Richard, to treat him with contempt, because that's how *I* felt about him. I didn't take *your* feelings into account."

"We've seen another side to Richard lately – and so have you," said Maggie. "You've got to admire a man who, when he made a mistake, took it on the chin, and knuckled down to the responsibility of minding his child. A less mature man would have run away."

"And he behaved impeccably during all the time that Jack was missing," added Olivia. "He could have thrown a tantrum, and blamed the hospital or harangued the police – instead, he appreciated everything that was done to help find Jack."

"That's true, I suppose," said Barbara grudgingly.

"Barbs, I'm going to tell you a little story," said Olivia firmly. "Once upon a time, there was a Professor and a PhD student who loved each other. But they had a silly quarrel, and the man left for a new job at a university in Australia. After he'd gone, the woman discovered that she was pregnant, but she was too proud to let him know, in case he thought she was trying to tie him down. He, in turn, was too proud to tell her how much he loved and missed her." Olivia smiled sadly. "Do you know whose story that is, Barbs? It's mine. And those two silly, headstrong people were my parents. *Are* my parents. The other day, Barbs, I discovered that Barney McDaid is actually my father."

Barbara's eyes were filling up with tears.

"Now my parents are together at last," continued Olivia, "but they wasted all those years because of stupid pride. And deprived me of the love of both parents for all that time."

Tears were now running down Barbara's cheeks. "Oh Liv, I'm so thrilled for you!" Leaping up from the table, she threw her arms around her friend.

"I'm not finished yet," said Olivia firmly. "This little story has a modern-day equivalent. There are two other people, not a million miles away from here, who love each other, but who are too stupid, or too full of pride, to admit it to each other. Have you any idea who I'm referring to?"

Reluctantly, Barbara nodded through her tears.

"Just don't spend your life regretting what might have been," finished Olivia.

Maggie's unruly hair bobbed up and down as she nodded in agreement. "Sometimes, a near-tragedy can offer us a second chance," she added. "You're being offered a second chance, Barbs – the question is, what are you going to do about it?"

"B-but what, I mean how . . ." Barbara fell silent, endeavouring to apply the lesson of Olivia's parents to herself. "But what will people think?" she said at last. "I felt so humiliated, so hurt, especially with everyone knowing about what he did to me . . ."

"Who gives a damn about other people?" retorted Olivia. "You're not living your life for anybody else – it's your life, and Richard's. If you want to be together, then to hell with everyone else." Then she grinned. "Besides, I'll get to be a bridesmaid at last!"

*   *   *

As they left the hospital building, having been photographed and given interviews to every newspaper and magazine in the country, Richard carried his son high on his shoulders. As they walked through the corridors to the front door, people constantly smiled at them, all of them relieved that tragedy had been averted. Richard held onto the child's legs tightly, as though to assure himself that his son was really there. He was terrified of losing contact with Jack ever again, even for a second.

"Daddy, Barbara's going to come and live with us."

"W-what?"

"When we were together on the train, I asked her to, and she didn't say no. I think she'd really like to." Jack looked down at his father. "And you want her to – don't you, Daddy?"

Richard nodded. "There's nothing I'd like better in the whole world," he said, smiling sadly. "Would you be happy if she lived with us, son?"

Jack nodded his head vigorously. "She said she loved me, Daddy. So we could all live happily ever after, couldn't we? Like in fairy stories."

Richard sighed, lifting Jack down from his shoulders as they reached the car park.

"If only things were that simple," he said sadly.

CHAPTER 71

The following weekend, Olivia was walking into Cloncullen to buy some fresh bread when Philip Lynch, accompanied by another Garda, pulled up in his patrol car. After making the necessary introductions, he looked pointedly at Olivia.

"Have you been to see Brendan Warren yet?" asked Philip.

Olivia nodded. "I went to the hospital last week, and apologised for hitting him."

"And?"

"And what?" replied Olivia, annoyed. "I haven't a clue what you mean."

"I thought you and Brendan liked each other."

Olivia blushed, and was even more annoyed with herself. "He's a very charming man. It'll be nice to have a good neighbour in the village."

Philip grinned provocatively at her. "Good neighbour? Oh dear! I thought there was a special spark between you two. Brendan told me himself how much he fancied you. What went wrong?"

"A vision in pink!" said Olivia, losing her cool completely. "This *creature* appeared at his bedside, and Brendan didn't seem to mind in the slightest that she virtually took over his life! She even sidelined my grapes!"

Philip laughed, then realised that Olivia was genuinely angry. "Oh, don't worry, Olivia – that sounds just like Evelyn."

"Well, he's welcome to her," said Olivia huffily. "He didn't even object when she virtually ordered me out, saying that he needed to rest!"

"She's actually Okay. She's very protective of Brendan, and wants to see him get well again. After all, he's been through a lot lately."

"But why did he lead me on?" said Olivia angrily. "He fooled me into thinking that he actually liked me, but I guess that's just his technique."

"Oh, he does like you – and Evelyn just wants to be sure that you're the right one for him."

"What do you mean?" asked Olivia, bewildered.

"Evelyn is Brendan's dental nurse," said Philip, smiling, "and she's married to Donal, the other dentist in the practice. But she has a tendency to take Brendan under her wing, even when he doesn't want her to!"

Olivia wasn't sure if she felt annoyed or relieved.

"But why didn't he say anything when she started ordering me around? He more or less allowed her to throw me out of the ward!"

Philip didn't seem particularly surprised. "Well, don't forget he's still recovering from his injuries, and gets tired very easily. Probably seeing you got him over-excited.

After all, he's been through a lot lately."

Olivia was angry that Philip appeared to be taking Brendan's side. "Huh! All I did was give him a little bang on the head – now he seems to be making a production out of it!"

Philip looked at her in amazement. "You don't know?"

"Know what?"

"Oh, my goodness! Brendan is one of Ireland's top rugby players!"

"And?"

"Don't you ever read a newspaper, Olivia?"

"Well, with all the problems over the house, and with Richard's son going missing, I haven't had much of a chance lately," she said, annoyed. "How on earth has reading newspapers got anything to do with Brendan Warren ignoring me?"

"Unless you've been living in cloud cuckoo land, you must know that we played the All Blacks in Lansdowne Road a few weeks ago."

Olivia looked from Philip to the other Garda uncomprehendingly.

"Oh Christ, I'm really going to have to spell this out to you!" said Philip in exasperation. "Brendan Warren, Ireland's leading wing three-quarter, was seriously injured in that game. He injured several vertebrae and took a blow to the head that knocked him unconscious, and he was airlifted to the new South City Hospital. Then, when he was considered out of danger, he was transferred back to the county hospital. And he's been in hospital ever since."

Olivia looked shocked.

"Well, it's not strictly true that he's been in hospital ever since," added Philip, grinning. "In fact, when he was released from hospital last week, he immediately went to see you – even though it was late at night – since he guessed you mightn't know why he hadn't been in touch." Philip's grin broadened as he watched Olivia's incredulous expression. "As soon as his parents collected him from hospital, took him home and fed him, then dropped him back to Blackberry Cottage, he had the promised visit from Evelyn. She was just making sure that he was okay, and fussing and faffing around as usual. Then, when he finally got rid of her, he headed over to your place. It was quite late by then, and he saw no light on upstairs so he figured you had already gone to bed. He decided against ringing the doorbell but, as he was leaving, he spotted a light on around the back of the house and wondered if you might be in the kitchen. So he went to sneak a look – I know – not much respect for your privacy! But he was really dying to see you! Then he saw the hole in the back wall and got the notion someone had broken in and you were being burgled! He went inside to investigate – stupid behaviour, I know, but the man had been hit on the head recently. Then you hit him over the head again, and put him back in hospital!"

The colour drained from Olivia's face as she realised several things all at once. Number one, she'd added horribly to poor Brendan's injuries. Number two, Brendan hadn't been ignoring her – he's been incapacitated in hospital! Number three, it was distinctly possible that Brendan Warren had actually meant what he'd said when he'd told her that she was the woman for him. A look of happiness began spreading over Olivia's face. Number four, she'd better get back to the hospital as fast as she could, and set the record straight!

As she turned to go, Olivia looked at Philip. "Did we win?" she asked mischievously.

"We did," said Philip, smiling back. "As usual, Brendan Warren saved the day."

*　　*　　*

Olivia sat by Brendan Warren's hospital bed, holding his hand.

"Are we an item, Olivia? I don't want to waste any more time."

"Yes, Brendan," said Olivia without a second's hesitation. Some things were just meant to be, and a woman had to follow her instincts.

"Phew! I'm glad that's settled," said Brendan. "Now I can go asleep again."

"I don't know anything about rugby," said Olivia apologetically.

"Don't worry, my love – I don't want you for your rugby skills."

"But maybe we could produce our own junior rugby team."

"Hang on – I want daughters!"

"Precisely."

Brendan grinned. "Uh oh, I can see I've a feisty feminist on my hands! Oh God, I can't wait to get out of this bed and have my wicked way with you, you gorgeous creature!"

"Speaking of creatures, how's Evelyn?"

"Don't know – I think she and Donal were in

yesterday, but I can't remember. It's the concussion, y'know."

"If you're still concussed, you might eventually regret getting involved with me," said Olivia.

"Never! The minute I laid eyes on you, I knew you were the woman for me. You were a stroppy cow, but I admired your spirit." Then he grinned. "Mind you, I wasn't quite so taken with your violent streak. Do all visitors to your house get walloped over the head, or am I just the lucky one?"

Olivia gazed adoringly at him. "I can't believe that we won't even have our first date until you get out of hospital!"

"First and last date. I doubt if people call it a date when they're engaged."

"We're getting engaged?"

"Of course. On the other hand, we could get married straight away. But by getting engaged first, we'll get an extra load of presents."

Olivia laughed. "You're incorrigible, Brendan Warren! Let's just shack up together and live in sin!"

Brendan solemnly shook his head. "That's definitely something Evelyn wouldn't approve of. No, I'll have to make an honest woman of you eventually, or I'll have Evelyn to answer to!"

Olivia smiled. She was liking Evelyn more and more by the minute.

CHAPTER 72

After Henry Morton's funeral, life at Bay Tree House developed a pleasant laid-back routine, with no one under any pressure, and an air of tranquillity about the house and gardens.

Ada no longer slept in the scullery – she now had her own room upstairs, and Laura insisted that neither Ada nor Mrs Collins would wear overalls any longer.

"That was Henry's way," she said, shuddering at the thought of him, "but it's not my way. You're both friends who just happen to work for me. And, Ada – I know Henry never paid you a penny – he felt that giving you a roof over your head was enough. But to me, that's exploitation, so we'll have to sort out a weekly wage for you."

Chrissie Delaney had also become a welcome and frequent visitor to Bay Tree House while she and her family were camping in Kilcolgan Wood. Her children were also invited to play in the large gardens beyond the summerhouse, and it pleased Laura to hear the sound of young voices having fun.

Laura also had plans for Ada's daughter. "Ada, now that Henry's gone and we all have a lot more freedom, why don't you invite Majella and her friends here for tea?"

"Really, Miss Laura? Sorry, I mean Laura." Ada's eyes shone. "That would be fantastic!"

"It would give you a chance to develop a closer bond with her," said Laura, smiling. "I wish we could adopt her and bring her to live here, but I know that's not possible, since unmarried people and widows can't adopt. But at least by bringing her here, you're welcoming her into your life."

"Oh Miss – sorry, Laura – things couldn't get better than that! Thank you so much!"

"It's me who should be thanking you," said Laura gently. "You've been a great support to me since you arrived here, despite all your own troubles – which my late husband substantially added to."

The two women smiled at each other.

"Everything's going to be wonderful from now on, Ada," Laura promised. "And while I love having you here, you don't have to stay if you don't want to. I'm going to talk to Chrissie about buying one of those little cottages at the end of the town for her, as and when one comes up for sale. Perhaps, Ada, you'd like your own place too? Or if you want to train for a career, or take a holiday abroad, just let me know. Now that Henry can't spend my money any more, there's plenty for everyone!" She smiled. "I must talk to Mrs Collins too – maybe she, Seamus and her son would like to take a holiday abroad – my treat, of course."

Ada was astonished at Laura's generosity. Holidays abroad were a rarity and very expensive, and having her own home was something she had never expected to have. She knew Chrissie would be thrilled too! Chrissie had been saving for years so that she could leave the road and settle in one place, but so far she'd never managed to get enough money together. The idea of having choices was an entirely new concept for Ada, and she revelled in the possibilities that Laura was generously offering her.

Laura was full of plans to use her wealth to spread happiness among those she cared about, and Ada was thrilled to see her friend so buoyant and happy at last.

"You're looking really well, Laura," she told her friend. "Cormac's fresh air treatment is really working – I never expected to see you walking about unaided, and – well, I can only say that you're blooming!"

"It's not only Cormac's treatment, Ada – you were the one who made me eat fruit and vegetables in the first place. I think I reached a turning point when I realised that there were people who genuinely wanted me to get well. You and Mrs Collins have been a tower of strength, and Cormac is trying every new kind of treatment that's available."

Ada eyed her friend shrewdly. "I see you're coping well with being a widow."

Laura laughed. "All I feel is relief! I'm finally in control of my life again, and the future is looking good."

Ada's eyes twinkled. "I don't suppose a certain doctor has anything to do with that?"

Laura blushed. "Oh Ada, I've been dying to tell you! Cormac and I have finally admitted that we love each other. Of course, nothing can come of it since he already has a wife and there's no divorce in this country."

Ada looked sympathetically at her friend. "Is that enough for you, Laura? Can you be happy with a relationship you can't acknowledge in public?"

Laura nodded. "Five minutes with Cormac is worth a lifetime with Henry," she said, smiling. Then she grinned impishly. "You're not shocked, Ada, are you? I mean, my *husband's barely in his grave —"*

Ada laughed. "Who am I to be shocked? I'm delighted for you both. No one deserves happiness more than you – after all you've been through."

"You've suffered so much more than I, Ada."

"Well, hopefully, it's all behind us both now," said Ada.

* * *

As the next few years slipped by, Ada continued to live at Bay Tree House, happy in the knowledge that she was near to her daughter, who was growing taller and stronger every day. During the winter months, Ada rarely managed to see Majella, since the nuns kept a tight rein on all the children in their care. But whenever she could, Ada would contrive to bump into Majella on her way home from school.

It was unbearably painful to be unable to hold her beloved daughter, or let her know that she was her mother, but Ada was grateful that at least the child was healthy and well cared for. According to Mrs Collins, Sister Angela had the children's interests at heart, and Dr McCarthy did his best to keep the nuns on their toes, ensuring that the children were all well nourished. Of course, there was no way she could let Sister Angela or Dr McCarthy know that she was the child's mother. Even though in her heart she didn't believe that either of them would sit in judgement on her.

During the summer months, however, when the nuns were away on holidays, Majella and her friends would visit Bay Tree House regularly. Then the house would ring with the sounds of childish laughter, and Chrissie's children would come down from their seasonal camping ground in Kilcolgan Wood to join in the fun. As Ada happily watched the large group of children, ranging in age from thirteen down to five, she was eternally grateful to Laura Morton for making it all possible. As she looked at her daughter, almost seven years old, her eyes full of mischief, her red-gold hair fanning out behind her as she ran, Ada could only marvel that such a wonderful child had come from such inauspicious beginnings.

* * *

One afternoon, in the summer that Majella was seven, Ada was taking a leisurely trip to the Post Office to post some business letters for Laura. But unlike in the past, when she'd made the same trip for Henry Morton, she could now take as much time as she wanted. Most days, she made a point of seeing Majella and talking to her and a bond was definitely growing between them. The children were now on their summer holidays from the local school, so it was a time of freedom for them too.

Today, Ada was even happier than usual at the thought of seeing her daughter. It was a glorious sunny day, all the nuns except Sister Angela were away on holidays, and she was going to invite Majella and her friends back to Bay Tree House for tea. When she'd left the house, Mrs Collins had been baking a batch of buns, her face pink with exertion from the heat of the oven, a happy smile on her face. They were all happier now, their lives under Henry Morton's control just a dim memory. Could life get any better than this?

It was one of those glorious sunny days, when the whole world seemed happy. Instead of the usual gloomy comments about the cold and dire forecasts of rain, everyone in the streets of Cloncullen greeted each other as though they were participating in one big open-air party. It was as though the sunny weather had spread a contagion of friendliness among them.

"Isn't the weather glorious?" said the normally taciturn Mr Larkin, greeting passers-by as he weighed potatoes outside the shop.

"We'll need to order extra supplies of ice cream if this heat continues," said the ever-practical Mrs Larkin.

As Ada walked along the main street of Cloncullen, she was greeted by people who'd previously barely muttered a greeting as they rushed by, heads bowed against the rain. Now, the same people lingered, their faces upturned towards the sun, as though paying homage to it, lest it disappear as quickly as it had arrived.

Just then, the delivery boy for Larkin's grocery store rode past on his bike, his basket laden with orders for local customers.

"Did you hear what's happened on Cloncullen beach?" he shouted, feeling very important at having such exciting news to relay, "A little girl from the orphanage has been drowned!" he called back as he whizzed past.

Ada's heart almost stopped. "W-what? Who is it?" she called after him.

"Don't know," the delivery boy called back, shrugging his shoulders. Who could tell one orphanage inmate from another?

Running towards the orphanage, Ada encountered several weeping children coming in her direction. "What's happened?" she implored them, "Oh my God, tell me what's happened!"

The younger children were so distraught they were unable to speak, but the oldest of the group, a girl called Julia, recognized Miss Casey from Bay Tree House.

"Oh Miss Casey!" she wailed. "One of the terrible twins is dead!"

"The terrible twins? What do you mean?" screamed Ada, almost shaking the girl in her anxiety to understand what she was talking about.

"S-Sister A-Angela calls them the terrible twins, because they're so alike!" Julia told her, in between sobs. "They went swimming this morning, and o-one of them drowned, b-but we don't know which of them it was!"

"What are their names?" Ada shouted, as the children looked at her in fear. They'd never heard Miss Casey raise her voice before.

"L-Lucy and Majella," Julia told her.

For a moment, Ada's world stood still. Just then, a younger child came running down the street to join her companions. "It's Lucy who's died!" she blubbed to the other children, and they all started to weep afresh.

In contrast, Ada felt relief flood through her. Thank you, God, she whispered inside her head, thank you! She felt guilty at wishing one particular child dead rather than another, but the strength of a mother's bond with her child had momentarily overwhelmed her. Quickly, she left the weeping children, and headed back to Bay Tree House, to tell Laura and Mrs Collins the terrible news.

* * *

Later that evening, Cormac McCarthy called to see Laura. As they embraced in the privacy of the summerhouse, where Laura was resting after walking around the garden, she could see from his face that he knew all about the tragedy at the orphanage.

"Oh Cormac, the poor child!" Laura whispered, as he held her close.

"Yes, I was the one who found them on the beach this morning," he told her sadly. "I tried to save the other one by giving her the kiss of life, but I was too late."

"Poor Sister Angela must be devastated too," said Laura, grimacing. "She dearly loves all those children."

"The poor kids had gone for a swim, since it was Lucy's last day at the orphanage," Cormac told her. "She was going to be adopted by some relatives of her late mother, and it was the last chance that she and the other girl had to be together."

"Majella."

"Pardon?"

"Majella is the name of the other girl." Laura sighed. "They were best friends. How tragic for Lucy to die, just before she was about to be adopted!"

Cormac looked surprised. "Oh, it wasn't her. Sister Angela told me it was the other child. Lucy's okay, and she's already left and gone to her new family."

"W-what?" Laura's face went pale with shock. Her legs buckled beneath her, and Cormac had to help her to sit, for fear she'd fall down.

"Are you sure, Cormac – there's no doubt at all?" Laura's voice was a whisper.

Cormac shook his head. "No, I'm certain, Laura. Personally, I couldn't tell one child from the other since they're so alike but Sister Angela told me it was Majella who died."

Laura clasped her hands together to stop them from shaking. She wished she could tell Cormac that Majella was Ada's child, but she had no right to do so without Ada's permission. So she stared at the ground, hoping that she could contain her grief, at least until Cormac left. While he'd obviously expect her to be distressed at the death of any child, if she started to cry now, she feared she'd never stop. And she needed to be strong for Ada's sake. She had to hold herself together, at least until she'd conveyed the tragic news to her friend.

Cormac stood up, picked up his medical bag and prepared to leave. "Look, love, I've several urgent house calls to make, so I must make a move. Will you be all right? You don't look the best – will I ask Ada or Mrs. Collins to come and sit with you?"

Laura shook her head, not trusting herself to speak.

"Well, then, will I call back later?"

Laura shook her head again. "No, Cormac – not this evening, thanks. I think I'll lie down for a while."

But when Cormac left, Laura did not head upstairs. Instead, using her stick for support, she made her way down to the kitchen.

It was as though some sixth sense made Ada look up and see the pain in Laura's face. As the tears welled up in Laura's eyes, Ada let out a groan of pain.

"No, not Majella!" she whimpered, as Laura nodded her head. "It can't be! The child said it was Lucy!" It was as though someone had run a knife through her. She couldn't breathe. This couldn't be happening. There must be some mistake.

Ada slipped to the floor as Mrs Collins and Laura rushed to catch her between them. The sunshine had betrayed her. That morning she had believed that it would ensure that nothing bad could happen on this beautiful day. Instead, it had lulled her into a false sense of security, then felled her with its sudden brutality.

As she gasped for breath, Ada would willingly have accepted any punishment from Henry Morton, Father Dineen, her parents or the nuns at the laundry, if she could just undo this moment in time. If she could just be as she was five minutes earlier, with no cares in the world, and a happy future *to look forward to.*

Dear God, she begged silently, if you're really there, don't you think I've suffered enough already? Just give me any other kind of punishment, and I'll accept it willingly. Send Henry Morton back from the dead, and he can rape me over and over again. Send me back to the convent laundry for all eternity, and I'll never complain. Just let Majella live, oh please, dear God!

CHAPTER 73

The three friends were sitting in Bay Tree House, having devoured a delicious meal cooked by Barbara. Olivia was making coffee in the kitchen, having just been to visit Brendan in the county hospital. She was deliriously happy, and couldn't wait to get Brendan out of hospital and into her arms. Permanently.

Her two friends had been shocked and stunned when out of the blue she'd announced that she and Brendan Warren were a couple!

"Come off it, Liv – you don't even have a man!" Maggie had told her, her unruly hair bobbing indignantly.

"Are you suffering from delusions?" Barbara asked solicitously, her dark eyes twinkling. "If so, I can probably pull a few strings and get you admitted to the Central Mental Hospital."

"Maybe she doesn't need a hospital, just a one-to-one session with a good psychologist," said Maggie.

"Then that rules you out!" Olivia said, laughing.

"Listen, you pair, it's really true! And you're just going to love Brendan!"

As she explained how and where she'd met Brendan, the misunderstandings that had occurred along the way, but their absolute certainty that they were right for each other, her friends were peeved and delighted in turn.

"Aha! So he was the rugby player who was airlifted to the hospital on the Saturday we had a huge backlog of patients," said Barbara, "Why on earth didn't you tell us before now? And when are we going to meet this guy?"

"How do we know he's good enough for you?" asked Maggie. "He'll have to get our seal of approval before we'll let this match go ahead!"

But seeing Olivia's glowing face, the two friends didn't doubt for a moment that their friend was blissfully happy, and had hopefully found her mate at last.

"How on earth have you managed to get it together so quickly, whereas I can't get Philip Lynch to do anything?" Maggie groaned.

"It certainly wasn't quick," Olivia informed her, smiling. "I met Brendan the first time I visited Bay Tree House, yet it's taken us all this time to sort out the misunderstandings between us."

"Well, the poor fellow couldn't exactly help being injured," said Barbara. "He was saving Ireland's pride on the playing pitch!"

"But how can this happen to you, Liv, whereas I can't even get a date!" Maggie had wailed.

Nevertheless, that very weekend, Philip finally invited Maggie out for a drink. Their first date was a great success, and they were planning to meet again the next Saturday night, assuming Philip could change his rota to be free at the weekend. If not, he was quite prepared to travel up to Dublin to meet her. Maggie was deliriously happy and Olivia was very relieved, but couldn't understand how Carmel Collins had got it so wrong. It was now clear to all of them that Philip had always been as keen on Maggie as she was on him. And Maggie had been the woman he'd been referring to when he'd told Olivia he didn't intend remaining single for much longer!

Just then, the doorbell rang, and Olivia looked up in surprise. She turned to Maggie and Barbara, but their expressions were equally blank.

"We're not expecting visitors, are we?" she asked, rising to her feet.

The other two shook their heads.

As she made her way to the door, Olivia could feel her heart thumping. She still experienced anxiety when she didn't know who was outside, a legacy, no doubt, from her frightening experience with Mark Cunningham.

But when Olivia tentatively opened the door, she was relieved to see Richard Devlin standing there, carrying a large bouquet of flowers.

"Is Barbara in?" he asked, somewhat unnecessarily, since her car was parked prominently in the driveway.

"Y-yes," said Olivia, ushering him inside. She was unsure of what his reception would be, but she intended to beat a hasty retreat before there was a chance to find out. "Maggie and I were just on our way out," she added hurriedly.

With that, she hurried into the kitchen, grabbed a surprised Maggie by the arm, and directed her towards the front door.

Richard smiled at her gratefully as he stepped into the large kitchen, where Barbara was still engrossed in her newspaper.

Seeing him, Barbara leaped to her feet. She felt rooted to the floor as Richard advanced towards her. Her mouth was dry and she felt unable to speak. Then she heard the front door close, followed by the sound of a car driving off. Now, she was all alone with Richard Devlin, and there was nobody to act as a buffer between them.

"Barbara, I never got a proper chance to thank you for finding Jack, and keeping him company on the train," said Richard softly, thrusting the flowers at her. "I'm in no doubt that he owes his life to you."

"No problem," said Barbara stiffly, finding her voice at last. "I was glad to be able to help. He's a marvellous little boy."

Taking the flowers over to the sink, Barbara found a vase to put them in, and filled it with water.

"Jack's very fond of you, Barbara – ever since we got home, he's been asking if he can see you."

Barbara's eyes lit up. "I'm fond of him too. In fact – " she looked quickly at Richard, "do you think I could take him out some day? Maybe go to the cinema?"

Richard's face broke into a big smile, and Barbara's heart took a lurch. "He'd love that, Barbs."

Barbara looked away, wishing that Richard would stop calling her Barbs, because it hurt too much. It reminded her of the time when they'd been a happy couple, deeply in love, and looking forward to their forthcoming wedding. Before the row, before everything else that had subsequently happened.

As though he could read her mind, Richard suddenly

spoke. "For what it's worth, Barbs, I've regretted our break-up every day since it happened." He looked at his watch. "Right now, it's exactly one thousand, seven-hundred and seventy-two days, fifteen hours and thirty-six minutes since we had that stupid row. Can you even remember what it was about?"

Barbara shook her head. She was so choked up that she couldn't speak. Richard had actually worked out the days, hours and minutes since they'd broken up! Suddenly, she thought of Olivia's parents, and the years they'd wasted, separated from each other by their stupid pride. As a result, Olivia had been denied the love of her father as she grew up.

Richard looked down at Barbara earnestly. "Look, I know you've someone else in your life now – but if you ever need a friend, I'll be here for you, Barbs. You deserve to be happy, and if this guy doesn't treat you right, I'll knock his block off!" He hesitated before speaking again. "I know I let you down in the past, and it's the biggest regret of my life. It's my own fault that I lost you, and I'll have to pay for that for the rest of my life." He shrugged. "Maybe seeing me miserable will give you some satisfaction. I certainly deserve it."

Barbara took a deep breath. "Richard, there's no man in my life. In fact, there's never been any other man since you."

Richard raised his eyebrows. "But – "

"I told you a lie, and I also asked Liv to tell you I'd a new man in my life." She laughed. "To salvage my stupid pride, I suppose. I felt so humiliated, so heartbroken, after we broke up. And then, when you got married – "

Richard looked shocked. "I assumed you'd moved on,

found someone new and relegated me to your past. Does this mean . . .?" He looked at her incredulously, hardly daring to hope.

"Yes," said Barbara, "I still love you, Richard." She smiled. "I've tried not to love you, but I don't seem to be able to do anything about it."

"Oh Barbs – what do we do now? I love you, you love me – is there any way forward for us?"

Barbara smiled. "I think Jack needs to be consulted about this, don't you?"

Richard grinned back. "Oh God, Jack will be thrilled if we get back together! He's already told me he wants you to live with us!"

"And what does his dad think?"

"There's nothing he wants more in the whole world."

Suddenly, they were in each other's arms.

CHAPTER 74

The phone in Bay Tree House rang.

"Hello?" said Olivia, still a little fearful of late night calls.

"Hi, Olivia – Gwen here."

"Oh hi, Gwen," said Olivia, marvelling at the happy, confident voice on the other end of the line. "How are you?"

"Never been better," said Gwen cheerfully. "I'm ringing to invite you, Maggie and Barbara to the hotel for a weekend – to thank you all for your support. I've filed for a divorce, and my solicitor is doing his best to ensure that Mark can't get his hands on either the hotel, or anything in it."

"That's great news!" said Olivia, relieved. "Since your soon-to-be-ex-husband has a court appearance lined up – and possibly a jail sentence – I hardly think he'll be in a position to contest anything!"

"You've all been wonderful friends," said Gwen softly. "You made me face up to my situation, even when

I didn't want to. If it hadn't been for your persistence, I might still be trying to justify Mark's behaviour."

Olivia blushed, and was grateful that Gwen couldn't see her. "No problem," she said, "we were very glad to help. Now about this weekend – I'm looking forward to it already!"

*   *   *

"Carmel – I think you know that Philip's discovered the name of the maid who used to work at Bay Tree House," said Olivia. "Her name was Ada Casey, and I have reason to believe that she was my great-aunt."

Carmel Collins spluttered as she spilt some of her tea on the table.

Olivia looked at her closely. "You worked there yourself – as housekeeper for the Mortons, so you must remember her." Olivia paused. "My grandmother and Great-uncle Eddie have tried all their lives to find out what happened to their sister."

"My memory's not what it used to be," said Carmel Collins, now recovered from her initial shock, and using the same excuse she'd used with Philip.

"Well then, let me refresh it for you," said Olivia, bracing herself to deal with Carmel's indifference. "I asked you about my great-aunt when I first met you, but you claimed you didn't know her, so there has to be a reason why you didn't want to tell me anything about her. You didn't want to talk about Laura Morton or the dead baby either. I didn't push you, because I didn't want to alienate you, but now that I know my aunt definitely lived at Bay Tree House, I'm begging you to tell me what happened to her."

Carmel Collins smiled. "So it's all right to alienate me now, is that what you mean?"

Olivia grinned. "Maybe I'm just getting desperate," she replied.

"Okay, so tell me what *you* know, first," said Carmel Collins. "At this point, I can't tell you anything, but I promise I'll find someone who will."

So Olivia told Carmel Collins about her visit to the graveyard, her discovery of the diaries, and Laura's choice of a separate burial. "I know now that nothing at Bay Tree House was as I expected," she finished.

"There's one thing I *can* tell you," said Carmel Collins, "and that is that Henry Morton was an evil and cruel man."

After Olivia left, Carmel Collins reached for the phone.

"She's found the diaries – behind the mirror in the drawing room."

There was a sigh at the other end of the phone. "We looked everywhere for them, didn't we? But we never thought of looking there."

"I think," Carmel Collins said, "she has to be told soon. I can't keep putting her off any longer."

"Yes," said the other person, "I realise we'll finally have to tell her about Ada. But let's hope she doesn't realise what else the diaries reveal."

*   *   *

"I'm having people around for a few drinks and a bite to eat next Saturday night," Carmel Collins told Olivia.

"Do you think you can manage to come? Your friends and family are welcome too. And will you bring your grandmother and great-uncle? I'll be able to tell them something about their sister Ada."

At first, Olivia looked excited, then her expression turned to one of dismay. "Oh, thanks, Carmel – but I'm not sure if they'll want to come. I mean, they haven't even visited Bay Tree House yet. I know they're scared, in case something awful happened to poor Ada. They're afraid that she may have died in terrible circumstances, maybe of TB, or in one of those awful convent laundries."

"Well, if they want to know the truth, you'll have to convince them that the journey will be worth their while," Carmel Collins replied. "Right now, I can't say any more than that."

CHAPTER 75

In the days before the funeral, Ada cried herself to sleep each night, and during the daytime, she tried to busy herself with the normal domestic minutiae of everyday life. While Mrs Collins and Laura were aware that there was no need for Ada to do anything but grieve, they realised that doing the chores regarded as household drudgery helped in some way to keep her from disintegrating. And Ada felt that they gave her some purpose to hold onto, when everything else in her life was falling apart.

She tried to hide her grief from both Laura and Mrs Collins so that she didn't disrupt the entire household, but they knew how she was feeling, and allowed her the dignity of dealing with it in her own way. They offered their silent support, but didn't crowd her when she clearly wanted to be alone. Mrs Collins made her regular cups of tea and tried to tempt her with tasty delicacies, all to no avail. But Ada knew they were there for her, and she drew some comfort from their love and concern.

Chrissie called several times, to sit silently with her in the garden at Bay Tree House. Chrissie, who had been present at

Majella's birth, seemed to know when no words were necessary, and her gentle undemanding presence soothed Ada, who felt she didn't need to pretend when her friend was around. She knew that Chrissie didn't mind her talking endlessly about Majella, and at times, when recalling some amusing incident, Ada would laugh, almost forgetting the reality of the situation. Then, the pain of loss would hit her with even greater force, and Chrissie would cradle her in her arms as all the grief poured out.

On the day of Majella's funeral, the heat wave continued and the sun continued to shine incongruously, and Ada felt that she'd never know a moment's joy again. As she stood with the others beside the gaping hole in the ground where the little coffin was being lowered, she felt like a zombie, a shell of a person who had no tears left.

Worst of all was being unable to tell anyone that Majella had been her own flesh and blood. While Laura, Mrs Collins and Chrissie knew about Majella, there was no one else she could share her story with. She could only express her grief among the people who knew the agony she was going through.

The nuns hadn't bothered to interrupt their holidays for a mere orphan, so the ceremony was a relatively private affair, attended only by Sister Angela and the children from the orphanage, Chrissie Delaney, Laura Morton on her walking stick, Mrs Collins and Ada.

Sergeant Murphy also attended, and at one point, when Ada became almost hysterical, he, Mrs Collins and Mrs Morton had accompanied her back to Bay Tree House and made her a strong cup of tea. He knew that Miss Casey was friendly with some of the orphans, but he was surprised at the intensity of her distress. Perhaps, he concluded, she was a highly strung individual, and any child's death would affect her that way. It was a sad day for the town, he concluded. But at least those hypocritical nuns had stayed away, and left the people who cared to grieve in peace.

*   *   *

As the summer wore on and the weather turned cooler, Ada was perversely relieved. She'd never trust the sunshine again. On the one occasion she'd relaxed and let down her guard, it had resulted in Majella's tragic death. On another level, Ada knew that her logic was flawed, but she had to place the blame for Majella's death somewhere. All she knew was that she'd never again know peace on a sunny day. While others might bask in its warmth and children reach for their buckets and spades, for her, it would be a stark reminder of the day she lost her reason for living.

But today, Ada was due to visit her friends, Mrs Collins and Laura Morton. Although she no longer lived at Bay Tree House, Ada still entered the house via the kitchen, where she stayed briefly chatting with Mrs Collins, who had just returned from her third overseas holiday. Although she'd returned to work several days earlier, Mrs Collins was still in a state of excitement as she relived every detail of her trip to Spain, courtesy of Laura Morton, showing Ada photographs of herself, Seamus and her son disporting themselves on a sunny beach. Mrs Collins had been amazed to discover that there were countries where good weather was actually the norm, and she declared herself a devotee of the continental holiday from then on.

Pleased and amused at her friend's excitement, Ada left the kitchen and stepped out into the garden, heading towards the summerhouse, where her other dear friend would be resting and reading.

In the garden, Laura stood up and silently embraced her beloved friend. She missed Ada's company on a daily basis, but nowadays their relationship was no longer employer-employee, but one of equals.

Initially, they chatted about Mrs Collins' holiday, and they both expressed their pleasure that she'd had such a wonderful time. But always, between them, the spectre of Majella still loomed. It could not be ignored, since it was central to Ada's very existence.

"Are you at peace now?" Laura asked her at last.

Ada gave a wistful smile. "I'm content, Laura – but I don't know if I'll ever experience peace again. Losing Majella was a wound that I don't think will ever heal."

Laura looked sadly at her friend, and wished that she could do something to ease her friend's pain. While money could buy lots of things, it couldn't buy the kind of happiness that Ada longed for.

For a few minutes, the two women sat in silence, enjoying the beauty of the garden. They never found any problem in being silent together, each of them thinking of the happy blue-eyed little girl, with the red-gold hair and freckled nose.

"When I die, I want to leave this house to you, Ada," Laura said at last.

"That's very kind of you, Laura – and I'm very grateful for the offer," Ada replied, reaching out to grasp her friend's hand affectionately, "but I don't need it. Besides, if you're not in it, it will have no meaning for me." Then Ada smiled mischievously. "Besides, who says you're going to go before me?"

"I'm older than you. And I want to make sure you're well taken care of, Ada."

"I have everything I need right now, Laura – honestly. But there are others who need your support more than me."

"Well, if you mean Chrissie, you needn't worry about her – I'm already in the process of buying her one of those little cottages on the outskirts of town. One has finally come on the market, and she's agreed to accept it," said Laura, smiling. "And I'll be leaving a sum of money to Mrs Collins. Cormac won't hear of me leaving him anything, since he's comfortably off already." Laura's eyes sparkled as she looked at her friend. "He says that all he wants is me!"

"That's all your friends want too," said Ada, a lump in her throat. "Now, no more talk of dying, or of leaving me anything. I want for nothing, and a house would only be an encumbrance."

The two women sat in silence again for several minutes.

"Ada," said Laura at last, "aren't you still curious about your brother and sister? Why don't you try to contact them again? Maybe you have nieces and nephews you know nothing about!"

Ada pursed her lips. "We've discussed this before, Laura, and you know my answer. Surely you remember the many times I wrote to Helen and Eddie at your insistence? And I never got a reply. It's obvious that they wanted nothing to do with me. So that's an end to it, as far as I'm concerned."

Laura said nothing. Yet she harboured an unquenchable belief that Ada had a family out there who cared about her. Maybe, she herself would have to be the one to find a way of bringing them all together . . .

CHAPTER 76

The following Saturday evening, the sitting room in Carmel Collins' house was full of guests. Philip, off-duty, was acting as bar man, ably assisted by Maggie, while Barbara and Richard sat holding hands on the big comfortable sofa in the corner. Jack had reluctantly agreed to stay overnight with friends of Richard's in Ballyesmond, so Richard was intending to stay overnight with Barbara at Bay Tree House.

Brendan Warren was still confined to hospital, so having kissed him a fond farewell, Olivia had driven up to the city to collect her grandmother and great-uncle Eddie. At first, they'd both been reluctant to even consider venturing down to Cloncullen, and Olivia had had quite a job persuading them.

"What can this woman possibly tell us about Ada?" her grandmother said. "I suppose if our sister worked in Bay Tree House fifty years ago, she might be able to tell us what happened back then, but does she know how Ada died? Oh Liv – I don't think I can face it!"

"C'mon, Helen – we've got to find out," said Eddie Casey. "Then we can let Ada rest in peace. We can even hold a memorial service for her when we know where she's buried. Assuming this Mrs Collins can tell us that."

Olivia's mother had also been invited, and was driving down separately with Barney, who was now fully recovered from his heart attack and looking forward to making up for lost time by marrying his beloved Doreen as soon as possible.

As the clink of glasses and the buzz of conversation grew louder, even more people began arriving. Dr McCarthy made his entrance, followed closely by the two nuns from the convent, the rearguard being brought up by Chrissie Delaney.

As she watched them arrive, Olivia suddenly had an inspired thought. The "Dr Mc" in Laura's diaries had been Cormac McCarthy, but as the time had gone by, Laura had started to use his first name, so "Dr Mc" had been phased out, and replaced by the more familiar "C!" Olivia's eyes twinkled. How far, she wondered, had their friendship gone?

Carmel Collins greeted everyone warmly. There was expectation in the air, and Olivia felt apprehensive as she introduced her grandmother and uncle Eddie to the other guests, found them a seat, and got them each a drink.

Olivia had made up all the beds at Bay Tree House, and got in supplies for breakfast the following morning, since she suspected no-one would be driving back to Dublin that evening. Whatever news Carmel Collins had to impart, it would be better received if people could safely drown their sorrows without the added worry about getting back to the city afterwards.

Despite her feelings of apprehension, Olivia suddenly smiled joyously to herself. Amid all the confusion of getting her family to come to Cloncullen, she hadn't even told them that she'd met an absolutely wonderful man! But it wouldn't have felt right anyway, to be revelling in her own happiness while they were on the brink of discovering what had happened to Ada. Olivia feared that the outcome was unlikely to be good, and she wanted to be there to support them.

As the evening wore on, plates of delicious food began to appear, and Olivia realised that she was starving. Soon, everyone in the room was tucking in to sausage rolls, salmon and brown bread, and a large selection of finger food. Olivia kept wondering when Carmel Collins was going to say anything about Ada. Although no on else was likely to notice, she was well aware that both her grandmother and great-uncle Eddie were tense and apprehensive.

As soon as the dishes had been removed to the kitchen and drinks replenished, Carmel Collins made a point of sitting down beside Olivia's grandmother and great-uncle Eddie.

"I believe," said Carmel Collins, "you want to know about your sister Ada."

As Helen and Eddie Casey nodded, a hush descended on the room. It was as though everyone else in the room was eager to hear the story too.

"Yes," said Helen, her voice sounding squeaky with emotion. For her and Eddie, this was the culmination of years of wondering, assuming that Carmel Collins could deliver what she'd promised.

"Around 1950, your sister Ada was sent by your

parents to one of the convent laundries, because she'd been raped and made pregnant by the parish priest," Carmel Collins told them.

There was an audible gasp, although no one could quite locate where it came from. Olivia glanced briefly at the two nuns to see how they were taking this news, but their expressions were implacable. She wondered if they were feeling uncomfortable at having the wrongdoings of their fellow religious exposed so publicly.

Carmel Collins gave a little smile. "But Ada tried to escape several times, and proved such a trial to the nuns that they sent her to Bay Tree House, to care for Laura Morton, who was dying of TB."

"If she was pregnant, what happened to her baby?" Olivia interjected.

"That, my dear Olivia, accounts for the baby in the chimneybreast of your kitchen."

Olivia was stunned. So it had been Ada's baby after all!

"But why didn't you tell me all this, when the Gardai were making enquiries?" Philip now asked his grandmother.

"It wasn't my story to tell," said Carmel. "I just happen to know what happened. Henry Morton broke the poor baby's neck."

"Presumably, you know this because you were the housekeeper there?" said Philip.

Carmel Collins nodded. "I knew Ada very well, and Laura Morton too. Henry Morton made everyone's life a misery. He was an appalling excuse for a man."

"So what happened to poor Ada?" Maggie piped up.

"We haven't reached that part of the story yet," said

Carmel Collins grimly. "Henry Morton raped poor Ada for a second time, and made her pregnant again. If the child was a boy, he intended keeping it and passing it off as his and Laura's son – which poor Laura didn't agree with either – so Ada secretly gave birth, and the baby girl was taken to the orphanage by our dear friend Chrissie Delaney."

Chrissie inclined her head as though to acknowledge her role in the event, and Sister Philomena looked pleased, as though the orphanage was going to emerge from this story with some credibility.

"But unfortunately, poor Majella was drowned when she was seven years old," Carmel Collins added.

People began to shift uncomfortably in their chairs, while Philip began topping up glasses. A general air of sadness permeated the room, and people seemed to be asking themselves if poor Ada Casey had ever had a moment's luck in her whole life.

"Poor Ada was a victim of Henry Moron's brutality until he mercifully died of a heart attack," Carmel Collins continued. "At one stage, Ada almost died herself, and was saved by another of my good friends, Dr Cormac McCarthy."

As all eyes turned towards the old doctor, who smiled gently in Carmel Collins' direction.

Olivia's grandmother, who'd sat in silence so far, her face pinched with misery, finally spoke. "Oh my God – our poor sister! All our lives, Eddie and I have wondered what happened to her. And while we feared the worst, we always hoped for the best." She looked towards the two nuns. "I'm sorry, Sisters, but I have to say this – the Catholic Church played a cruel and vindictive role in treating women like second-class citizens, and I don't think the children in orphanages fared much better."

Everyone looked tentatively in the direction of the two nuns, unsure of how they'd react to this attack on their vocations and lifestyles. Would they walk out in anger? Would Carmel Collins' party turn into a mêlée?

But instead, Sister Maria stood up and walked over to Olivia's grandmother and uncle Eddie. "Thank you for that, Helen," she said smiling. "I'm so thrilled to meet you and Eddie again. I'm your sister Ada."

Suddenly, Olivia's grandmother and great-uncle Eddie were weeping, flinging their arms around the little nun. "Oh God, Ada!" Eddie groaned. "We thought you were dead! We never thought we'd see you again!"

Tears flowed freely, and every person in the room was wiping their eyes.

At last, Olivia's grandmother found her voice. "But when Olivia started spending weekends at Bay Tree House, why didn't you make contact then?"

"I had to be sure that your attitude towards me had mellowed over the years," said Ada. "For all I knew, maybe you still disapproved of me and considered that I'd disgraced the family."

"We never thought that – not even for a moment!"

"Well, you never replied to any of the letters I sent you."

"We never got any letters!"

Ada pursed her lips. "Then, obviously, our parents managed to destroy them."

Realisation suddenly dawned on Eddie's face, and his surprise turned to fury. "So that's why we were forbidden to collect the post at the gate any more!"

Ada wiped her eyes resolutely. "Oh dear, we've all wasted so much time! Let's never lose contact again!"

Just then, they were joined by Carmel Collins, who hugged each of them in turn.

Ada and Carmel embraced, then Ada turned to face her newfound family again. "I gave Carmel the job of finding out about your attitude." She chuckled, looking directly at Olivia. "Poor Carmel also had to ward off a lot of Olivia's awkward questions!"

"I'm sorry, Olivia – I wasn't very cooperative when you started questioning me," said Carmel Collins apologetically. "It's just that you were getting a bit too close to the truth, and I wanted to find some way of making you back off a bit. That was why I implied that Philip fancied you rather than Maggie, so you'd stay well away from him – and me – in support of your friend. Which, of course, you did."

Maggie's eyes were like saucers. "Wow! I never knew that all this was going on!" She began to chuckle. "My God – you thought Philip fancied you!"

"Eh, not really," said Olivia, looking embarrassed, and wanting to strangle Carmel Collins.

"You're a devious one, Gran," said Philip, smiling as he slipped his arm around Maggie's shoulders. "I couldn't understand why Olivia was suddenly so distant towards me." He grinned at Olivia. "I started to worry in case you thought I wasn't good enough for your friend."

"Never!" said Maggie, looking adoringly into Philip's eyes. "I fancied you from day one – Liv will tell you that."

Olivia nodded, grinning at her friend. "You weren't exactly subtle. Your tongue was permanently hanging out every time he was around!"

Smiling, Philip turned back to Olivia. "I assumed you always knew that I was dying to ask Maggie out! But I was afraid to do it while I still had official business with you over the baby in the chimneybreast. It would've been downright embarrassing – and painful – if she'd rejected me."

As all eyes focussed on her, Olivia blushed, embarrassed at being the centre of such unwanted attention. "When you first hinted to me that you fancied someone, Philip, I was worried in case it *wasn't* Maggie," she told him. "Then, when Carmel hinted that you might fancy *me*, I was terrified that Maggie might get hurt. I can assure you, Philip – I'd rather have killed you than chatted you up!"

When the laughter died down, Helen turned to her newfound sister. "But why, Ada, after all the nuns did to you, did you become one yourself?"

Ada gave a gentle smile. "It's a long story, Helen. After Majella drowned, I felt I had nothing to live for." She smiled. "Not the most ideal vocation, you'll agree, but I felt that I could help the remaining children in the orphanage, since Sister Angela, the wonderful old nun who loved the children, was due to retire. She died shortly after I entered, and I took on her role as protector of the poor orphans." She grimaced. "I suppose I felt that in some way I could honour my daughter's memory in that way."

Olivia smiled at her great-aunt. "You told me a few porkies yourself, Great-aunt Ada, when you came to Bay Tree House recently, and pretended you'd been there as a nun!"

Ada smiled impishly. "I fooled you too, didn't I? And I've been fooling poor Sister Philomena for years." She smiled across at the other nun. "Any time she and I have been in town together, and we've bumped into any of my close friends, I've had to address them all formally, and pretend I hardly know them!"

Suddenly, Olivia remembered her visit to the graveyard – and the grave of the seven-year-old girl called Majella that she'd seen there.

"I've seen Majella's grave, Great-aunt Ada," said Olivia. "It's beautifully kept."

Ada nodded. "I often go there, to talk to her, and to keep it tidy. It's a lovely peaceful spot." She sighed. "As for the other poor baby," she said softly, "she didn't live long enough to be given a name. If it wasn't for Henry Morton, she'd be fifty-seven now." She looked sadly at Olivia. "I still think of both my babies, Olivia. If Majella had lived, she'd be in her fifties today. And maybe she'd have had a family of her own."

Olivia reached across and gripped her great-aunt's hand, realising that even after half a century, Ada Casey still suffered from a broken heart.

As Ada sat down beside her long-lost brother, he was still looking puzzled. "But why did Laura leave the house to us?" Eddie asked. "It doesn't make any sense."

Ada smiled, remembering her late friend. "Dear, mischievous Laura! She was always urging me to get in touch with you, but I refused, believing that you'd sided with our parents. She'd offered to leave the house to me, but I'd no need of it as a nun. She did, however, insist on paying my dowry for the convent, so that I'd be treated with respect." Her eyes crinkled up in a smile. "There's more snobbery in a convent than anywhere else on earth! If I hadn't been able to produce a dowry, I'd have been treated like dirt."

"But the house," Eddie prompted.

"Laura didn't tell me she was leaving the house to you," Ada told Helen and Eddie. "I think she wanted to prompt communication between us. She never believed, as I did, that you'd all rejected me. So she was right and I was wrong. And now, she's finally had her wish." She raised her glass. "I'd like to make a toast to my dear and late friend, Laura Morton! Thank you, Laura, for bringing me and my family back together!"

Everyone in the room raised their glasses and clinked them against their neighbours'.

Just then, the group was joined by Olivia's mother and Barney. Up until now, the couple had stood on the sidelines, allowing the immediate family to share their own recollections.

Doreen wiped a tear from her eye. "Isn't it wonderful?" she whispered.

Olivia nodded, feeling emotional herself, especially since she'd rarely seen her mother cry before.

"I'm clearly joining a very interesting family!" whispered Barney, grinning, "If it's like this at the first family get-together, how many more dramas can I look forward to?"

Olivia laughed, giving her father a spontaneous hug.

Looking across the room, she noticed that Sister Philomena was looking rather forlorn. Clearly she'd known nothing about Ada's previous life! Olivia went over to join her.

"Are you all right, Sister?" she asked.

Sister Philomena nodded, her eyes wet with tears. "Poor Ada – I never knew she'd been treated so cruelly!

The Church back then had a lot to answer for."

Nevertheless, Olivia couldn't resist a dig at the poor nun. "And you, Sister – were you one of the baddies?"

"Oh dear!" The little nun became flustered. "I hope not! I was one of those who couldn't produce a dowry, so my role in the convent was to do menial jobs all my life!" She sighed. "They were bad times for women, and many nuns took out their aggression on the children in their care, because they were just as much trapped themselves." She took a deep breath. "While I'm not defending their behaviour for an instant, many nuns were victims too. Often, a so-called vocation was their only career option, since the family farm always went to the son in the family, and his wife would want any of her husband's sisters out of her domain." She shuddered. "Can you imagine the cruelty of a Church that put women – many of whom would have loved children of their own – in charge of other women's illegitimate children? And in the laundries, the nuns were forced to look daily at women who were fulfilling their biological function, yet the nuns were denied theirs. Both institutions were recipes for disaster!" She suddenly reddened. "Sorry, Olivia, I'm waxing a little too lyrical. I think I've had too much sherry!"

Olivia smiled. She liked the little nun, and was glad that she was fully supportive of Ada. Hopefully, the Church had learned some lessons from the previous century.

So far, Olivia hadn't had a chance to speak to Chrissie, and she now left Sister Philomena chatting to her mother and Barney, and crossed the room to greet her and old Dr McCarthy.

She gave them both a hug. "It's been quite a day, hasn't it?" she said, and they both nodded, looking pleased.

"Chrissie, Laura, Carmel, Ada and I have all been friends for more than half a century now," said the doctor, "and it's wonderful to see Ada finally making contact with her family. I never thought I'd live to see the day."

Chrissie smiled at Olivia. "Will you be down in Cloncullen next weekend? I'm having a few close friends round on Saturday night, and I'd be thrilled if you could come. Now that you're more or less living here, it'll be a chance for us to get to know you better."

"Thanks, Chrissie – I'd be delighted to accept."

Olivia smiled to herself in amusement. Her new social life in Cloncullen seemed to involve hanging out with eighty-year-olds!

"I'm only asking a few people, mainly old friends who know my dear friend, Julia Gleeson. Julia's coming to stay with me for a quiet break before her next big tour."

Olivia raised her eyebrows. "Is that Julia Gleeson, the world-famous mezzo soprano?"

Chrissie nodded proudly. "Yes, Julia has always been like a daughter to me. Did you know she grew up in the orphanage in Cloncullen? She was there until she was thirteen." Chrissie chuckled. "Julia is quite a character – I think you'll like her."

The old doctor smiled. "I remember Julia well, too – she was a wild young girl, who was always in trouble with the nuns. Mind you, all the poor children were endlessly in trouble with the nuns. But thanks to Chrissie and the late Sister Angela, Julia grew into a bright, caring and talented woman."

Olivia shuddered. "It must have been awful for those kids, Dr McCarthy."

"The name is Cormac," said the doctor, smiling. "I know I'm a very old man, but such formality makes me feel even older!"

"And Cormac played his part in making sure those kids were well cared for too," Chrissie added stoutly.

As the party broke up, Olivia led her grandmother, great-uncle Eddie, Doreen, Barney, Maggie, Barbara and Richard back to Bay Tree House. She'd surmised correctly that no one wanted the hassle of driving home that night, especially after drinking, and they were all grateful for a comfortable bed. Besides, her grandmother and great-uncle Eddie wanted to be close to Ada, now that they'd found her again. They'd be seeing her again for breakfast, the following morning, at Bay Tree House.

Grinning to herself, Olivia noticed the lingering farewells outside Carmel's house as Maggie and Philip took leave of each other. And she thought fondly of her own beloved Brendan, still in his hospital bed, hopefully dreaming sweet dreams of their new life together. Olivia yawned. Hopefully, she'd soon be dreaming of Brendan too.

CHAPTER 77

Olivia was thrilled and relieved that the search for Ada had ended happily, at least for her grandmother and Great-uncle Eddie. It was impossible to forget what Ada had suffered at the hands of Henry Morton, and the death of her two children must have been more than any normal woman could bear. Majella's death was particularly poignant, having reached the age of seven, and already established a close bond with her mother. Olivia could only hope that the passing of the years had dulled Ada's pain, although she knew it would never go away.

Ada was arranging to take leave from the convent to go and stay with her sister and brother, and they were planning a big family reunion of their own. Olivia smiled as she made endless pots of tea at Bay Tree House the following morning. Her grandmother, great aunt and great-uncle had been huddled together all morning, laughing, hugging, and sharing the milestones of their cruelly separated lives.

As she poured out the hundredth mug of tea, she heard snatches of conversation, as her grandmother and Uncle Eddie explained how as children, they'd always missed Ada, and had done their best to keep her memory alive.

"We devised games, you know – one in particular was called 'Let's Hunt for Ada'," uncle Eddie recalled. "Helen and I would spread out across the fields, riverbank and woods in search of clues that might help us discover where you'd gone. Somewhere in the back of our minds was the notion that we might stumble on a hairclip or a ribbon – something that might point us in the right direction." He sighed. "But even when we did find things, we never knew if they'd actually belonged to you, Ada, or if they could help us in any way. Occasionally, we found things like pencils or broken toys in the woods, and we hoarded these things, which acquired an almost mystical value. We stored them in our tree house, and on rainy days, we'd sit in there and examine each of them in turn, wondering if they'd actually belonged to you, or perhaps even the people who'd abducted you."

Ada sat there, tears streaming down her face, thrilled and humbled to know that all this time she'd been deeply loved and sorely missed.

Olivia's grandmother smiled whimsically. "We evolved another game in which everyone in the locality assumed the role of villain and abductor. The postman, the parish priest, the vicar from the Church of Ireland chapel, our own teachers – they all became evildoers, who might have played a part in your capture or disappearance. We'd set out to find you and free you, but we always returned home empty-handed, and tired out from our game. I don't think we ever expected to find you, but we felt that in some small way, we were keeping your memory alive."

"Now I understand why you two are so close," said Olivia, looking fondly at her grandmother and great-uncle. "Grief for your sister united you."

Just then, Doreen and Barney arrived down for breakfast, and after hugging everyone, perched themselves on the arms of the sofa, listening as the trio continued to share reminiscences.

"There were special times of the year that were particularly difficult to deal with, like Christmas and our own birthdays," Olivia's grandmother added, wiping her eyes yet again. "But the worst day of all was your own birthday, Ada. Our parents ignored the occasion, but Eddie and I would retire to the tree house, light candles and quietly sing 'Happy Birthday to You' in honour of the sister we'd lost. Then we'd take turns in blowing them out, and we'd make a silent wish that you, dear Ada, wherever you were, might somehow know that we still cared about you."

"I remember that tree house so well," said Ada, smiling through her tears.

"Thankfully, our parents didn't know what we were doing," Uncle Eddie continued. "It was our secret ritual. We'd buy the candles from the local shop with our pocket money." His eyes twinkled. "But we were clever enough to buy them well in advance of your birthday, Ada, so that no-one would ever make the connection between the two events."

Tenderly, Helen squeezed her sister's hand before continuing. "But now that we've found you again, and when we've managed to fill in all the gaps, it'll be like you never left us at all."

Just then, as Olivia was beginning to serve a big fry-up to everyone, a bleary-eyed Maggie, Barbara and Richard appeared. Quickly, they all mucked in, and soon everyone was seated around the dining-room table, alternately talking, laughing, weeping and eating.

Olivia smiled as she surveyed the scene, and wondered what Laura Morton would make of it all. Olivia suspected that she'd be thrilled to see, at long last, her house so full of happiness.

CHAPTER 78

"You're very welcome," said Chrissie Delaney, as Olivia stepped into her cosy cottage at the other end of Cloncullen the following Saturday night.

In the sitting room, Cormac McCarthy rose to greet her, introducing a tall, dark-haired woman, probably in her late fifties. "I'd like you to meet Julia Gleeson," he said.

The two women shook hands, and Olivia found that she liked the other woman straight away. As Julia poured Olivia a glass of wine, Olivia suspected that the older woman would be fun to spend time with. She had a mischievous air about her, and Olivia could already imagine a younger version of her being continually in trouble with the nuns at the orphanage.

Next to arrive was Carmel Collins, and Olivia concluded that she herself was the youngest of the guests by at least a quarter of a century! Yet despite the disparity in ages, Olivia found herself enjoying the evening immensely. Julia was a brilliant raconteur, and had them all in stitches with tales from her travels, and from her singing tours abroad. Despite her considerable fame and wealth, she was a warm, down-to-earth woman, and it was clear that Chrissie was very important to her.

Olivia wondered how the two were so close, and wondered if it would be rude to ask. Olivia knew that Chrissie had four adult children, but she treated Julia as though she was a child of hers too.

After yet another glass of wine, Olivia picked up her courage, and asked. Chrissie and Julia smiled at each other before Julia began to speak.

"Chrissie gave me a home when I ran away from the orphanage at the age of thirteen," Julia informed her. "I stayed with the travelling community for two years, living in a caravan with Chrissie, her late husband Mikey and their four children. They were unbelievably kind to me, and Chrissie was like a mother to me."

Chrissie beamed. "I've always told people I had five children. As far as I was concerned, Julia was my fifth child."

Julia smiled back at her before continuing with her story. "Then, when it was time for me to leave the Travellers, Chrissie gave me all her savings, so that I could get somewhere to live, and take singing lessons. Without Chrissie's generosity, I'd never have managed to achieve my dream. Any success I've had is all due to Chrissie."

Doing her sums, Olivia was amazed to think that a fifteen-year-old girl could survive on her own, with only a sum of money and her willpower to sustain her.

"You must have had great drive to achieve all that alone," she said.

Julia gave a tinkling laugh. "Oh, I wasn't entirely alone – my friend Betty ran away from the orphanage and came with me. Together, we made our way to Dublin, where another friend of ours, Lucy, had gone to live after being adopted."

"But how did you manage to achieve so much – I mean, you're now an international star." Olivia smiled. "I have several of your CDs myself!" She jumped up, remembering that her own Julia Gleeson CDs were in her car. "Would you mind signing my CD sleeves for me? It'll make me the envy of everyone I know!"

Julia smiled. "I will, if you really want me to, but believe me, the unsigned ones are probably a lot more valuable!"

Olivia marvelled at how self-effacing and genuine Julia was. Olivia liked the fact that the woman didn't take life, or her own fame, too seriously.

Nevertheless, Olivia went out to her car, returning with the CDs, which she placed in front of Julia. It also provided her with the opportunity of letting Julia see that she was a genuine fan.

After a light supper and lots more wine, Carmel Collins stood up to go home, and Cormac McCarthy moved to help her. Olivia was genuinely sorry to see both of them leave, but they assured her that since it was midnight it was already long past their bedtime!

Cormac said he'd see Carmel to her door before making his own way down the street to his home out the other end of town.

"Dr McCarthy – I mean, Cormac – do you think I could come and visit you soon?" asked Olivia. "There's something personal I'd like to discuss with you."

Olivia thought she noticed a flicker of fear in the old man's eyes, then it was gone. "Of course," he said graciously. "When would suit you best?"

Having arranged a date and time, Olivia reached for her own jacket as a prelude to leaving herself.

"Don't go yet, Olivia," Julia said. "I'm really enjoying your company. You know, you also remind me very much of a dear friend of mine . . . you've very similar colouring, same blue eyes, same red-gold hair."

"Yes, do stay and keep Julia company, Olivia," said Chrissie, pleased that the two women were getting on so well together. "I'm exhausted, so if you don't mind, I'll head off to bed myself, but there's plenty of booze in the cupboard, so just help yourselves!"

"Well, if you're sure," said Olivia, sitting back down. There was no need to go back to Bay Tree House yet. In contrast to the week before, she had no guests staying this weekend. Her relatives had all returned home, and her two friends were off about their own romantic endeavours!

As Chrissie ambled off to bed, Julia opened another bottle of wine, and the two women began chatting once again. Olivia learnt that Julia had a grown-up family of her own, that her friend Betty had married a farmer, and that Lucy, her friend in Dublin, was married with three grown-up children and three grandchildren.

In turn, Olivia told Julia all about being given the house by her grandmother and great-uncle, her parents' re-union, her friends Maggie and Barbara, and about meeting Brendan Warren, and her plans for their future. Before long, the two women felt that they'd known each other all their lives.

"Tell me about the orphanage," urged Olivia. "It must have been a awful place!"

"It was," said Julia, nodding. "Except for Sister Angela – she was wonderful to us all. If it wasn't for her and Dr McCarthy, we'd probably have died of starvation. The rest of the nuns didn't give a damn about us."

"I've recently discovered that my own great-aunt is one of the two remaining nuns at the convent now," Olivia told her, "and she's told us that she became Sister Angela's replacement. She loved the children too, and did her best to protect them from the other nuns."

Julia nodded. "Yes, Chrissie mentioned that you'd recently found your long-lost aunt." She took another sip of her wine. "I'm glad to hear that the kids had someone to take over when Sister Angela died. That woman was an absolute saint."

"How did you end up in the orphanage, Julia?" Olivia asked, feeling brave after almost finishing a third bottle of wine. "Of course, if you don't want to answer . . ."

Julia grimaced. "It took me years to come to terms with what happened, but I was sexually abused by my father. When my mother found out, she became hysterical, and was taken away to a mental institution. There was no one left to care for me, so I ended up in the orphanage."

"Oh," said Olivia, "I'm sorry – I should never have asked anything so personal."

"Don't worry," said Julia, pouring them both another glass. "Thankfully, this country seems to have stepped out of the Dark Ages at last. Back then, everything was swept under the carpet. Maybe, in some instances, it still is." She sighed. "I presume you know how women back then were punished for having a child outside marriage? They were sent off to these awful laundries, their babies taken away and placed in orphanages. Undoubtedly, many of my friends in the orphanage were born into situations like this."

"That's exactly what happened to my great-aunt – before she became a nun," said Olivia sadly. "She was raped by the local priest, then sent away to one of those laundries. When she proved troublesome, she was sent to care for a woman with TB." Olivia waved her wine glass in a gesture of disgust. "Can you believe the callousness of the nuns, in sending her to look after someone who was likely to infect her? Luckily, she survived, and so did the sick woman, until quite recently. In fact, Laura Morton only died recently – that's how I got the house I was telling you about."

Julia nodded, her eyes quite glazed from all the wine she'd drunk. Then suddenly, she sat up. "Laura Morton – that name rings a bell. Let me think – what was your great-aunt's name?"

"Ada. Ada Casey."

"Ah! I remember now!" said Julia, all trace of inebriation gone. "She was the maid at Bay Tree House, that beautiful Victorian place just outside the town. I remember her well – she was the one who wept bitterly at Lucy's funeral. It was an unbelievably sad day for all of us in the orphanage, but I never knew why it upset that poor woman so much."

"Well, for one thing – you got the child's name wrong. You've just called her 'Lucy', but wasn't that the name of the friend you've just mentioned? It was Majella who died, and Majella was Ada's daughter. But of course, nobody knew that back then. Henry Morton had raped her, but since she didn't want him to get his hands on the child, Chrissie took it to the orphanage for her."

Julia was silent for so long that Olivia began to think she'd fallen asleep. Olivia was beginning to feel quite tired herself, and looked at her watch. Good God, it was two o'clock!

Just as Olivia was about to stand up from the table, Julia suddenly spoke.

"Olivia," she said, "I know my brain is fuddled from all the wine we've been drinking, but you said that Majella was Ada's daughter."

Olivia nodded.

"Are you absolutely certain of that?"

Olivia nodded again. How could she not be certain? Her aunt had told her, at Carmel Collins' house only the week before, that her daughter had been called Majella. And that Majella had drowned at Cloncullen beach.

"Yes, Julia, I'm absolutely certain."

Suddenly, Julia stood up. "I have a very urgent phone call to make."

Olivia laughed. "But it's two o'clock in the morning!"

Julia, now fully awake, reconsidered, her eyes sparkling with excitement. "You know, Olivia, you're right," she said, smiling. "This business has waited for so many years that it can wait a little bit longer."

CHAPTER 79

Ada held tight to her daughter's hand, as though she would never let go. She could hardly believe that this tall willowy woman, with red-gold hair and a pretty freckled face, was her long-lost daughter Majella. Although now, she'd have to learn to call her Lucy!

Ada felt she was going to burst with joy. From having no family at all, she suddenly had a sister and brother, niece, great-niece – and most miraculous of all, her own daughter, who was alive and well, with a husband, three children and grandchildren of her own in Dublin. Now Ada had more relatives than she'd ever imagined possible!

"It was just a matter of putting the two pieces of the jigsaw together," said Julia happily. "Obviously, I knew that Lucy had once been Majella, and when Olivia said that Majella had been the name of Ada's daughter, well, all the alarm bells began to ring inside my head." She laughed. "I suspect I'd never have figured it out if I'd been sober!"

Olivia, however, was still confused. "Julia, explain it all to me again," she said. "There are still parts of this story I can't figure out."

"Okay," said Julia kindly. "It all began when Lucy – the real Lucy – discovered she was going to be adopted. But when she drowned on Cloncullen beach, Sister Angela decided to let Majella go in her place, since the girls looked so alike. The other nuns were away on holidays, and the people due to adopt Lucy – the real Lucy – had no idea what she looked like either. Sister Angela felt that it was an opportunity to give Majella a chance of a better life."

"And I've had a great life!" Ada's daughter interjected, hugging Ada tightly. "All due to Sister Angela's deception – but in the process, poor Ada here has paid a terrible price." The tears ran down her face. "I can't begin to think how you must have felt, thinking that it was me, rather than Lucy, who had died."

"Go on," said Olivia, urging Julia to continue the story.

Julia nodded happily, resuming her narrative. "After I left Chrissie and her family, and headed to Dublin with Betty, we went looking for Lucy, and we were stunned to discover that she was really Majella, using Lucy's name! She told us all about Sister Angela making the swap, and we were both sworn to secrecy. I've never told anyone, not even my nearest and dearest, since we'd have jeopardised our friend's happy life if we done so." Julia smiled. "We've called her Lucy for so many years now, that I'd find it impossible to think of her as Majella any more!"

Ada smiled, unable to take her eyes off her new-found

daughter. "Whereas for me, it's the reverse. I find it difficult to think of you as Lucy rather than Majella," she said, smiling through her tears, "but I'm sure I'll get used to it in time."

"Well, Ada – Sister Maria – Mum – you can call me whatever you want," Lucy replied, "but don't forget, it's odd for me too – to be hugging my long-lost mother, who's now a nun!"

"Do you remember your mother from the time you were in the orphanage?" Olivia asked.

Lucy nodded, smiling. "Of course I do! She was Miss Casey from Bay Tree House back then, and I used to love chatting to her. She also used to give me an occasional sixpence, but I could never spend it, because I was terrified the nuns would find out!"

"How ironic that you even worked alongside Sister Angela yourself, shortly before she retired," Olivia said to Ada.

Ada nodded. "She'd never have mentioned the swap to me, in case I disapproved of what she'd done and wrecked Majella's – sorry, Lucy's – chances. And since giving birth to Majella was *my* secret, I'd never be likely to mention it to her, in case she, in turn, disapproved of me. Neither of us could afford to take that chance."

Olivia sighed. "So many secrets, so many misunderstandings, so many things hushed up."

"Well, next on the agenda," said Lucy, "is to introduce you to my husband and my three adult children – your grandchildren – and *their* children."

Ada was still smiling, even though the tears were still flowing, and she felt overwhelmed by all that was happening. "And I'm looking forward to bringing you to meet *my* family – the new family that I've only just found. And my wonderful friends of old – Carmel Collins, Cormac McCarthy, and Chrissie Delaney."

And of course, she would never forget Laura Morton, who indirectly made all of this possible. I hope, dear Laura, thought Ada, wherever you are, you can see how happy you've made me. Thanks to you, I've got my family back.

CHAPTER 80

A few days later, Olivia was sitting in Cormac McCarthy's parlour. He'd insisted on making tea, even though neither of them really wanted it. But there were niceties to be observed, and they gave Cormac a brief respite in which to compose himself.

At last they were sitting opposite each other, although Cormac seemed unable to stop moving the milk jug and sugar bowl about. He's nervous, thought Olivia. He probably knows what I'm going to say. Then she realised that she was nervous too.

"I know what happened to Henry Morton, Cormac."

Cormac McCarthy looked at Olivia through bleary eyes. He suddenly looked defeated as he spoke. "Carmel, Chrissie and I searched everywhere for Laura's diaries, and eventually figured that she must have destroyed them herself."

"No, they were lodged behind the big mirror over the mantelpiece in the drawing room. I only found them when I decided to tighten the screws holding the mirror to the wall."

Cormac sat there, as though in a daze, saying nothing. Then he took a deep breath. "When Carmel told us you'd found Laura's diaries, we were all panic-stricken. We hoped you wouldn't read them, or if you did, you wouldn't realise the significance of certain things." He looked into the distance, remembering. "Laura was always an avid diary-keeper. Being confined to bed for so many years, it gave her something to do. Most of it was just musings about the household, and rants against Henry Morton, but we all felt certain she'd include something as important as – " He left the sentence hanging.

"I wanted to get close to her," Olivia said softly, "that's the only reason I read her diaries. I also hoped they might tell me something about Ada, since no one else would. Besides, since Laura was dead, it didn't seem to matter any more."

"I loved Laura, y'know," said Cormac at last. "And she loved me."

Olivia smiled. "I know – she mentioned that in her diaries too."

"We would have married, if it weren't for the fact that I had a wife. But they were very different times back then – leaving one's spouse or getting divorced abroad could – and did – cause huge scandals. After Henry died – "

Olivia smiled, noting that he didn't say 'was murdered'.

"– we talked about leaving Cloncullen and going abroad ourselves. But always, we found some reason to put it off. Laura had dear friends here, whom she'd miss terribly, and I felt responsible for keeping an eye on the children in the orphanage. I'd made a promise to Sister Angela – a wonderful woman – that I'd see that the children were properly cared for." He sighed. "Having no kids of my own, I suppose they were, in some ways, a surrogate family. So Laura and I settled for whatever time we could have together." He smiled sadly, his eyes gazing into the distance. "We even talked again about getting married after Sally, my wife, died, but by then Laura and I were both old, and there seemed little point." He smiled bleakly. "And no, I didn't poison my wife . . ."

"So that's what she used – poison."

Cormac McCarthy said nothing, but inadvertently he'd told her what she wanted to know.

"Don't worry, Cormac," said Olivia gently, "my interest is purely academic. Just curiosity, really."

"In a way, it was a heroic act," said Cormac suddenly. "If she'd regained her health earlier, I suspect she'd have done it sooner. Henry Morton, and people like him, destroyed so many lives."

"And you covered up for her."

"You're a very bright young woman."

"She says in her diary that she was helped by someone called C."

"That wasn't me." Then, realising that inadvertently he'd exposed the only other person whose name began with C, he clamped his hand over his mouth.

"I never thought it was you," said Olivia. "Besides, it doesn't matter anyway."

"She just wanted to protect us all," said Cormac earnestly. "Ada had already suffered terribly at Henry's hands, and Laura feared that I, by my outspokenness, would soon land myself in trouble too."

Olivia nodded. Laura Morton's only concern had been to protect those she loved.

Cormac's voice was hoarse. "You won't destroy her memory, will you?"

"Of course not. Nothing would be gained by exposing what happened, but a lot of people could get hurt." Olivia smiled at Cormac's sad wrinkled old face. Reaching out, she covered his hand with hers. "I think it should stay between us, don't you agree?"

He nodded, visibly relieved.

"And her diaries – will we burn them together?"

Again, he nodded, this time with tears in his eyes.

CHAPTER 81

It was a blustery day as Olivia's family and friends gathered together at the Angels' Plot in Glasnevin Cemetery. They'd come to pay tribute to Ada's other child, the baby from the chimneybreast at Bay Tree House. Ada and Lucy held tightly to each other, as they stood before the communal grave that held Lucy's older sibling, the sister she'd never known. Lucy's husband, sons, daughter and their families stood respectfully in the background. The kind cousins who'd adopted her were long dead, so there was no one else to be hurt by the knowledge that she was really Majella.

Friends were there too. Carmel Collins was in attendance, leaning on her grandson Philip's arm, Chrissie Delaney and some of her children were there, as was Julia, Betty and their families, Cormac McCarthy, Sister Philomena and Maggie. Barbara and Richard had brought Jack with them, and as he clutched his toy police car, Barbara smiled to herself. She'd been right – his ride in the Garda patrol car had supplanted trains as his preferred toy!

Earlier that day, they'd all been to Majella's grave in Cloncullen Cemetery. And Lucy had gazed at the grave where Ada had believed her daughter had rested for over fifty years. It was a deeply moving moment, and those who could remember thought back to the lively little girl – the other terrible twin – who'd been so much looking forward to being adopted.

Then Julia, Betty and Lucy had made their own personal pilgrimage – to Sister Angela's grave over in the corner of the cemetery.

Finally, there was one more grave to be visited – Laura Morton's in Ballyesmond Cemetery.

"I'm going to be buried alongside her, when my time comes," Cormac McCarthy told Olivia, linking arms as they walked along the pathway between the graves. "Even though we couldn't be together in life, we promised each other that we'd at least be together for all eternity."

Olivia nodded, unable to speak as a lump had risen up in her throat. So many deaths, so much sadness, so many things hushed up, she thought sadly. Has anything been learnt by what had gone before? She could only hope so. If lessons weren't learnt, then there wasn't much hope for the human race.

As they all walked back to Bay Tree House later that day, Maggie, now holding Philip's hand, was anxious to move the discussion on to a more positive topic.

"When will Brendan be out of hospital?" she asked Olivia.

"Hopefully, the day after tomorrow."

"Are you taking him back to Bay Tree House?"

Olivia nodded, blushing. She felt sure that everyone listening knew exactly what she and Brendan would be doing, as soon as they were finally alone! Of course, Brendan's injuries might slow them down a little, and they had plenty of talking to do as well. It would be a while before Brendan could return to work – and even longer before he could play rugby again – but that meant they'd have lots of time to revel in the joy of being a couple. Maybe they'd even invite Donal and Evelyn round for a meal!

* * *

At last, Olivia and Brendan stood on the front steps of the county hospital. Before they'd been allowed to leave, they'd had to pose for photographs with the staff on duty, all of whom gathered round to wish Ireland's rugby hero well, and get autographs signed by him. Outside the hospital, there were rugby fans with banners, and journalists trying to outdo each other by getting the first few words from the country's top rugby player, and photographs of him with his new partner.

At last, the duo managed to escape to the car park and head for Olivia's car.

"I can't believe we're together at last!" said Brendan, holding her hand tightly. "Do you know something, Sweet Pea? The thought of you was the only thing that kept me going when I was lying in hospital. I knew we were meant for each other, and I knew that you knew it too."

"Well, yes."

Fleetingly, Olivia thought of Mark Cunningham and

her very nearly disastrous relationship with him. Saved by the bell, in this case by Barney, her own father.

"You'll have to meet my family soon, my darling Olivia."

"And you'll have to meet mine."

Brendan grinned. "My mother is a doting fusspot, who thinks I'll die of starvation if she doesn't feed me regularly. My dad and brother are reasonably normal, I think. What about yours? A woman as gorgeous as you has to have some hidden flaw, so am I joining the family from hell?"

Olivia laughed. "Not exactly, but we're not as conventional as you might expect."

"Uh oh! So Dad's a Hell's Angel and Mum's a flower child of the sixties. Well, I think I can cope with that."

"Not quite. But your first duty as my partner will be to attend my mother's wedding. She's getting married next month – and the reception's at the Glen Hotel, near Ballyesmond. Gwen, the owner, is a friend of ours."

"I look forward to it! I hadn't realised your mother was a widow."

Olivia shook her head. "She's not."

"So she's divorced?"

"No, she's not divorced. It feels really strange saying this, but – " she smiled, "she's actually getting married to my father."

Brendan laughed. "Well, my love, with you, I'm learning to expect the unexpected!

I don't suppose you have any other bizarre family relationships you need to tell me about?"

"Well, now that you mention it, my great-aunt is a nun at the convent in Cloncullen. You'll meet her and her daughter and her daughter's family soon. I've only just met them myself recently, but they're great, and I love them all already."

Brendan grinned. "A nun with a daughter – that's a difficult one to beat. Looks like nothing's ever going to be straightforward with you! And you say you've only met them recently?"

"Yes – while you were in hospital."

"It looks like I missed all the excitement again," Brendan said, putting on an exaggeratedly sad face.

"Don't worry, Brendan – I'm going to ensure that you've as much excitement in your life as you can cope with!"

"Is that a promise, Olivia? Then I can't wait!"

Taking her in his arms, he kissed her passionately. And Olivia knew that dreams really do come true . . .

THE END

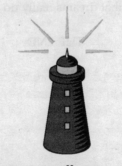